# LISA JACKSON

## DISCLOSURE:
### The McCaffertys

HARLEQUIN®
entertain, enrich, inspire™

ISBN-13: 978-0-373-77804-1

DISCLOSURE: THE McCAFFERTYS

Copyright © 2013 by Harlequin Books S.A.

The publisher acknowledges the copyright holder
of the individual works as follows:

THE McCAFFERTYS: SLADE
Copyright © 2002 by Susan Crose

THE McCAFFERTYS: RANDI

First published in 2004 by Harlequin Enterprises Limited
under the title BEST-KEPT LIES

Copyright © 2004 by Susan Lisa Jackson

Reissued April 2007

This edition published January 2013

Recycling programs
for this product may
not exist in your area.

**Printed in U.S.A.**

# CONTENTS

# Book One:
# SLADE

# Prologue

*There he was, sitting in his damned rocking chair as if it were a throne.*
Slade McCafferty gnashed his back teeth and felt the taste
of crow on his tongue as he glared through the bug-spattered
windshield of his truck to the broad front porch of the ranch
house he'd called home for the first twenty years of his life.

The old man, John Randall McCafferty, sat ramrod straight.
In a way Slade respected him for his tenacious hold on life, his
stubbornness, his determination to bend all of his children's
wills to meet his own goals. The trouble was, it hadn't worked.
The eldest McCafferty son, Thorne, was a hot-shot attorney,
a millionaire who ran his own corporation from Denver, and
the second-born, Matt, had struck out on his own and bought
himself a spread near the Idaho border. Randi, the youngest,
Slade's half sister, lived in Seattle, and wrote her own syndicated column for a newspaper there.

That left Slade.

Ever the black sheep.

Ever the rogue.

Ever in trouble.

Not that he gave a damn.

As Slade eased out of the truck, a sharp pain shot through his hip and he winced, feeling the skin tighten around the barely visible scar that ran down one side of his face, a reminder of deeper marks that cut into his heart, the pain that never really left him. Well, no doubt he'd hear about that, too.

He paused to light a cigarette, then hobbled up the path through the sparse, dry grass that served as a lawn. Though it was barely May, it had been a dry spring, hotter than usual for this time of year, and the sun-bleached grass was testament to the unseasonable and arid weather.

John Randall didn't say a word, didn't so much as sway in the rocker as he watched his youngest son through narrowed eyes. A breeze, fiery as Satan's breath, scorched across the slight rise that supported the old ranch house. Two stories of weathered siding with dark-green trim around each window, the house had been a refuge once, then a battlefield, and later a prison. At least to Slade's way of thinking.

He sucked hard on his filter tip, felt the warmth of smoke curl through his lungs and faced the man who had sired him. "Dad." His boots rang as he hitched up the steps and John Randall's old hunting dog, Harold, lifted his graying head, then thumped his tail on the dusty planks. "Hi, boy."

More thumps.

"I thought you might not come."

"You said it was important." Jeez, the old man looked bad. Thin tufts of white hair barely covered his speckled pate, and his eyes, once a laser-blue, had faded. His hands were gnarled and his body frail, the wheelchair parked near the door evidence of his failing health, but there was still a bit of steel in

John Randall's backbone, a measure of McCafferty grit in the set of his jaw.

"It is. Sit." He pointed toward a bench pushed under a window, but Slade leaned against the rail and faced him. The sun beat against his back.

"What's so all-fired important?"

"I want a grandson."

"What?" Slade's chest tightened and he felt the same old pain pound through his brain.

"You heard me. I don't have much time, Slade, and I'd like to go to my grave knowin' that you've settled down, started a family, kept the family name alive."

"Maybe I'm not the one you should be talking to about this." Not now, not when the memories were so fresh.

"I've already had my say with Thorne and Matt. It's your turn."

"I'm not interested in—"

"I know about Rebecca." Slade braced himself. "And the baby."

Slade's head pounded as if a thousand horses were running through his brain. His scar seemed to pulse. "Yeah, well, it's something I've got to live with," he said, his eyes drilling into the old man's. "And it's hell."

"It wasn't your fault."

"So I've heard."

"You can't go beating yourself up one side and down the other the rest of your life," his father said with more compassion than Slade thought him capable of. "They're gone. It was a horrid accident. A painful loss. But life goes on."

"Does it?" Slade mocked, then wished he could call back the cruel words. He'd said them without thinking that his father was surely dying.

"Yes, it does. You can't stop living because of a tragedy." He reached into the pocket of his vest and pulled out his watch, a silver-and-gold pocket watch engraved with the crest of the Flying M, this very ranch, his pride and joy. "I want you to have this."

"No, Dad. You keep it."

The old man's lips twisted into an ironic grin. "Don't have any use for it. Not where I'm goin'. But you do. I want you to keep it as a reminder of me." He pressed the timepiece into Slade's palm. "Don't waste your life, son. It's shorter than you think. Now, it's time for you to put the past behind you. Settle down. Start a family."

"I don't think so."

A fly buzzed near John Randall's head and he swatted at it with one gnarled hand. "Do me a favor, Slade. Quit moving long enough to figure out what you want in life. Whether you know it or not, what you need is a good woman. A wife. A mother for your children."

"You're a fine one to talk," Slade growled, dropping his cigarette to the floorboards where he crushed out the butt with his boot heel.

"I made my share of mistakes," his father admitted.

Slade didn't comment.

"I was young and foolish."

"Like I am now? Is that what you're trying to say?"

"No. I'm just hoping you'll learn from my mistakes."

"Mistakes. You mean, your two marriages? Or your two divorces?"

"Maybe both."

Slade glanced over his shoulder to the rolling hills of the ranch. Dust plumed behind a sorry old tractor chugging over one rise. "And you think I should get married."

"I believe in the institution."

"Even though it stripped you clean?"

John Randall sighed. "It wasn't so much the money that mattered," he said with more honesty than Slade expected. "But I betrayed a good woman and let you boys down. I lost the respect of my children, and that…that was hard to take. Don't get me wrong, if I had to do it again, I would. Remember if I hadn't taken up with Penelope, I would never have had my daughter."

"So it was worth it."

"Yes," he said, pushing the rocker so that it began to move a bit. "And I only hope that someday you'll forgive me, but more than that, Slade, I hope you find yourself a woman who'll make you believe in love again."

Slade pushed himself upright. "Don't count on it." He dropped the watch into his father's lap.

# Chapter 1

*Seven months later*

*The McCaffertys! Why in the world did her meeting have to be with the damned McCafferty brothers?*

Jamie Parsons braked hard and yanked on the steering wheel as she reached the drive of her grandmother's small farm. Her wheezing compact turned too quickly. Tires spun in the snow that covered the two ruts where dry weeds had the audacity to poke through the blanket of white.

The cottage, in desperate need of repairs and paint, seemed quaint now, like some fairy-tale version of Grandma's house.

It had been, she thought as she grabbed her briefcase and overnight bag, then plowed through three inches of white powder to the back door. She found the extra key over the window ledge where her grandmother, Nita, had always kept it. "Just in case, Jamie," she'd always explained in her raspy, old-lady voice. "We don't want to be locked out now, do we?"

*No, Nana, we sure don't.* Jamie's throat constricted when she thought of the woman who had taken in a wild, rebellious teenager; opened her house and her heart to a girl whose parents had given up on her. Nana hadn't batted an eye, just told her, from the time she stepped over the front threshold with her two suitcases, one-eyed teddy bear and an attitude that wouldn't quit, that things were going to change. From that moment forward, Jamie was to abide by her rules and that was that.

Not that they'd always gotten along.

Not that Jamie hadn't done everything imaginable behind the woman's broad back.

Not that Jamie hadn't tried every trick in the book to get herself thrown out of the only home she'd ever known.

Nana, a God-fearing woman who could cut her only granddaughter to the quick with just one glance, had never given up. Unlike everyone else in Jamie's life.

Now the key turned easily, and Jamie walked into the kitchen. It smelled musty, the black-and-white tiles covered in dust, the old Formica-topped table with chrome legs still pushed against the far wall that sloped sharply due to the stairs running up the other side of the house from the foyer. The salt and pepper shakers, in the shape of kittens, had disappeared from the table, as had all other signs of life. There were light spots in the wall, circular patches of clean paint where one of the antique dishes Nana had displayed with pride had been taken down and given to some relative somewhere in accordance with Nita's will. A dried cactus in a plastic pot had been forgotten and pushed into a corner of the counter where once there had been a toaster. The gingham curtains were now home to spiders whose webs gathered more dust.

If Nana had been alive, she would have had a fit. This kitchen had always gleamed. "Cleanliness is next to godliness," she'd preached while pushing a broom, or polishing a lamp, or scrubbing a sink. And Nana had known about godliness; she'd read her Bible every evening, never missed a Sunday sermon and taught Sunday school to teenagers.

God, Jamie missed her.

The bulk of Nana's estate, which consisted of this old house, the twenty acres surrounding it and a 1940 Chevrolet parked in the old garage, had been left to Jamie. It was Nana's dream that Jamie settle down here in Grand Hope, live in the little cottage, get married and have half a dozen great-grandchildren for her to spoil. "Sorry," Jamie said out loud as she dropped her bags on the table and ran a finger through the fine layer of dust that had collected on the chipped Formica top. "I just never got around to it."

She glanced at the sink where she envisioned her short, round grandmother with her gray permed hair, thick waist and heavy arms. Nita Parsons would have been wearing her favorite tattered apron. In the summertime she would have been putting up peaches and pears or making strawberry jam. This time of year she would have been baking dozens upon dozens of tiny Christmas cookies that she meticulously iced and decorated before giving boxes of the delicacies to friends and relatives. Nana's old yellow-and-white spotted cat, Lazarus, would have been doing figure eights and rubbing up against Nita's swollen ankles, and she would have complained now and again about the arthritis that had invaded her fingers and shoulders.

"Oh, Nana," Jamie whispered, glancing out the window to the snow-crusted yard. Thorny, leafless brambles scaled the wire fence surrounding the garden plot. The henhouse had nearly collapsed. The small barn was still standing, though the roof sagged and the remaining weed-strewn pasture was thankfully hidden beneath the blanket of white.

Nana had loved it here, and Jamie intended to clean it up and list it with a local real estate company.

She glanced at her watch and walked outside to the back porch. She couldn't waste any more time thinking maudlin, nostalgic thoughts. She had too much to do, including meeting with the McCafferty brothers.

*Boy, and won't that be a blast?* She carried in her bags and, despite the near-zero weather, opened every window on the first floor to air out the house. Then she climbed up the steep wooden stairs to her bedroom tucked under the eaves. It was as she'd left it years ago, with the same hand-pieced quilt tossed over the spindle bed. She opened the shades and window and looked past the naked branches of an oak tree to the county road that passed this stretch of farmland. All in all, the area hadn't changed much. Though the town of Grand Hope had grown, Nana had lived far enough outside the city limits that the fast lane hadn't quite reached her.

Jamie unpacked. She hung some clothes in the old closet, the rest she stowed in the top two drawers of an antique bureau. She didn't allow her mind to drift back to the year and a half she'd lived with Nana, the best time of her life...and the worst. For the first time in her seventeen years she'd understood the meaning of unconditional love, given to her by an elderly woman with sparkling gold eyes, rimless glasses and a wisdom that spanned nearly seven decades. Yet Jamie had also experienced her first love and heartbreak compliments of Slade-the-bastard-McCafferty.

And whoop-de-do, she probably was going to meet him again this very afternoon. Life was just chock-full of surprises. And sometimes they weren't for the best.

It took two hours to check in the barn and find that Caesar, Nana's old gelding, was waiting for her. A roan with an ever-graying nose, Caesar was more than twenty years old, but his eyes were bright and clear, and from the shine on his winter coat, Jamie knew that the neighbors had been taking care of him.

"Bet you still get lonely, though, eh, boy?" she asked, seeing to his water and feed and taking in the smell of him and the small, dusty barn. He nickered softly, and Jamie's eyes burned with unshed tears. How could she ever sell him? "We had some good times together, you and I, didn't we? Got into our share of trouble."

She cleared her throat and found a brush to run over his shoulders and back as memories of racing him across the wide expanse of Montana grassland flashed through her eyes. She even rode him to the river where he waded into the deeper water and swam across, all at the urging of Slade McCafferty. Jamie had never forgotten the moment of exhilaration as Caesar had floated with the current. Slade's blue eyes had danced, and he'd showed her a private deer trail where they'd stopped and smoked forbidden cigarettes.

Her heart twisted at the memory. "Yep, you're quite a trouper," she told the horse. "I'll be back. Soon." Hurrying into the house, determined to leave any memory of Slade behind her, she worked for the next two hours getting the ancient old furnace running, turning on the water, adjusting the temperature of the water heater, then stripping her bed only to make it again with sheets that had been packed away in a cedar chest. She smiled sadly as she stretched the soft percale over the mattress. It smelled slightly of lavender—Nana's favorite scent.

Again her heart ached. God, she missed her grandmother, the one person in the world she could count on. Rather than tackle any serious cleaning, she set up a makeshift office in the dining room compliments of her laptop computer and a modem; she only had to call the phone company and set up service again; then, she could link to the office in Missoula.

She checked her watch. She had less than an hour before she was to sit down with Thorne, Matt and Slade McCafferty. The Flying M ranch was nearly twenty miles away.

"Better get a move on, Parsons," she told herself, though her stomach was already clenched in tight little knots at the thought of coming face-to-face with Slade again. It was ridiculous, really. How could something that happened so long ago still bother her?

She'd been over Slade McCafferty for years. *Years.*

Seeing him again would be no problem at all, just another day in a lawyer's life, the proverbial walk in the park. Right? So why, then, the tightness in her chest, the acceleration of her heartbeat, the tiny beads of sweat gathering under her scalp on this cold day? For crying out loud, she was acting like an adolescent, and that just wouldn't do. Not at all.

Back up the stairs.

She changed from jeans and her favorite old sweater to a black suit with a silk blouse and knee-high boots, then wound her hair into a knot she pinned to the top of her head, and gazed at her reflection in the mirror above the antique dresser. It had been nearly fifteen years since she'd seen Slade McCafferty, and in those years she'd blossomed from a fresh-faced, angry eighteen-year-old with something to prove to a full-grown adult who'd worked two jobs to get through college and eventually earned a law degree.

The woman in the reflection was confident, steady and determined, but beneath the image, Jamie saw herself as she had been: heavier, angrier, the new-girl-in-town with a bad attitude and even worse reputation.

A nest of butterflies erupted in her stomach at the thought

of dealing with Slade again, but she told herself she was being silly, reliving those melodramatic teenage years. Which was just plain nuts! Angry with herself, she pulled on black gloves and a matching wool coat, grabbed her briefcase and purse, and was down the stairs and out Nana's back door in nothing flat. She trudged through the snow to her little car, carrying her briefcase as if it were some kind of shield. Lord, she was a basket case. So she had to face Slade McCafferty again.

So what?

So far, it had been a bad day.

And it was only going to get worse.

Slade could feel it in his bones.

He leaned a shoulder against the window casing and stared out the dining room window to the vast, snow-covered acres of the Flying M ranch and the surrounding forested hills. Cattle moved sluggishly across the wintry landscape, and gray clouds threatened to drop more snow on this section of the valley. The temperature was hovering just below freezing, and his hip ached a little, a reminder that he hadn't quite healed from last year's skiing accident.

Thorne was seated at the long table where the family gathered for holidays and special occasions. He'd shoved the holly and mistletoe centerpiece to one side and had spread out documents in neat piles. He was still wearing a leg brace from a plane crash that had nearly taken his life, and he propped that leg on a nearby chair as he sorted through the papers.

Damn, he was such a control freak.

"You're sure you want to sell?" he asked for the dozenth time.

They'd been over this time and time again.

Slade didn't bother answering.

"Where will you go?"

"Not sure." He shrugged. Craved a smoke. "I'll hang around for a while. Long enough to nail the bastard who messed up Randi."

White lines bracketed Thorne's mouth. "I can't wait for the day." He shoved his chair back. "It won't come soon enough for me."

"Me, either."

"You heard anything from Striker?" Thorne asked, bringing up the P.I. whom Slade had brought into the investigation.

"Nope. Left a message this morning."

"You sure about him?" Thorne asked.

"I'd trust my life with him."

"You're trusting Randi's."

"Give it a rest, will ya?" Slade snapped. Everyone's nerves were stretched to the breaking point. Slade had known Kurt Striker for years and had brought him in to investigate the attempts on their half sister, Randi's, life. Kelly Dillinger, Matt's fiancée, had joined up with Striker. She'd once been with the sheriff's department; she was now working the private side.

"You doubt Kurt Striker's ability?"

Thorne shook his hand. "Nah. Just frustrated. I want this over."

"You and me both."

Slade would like to move on. He'd been restless here at the Flying M, never did feel that this old ranch house was home, not since his parents' divorce some twenty-odd years earlier. But he'd planned to stay in Grand Hope, Montana, until the person who was terrorizing his half sister and her newborn baby was run to ground and locked away forever. Or put six feet under. He didn't really care which.

He just needed to find a new life. Whatever the hell it was. Ever since Rebecca… No, he wouldn't go there. Couldn't. It was still too damned painful.

*Now, it's time for you to put the past behind you. Settle down. Start a family.* His father's advice crept up on him like a ghost.

Bootsteps rang in the hallway.

"Sorry I'm late—" Matt apologized as he strode in. Propped against his shoulder was J.R., Randi's baby, now nearly two months old. The kid had captured each one of his uncles' jaded hearts, something the women around this neck of the woods had thought impossible.

Matt adjusted the baby on his shoulder, and J.R. made a strange gurgling sound that pulled at the corners of Slade's mouth. With downy, uneven reddish-blond hair that stuck up at odd angles no matter how often Randi smoothed it, big eyes that took in everything, and a button of a nose, J.R. acted as if he owned the place. He flailed his tiny fists and often sucked on not only his thumb, but whatever digit was handy. "I was busy changing this guy."

Thorne chuckled. "*That's* your excuse for being late?"

"It's my *reason*."

Slade swallowed a smile, his mood improving. The little one; he was a reason to stick around here awhile.

"Okay, so let's get down to business," Thorne suggested. "Aside from the papers about the land sale, I'm going to ask about checking into the baby's father, seeing what his rights are."

"Randi won't like it," Matt predicted.

"Of course she won't. She doesn't like much of anything these days."

*Amen,* Slade thought, but he didn't blame his sister for being restless and feeling cooped up. He'd experienced the same twinges. It was time to move on…as soon as the bastard who was terrorizing her was put away.

Thorne added, "I'm only doing what's best for her."

"That'll make her like it less." Slade rested a hip on the edge of the table.

"Too bad. When Ms. Parsons arrives, I'm going to bring it up."

*Ms. Jamie Parsons, Attorney-at-Law.*

Slade's back teeth ground together at the thought of her. He'd never expected to see her again; hadn't wanted to. Still didn't. He'd dated her for a while, true, and there had been something about her that had left him wanting more, but he'd dated a lot of women in his lifetime, before and after Jamie Parsons. It wasn't a big deal.

"Why do I think you've been discussing me?" Randi asked as she appeared in the doorway to the dining room. She was limping slightly from the accident that had nearly taken her life, but her spine was stiff as she hobbled into the room and pried the baby easily from Matt's arms.

"You always think we're talkin' about you behind your back," Matt teased.

"Because you always are. Right?" she asked Slade.

"Always," he drawled.

"So when's the attorney due to arrive?"

Thorne checked his watch. "In about fifteen minutes."

"Good." Randi kissed her son's head and he cooed softly. Slade felt a pang deep inside, a pain he buried deep. He touched the scar on the side of his face and scowled. He wasn't envious of Randi—God, no. But he couldn't help being reminded of his own loss every time he looked at his nephew.

And his sister had been through so much. Aside from the fact that she still moved with difficulty, wincing once in a while from the pain, there was the problem with her memory. Amnesia, if she could be believed.

Slade wasn't convinced. Nope. He wasn't certain his half sister was being straight with them. Her memory loss smacked of convenience. There were just too many questions Randi didn't want to answer, questions concerning her son's paternity. When her jaw had been wired shut and her arm in a cast, communication had been near impossible, but now she was well on the way to being a hundred percent again. Except for her mind. To Slade's way of thinking, amnesia made everything so much easier. No explanations. Not even about the damned accident that had nearly ended her life.

What the hell had happened on that icy road in Glacier Park? All Slade, his brothers and the police knew was that Randi's Jeep had swerved off the road and down an embankment. Had she hit ice? Been forced off the road? Kurt Striker, the private investigator Slade had contacted to look into the accident, was convinced another car, a maroon Ford product, had forced Randi off the road. The police were checking. Only Randi knew for certain. And she wasn't talking.

The result of the accident had been premature delivery of the baby, internal injuries, concussion, lacerations, a broken jaw and a fractured leg. She'd spent most of her recuperation time in a coma, unable to communicate, while the brothers had searched for whoever had tried to harm her and her baby.

So far, they'd come up empty. Whoever had tried to kill Randi had taken a second shot at it, slipping into the hospital, posing as part of the staff and injecting insulin into her IV. She'd survived. Barely. And the maniac was still very much at large.

Slade's fists clenched at the thought of the bastard. If he ever got his hands on the guy, he'd beat the living tar out of him.

But Randi wasn't helping much. She'd emerged from her coma fighting mad and unwilling to help. If only she'd help them, give them some names, let them know who might want to harm her.... But no. Her memory just kept failing her.

Or so she claimed.

Bull.

Slade figured she was hiding something, covering up the truth, protecting someone. But why? Who?

Herself? Her baby? Little J.R.'s father, whoever he was? Or someone else?

"Hell," he growled under his breath.

Maybe Thorne was right. Maybe they should enlist Jamie Parsons and the firm of Jansen, Monteith and Stone to try to locate the baby's father and to take the legal steps to ensure that J.R.'s daddy wouldn't show up someday and demand custody. If that was even possible.

Slade just wished the lawyer assigned to their case was someone other than Jamie Parsons.

Randi settled into the chair directly across the table from Thorne. "Since the attorney's dropping by anyway, I want to talk about changing the baby's name legally. J.R. doesn't cut it with me."

"Do what you want. We needed something for the birth certificate." Thorne glanced at his nephew. "But I think J.R. fits him just fine."

"So do I," Slade agreed. "Since you were in a coma, we agreed on the initials."

"Okay, okay, so it served a purpose and now everyone is calling him J.R., but I'm going to change his name officially to Joshua Ray McCafferty." She glanced around the room, and if she saw the questions in her brothers' eyes, ignored them.

J.R.'s paternity was a touchy subject. With everyone. Particularly Randi, who was the only one who could name the father. But she wasn't talking. Unmarried and, to her brothers' knowledge, not seriously involved with anyone, she refused to name the man.

Why?

"He's mine," she'd say when asked about the baby. "That's all that matters."

But it bothered Slade. A lot. He couldn't help but think her reticence to name the man and the attempts on her life were related.

"He's your kid. You can name him whatever you want," Thorne said agreeably, "but I didn't warn the attorney that we'd have more issues than the property division."

"He'll handle it." Randi adjusted the drool bib around her son's tiny neck.

"She," Thorne clarified. "Chuck Jansen is sending a woman associate. Jamie Parsons. She grew up around here."

"Jamie?" Randi's eyes narrowed thoughtfully and Slade envisioned the gears in her mind meshing and spinning and spewing out all kinds of unwanted conclusions. Yep. She glanced his way.

"She lived with her grandmother outside of town." Thorne winced as he adjusted his bad leg on the chair next to him.

"Nita Parsons. Yes, I remember. Mom made me take piano lessons from Mrs. Parsons. Man, she was a taskmaster."

None of the men commented. They never liked to be reminded that Randi's mother had been the reason their parents had divorced. John Randall had fallen in love with Penelope Henley, promptly divorced Larissa, their mother, and married the much younger woman. Six months after the nuptials, Randi had come into the world. Slade hadn't much liked his stepmother or the new baby, but over the years he'd quit blaming his half sister for his parents' doomed union.

Randi looked up at Slade and he felt it coming—the question he didn't want to face. "Weren't you and Jamie an item years ago?"

"Hardly an item. We saw each other a few times. It wasn't a big deal." He shoved his hands into the back pockets of his

jeans and hoped that was the end of it. But he knew his reporter sister better than that.

"More than a few. And, if I remember right, she was pretty
gone on you."

"Is that right?" Matt asked, a smile crawling across his
beard-shadowed chin. "Hard to believe any woman would
be so foolish."

"Isn't it?" Randi said as J.R. tried to grab her earring.

"Funny. I wouldn't think you'd *remember* anything."

Randi's eyes flashed. "Bits and pieces, Slade. I already told
you, I just remember a little of this and a little of that. More
each day."

But not the father of her child? Or what happened when
she was forced off the road?

"Then you'd better focus on who wants to see you dead."

"You were involved with the lady lawyer?" Matt asked.

Slade lifted one shoulder and felt the weight of his brothers'
gazes on him. "It was a long time ago." He heard the whine
of an engine and his muscles tightened. He turned toward
the window.

Through the frosty panes he caught a glimpse of a tiny blue
car chugging its way along the drive. Slade's gut clenched. The
compact slid to a stop, narrowly missing his truck. A couple
of seconds later a tall woman emerged from the car. With a
black briefcase swinging from her arm, she hesitated just a second as she looked at the house, then taking a deep breath, she
squared her shoulders and strode up the front path where the
snow had been broken and trampled.

Jamie Parsons in the flesh.

*Great. Just...great.*

She was all confidence and femininity in her severe black
coat. Sunstreaked hair had been slicked away from a face that
boasted high cheekbones, defined chin and wide forehead.

He couldn't make out the color of her eyes but remembered they were hazel, shifting from green to gold in the sunlight or darkening when she got angry.

For a second he flashed upon a time when the two of them had been down by the creek, not far from the swimming hole where Thorne had almost drowned.

It had been a torridly hot summer, the wildflowers had been in bloom, the grass dry and the smell of fresh-cut hay had floated in the air along with the fluff from dandelions. He'd dared her to strip naked and jump into the clear water. And she, with the look of devilment in those incredible eyes, had done just that, exposing high, firm breasts with pink nipples and a thatch of reddish hair above long, tanned legs. He'd caught only a glimpse before she'd dashed into the water, submerged and come up tossing her wet hair from her eyes. He could still hear her laughter, melodious as a warbler's song.

*God, where had that come from? It had been eons ago. A lifetime.* The bad day just got worse.

From somewhere on the front porch Harold gave up a deep "woof" just as the doorbell chimed.

"You gonna get that?" Matt asked, and Slade, frowning, headed along the hallway toward the front door.

From the kitchen Juanita, the housekeeper, was rattling pans and singing softly in Spanish, while in the living room a fire crackled and Nicole, Thorne's wife, was playing a board game with her four-year-old twin daughters. Giggles and quiet conversation could be heard over the muted melodies of Christmas carols playing from a recently purchased CD player. At the sound of the front door chimes, two little voices erupted.

"I get it! I get it!"

"No. Me!"

Two sets of small feet scurried through the living room as Molly and Mindy, their dark ringlets flying, scrambled into the entry hall and raced for the door. Small hands vying for the handle, they managed to yank the door open and there on the front porch, looking professional, feminine and surprised as all get-out at her reception, stood Jamie Parsons, Attorney-at-Law.

# Chapter 2

"Who're *you?*" Molly demanded, her brown eyes trained on the woman in black.

"I'm Jamie." With one quick glance at Slade, she bent down on one knee, mindless that her coat was getting wet in the snow melting on the floorboards of the porch. Good Lord, he'd gotten better-looking! "And who are you?" she asked one girl.

"Molly," the bolder twin asserted, rubbing a hand on her pink sweatshirt.

"And you?" Jamie's eyes moved to Molly's identical sister. They were Slade's daughters, she thought wildly. Surprised that she cared. "What's your name?"

Mindy took a step behind Slade's jeans-clad leg. Her small arms wrapped around his knee and she hid her face.

"She's Mindy and she's shy," Molly stated.

"Am not." Mindy's thumb was suddenly in her mouth as she peeked around Slade's thigh. Slade was amused as he read

Jamie's case of nerves. Another set of footsteps announced Nicole's arrival. Tall, slender, with amber eyes and blond-streaked hair, she was a doctor at St. James Hospital and the mother of the imps, not to mention the reason Thorne wore a smile these days.

"Hello," she said to Jamie. "I'm Nicole McCafferty." She extended a hand and tossed a lock of hair off her shoulder. "And these two tornados—" she indicated the twins with her chin "—are my daughters."

Straightening, Jamie accepted Nicole's handshake. She glanced at Slade, and something dark shifted in her hazel eyes. Her smile became a little more forced, her voice more professional and cool. "Pleased to meet you. All of you."

"I take it you already know Slade?" Nicole said as she peeled Mindy from Slade's leg and gathered the shy girl into her arms.

"Yes...we've...we've met. Years ago." Jamie's voice was husky and she cleared her throat.

Slade noticed that she inched her chin up a fraction as she turned to him and, gesturing to the girls, said, "You've been busy."

He lifted one eyebrow.

"Your daughters...they're lovely," she added.

"Why thank you," he drawled, smothering a smile at her discomfiture—now what was that all about? "But they're not mine."

"Oh. I'm sorry. I was married before," Nicole explained. "I just recently joined this family."

"I see."

Nicole laughed as she finally caught on. "Oh. No. *No!* It's not what you think. Slade's my brother-in-law. I'm married to Thorne."

"Poor woman," Slade drawled, and Nicole sent him a dirty look. He witnessed a blush steal up Jamie's neck. He remembered that. How easily her fair skin would color a soft, embarrassed pink.

"Oh. Well. My mistake." Was she relieved? "There wasn't any reference to wives in the documents."

"*That* will have to be changed." Nicole chuckled and stepped out of the doorway as a black-and-white-spotted cat darted up the stairs. "Come in. It's freezing out there. Let me take your coat, and Slade—if he has a gentlemanly bone in his body, which is highly unlikely in my opinion—can show you into the dining room where the rest of the clan is waiting."

"I can manage that," Slade allowed.

"I hope so." Nicole transferred a squirming Mindy to the floor. "Meanwhile, I'll see if Juanita can scrounge up some coffee or tea."

Jamie was working the buttons of her coat. "That would be great."

"I'll take that," Slade offered as Nicole headed toward the kitchen, her daughters trailing after her like ducklings behind a mother duck.

Jamie set her bags down and shrugged out of her overcoat with Slade's help. His fingers brushed her nape for the briefest of seconds and he thought she stiffened, but he might have imagined it. She probably barely remembered him.

All business in a black suit and shimmery blouse, she picked up her bags again. "Ready?" she asked.

"As I'll ever be." He showed her along the hallway to the dining room. They passed by what he referred to as the McCafferty Hall of Shame where photos of the family were mounted. With cool disinterest Jamie's eyes skimmed pictures of Thorne in his football uniform, Randi going to the prom, Matt on a bucking bronco and Slade skiing downhill as if the devil were on his tail. Jamie didn't react, just walked smartly into the dining room.

"Hi," she said. "You all probably know this, but I figured I'd better get the formal introductions over. I'm Jamie Parsons with Jansen, Monteith and Stone." Thorne had some trouble scrambling to his feet as one of his legs was in a brace, but Matt reached forward to shake her hand. Slade made quick introductions. "All right," she said, offering them each a smile that Slade was certain she'd practiced a thousand times in front of a mirror, "let's get started."

Everyone settled into a chair. Jamie flipped open her briefcase and distributed copies of legal documents. "The way I understand it is that Matt—" she pinned the middle McCafferty brother in her gaze "—wants to sell his place north of Missoula on contract to Michael Kavanaugh, his neighbor. He then wants to buy the two of you—" she motioned to Slade and Thorne "—out, so that he'll own half of this place and, Randi, you'll own the other half."

"That's right," Matt confirmed.

"Matt's agreed to run the ranch," Randi contributed. "Then he…well, he and Kelly, since they're going to be married soon…can live here."

"What about you?" Thorne asked, his brows beetling.

Randi shook her head and flipped a palm toward the ceiling. "I do have a life in Seattle, you know."

Thorne's scowl deepened. "Yeah, I do know. But until we're certain you're safe, I don't want you going anywhere. Not until we figure out who's been trying to kill you and he's safely behind bars."

With a smile that dared her oldest brother to try to tell her what to do, she arched a dark brow. "I'm not arguing about it now, okay? I think Ms. Parsons has business here and she'd like to get down to it."

"Jamie. Let's keep this casual."

Slade stiffened.

"We're all from around here, so there's no reason to be formal," Jamie said coolly. "Okay, you've all got a copy of the paperwork, so let's go over it."

Slade tried not to notice the slope of her jaw, or the way she flashed a smile or how her eyebrows knitted in concentration as she read through the documents. What had happened between them was ancient history. *Ancient.*

Besides, he didn't like lawyers. Any of 'em. He reached into his shirt pocket, his fingers searching for a nonexistent pack of cigarettes. He was trying to cut down and had left his smokes in his truck. Not that anyone would let him light up in here anyway.

Nicole brought in a tray of coffee, tea and cinnamon cookies, but Jamie seemed to barely notice. The baby started to fuss and she glanced at J.R. for just a second, her eyes turning wistful for the barest of moments before she became all business again.

Apologizing in Spanish and English, Juanita bustled in. Dark eyes flashed with pride as she fixated on the baby. "*Dios,* little man, you are a loud one." Expertly she plucked the infant from Randi's arms. "He is hungry, *sí?*"

"Big time," Randi said, starting to climb to her feet.

"Sit, sit…you have business." Juanita waved Randi back into her chair. "I'll see to him." Before Randi could protest, Juanita turned on her heel and, cradling the baby close, swept out of the room.

Jamie barely broke stride. "Let's look at page two…"

A professional attorney through and through, Slade thought, staring at her. Where was the wild, rebellious girl he remembered? The one who had turned his head and made him, for a few weeks, question what he wanted? The girl in tattered jeans who had, behind her grandmother's back, drunk, smoked and gone to a tattoo parlor, only to be kicked out before the deed was done as she was underage? If Slade's recollection was right, Jamie had planned to have a small butterfly etched into one smooth shoulder.

Glancing at the thick sheaf of neatly typed pages in front of him Slade wondered if Jamie, once she'd finally turned eighteen, had ever gone back for the body art? Or had her transformation into this all-business woman already begun? Who was she these days? Just another corporate attorney with her hair pulled harshly away from her face, her nails polished, her smile forced? Where was the free spirit who had attracted him so many years ago? Where was the rebellious creature who could spit as well as any boy, swear a blue streak and ride bareback under the stars without a second's hesitation? He watched her through eyes at half-mast and hardly caught a glimmer of the girl she'd once been. For today, at least, she was all business—an automaton spewing legal jargon.

Every once in a while one of the brothers or Randi asked a question. Jamie always had an answer.

"I'll want to put my fiancée's name on the deed," Matt said, his dark eyes thoughtful.

"So you're getting married." Jamie scribbled a quick note on her copy of the documents. "When?"

"Between Christmas and New Year's. I tried to talk her into eloping, but her family had a fit. As it is, it's pretty short notice."

Jamie lifted an arched brow. "So another McCafferty bachelor bites the dust."

"Ouch," Thorne said, but one side of his mouth curved upward. "That just leaves Slade."

For a second the Ice Woman seemed to melt. Her hazel eyes found his. A dozen questions lurked therein. "I thought you were married."

"Never," he replied. Seated low on his spine, sipping coffee, he stared straight into those incredible eyes.

"But...I mean..." She seemed confused, then quickly shoved whatever she was thinking out of her mind and pulled her corporate self together. "Not that it matters. So..." She swung her head toward Matt who was seated at the head of the table near the china closet. "What's your fiancée's name?"

"Kelly Dillinger, but it will be McCafferty by the end of the month."

"She's the daughter of Eva Dillinger, who was our father's secretary." Thorne's mouth turned down and Slade's stomach twisted at the thought of his old man. He missed him, true, but the guy had been a number-one bastard most of Slade's life. "The deal is this. Dad reneged on paying Eva the retirement that he'd promised her and so we—" he motioned to include his brothers and sister "—through the trust, decided to make it good. Your firm handles the disbursements."

Jamie gave a quick nod as if she suddenly remembered. "I've got the papers on the trust with me," she said, riffling through her briefcase and withdrawing another thick file.

"Good." Thorne nodded.

"But Kelly's name needs to be on the deed to the ranch," Matt insisted.

"Duly noted." Jamie penned a reminder on the first page of the contract allowing Matt to buy out his brothers. "I'll see that she's included in the final draft, then she'll have to sign, along with the rest of you, and Mr. Kavanaugh. I'll leave you each a copy of what I've drawn up and you can peruse everything more closely. If you all agree, I'll print out final copies and we'll sign."

"Sounds good." Matt picked up his set of papers as Jamie straightened her pile and thumped it on the table. With a well-practiced smile that didn't light her eyes, she glanced at each

McCafferty sibling before sliding all the documents into her briefcase.

So rehearsed, so professional, so un—Jamie Parsons. At least the Jamie he remembered. As he observed her, Slade wondered what it would take to catch a glimpse of the girl hiding beneath the neatly pressed jacket and skirt.

"So...Matt, you and your wife will be living on the property... Thorne and Nicole are building nearby and Randi will eventually move back to Seattle. I've got all your addresses except Slade's." She stared straight at him. "Where do you call home these days?"

"I've got a place in Colorado, outside of Boulder, but...I haven't decided if I'll stay there or sell it. In the meantime, I'm here, so you can use the address of the Flying M."

"Fair enough." She glanced again from one McCafferty sibling to the next. "Anything else?" she asked.

"Yeah." Thorne glanced at his sister. "We've got a little situation and I'd like some advice on it. As you know, Randi, here, had a baby a couple of months back and the father hasn't stepped forward and made any claim of custody yet, but—"

"Hey!" Randi shot out of her chair and skewered her brother with a don't-even-go-there glare. "Let's not get into this. Not now."

"We have to, Randi." Thorne was serious. "Sooner or later J.R.'s dad is gonna show up. I'll bet on it. And he's gonna start talking about custody and his rights as a father and I'd like to know what we're up against."

"This is *my* problem, Thorne," Randi said, leaning over the table. Pushing her face as close to her oldest brother's as was possible, she hooked a thumb at her chest. "Mine. Okay? Not yours. Not Matt's. Not Slade's. And certainly not Jansen, Monteith and Stone's!" Her eyes snapped fire, her cheeks flushed and she glared at Thorne for a long moment. No one said a word. Finally, Randi swung her gaze toward Jamie. "No offense, okay, but I can handle this. My brothers are just mad because I haven't told them who the baby's father is. Not that it's *any* of their business."

"There's a reason for that," Slade reminded her. "Someone's trying to kill you."

"Again, it's nobody's business."

"Like hell." Slade glowered at his sister. Sometimes Randi could be so bullheaded she was just plain stupid. "Your safety is our business."

"I can take care of myself."

"You can't even remember what happened!" Slade countered, disgusted with his half sibling. "At least that's what you claim."

"It's true."

"Okay, fine, then help us out. We're just trying to keep you safe. To keep J.R., or whatever the hell you call him, safe, okay? So quit being so damned bristly and give us a clue or two! Who's the kid's dad?"

"This isn't the time or place," she warned, every muscle tightening.

Thorne held up a hand as if to somehow quiet Slade. "We're just trying to help."

"Back off, Thorne. I said I can handle it. He's my baby and I would never, *never* do anything to put him in jeopardy, for God's sake. Now, I agreed to stay here for a while, until this whole mess is cleared up, but that doesn't mean my life is going to stop, so just back off!"

Matt shook his head and stared out the window.

"Women," Slade growled, and Jamie's spine stiffened.

Instead of snapping back at his remark, she visibly shifted, as if deciding it was her job to defuse the argument rather than aggravate it. "Custody rights aren't my area of expertise, but, if you decide you do want some legal advice, I can hook you up with Felicia Reynolds. She handles all the custody cases for the firm."

"Thanks. Maybe *I'll* contact her." Randi shot Thorne another warning glare before dropping into her chair. "Maybe."

Jamie snapped her briefcase closed. "Let me know if you want to get in touch with her."

"I will," Randi said, firing Thorne a look meant to not only kill but to eviscerate, as well.

"Okay." It was Jamie's turn to stand. "If any of you has any questions, you can call me through my cell phone, as I don't have a phone number here in town yet, or you can leave a message with the office and they'll get in touch with me. I'm staying at my grandmother's place and as soon as the regular phone is hooked up, I'll let you know."

The meeting was over.

Everyone shook hands.

All business.

Somehow it galled the hell out of Slade, but he found her coat and helped her into it.

Without a backward glance, she walked out the door, her black coat billowing behind her, her briefcase swinging from one gloved hand. Slade hesitated, couldn't help but watch as she climbed into her car and drove away, tires spinning in the snow.

"Randi's right. You did date her," Matt said as Slade closed the door and, hands in the front pockets of his jeans, strolled back to the living room where his brothers were waiting. Matt knelt at the fire, prodding the blackened log with a poker while Thorne rummaged in the old man's liquor cabinet.

"I saw her a few times," Slade admitted, leaning one hip on the windowsill. This conversation was getting them nowhere and he didn't want to discuss it. Seeing Jamie again had brought back a tidal wave of memories that he'd dammed up a long, long time ago.

"Oh, come on, Slade. You saw her more than a few times." Randi hobbled into the room, then fell onto the leather couch. "Let's see," she said, her features pinching as she tried to recall images from the past. Slade sensed he wasn't going to like what was coming next and he braced himself. "The way I remember it, you dated Jamie for a couple of months while you were broken up with Sue Ellen Tisdale, right?"

"I remember you with Sue Ellen," Thorne added.

Great. Just what he needed: his family dissecting his love life.

"But," Randi added, "once Sue Ellen came to her senses and came running back, you dropped Jamie like a hot potato. I thought you were going to marry Sue Ellen."

Slade snorted; didn't comment.

Thorne pulled out a bottle of Scotch. "So did I."

"Everyone did." Randi wasn't about to let up. "Probably even Jamie."

"Again, your memory amazes me," Slade commented.

"As I said, 'bits and pieces.'"

"Is that right?" Matt prodded the fire with a poker. "You really tossed Jamie over for Sue Ellen Tisdale?" His tone implied that Slade was a first-class idiot.

"That's not exactly what happened. Besides, it was years ago."

"Doesn't matter when it happened." Randi rested one heel on the coffee table. "Face it, Slade," she said as the fire began to crackle, "whether you want to admit it or not, about fifteen years ago, you were the son of a bitch who broke Jamie Parsons's heart."

# Chapter 3

"Well, that went swimmingly," Jamie rumbled under her breath as she carried her briefcase and a sack of groceries into her grandmother's house. Driving into town from the Flying M she'd second-guessed herself and cursed C. William "Chuck" Jansen a dozen times over for assigning her to the McCafferty project.

"Since you're heading to Grand Hope anyway, I thought you could help the firm out," Chuck had said as he'd sat familiarly on the corner of the desk in her office, one leg swinging, his wing-tip gleaming in the soft lighting. His boyish smile had been wide, his suit expensive, his shirt, as always, starched and crisply pressed. He'd tugged at his Yves St. Laurent tie. "I think it would be a good idea to put a face on Jansen, Monteith and Stone for the McCafferty family. John Randall McCafferty was an excellent client of the firm and the partners would like to keep the McCaffertys' business. Maybe even get a little more. Thorne McCafferty is a millionaire several times over in his own right, and the second son, Matt—he owns his own place. He's basically a small-time rancher, but he also seems to have some of that McCafferty-Midas touch. The third son…"

Jamie recalled how Chuck's brows had knit and his lips had folded together thoughtfully while she had conjured up a few unwelcome memories of Slade and nearly snapped her pen in two. "Well, there's always one in the family, I suppose. The third son, Slade—he never amounted to much. Lots of potential, but couldn't get it together. Too busy raising hell. He drove race cars and rode rodeo and even led expeditions for extreme skiing, I think. Always on the edge, but never getting his life together.

"But John Randall's only daughter, Randi—she's a real firecracker—takes after the old man. No wonder she was named after him."

Jamie tried to ignore the comments about Slade and concentrated on his half sister. She remembered Randi as being smart, sassy and McCafferty-stubborn.

"She's got her own daily column, 'Solo' or 'Being Single' or something," Chuck had continued. "Writes for a Seattle newspaper. There's some talk of syndication, I think. And Thorne mentioned that she could have been working on a book at the time of the accident."

"Thorne McCafferty used to work here, didn't he?" Jamie had asked, twiddling her pen and not liking the turn of the conversation. Especially not any reference to Slade.

"Yes, yes, that's right. He was a junior partner years ago. Then went out on his own. Moved to Denver. But he still throws us a bone once in a while. So, I've been thinking. Wouldn't it be a plum to nail down the corporate account, steal it away from that Denver firm he deals with?" Chuck's eyes had sparked with a competitive fire Jamie hadn't witnessed in a while.

"I thought you were going to retire."

"In a couple of years, yes," he'd admitted, winking at her. "But why not go out in a blaze, hmm? It'll only make my share of the firm worth more, hence my retirement…we could buy a sailboat and sail to Tahiti or Fiji or—"

"I'll still have a job."

"Not if you marry me."

She'd squirmed. Chuck had been pressuring her lately and she wasn't sure what she wanted to do with the rest of her life. There had been a time when she'd thought that enough money could buy happiness, that the reason Slade McCafferty hadn't been interested in her was because she was poor, from the wrong side of the tracks and didn't have the social status of Sue Ellen Tisdale. But over the years she'd changed her opinion about financial success and its rewards. She'd met plenty of miserable millionaires.

"Listen." Chuck had rapped his knuckles on the desk as he'd straightened. "Think about it when you're in Grand Hope. Being Mrs. Chuck Jansen wouldn't be all that bad, not that I'm pressuring you."

"Right," she'd said, and managed a smile.

"We'll talk when you get back." He'd said it with the same confidence he oozed in a courtroom.

"What a mess," Jamie muttered to herself as she adjusted the thermostat while, presumably, back in Missoula, Chuck was waiting, expecting her to get off the fence and accept his proposal.

But she couldn't. Not yet.

Why?

Chuck was smart. Educated. Clever. Good-looking. Wealthy.

His share of the business was worth a bundle and then there was his stock portfolio and two homes.

*He also has a bitter ex-wife,* her mind nagged. *And three college-age kids. He doesn't want any more.*

Jamie thought of Randi McCafferty and her newborn son, the way the baby's eyes had twinkled in adoration at his mother. Her heartstrings tugged. God, how she wanted a baby of her own, a baby to love. Could she marry Chuck, become a stepmother to nearly grown children, never raise a daughter or son of her own, one she conceived with a husband who made her heart pound and brought a smile to her lips? For a second Slade's face flashed through Jamie's mind. "Oh, stop it," she growled at herself in frustration. Just because she'd been thrown back here and had to face him, she'd started fantasizing. "You're pathetic, Parsons. Pa-thetic." She started to unpack the groceries, but couldn't forget how surprised she'd been at Slade's easy manner with his twin nieces and tiny nephew. Who would have thought?

Ironic, she thought, touching her flat abdomen. But, once upon a time...

"Don't even go there," she chastised herself, stocking the cupboard with a few cans of soup and a box of crackers, then stuffing a quart of milk and jug of orange juice into the old refrigerator.

She remembered turning into the lane of the Flying M this afternoon. Her nerves had been stretched tight as piano wire, her hands sweating inside her gloves. But that had been just the start of it. Finally facing Slade again—oh, Lord, *that* had been the worst; more difficult than she'd even imagined.

He'd changed in the past fifteen years. His body had filled out, his shoulders were broader, his chest wider, though his hips were as lean as she remembered. At that thought, she colored, remembering the first time she'd seen him without clothes—at the swimming hole when he'd yanked off his cut-offs, revealing that he hadn't bothered wearing any underwear. She'd glimpsed white buttocks that had contrasted to his tanned back and muscular legs, and caught sight of something more, a part of male anatomy she'd never seen before.

Oh, God, she'd been such an innocent. Of course he'd changed physically. Hard-living and years had a way of doing that to a body. Slade's face was more angular than it had been; a thin scar ran down one side of his face, but his eyes were still as blue as a Montana sky.

She'd noticed that he'd limped slightly. And there was something in his expression, a darkness in his eyes, that betrayed him, a shadow of pain. Okay, so he had his war wounds; some more visible than others. Didn't everyone? She folded the grocery sack and slipped it into the pantry.

She couldn't help but wonder what had happened between Sue Ellen and him, though she imagined Sue Ellen was just one of dozens. The McCafferty boys had been legendary in their conquests. Hadn't she been one?

"Who cares," she growled as she picked up her coat and hung it in the hall closet where Nana's vacuum cleaner still stood guard. All the McCafferty boys had been hellions, teenagers who had disregarded the law. Slade had been no exception. While Thorne had been an athlete, and toed the line more than either of his brothers, Matt had been rumored to be a lady-killer with his lazy smile and rodeo daring, and Slade had gained the reputation of a daredevil, a boy who'd fearlessly climbed the most jagged peaks, kayaked down raging rivers and skied to the extreme on the most treacherous slopes—all of which had been accomplished over his father's vehement protests.

But it had been a thousand years ago. She'd been a rebellious girl trying to fit in. Not a grown woman with a law degree. Sensible, she reminded herself. These days she was *sensible.*

And sometimes she hated it.

"Don't lecture me," Randi ordered as Slade walked into the den. She was seated at Thorne's computer, glasses propped on the end of her nose, the baby sleeping in a playpen in the corner.

"Did I say a word?"

"You didn't have to. I can see it in your face. You're an open book, Slade."

"Like hell." He propped a hip against the edge of the desk. "I think you and I need to clear the air."

The corners of her mouth tightened a fraction. "Just a sec." Her fingers flew over the keyboard. "You can't believe how much email I've collected…" With a wry smile, she clicked off and added, "It's great to be loved. Now, as I was saying, don't start in on me about the baby's father. It's my business. So if that's what you mean by 'clearing the air,' let's just keep it foggy."

"Someone tried to kill you."

"So you keep reminding me, over and over." Something darkened her eyes for a heartbeat. Fear? Anger? He couldn't tell, and the shadow quickly disappeared. Standing slightly, she leaned over the desk, pushing aside a cup of pens and pencils. "I get enough advice from Thorne. And Nicole. And Matt and even Juanita." Pointing an accusing finger at his nose, she said, "From you, I expect understanding."

"I don't know what you're asking me to understand."

"That I need some space. Some privacy. Come on, Slade, you know what it's like for the whole damned family to be talking about you, worrying about you, clucking around like a bunch of hens. It's enough to drive a sane person crazy.

That's why you and I both moved away from Grand Hope in the first place."

"So who says you're sane?"

"Oh, so now you're a comedian," she quipped, smothering a smile as she took off her glasses and leaned back into her chair. Large brown eyes assessed him. "What's with that private detective?"

"Striker?"

"Yeah, him. I hear he's your friend."

"He is."

"Humph." She frowned, fluffing up her short locks with nervous fingers. "There's a reason they're called dicks, you know."

He snorted. "Testy, aren't we?"

"Yes, *we* are. *We* don't like being watched around the clock, spied upon, our lives being dissected. Tell him to lay off. I don't like him digging around in my personal life."

"No way, kiddo. It was my idea to bring him into the investigation."

"And it was a bad one. We don't need him." She was adamant. "We've got the sheriff's department. Detective Espinoza seems to be doing a decent enough job. Kelly should never have quit the department to work with Striker."

Something was going on here; something Randi wasn't admitting. "Is it Striker you don't like? Or P.I.s in general?"

"Both. Aren't the police enough?"

"No."

"But—"

"Kurt's just trying to help us find the bastard who wants you dead. You might be a little more helpful, you know. It's like you're hiding something."

"What?"

"You tell me."

"I would if I could," she snapped. "But that's just not possible right now. However, if I remember anything, anything at all, you'll be the first to know."

"Yeah, right. Then try concentrating on something besides people I dated fifteen years ago."

Randi's eyes narrowed. "It bothers you, doesn't it? What happened with Jamie?"

"I haven't thought about it much."

"Until now." His sister's smile was nearly wicked. "What are you going to do about it?"

"Nothing," he said, knowing as the word passed his teeth it was a lie. Jamie had gotten to him. Already. And he felt an unlikely need to explain himself, to set the record straight about the Sue Ellen thing.

*Or is that just an excuse to see her again? Face it, McCafferty, you haven't been interested in a woman since Rebecca, but one look at the lady attorney and you've barely thought of anything else.*

"So what're you working on?" He pointed at the computer and shoved his nagging thoughts aside.

"Catching up on a billion emails," she said. "I've been out of the loop awhile. It'll take days to go through all of these and I've got to get my own laptop back. This one is Thorne's and I don't think he appreciates me monopolizing it as it's his main link to his office in Denver."

"He's got a desktop ordered. It should be here any day."

"That'll solve some problems."

"Where's your laptop?"

She bit her lip. "I don't know...I can't remember...but...why don't you ask Kurt Striker. I hear both he and the police have been in my apartment. Damn." She raked her fingers through her short, uneven hair, and when she looked up at Slade, her expression was troubled. "I'm really not trying to be a pain, Slade. I know everyone's trying to help me, but it's so frustrating. I feel like it's really important for me to get back home, to look through my stuff, to write on my own computer, but I can't remember what's on the damned thing, probably just ideas and research for future columns, but I feel like it could help—that it might be the reason some psycho is after me."

"Maybe it is," he said. "Juanita said you were working on a book."

"So I've heard. But..." She sighed loudly. "I can't remember what it's about."

"Then I guess we'll just have to find the damned laptop, won't we? Striker's still working on it."

"Striker. Oh, great," she muttered as Slade left her.

In the kitchen, he yanked his jacket from a hook near the back door and walked outside. The late-afternoon sky was already dark, the air brisk.

Overhead, clouds threatened to dump more snow. Not that he cared. He climbed into his pickup, started the engine and cranked on the wheel. He'd drive into town, have a drink and...and what?

*See Jamie again* ran through his mind.

"Damn it all to hell." He threw the truck into First and reached for his pack of smokes. He'd always gotten himself into trouble where women were concerned and he knew, as the tires slid on a slick patch of packed snow, that he hadn't changed over the years.

He could deny it to himself up one side and down the other, but the truth of the matter was, he intended to see Jamie again and he intended to do it tonight.

Shivering, Jamie changed into soft jeans and her favorite old sweatshirt before she clamored down to the kitchen where she found a pan, washed it, heated the soup and crushed oyster crackers into the beef and vegetable broth. She imagined

Nana sitting across the table from her, insisting they say grace, watching her over the top of her glasses until Jamie obediently bowed her head and mouthed a prayer.

It wasn't that Jamie hadn't believed in God in those days, she just hadn't had a lot of extra time to spend on her spiritual growth—not when there were boys to date, cars to carouse in and cigarettes to smoke. It was a wonder she'd graduated from high school, much less had been accepted into college.

"God bless the SATs," she said, smiling at her own prayer. "And you, Nana, wherever you are. God bless you." She left the dishes in the sink, then started cleaning, room by room, as the ancient furnace rumbled and heat slowly seeped into the house. She'd considered hiring a cleaning service, but figured the scrubbing was cathartic for her and somehow—wherever she was—Nana would approve. "A little hard work never hurt anyone," she'd lectured when Jamie had tried to weasel out of her chores.

Nita Parsons had realized her granddaughter was a troubled girl who had one foot headed to nowhere good. And she had decided she wouldn't make the same mistakes with Jamie as she had with Jamie's father, an alcoholic who had abandoned his wife and daughter two days after Jamie's eighth birthday. Barely nine years later, Jamie's single mother had gotten fed up with a rebellious teenage daughter who seemed hell-bent on ruining both their lives.

That's when Nana had stepped in.

And how had Jamie repaid her? By giving her grandmother more gray hairs than she'd already had.

"Sorry," Jamie whispered now as she rubbed polish into the base of a brass lamp. She intended to scrub Nana's hardwood and tile floors until they gleamed, paint the rooms in the soft yellows Nana had loved and repair what she could afford.

And then sell the place?

Inwardly Jamie cringed. She could almost hear the disappointment in her grandmother's voice. How many times had she heard Nana say, "This will be yours one day, Jamie, and don't you ever sell it. I own it free and clear and it's been a godsend, believe me. When times are lean, I can grow my own food. Twenty acres is more than enough to support you, if you're smart and work hard. I don't have to worry about a rent payment or a landlord who might not take a shine to me." She'd wagged a finger in front of Jamie's nose on more than one occasion. "I've lived through wars and bad times, let me tell you, and I was one of the lucky ones. The people who had farms and held on to them, they did okay. They might have had patches on their sleeves and holes in their shoes but they had full bellies and a roof over their heads."

Jamie had thought it all very dull at the time and now as she wiped at a network of cobwebs behind the living room blinds, she felt incredible guilt. Could she really sell this place, the only real home she'd had growing up? And what about Caesar? Could she offer up the roan to some stranger for a few hundred dollars? Biting her lip, she looked at the rocker where Nita had knitted and watched television, the coffee table that was cluttered with crossword puzzle books and gardening magazines and the bookshelf that held her grandfather's pipes, the family Bible and the photo albums. In the corner was Nana's old upright piano, and the bench, smooth from years of sitting with students.

Nostalgic, Jamie glanced out the window.

A shadow moved on the panes.

Her heart nearly stopped. The shadow passed by again and then, behind the frosted glass a tiny face emerged—gold head, whiskers, wide green eyes.

"Lazarus!" Jamie cried, recognizing her grandmother's precious pet as he jumped onto the windowsill. He cried loudly,

showing fewer of the needle-sharp teeth than he had in
the past.

Grinning, Jamie sprinted to the front door, pulled it open
and flipped on the porch light. Cold air followed the cat inside. "What are you doing here, old guy?" she asked as Lazarus slunk into the living room and rubbed against her legs.
She gathered him into her arms and felt tears burn the backs
of her eyelids. When Nana had died, the neighbors, Jack and
Betty Pederson, had offered to take in the aging cat, Jamie
had never expected him to show up.

"You escaped, did you?" she said, petting his silky head.
"You're a bad boy."

His purr was as loud as it had been when he was a kitten.
"Like a damned outboard motor," her grandfather, when he'd
been alive, had complained.

Now, the sound was heavenly. "Come on, I've got something for you," she whispered, kicking the door open and starting down the hall. Lazarus trotted after her. In the kitchen
she poured a little milk into a tiny bowl, took the chill off of
it on the stove and set the dish on the floor. "There ya go."

The words were barely out of her mouth when she heard
footsteps on the front porch. The doorbell chimed. "Uh-oh,"
she said to the cat. "Busted."

She expected to find a frantic Betty or Jack on the front
porch. Instead, as she peered through one of the three small
windows notched into the door, she recognized the laser-blue
eyes of Slade McCafferty.

# Chapter 4

*This is the last thing I need,* Jamie thought. *The very last thing.* Her stupid heart skipped a beat at the sight of him and if she were honest with herself she would admit that her breath caught in her throat nonetheless. If she had any sense at all, she'd tell him to get lost.

*You can't do that, Jamie-girl. He's a bona fide paying client now, remember? Like it or not, you have to deal with him and you* have to *be professional. No matter what kind of a lying bastard he might be.*

"Something I can do for you?" she asked as she cracked open the door, then, feeling foolish threw it wide enough to let in a gust of frosty air and give her full view of the man she'd sworn to despise.

"You said to call or drop by if any of us needed anything." Snowflakes clung to the shoulders of his jacket and sparkled in his dark hair.

"That I did." She'd never in a million years thought he'd take her up on it.

"I think you and I...we should clear the air."

"Does it need clearing?"

"I think so." His eyes didn't warm. Every muscle in her body was tense. "The way I see it, you and I, we're gonna be stuck with each other for a couple of weeks."

"Is that a problem?" she asked, sounding far more cool and professional than she felt.

"Could be. I don't want anything from the past making either one of us uncomfortable."

*Too late.* "I'm not uncomfortable."

"Well, I am," he said, one side of his mouth twisting upward in a hard semblance of a smile. God, he was sexy. "I'm freezing my rear out here." A pause. She didn't move. "Are you gonna invite me in or what?"

*This is going to be dangerous, Jamie. Being alone with Slade isn't a good idea.*

"Sure," she said, pushing the door even wider. "Why not?" *A million reasons.* None worth examining. The faint hint of smoke and a blast of cold air swirled into the foyer as he walked into the small hallway. Quickly she closed the door and leaned against it. She didn't offer him a chair. "So, what's on your mind?"

"You."

She nearly fell through the floor.

"Me?"

"More specifically us."

"Us?" Her heart catapulted. This wasn't what she'd expected. The professional smile she'd practiced all afternoon cracked and fell away. "There is no 'us,' not anymore, Slade," she said, clearing her throat. "Where's this coming from?"

"Guilt, probably."

"Well, forget it. What happened was a lifetime ago. We were just kids and...and it's just easier if we forget there ever was. We only saw each other for a couple of months. I'm surprised you remember."

"Don't you?"

*As though it was yesterday!* "Vaguely," she lied. "You know, little flashbacks, I guess, but not much. It's been a long time, more like a lifetime," she said, gathering steam. "You and I, we've got to deal with each other professionally for the next few weeks, so let's just forget that we ever knew each other, okay? Let the past stay right where it is. After all, it wasn't much more than a blip in our lives."

"Bull."

"Excuse me?"

"It was more than that."

"At the time."

"I'm not buying that you don't remember."

"I said I do, some of it, probably more than I wanted to when I drove back here, but let's just keep things in perspective."

"Perspective?"

"I'm an attorney working for you. You're the client."

"Hell's bells, Jamie, we slept together."

"That's really not so unique, is it? Not for you. Not with the girls around here."

His jaw tightened and he took a step forward. "You were different."

"Like hell, McCafferty. I'm going to be honest with you, okay? There was a time when I would have done anything, *any*thing to hear you tell me I was different, special, someone you never forgot... But that was eons ago, when I was just a wounded little girl. I'm over it and I don't want to go back there and I don't believe for an instant, not one instant, that you've had even the slightest bit of regret for what happened.

"So just because I'm in town and you feel…what? Compelled to 'clear the air,' forget it. I have."

"Nice speech you're peddling," he said, looking down at her. "But I'm not buying it."

God, his eyes were blue. "You don't have to. You can take it or leave it." She wanted to step away from him. He was just too damned close, but she held her ground, determined to show him that she wasn't going to be intimidated or bullied. Those days were over.

"You're scared."

"And you've got one hell of an inflated ego, McCafferty. But then some things just don't change, do they?"

"That's what I've been trying to tell you. And you do remember, Jamie. You're too smart to have forgotten."

"Flattery won't work—hey!" To her surprise he grabbed her wrist in his gloved fingers. Worse yet, she felt a jolt of electricity—that same damned charge that had gotten her into all kinds of trouble years ago.

"What will?" he asked, too close…much too close.

"Nothing! It's over, Slade. Don't come on to me, okay? Just because I'm here and it's convenient, let's not go there." She tried to pull her hand out of his grasp, but he only gripped her tighter, and her heart began to pound, her pulse race… She swallowed hard, reminding herself that this man was the cause of much of the pain in her life, that it would be incredibly stupid to come under his sensual spell once again….

"Admit it, you remember."

"For the love of God, yes. I remember that we dated, but that's about it. No reason to lie and make it a bigger deal than it was—" she glanced down at her hand "—and you don't have to act like I was important to you."

"You were."

"So important that you threw me over for... Oh, wait a minute, I'm not going there, okay?" She looked pointedly at the gloved fingers surrounding her wrist. "Let go," she ordered a tad too breathlessly. When he didn't comply, she managed to yank her hand away. "Let's just keep this professional."

"Randi accused me of breaking your heart."

She froze. All of her poise threatened to seep from her body and through the floor. "Boy," she whispered. "You...you just get right down to it, don't you?" Heat crawled up her neck as her pride crumbled. She tried to shrink away but he grabbed her again, his grip strong.

"No reason to beat around the bush." The sounds of the night closed in on her, the hum of the refrigerator, the ticking of the clock, the sigh of the wind outside, and the crazy beat of her own silly heart. She had to end this conversation now. Before she was seduced into thinking that he actually cared.

"Look, Slade," she said, jerking her arm away again but stepping closer, angling her chin upward so that she could stare into those hot blue eyes. "I don't know what you thought you would accomplish by coming over here tonight, but unless it's about business, then I don't see that we need to be talking. Consider the air cleared."

She eased into the living room and propped her rear on the edge of the couch as much to put some space between them as to brace herself. Folding her arms over her chest, she added, "Anything else?"

The house had seemed to shrink, not only filled by the man himself but by the memories of a misspent youth, a few weeks that had changed the course of her life forever. She reached over to one of Nana's end tables and snapped on a lamp.

"I've got a couple of questions."

*Me, too. About a billion of them, but I'm not asking.*

"Why were you assigned to our case? I thought Chuck Jansen was handling it."

"I think he called Thorne and explained that he couldn't get away and since I was coming to Grand Hope to put my grandmother's house on the market, he thought I could handle it."

"Is he your boss?"

She bristled slightly. "A senior partner."

"And you?"

"Junior partner."

He frowned, his lips folding in on themselves, a furrow deepening between his brow. "I never figured you for a lawyer."

"But then you really didn't stick around to find out too much about me, did you?" she snapped, then bit her tongue. She was the one who didn't want to talk about the past. Before he could accuse her of just that, she added, "If you want to talk about what happened between us, consider the subject closed, but, if you came by because you want to talk about the sale of the ranch, maybe we should go into my office," she offered, pushing up from the arm of the sofa.

"That would be a good idea."

She led him down the short hallway to the tiny dining room at the back of the house. She snapped on the overhead fixture and wished it had brighter, harsher bulbs, anything to keep the house from feeling cozy or intimate. "Could I get you something? Coffee?"

"Not without a shot of whiskey in it."

"Fresh out. My grandmother was a teetotaler." She managed another tight smile, motioned toward a caned-back chair near the window, then took one herself on the opposite side of the table.

"For the record, Jamie? What we shared? It was more than a blip."

*Oh, if you only knew.* "I thought we agreed not to discuss this."

"I didn't agree to anything." He pulled off his gloves and unbuttoned his jacket as if he were settling in. "That was your idea."

Obviously he couldn't be budged. She took a new tack. "Okay, but let's keep what happened between us in perspective. It wasn't that big of a deal, right? We saw each other for six weeks, maybe two months at the most?"

He wasn't buying. "That can be a long time when you're a kid."

"That's the point, we were kids."

"But we're not any longer." He shrugged out of his sheepskin jacket. "I figure we're going to see a lot of each other in the next week or so, whether we want to or not." He was undeterred. She remembered that about him, how focused he could be. Stubborn. Nearly obsessive. It had appealed to her at seventeen. Now, it was a pain.

He hesitated, looked away for a second as if studying the reflection of the room in the paned windows, then said, "I thought maybe I should explain what happened."

There seemed to be no way around it. "You went back to Sue Ellen. End of story." If only she believed it herself, could dismiss her feelings as a high school girl's crush...first love... but there had been more to it.

A lot more.

Of course he hadn't known about the baby. Would never. There wasn't any reason to tell him.

"Listen, this isn't easy for me."

"Nor me." To diffuse the tension, she scooted back her chair. "I don't know about you, but I could use some coffee."

"You're avoiding the issue."

But she'd already walked into the kitchen. She heard the

scrape of his chair as he followed, only to lean one broad shoul-der against the archway separating the rooms.

"There is no issue." She pulled out a jar of coffee crystals. Oh, damn, she forgot there was no microwave. Nana hadn't believed in them. Scrounging around a cupboard she found a saucepan, filled it with tap water and set it on a burner. "It was a fling."

"That's all?"

"That's all," she lied. There was just no reason to dig it all up again. All the old feelings, the painful emotions, the an-guish she'd been through, were long buried. From the corner of her eye, she spied Lazarus. He'd been hiding in the pantry, but had slipped through the door that had been left ajar to rub up against Slade's legs, doing figure eights as if he'd missed the man. "So you came over here, explained yourself, cleared your conscience and now that's not hanging over our heads anymore, let's just forget it."

God, his eyes were blue. "Right." Sarcasm.

Time to change the subject. "How'd that happen?" She motioned to his face and the thin scar slicing down one side. "A fight?"

"Yeah. You should see the other guy." His lips twitched. "Not a scratch on him."

She couldn't help but laugh as she found a couple of mugs, rinsed them quickly, then measured dark coffee crystals from the jar as steam began to rise from the water heating on the stove. "I can't see you in a knife fight."

"I wasn't." He fingered the scar and frowned. "It happened early last winter. I was skiing."

"And you fell?"

"Avalanche."

"Really?" she said, thinking he was kidding again, but his

expression had turned serious. "But obviously not a bad one. You survived."

"I guess I was lucky," he said, though she heard the irony in his words and noticed as he leaned against the refrigerator that the edges of his mouth pulled tight.

"There were others," she guessed, carefully pouring hot water into the cups, then stirring the coffee crystals as they dissolved. "You weren't alone."

A muscle worked in his jaw and he stared at the floor for a heartbeat. "That's right." The silence was only disturbed by the hum of the refrigerator and the clink of her spoon against one of the cups.

"You had a friend with you?"

"Yeah."

More than a friend, she figured. From the devastation in his expression, she felt a sliver of envy for this unknown woman. "Is...is she okay?"

"She died."

"Oh, Lord." The floor seemed to buckle. "I didn't know... I'm sorry." Her heart dropped and she felt guilty for having felt any bit of envy for the poor woman. The seconds ticked by, meted off by Nana's clock in the living room. "I...I don't know what to say."

"Nothing. There's nothing to say." His eyes held hers for a second, then moved to the window again. So that was it. The pain she'd thought she'd glimpsed in his gaze. He was still grieving.

She handed him a mug and she saw how much he'd cared for the woman, enough that he was still raw. Or maybe there was more than simple grief in the shadows in his eyes; perhaps there was a twinge of guilt on his part because he was the one who had survived.

"Do you want to talk about it?"

"Nope." He sipped from his cup.

Her cell phone jangled from the dining room. "Excuse me." Jamie switched off the stove, nearly burning herself. "I've got to get that."

Slade nodded as she swept past him and retrieved her phone from the table in the dining room. "Hello?"

"Hi." Chuck's voice echoed in her ear.

"Hi." Oh, Lord, why now? She cast a look through the archway to the kitchen where Slade was watching her unabashedly, as if it was his damned right. Turning her back to him, she wrapped one arm around her middle and tried to concentrate on the conversation.

"How's it going? You meet with Thorne McCafferty and his brothers today?" Chuck asked.

"Earlier. Yes." She nodded, keeping her voice low.

"And it went well?"

*Professionally, yes. An ace. Personally? A disaster.* "I think I'll wrap up everything pretty quickly."

"What about your grandmother's place?"

She swept a glance over the dust in the china cabinet, the walls that needed at least two coats of paint, the windows that had to be resealed. "That'll take a little longer." Looking through the window to the backyard where the snow shined silver in the moonglow, she saw the faint image of her reflection in the glass. As she watched, Slade appeared behind her, holding out a steaming cup of coffee. She turned, accepted the mug and her gaze connected with his for just an instant. A heartbeat. She lost the thread of the conversation.

"Jamie?" Chuck's voice brought her back.

"Oh, what?"

"I asked how long?"

"I'm not sure. I'm still taking stock," she said. "But...but I'll come back to Missoula ASAP."

Slade walked into the dining room again and dropped into his chair. The legs scraped against the hardwood and Jamie inwardly cringed; she didn't want to explain this particular scenario—that she was alone with the man to whom she'd lost her virginity—to her boss and the man who swore he was in love with her. It was just too complicated.

"I already miss you," Chuck said, and she felt herself blush.

"All talk, Jansen," she teased. "All talk."

"No way." He chuckled and her cheeks burned hotter.

"Don't suppose you talked to Thorne about sending more of his legal business our way?"

"Not yet."

"Well, work it in. Do it smoothly though. Start by doing a good job on this land transfer and...oh, hold on a minute." He turned, answered a question that she couldn't hear, then said, "Wasn't there something else he wanted? What was it?" A snap of fingers. "That's right. How could I have forgotten? The last time I talked with Thorne he mentioned a custody situation with his half sister's baby. Something he wanted cleared up, but I don't have the particulars."

"Neither do I."

"Maybe you should get them, forward the info on to Felicia. Do some prelim stuff, dazzle McCafferty, you know, show you're interested in his family, take the whole family out to dinner on the firm. Just play the game."

*The game.* She was beginning to hate the game. "Don't you think he'd see it for what it is?" she asked, embarrassed that Slade could hear every word of her end of the conversation. She walked back to the kitchen, put some space between her voice and his ears.

"Oh, yeah, Thorne will. He knows what's up, and that sister, she probably will, too. The other brothers, I don't know. I think we already talked about them, didn't we? I think I mentioned that one of the other boys is a rancher, the other kind of a nothing, I take it. The loser or black sheep, I'd guess. Never has settled down with a wife or a steady job, kind of into himself the way I hear it."

"Is that the way you hear it?" Jamie couldn't keep the edge out of her voice as she turned in the kitchen and, from her vantage point, saw the squared-off toes of Slade's boots as his legs, ankles crossed, were stretched under the dining room table.

"Well, he's probably pretty sharp. They all are. The old man, John Randall, wasn't behind the door when they passed out the brains. The youngest son was probably just pampered and lazy." She thought of Slade, his hard edges, his fixation with extreme sports, his raw energy. Pampered? Lazy? No way. "Anyway, do what you can," Chuck rambled on. "Schmooze them, work your magic, bat your pretty little eyes, anything it takes."

"Anything?" she threw back at him, and he chuckled again, deeper this time.

"Within limits, okay? We do have a loose code of morals here at Jansen, Monteith and Stone."

"Very loose," she said. He was kidding around of course, but tonight it rubbed her the wrong way, caused her hackles to rise.

"I'll phone you again tomorrow for an update," he said. "I've got another call coming in and I'd better take it. I imagine one of my kids is out of spending money again. It just doesn't end. Love ya, babe," he said, and hung up.

She took a long, slow breath, then, trying to get her bearings again, stopped by the refrigerator and pulled out the carton of milk. "I think I'll doctor this up," she said as she walked into the dining room and poured a splash of two-percent milk into her cup. Pointing the spout at Slade's, she asked, "You?"

"Mine's fine," he drawled, then looked pointedly at the phone. "Your boss?"

"Mmm-hmm." She tested the coffee. Not freshly ground French roast, but it was hot and not half bad with the milk.

"Among other things," Slade guessed.

"What other things?"

"I'm figurin' he's your boss *and* your boyfriend. Maybe even more."

"Is that what you figure?"

Quickly he reached across the table and grabbed her left hand. A few drops of coffee slopped from her cup onto her papers. "What're you doing?" Jamie asked.

"Lookin' for hardware."

"What?"

"A ring."

The warmth of his fingers was too intimate. He rubbed the back of her ring finger with his thumb, then let it go.

"I'm not engaged."

"Yet. But your boyfriend—"

"I'm too old for a boyfriend," she said quickly. It was hard to imagine Chuck, fifty, gray-haired and forever worried about his nearly grown kids, as a boy—any kind of boy. She wondered if he'd ever been one. All his life he'd been so damned responsible. High school, the army, college, law school, then straight to a firm in Seattle before settling in Missoula. He'd married his college sweetheart and started having babies right away.

Obviously, Slade didn't believe her protests. "Whatever you say," he muttered, but there was skepticism in his voice, a hint of amusement in his eyes that bugged the heck out of her as she found a towel in the kitchen and dabbed at the spilled drops of coffee.

"I say it's none of your business."

One side of his mouth lifted into a smile that could only be classified as wickedly sexy. "We'll see about that."

Her foolish heart knocked wildly. "Is there a reason you're here—I mean a reason pertaining to business?"

"Nope." He drained his coffee cup and stood. "I just dropped by to see you again." Shrugging into his coat, he rounded the table—then, to her surprise, dropped a chaste kiss on her cheek.

She nearly jumped out of her skin. How could something so seemingly innocent, a simple brush of lips on skin, burrow so deep, make her want more? Her silly pulse fluttered as she pulled away and saw the mockery in his eyes...damn the man, he knew how he affected her.

"Don't bother showing me the door." He had the audacity to wink...*wink* at her! "I think I can find it on my own." With a knowing grin, he turned and was gone, boots ringing against the polished hardwood, the door creaking loudly as he strode outside.

Jamie walked to the living room and, as she parted the curtains, touched that sensitive spot where the impression of his kiss still lingered. Dear God, what was it about Slade that burrowed right to her very core? How could he so easily bulldoze through all her well-constructed walls to keep him at arm's length? She watched the taillights of his pickup disappear into the night.

Sighing, she sagged onto the old couch. Lazarus jumped into her lap, and she stroked his silky head. "This is gonna be bad," she predicted as the cat began to purr loudly. "Even worse than I'd imagined."

# Chapter 5

"I *don't* need a babysitter." Randi glared at her brother as she hobbled toward an SUV that Larry Todd, the foreman, used when he was at the ranch. Keys jangled from her gloved fingers and she was slowly making her way through the soft snow.

"Do you have doctor's permission to leave the house?" Slade was with her every step of the way, ready to ensure that she didn't fall.

"That's another thing I don't need."

"Randi—"

"Quit acting like I'm a two-year-old. If it's so important that a doctor say I can leave, I'll just have Nicole do it."

"She wouldn't."

"I think she'd understand. As for you, quit treating me like a two-year-old."

"Then quit acting like one."

Randi rolled her eyes expressively as she reached the vehicle and yanked hard on the icy driver's side door. With obvious effort, she struggled to reach the handhold above the door, then winced as she hoisted her body into the cab.

"You're not ready for this."

"Sure I am," she insisted, settling herself behind the steering wheel. "Look, I'm going stir-crazy, okay? I just need to get out, even if it's only as far as Grand Hope."

"Then I'm coming with you."

"Super," she mocked. "My own private bodyguard." Her eyes met his. "You don't have to do this, you know. I'll be *fine*." Slamming the door shut, she waved her fingers at him then cranked on the ignition. Slade was around the truck and opening the passenger door before she realized he hadn't given up.

"For the love of God, Slade. This is ridiculous. Beyond ridiculous!"

"I need some things in town anyway."

"Sure you do." She didn't bother hiding her sarcasm. "Put on your seat belt. The last time I got behind the wheel it didn't turn out so well." She adjusted the seat and flipped on the wipers, then eased out of the drive.

She didn't look too bad, Randi figured with a glance into the rearview mirror. All things considered. The bruises on her face had disappeared, the wires holding her broken jaw together had been removed, as had the cast on her leg, and her hair, shaved short while she'd been in the hospital, was beginning to grow out unevenly. That was the reason for the trip. She wanted a professional hairdresser to trim her locks, give her some style, even if the result was a punk-rock do.

"I don't know why you're still hanging around," Randi mumbled as she flipped on the radio, pushed a few buttons and then, sighing, settled for a country-western station.

"Still have to sign the papers to sell the place."

"And when that's accomplished, what? You going to take off?" she asked as the SUV blasted down the long lane to the main highway.

"Not quite yet," he said, looking out the side window to an area they called the big meadow. It was now snow-covered, the creek that cut through the field frozen; only a small, sparse herd of thick-hided cattle wandered toward the barn.

"Don't tell me. Seeing Jamie Parsons again changed your mind."

His jaw tightened. Randi's observation cut too close to the bone. The truth of the matter was that seeing Jamie again had brought back memories he thought he'd forgotten. He'd lied to her last night, telling her that she hadn't been far from his thoughts. That was just a line, one so transparent she'd seen right through it. But she did intrigue him. Now more than ever. He wondered about her, about the wild girl hidden behind the sophisticated don't-mess-with-me lawyer attitude. Yeah, Jamie made things more interesting, but the real reason he was still at the ranch was to make sure his sister lived to see her thirtieth birthday. He'd decided to appoint himself her own personal bodyguard, which she'd figured out and hated. "I haven't really decided what I'm gonna do," he hedged, fiddling with the knob of the defroster. "But I figured I'd hang awhile."

"Not on my account, I hope." She wheeled onto the main road and gunned the engine.

"That's part of it."

"Don't bother. As I said, I don't need a keeper."

He slashed her a harsh look that silently called her a fool and she reacted in typical Randi fashion.

"Believe me, I'm serious! As soon as I'm able, I'm going to take Josh and head back to Seattle." She arched an eyebrow and glanced his direction as she shifted down for a corner. "You gonna follow me?"

"I haven't decided."

"Damn it, Slade, just leave it alone."

He ignored that. "I don't know why you're planning on heading West so fast."

"Let's start with my job." She lifted her thumb away from the steering wheel. "If I don't get back pretty soon, I won't have one. Then there's my apartment. You know, the place I call home." One finger shot up to join her thumb. "I've got friends and a social life and—"

"—and no babysitter, no car. You still can't walk without a limp. And someone's definitely determined to see you dead, if you haven't noticed. Now if you don't give a lick about your life, well, fine, that's your business, I suppose, but you're a mother. That little boy back there depends on you and only you seein' as you're not telling us who his father is, so you need to keep yourself alive. For the kid."

"Don't tell me how to run my life."

But Slade wasn't finished. "The way I figure it, J.R.—er, Josh, is a whole lot better off staying at the ranch with people who love him. He's got uncles and aunts and cousins, and Juanita, and you can't beat her. She raised us."

"I'm not sure that's a recommendation."

"Well, the baby's safe at the ranch. Why in the hell would you go back to an apartment in a city full of strangers?"

He snorted and thought he saw her chin wobble a little as she gripped the steering wheel so hard her knuckles blanched white. "That's where I live, Slade."

"Alone. Do you have a babysitter?"

"I—I don't know," she admitted as the frigid countryside rolled past, rolling hills covered with snow. "I, um, I thought that if I went to Seattle, back home, maybe my memory would return." She stole a glance his way. "There are such big holes. Somehow I've got to fill them. I've got to find a way to remember and get my life back." She swallowed hard and blinked as if fighting tears.

Was she on the up-and-up? She seemed so sincere, but then, Randi had always been a schemer. And a great actress. He'd been fooled before.

"Do you remember firing Larry Todd?" he asked.

She gave it a moment's thought, then, sighing, shook her head. "No. I can't imagine doing that."

"Well you did and he was mad about it, let me tell you. Thorne had to talk like hell to get him to come back to run the place. He'd been the foreman for years, you know. A good man. Why in the world would you let him go?"

"I wish I knew." Scowling, she frowned at the road ahead and chewed on her lower lip. "But then I wish I knew a lot of things." Faith Hill's voice floated through the speakers and before the love song really took off, Randi punched the button for another station.

"What about the book you were writing?" Slade asked.

Randi sighed and tapped a finger on the steering wheel. "I told you...I don't remember. But I've always wanted to write a book, that much I'm pretty sure of. It's all so foggy." Lines of concentration marred her brow. "I'd have to go home, back to Seattle, check my computer files, go into the office..." Her voice drifted away.

The wipers scraped away snowflakes that caught on the windshield as a radio commercial for a local car dealership blasted through the speakers. "So why don't you tell me what, exactly, you do remember?"

"That you dated Jamie Parsons." She slid him a teasing glance and he couldn't help but smile. Randi, for being a royal pain in the backside, was charming as all get-out when she wanted to be.

"Okay, okay, but beyond *my* love life, is there anything?"

"Some things…but they're out of sync, kind of in soft focus, if you know what I mean. And it isn't that I just remember you dating Jamie, it's that I recall most of my childhood. You know, Mom and Dad, you guys as teenagers getting into trouble while I was riding horses and bikes, that kind of thing, but…then it gets fuzzy." She thought long and hard as the announcer on the radio gave the weather report.

Snow, snow and more snow.

Montana in winter.

So what else was new?

Slade watched the snow-drifted fields give way to subdivisions as Randi drove past the sign announcing Grand Hope's city limits. "I do remember some of the recent stuff," she admitted, driving past the old train station with its distinctive redbrick tower and clock face. "My job at the *Clarion* and my boss, Bill Withers, and a few of my coworkers, especially Sara and Dave." Slade knew the names by heart. Bill Withers was the editor of the *Clarion,* while Sarah Peeples wrote movie reviews in a column called "What's Reel" and Dave Delacroix was a sports writer.

"What about Joe Paterno?"

"Joe?" she repeated, her teeth sinking into her lower lip as she drove over the bridge spanning Badger Creek. "He…he works at the paper, too, I think."

"Freelance photographer. You dated him."

"Oh." Did she show a spark of recognition? Or was it his imagination? "So you're fishing again? Hoping I would tell you that he's Josh's father?"

"Just tryin' to help," Slade drawled.

She didn't reply, and when he brought up Brodie Clanton

and Sam Donahue's names, trying to work them casually into the conversation, she rolled her eyes. Brodie Clanton was a lawyer. Sam Donahue a cowpoke.

"Don't take up private detective work, okay, Slade?" she suggested, easing into a parking space at the curb near the Bob and Weave Hair Salon. "You're about as subtle as a Mack truck." She parked, pocketed the keys, opened the door and slid out of the SUV and into the street where traffic rolled slowly through town. "And speaking of private detectives, be sure to tell your friend Striker that I've told him everything I know. Everything. If I think of anything else, *I'll* get in touch with him." She glanced over her shoulder as she reached for the door handle to the little shop.

Inside the salon three stations were filled with women in various stages of beautification. If that's what you'd call it, Randi silently chuckled. One of the patrons held her head forward while the beautician shaved the back of her neck, another had huge curlers in her hair and the third looked as if she could pick up radio signals from outer space with all the pieces of tin foil stuck to her head.

"I'll meet you over at the Pub 'n' Grub when you're finished," he said, hitching his chin down the street.

"And I'll be a new woman."

"Just as long as you're a new *and improved* woman," Slade said with a smile.

"I'll try, but it's so damned hard when you start out perfect."

He laughed as she pushed open the door and started talking immediately to Karla Dillinger, the woman who owned the shop and also happened to be Matt's fiancée's sister. Her own hair was a mixture of blond and red and through the plate-glass window she cast a glance at Slade as if he were the devil incarnate. Though Kelly Dillinger was marrying into the McCafferty family, obviously Karla had deep reservations about her sister's choice. He winked at her and she blushed and quickly turned back to her client.

Hands tucked into the pockets of his jacket, Slade started down the street when he noticed the car, the little blue compact parked in front of a local realty company. One glance confirmed that the car belonged to Jamie Parsons. A quick look inside and he saw her seated at the desk of a petite blonde woman.

He should just walk on by, but he couldn't. Not until he'd talked with her. Last night he hadn't gotten anywhere, hadn't explained what had happened between them, hadn't broken through her icy veneer.

Through the window he saw Jamie stand and sling the strap of her purse over her shoulder. She must've caught a glimpse of him because he saw her tense, her eyes lifted to his and then small lines of disapproval gather at the corners of her mouth. With a quick word to the Realtor, she walked to the door and joined him on the street.

"You know, McCafferty," she said without so much as a hello, "I get the feeling that you're following me."

"Do you?" No reason to try to explain.

"What is it you want?" She was walking to her car now, using a remote to unlock the doors. "And don't start coming up with explanations about the past, because we've covered that territory already."

She offered him a cold, professional, guaranteed-to-put-pushy-males-in-their-place smile, but beneath her icy exterior he caught a glimpse of something more, emotions that she tried to deny.

"I was just walking by."

"Right."

"I dropped my sister off at the beauty parlor up the street."

He hitched his thumb over his shoulder. "Then I thought I'd get a beer, and saw your car."

"So you decided to wait for me."

"I guess." Leaning a hip against the fender of her compact, he watched as a couple of teenagers ran down the sidewalk, backpacks slung over their shoulders, snowballs formed in their gloved hands. Laughing and shouting, they hurled their icy missiles at each other before rounding the corner. "You act like I'm stalking you."

"Are you? I hope not. Because there are laws against that kind of thing."

"It's not my style."

Her icy facade cracked a little. "I know that. I just don't understand what you want from me."

"Just some of your time."

"I don't know, it's pretty precious. The current rate is a couple of hundred dollars an hour, but for you I've got a deal. I'll make it three hundred." She arched a reddish eyebrow, silently challenging him.

He let out a low whistle. "That's pretty steep."

"Oh, come on, you can afford it. You're a rich man. A McCafferty."

"Three hundred bucks an hour?" He eyed her up and down. She was wearing slacks and a sweater, a long coat and boots; her hair was twisted into some kind of knot at the back of her head. "You think you're worth it?"

"Every cent," she said, and slid into the car. "Don't you?" She closed the door and as he straightened from the fender, she punched the accelerator and tore away from the curb. He should take her advice and leave her alone. Let that be the end of it.

But he couldn't. Whether she intended to or not, Jamie Parsons had thrown down the gauntlet.

Slade had never been one to back down from a challenge, and he sure as hell wasn't going to start now.

Why had she baited him? Why hadn't she left well enough alone? Been coolly disinterested? Or professional? Or just plain civil? What was *wrong* with her? Ever since setting eyes upon Slade McCafferty again, she'd been acting like a fool. She couldn't stop her pulse from skyrocketing at the sight of him, nor could she slow her heartbeat. The man got to her.

Jamie tossed her pen onto the dining room table and glowered down at the brochure she'd picked up from the real estate company. Her mind wasn't on putting her grandmother's house up for sale, nor was it focused on the buyout agreement for the McCafferty ranch, or even on the mystery surrounding Randi McCafferty. No. Her thoughts were filled with Slade, Slade, Slade.

Which was just plain ridiculous. She took a sip of tepid coffee, walked into the kitchen and tossed the rest of it into the sink.

She'd managed to keep him out of her brain for more than fourteen years. Every time his image had dared venture into her thoughts, she had mentally drop-kicked it into the next county, never daring to dwell on what had happened between them, what they'd shared and what they'd lost.

Absently she touched her abdomen. Their child would be fourteen years old now, going on fifteen. In high school, learning to drive. Maybe a cheerleader or an athlete or a bookworm.

*Or a hellion.*

It didn't matter...if only the baby had lived. She would have raised it alone or maybe told Slade the truth. But it hadn't happened. The miscarriage had taken care of that.

What she'd shared with Slade, that little piece of one summer, was over.

He was out of her life.

Until now.

"Damn, damn, damn and double damn," she muttered, cringing a little as if she expected her God-fearing grandmother to appear and wash her mouth out for cursing in her house. "Oh, Nana," she whispered, "what am I gonna do?"

*You forget that McCafferty boy, y'hear. He's no good. Wild. Never goes to church. Lord, Jamie, you're so much better than all those Mc-Cafferty hellions rolled into one!*

Jamie had heard the lecture before and it seemed to echo through the chilly hallways of Nita Parsons's cottage. She was cold from the inside out. All because of Slade... *Don't go there,* she told herself as she rubbed her arms to warm herself up. Lord, it was cold...she listened and realized that the furnace had quit rumbling. "Now what?"

She found the thermostat, noticed that the arrow designating the desired temperature was steadfastly pointed at sixty-eight. "No way," she muttered, notching it up a couple of degrees. Nothing. She tried again, pushing the indicator to eighty. Nothing happened. No reassuring click or whoosh of air. The dial was pointed to eighty but nothing happened. Knowing it was futile, she walked to the vent in the living room and splayed her fingers over the duct. Sure enough, not a whisper of warm air was blowing through the old ductwork.

"Just what I need," she muttered as she found her grandfather's old toolbox in the pantry and made her way down the narrow staircase to the unfinished basement. Lazarus, ever curious, shot down the stairway ahead of her.

Lit by two dim bulbs screwed into ceramic outlets, the basement smelled musty. Dust covered every inch of the floor and cobwebs draped from the low ceilings. The furnace stood in the middle of the room, a behemoth with tentacle-like ducts stretched to the far corners of the ceiling. It had originally been wood-burning, her grandmother had explained, but had been converted to electric sometime in the seventies. Jamie placed a hand upon its dusty side. Stone-cold. Not a sound emitting from the monster.

There were instructions on the side and she wiped the dirt away and shone the beam of her grandfather's old flashlight on the panel, then unscrewed the cover and looked at the workings. "Now," she said as Lazarus walked around the cracked cement floor, "all I need is a degree in electrical engineering." The cat meowed as if he understood just as the phone shrilled upstairs. Leaving the tools behind, Jamie dashed up the stairs, flew into the kitchen and snagged the receiver by the fourth ring. "Hello?"

"Jamie?" a male voice asked.

"Speaking."

"Oh, good. It's Jack. Next door." She relaxed when she recognized the neighbor's voice. "Betty and I, we got your message about you being over at the house. Now you're sure you don't need any help with Caesar or Lazarus?"

"I can handle them," she said, and decided she wouldn't mention the furnace.

Lazarus appeared at the top of the stairs. He rubbed up against Jamie's legs as she listened to the neighbor prattle on, the gist of the conversation being that Jamie was welcome to keep Lazarus as long as she wanted because Betty and Jack, who had two dogs and three other cats of their own, thought Jamie might be lonely by herself. As for the horse, Jack gave her specific instructions as to his feed, water and exercise. "He's not as young as he used to be and we old fellas like to stick to our schedules," he added with a chuckle.

Jamie grinned. "I'll keep that in mind."

"If it was up to me, I'd rather you have Rolfe with you, he's our three-year-old German shepherd, y'know, and one helluva watchdog. He'd be more company for you, too. More than the cat. Me and the missus, we'd loan him to ya, if ya wanted."

"Thanks, but I think Lazarus and I will be fine," Jamie assured him as from the corner of her eye, she saw headlights flash through the window as a truck pulled into the drive. A second later her little car was illuminated in the glare. "I'd better go," she told Jack. "I think I've got company."

She hung up and leaned over the sink to get a better view outside.

There, big as life, was Slade McCafferty.

Again.

She strode to the front of the house and before he had a chance to knock, she yanked open the door. "Well, well, well, Mr. McCafferty," she drawled. "This seems to be getting to be a habit."

"Does it?"

"Mmm-hmm. A bad one."

He flashed her a devastating smile. "And you love it, Counselor, admit it."

"In your dreams."

"And in yours." His lips curved into a wicked little smile that caused her heart to flutter stupidly.

"Don't flatter yourself. To what do I owe the honor?" she asked.

His eyes darkening with the night, he held up three crisp one-hundred-dollar bills.

# Chapter 6

"This buys me one hour, right?" Slade asked.

"Oh. I was only kidding around. I would never—"

Quick as a striking snake, he grabbed her hand and curled her fingers around the cash, then looked pointedly at his watch. "The clock's running."

"Slade, this is a joke, right?"

"Take it any way you like."

This was getting her nowhere, so she stepped aside and he released her hand. "Fair enough. Since the clock is ticking, come on in," she said, "but you'd better bring a wool blanket. The furnace is on the fritz."

"Maybe I can do something about that."

"If you can, I'll be forever in your debt."

Blue eyes sparked. He glanced down at the money curled in her fist. "In *my* debt? Is that so?" A crooked grin slashed across his jaw. "I like the sound of that. You're on."

He strode inside and as she closed the door, he found the thermostat, fiddled with it, then looked over his shoulder at her. "Is the furnace in the basement?"

"Yes. The stairs are through the kitchen, right next to the pantry..."

He was already charging down the short hallway and through the open door with Jamie tagging behind. Ducking his head to avoid low-hanging beams, he made his way to the nonfunctioning behemoth. "Not exactly the newest model around," he commented, grabbing the flashlight and screwdriver from the open toolbox and flipping open a dusty panel.

"Anything I can do?"

"Besides pray?"

"Very funny."

"When was the last time the filters were cleaned or it was serviced?"

"Beats me."

"Humph." He tinkered some more and rather than hover over him like a useless female, she climbed the stairs and, after having secured his money on the windowsill with one of Nana's jelly jars, heated water for coffee.

Damn the man, he'd paid her. Actually had the gall to hand her cash. Well, it served her right for being so flip on the street today.

The two cups they'd used the night before were still in the drainer. With icy fingers she poured dark crystals into the mugs, then added hot water. From the basement came sounds of clanging, banging and clicking, but no familiar whoosh of hot air rushing through the old ducts.

"Try the thermostat now," Slade yelled up the stairs. "Turn it off, then on again."

"Aye, aye, captain," she muttered under her breath, but did as she was asked. Several times. To no avail.

A few minutes later she heard the sound of boots pounding up the old wooden stairs. Frustration tugged his eyebrows together as Slade appeared. "I give," he admitted. "I guess you're off the hook. You won't be beholden to me, after all."

"There's a relief."

"I'll bet."

"But you can't fix it?"

"No, ma'am," he drawled, finding a towel and wiping the dust from his hands. "I think you're going to have to call the repairman."

"Which is the same conclusion I'd drawn myself, but here—" She finished stirring crystals into the hot liquid and handed him a mug. "For your efforts."

"Futile as they were."

She couldn't help but laugh. "I won't hold it against you."

He snorted. "That's something, I suppose. I think I have enough black marks as it is."

*More than you know, McCafferty.* "We're not going there, remember?" she reminded him as she sampled her coffee, wrinkled her nose and pulled a quart of milk from the refrigerator.

"Your rules."

"My house."

"Until you sell it."

"Yes." Pouring a thin stream of milk into her cup, she nodded and refused to acknowledge that the man was getting to her on a very primal level, forcing her to remember how easily he'd seduced her. Nor would she think of what her grandmother might say to that sorry fact.

"Don't want to keep it for a vacation retreat?"

"Oh, right. I could leave my condo in Missoula for the change of scenery here in Grand Hope." She glanced out the window into the frigid winter night, tried to keep her mind set, attempted to ignore how downright sexy Slade was, how her heart raced at the sight of him. Lord, it was hard with Slade. It always had been. "Your idea's tempting, I'll give you that, but I was thinking maybe somewhere where the temperature is above freezing. You know, like Hawaii or Palm Springs or the Bahamas."

"Wimp."

"Sticks and stones, McCafferty. At least I'd be a warm wimp."

"So you don't want to keep it as a rental?"

"Don't think so." She set the milk carton on an empty shelf in the refrigerator. "I think selling it and getting out clean would be the best."

"No muss. No fuss." Serious eyes regarded her over the rim of his mug.

"Precisely."

"But in the meantime you could freeze. Let's see if we can get this place warmed up. Got any firewood?"

"I think so…on the back porch, or maybe in the garage."

He started for the door, ready to brave the elements for a stick of kindling and a log, but Jamie wasn't interested in any more of his help. A crackling fire sounded far too cozy, too intimate, and she'd already found herself enjoying his companionship far too much, looking forward to seeing him again. There was just no point to it. "I can build a fire by myself, you know."

"I'm sure, but since I failed Furnace 101, I've got to find some way to salvage my wounded male pride."

"Wounded pride? That'll be the day, McCafferty."

His lips twitched and his eyes sparkled blue devilment, but he kept whatever was on his mind to himself. He drained his cup, left in on the counter and, with a bad Arnold Schwarzenegger impersonation of "I'll be back," was out the back door, the screen door slapping behind him.

"There's no kindling," she called through the mesh as an icy wind swept inside and rattled the windowpanes.

"There will be. Got an ax?"

"I assume so." Rubbing her arms, Jamie added, "There used to be one. But I think it's probably locked in the garage."

"How about a key?" He stared at her through the rusted, patched screen and all at once the mesh seemed a thin, frail barrier between them. Standing in the pool of light from the single bulb on the porch, with his breath fogging, his skin flushed from the cold, he looked more like the boy she remembered, the boy she'd tried so hard to forget.

"That's a good question."

"See if you can find it."

She should just ask him to leave, tell him she didn't need his help, that a woman could chop kindling if she wanted to. Besides, he was bossing her around, as if they were still kids. Still friends. If she had any brains at all, she'd keep her relationship with each of the McCaffertys, especially Slade, strictly professional, but she wasn't up to arguing and the house was getting colder by the minute. She opened the pantry door, and found a key hanging on a nail by the shelf that used to hold jars of home-canned peaches.

She plucked the key from its resting spot. "Really, Slade, I can do this."

"You'll probably have to. Tomorrow." Slade opened the door and she passed the key through. Knowing she was making another big mistake, Jamie snagged her coat from the closet and made her way outside, following the path he'd broken in the snow.

By the time she reached the garage he'd already unlocked the side door and had flipped on the lights. He slid a quick glance in her direction as she entered, then focused on Nana's old car—a vintage 1940 Chevrolet. It had actually been Grandpa's while he was alive and Nita Parsons hadn't had the heart to sell her husband's pride and joy, even though she, herself, had gone through a succession of small, imported pickups.

Jamie ran a finger over a front fender. The Chevy had once been waxed every other week, but now the exterior had lost most of its gloss and cat tracks and dust had collected on the fenders, top and hood.

"This is a classic," Slade said, walking around the car and appraising it slowly.

"Probably. It belonged to my grandfather."

"And now it's yours."

"Yeah."

"Don't ever sell it."

Jamie laughed and rubbed her hands together. "You sound like my grandmother."

"I doubt it." But he grinned just the same and the tiny, dilapidated garage seemed a few degrees warmer. Dry wood was stacked in a corner and gardening tools, saws and hubcaps were mounted on the wall that stretched behind a long workbench. Jamie fingered the cold steel of her grandfather's vise, twisting the grip as she reminded herself not to fall victim to the McCafferty charm again.

"I really don't know what I'm going to do with the car," she admitted. "I had intended to sell everything. The house, the furniture…this." She rapped her fingers on the hood, then rubbed out a spot of dirt on one headlight. "Even Caesar."

"Caesar?" Slade repeated, and then, as he remembered, a grin stretched across his face. "He's still alive?"

"And kicking."

Slade nodded. "Good for him." Leaning jeans-clad hips against one fender, he eyed Jamie. "You'd really sell your horse?"

Guilt cinched tight around her heart but she tried to make

light of it. "He wouldn't fit in my condo. Besides, I don't think he's house trained."

"The girl I used to know would never have sold him."

"The girl you used to know grew up," she countered, but didn't add how much he'd influenced the rate with which she'd catapulted into womanhood. Being pregnant and jilted had a way of crushing girlhood dreams.

"That she did," he said, and she felt the weight of his gaze slide slowly from her toes upward, past her hips, waist and breasts, only to stop at her own eyes. She swallowed hard, refused to glance away. "You look good, Jamie. You're a beautiful woman."

She warmed under the compliment, but didn't let her silly feminine heart take flight. "Thanks, but…let's cut through all this, okay? If you're trying to come on to me, Slade, it's not going to work." She stopped fiddling with the vise. "I learned a long time ago that you can never go back. That's why I'm selling this house and yes, the horse, and probably the car. I pride myself in not wallowing in nostalgia."

"A businesswoman through and through."

"Yes."

"So you never married?"

"Not that it's any of your business," she reminded him.

"No kids?"

Her heart twisted. She had to force the word past her lips. "None."

"But the boyfriend, the senior partner, he's going to give you some?"

She didn't reply.

"Touchy subject?"

"Personal."

"Let me guess." He walked to the woodpile, selected a dusty chunk of pine. "He doesn't want any."

"Chuck's got three kids already. They're in college—well, the youngest one hasn't graduated from high school yet, but... wait a minute." She shook her head. "Why am I telling you this? As I said, it's none of your business."

"But this is my hour, remember? I've already paid for it."

Rather than comment, she sent him a look that would cut through stone.

He got the hint. Rapping his knuckles on the hood, he said, "Just for the record, you should keep this as an investment."

"So now you're a financial analyst?"

"Jack-of-all-trades. Master of none. Today, I'm a furnace repairman and stockbroker."

His self-deprecating smile touched a forbidden part of her heart and she forced herself behind her carefully constructed barriers against this man. Emotionally he was a nightmare to her. Despite all her warnings, all of the pain, she still reacted to him, still wondered what would be the harm in letting him kiss her and touch her...

Oh, God. She cleared her throat and ignored the heat suddenly rushing through her blood. What had they been talking about...oh, yes...

"You're a repairman? Not much of one tonight."

White teeth flashed. "But a helluva lot better than I am as a financial analyst."

"Is that so?"

"Yep. I can guarantee you a fire, though. I'm a master craftsman when it comes to that. It's my primitive side."

"Cro-Magnon or Neanderthal?"

"Take your pick." He found an ax near the door and pulled it from the wall.

"How about a little of both?"

"Whatever floats your boat." He set the piece of pine on a scarred chopping block and swung the ax down hard.

*Crack!*

The chunk of pine split, the two pieces tumbling to the old cement floor. He picked up one of the pieces, set it on the block, then swung again. Wood splintered. Kindling clattered noisily to the floor. "What did I tell you? A master craftsman, here."

He grabbed another piece and set to work. Within minutes there was a pile of kindling near the door and the air inside the garage was filled with the scent of dry wood and disturbed dust.

"Enough?"

"Plenty. Thanks."

"No problem." He hung the ax back on the wall, grabbed an armload of the split wood while she picked two larger pieces and headed into the house.

"You don't have to do this," she said when they were in the living room and he, on one knee, checked the flue. Soot fell from the chimney.

"I know. I don't *have* to do anything."

"I mean, I don't think…"

"Are you trying to kick me out?" He looked over one shoulder.

"Yes."

"To quote the vernacular, 'it ain't workin'.'"

"It should."

He glanced pointedly at his wrist and she noticed the five-o'clock shadow darkening his jaw, the way his hair fell over his forehead despite the fact that he kept pushing it out of his eyes. "The way I see it, you still owe me a few minutes."

"I'm not taking your money, Slade."

Satisfied that the flue would vent properly, he stuffed an old newspaper around the kindling, flicked a lighter to the yellowed edges and as the flames devoured the Want Ads, he rocked back on his heels to survey his work.

"I think I should tell you about Sue Ellen."

"I thought we weren't going to discuss the past."

"That was your rule last night, not mine."

"Nothing you can say will change things, Slade."

"You don't know that."

"I do."

"You're afraid of the truth," he charged, standing, staring at her hard.

"No way," she snapped, suddenly angry. "I just don't think it's relevant. Not anymore. What happened between us—"

"The 'blip,' isn't that what you called it?"

"That's right. The blip. It's over. Forget it."

"I can't, damn it." Blue eyes regarded her. "Not since seeing you again."

"Oh, save me."

"It's true."

"There was a time when I would have clung to those words, Slade, but no more." His gaze drilled into hers, silently accusing her of the lie, and she wanted to squirm away. But she didn't. "I don't want to hear whatever it is you're so hell-bent on saying."

"Well, maybe, Counselor, just maybe, this isn't so much about you, as it is about me."

"Oh, great, so now I get to be your confessor? Now, after fifteen damned years, I get to listen to some weak excuse as to why you tried so hard to seduce me, just to throw me away when your rich girlfriend came running back to you? Well, no thanks. I'm not a priest."

"It wasn't because she was rich."

Jamie didn't comment. "Then she was more beautiful or more exciting or—"

"No way. She was…safe, okay? Safe. I knew what to expect from her. With you…"

"What?"

"You gave as well as you got, Jamie. Anything I dared you to do, you did it and then dared me right back. I thought we were on a collision course."

"That's what I thought you liked."

"I did. Too much. It was just too much. Too fast. Too hot. Too dangerous."

"You know, those should be my lines, because the way I remember it, you were the one always pushing the envelope, pushing me, convinced that we were both invincible." She stepped closer to him and poked a stiff finger at his chest. "You scared me, McCafferty, you scared the hell out of me and I liked it."

"Me, too."

The silence stretched between them. A hundred memories flashed through Jamie's mind. A dozen reasons to tell him to take a hike or to jump in a lake or to go to hell flitted through her brain, but she held her tongue.

Like it or not, he was her client.

As if reading her mind he said, "Yeah. That's the way I remember it." His jaw slid to one side and his lips barely moved as he said, "But, no matter what happened way back when, the reality is that you and I are gonna be dealing with each other a lot in the next couple of weeks and we'll have to find a way to get past what happened. So…I thought I'd come by and set the record straight, okay?"

*No,* she thought, *it isn't okay. Nothing is with you.* But she couldn't let him know.

"Okay?" he persisted.

"Fine, Slade," she said, dropping onto the arm of Nana's overstuffed couch and trying vainly to hold on to her rapidly escaping poise, the poise that always seemed to elude her whenever she was near Slade. Damn the man, why wouldn't he just leave well enough alone? Why couldn't he leave her alone, and why in the world couldn't she stop reacting to him? "If you're so all-fired intent on unburdening yourself, then, by all means—" she waved her fingers in the air as if she didn't care "—spill your damned guts."

"Good."

*No, it's not. Nothing good will come of this,* she thought, but again held her tongue as she noticed the stretch of denim against his thighs and buttocks as he warmed the backs of his legs near the hungry, crackling flames... She tore her eyes away.

*Don't go there, Jamie, don't!*

But the man's pure sexuality was hard to ignore, from the slight cleft in his chin to the breadth of his shoulders. She remembered clinging to those muscular, sinewy shoulders, feeling the heat of his body, a mirror of the fire in her own bloodstream...she hadn't had thoughts like these in years, not since...Slade. Always Slade. Suddenly the room was far too cozy, too intimate, too close. Though it was freezing out, she wanted to throw open the windows.

He was staring at her. She cleared her throat, pretended she was in a courtroom, and tried desperately to keep the emotions swirling deep inside. "Okay," she said, hating the breathless sound of her voice. "Here's your big chance to explain every-thing. Go for it."

His expression turned serious. "First of all, you should know that I was never in love with Sue Ellen Tisdale."

"You could have fooled me." Oh, God, she really shouldn't hear this...couldn't allow herself to believe his lies.

Lazarus jumped into her lap and absently she stroked his head as the old pain of Slade's rejection, the dull ache of knowing he hadn't cared for her, that he'd used her, settled over her. It was silly, of course. Downright ludicrous. But undeniable.

"I fooled everyone. Maybe even myself," he admitted, his voice low. "It seemed the right thing to do."

"As I said, it's ancient history." She tried to sound flip, but her words seemed hollow.

He didn't immediately respond, not until she looked up and found him staring at her. His gaze was intense, the muscles in his neck tight. For the first time she realized how difficult this was for him.

"The plain truth of the matter is, Jamie, you were the girl I wanted."

"*I* was the girl you wanted?" She nearly laughed. "Oh, give me a break. This is like some kind of cruel joke," she said, though deep in her heart a very feminine part of her wanted desperately to believe him. How many times had she conjured up just this very admission? But, of course, it was a lie.

"No joke."

"Whoa—just wait a minute." She held up a hand and shook her head. "I don't know what you're trying to do here, but it's…way out of line. You didn't give two cents for my feelings. If you had wanted me then, you could have had me. I was nuts about you."

"So it was more than a 'blip.'"

"A schoolgirl crush. A short one. Look, I don't know what's gotten into you, but this…this is crazy," she insisted. How long had she wished, prayed, she would hear those words he'd just said? *You were the girl I wanted.* How many nights had she cried herself to sleep hoping foolishly that Slade would come to his senses, that he would love her? That he would track her down, spin her around and tell her that letting her go was the worst mistake of his life?

Just like a poorly plotted scene in some bad B movie.

"Let's just forget we had this conversation," she suggested. "Whatever we had, it's over. Has been for a long time."

He frowned, looked at the toes of his boots and then glanced up. "If you say so, Counselor."

"I do."

"Then I guess that's settled." He started for the door, but as he passed her one arm reached out, grabbed her around the waist and pulled her to her feet.

"Hey! Wha—" The tip of his nose touched hers.

"You know what, Jamie Parsons? You're the worst liar I've ever met in my life, and that's not good, what with you being a lawyer and all. You're supposed to be good at twisting the truth around."

"I haven't lied—"

"Bull."

"Honestly, Slade—"

"You want me to kiss you," he said, his eyes darkening to a seductive blue that caused the pulse in her throat to pound erratically.

"What? No!" She tried to pull out of his embrace.

"You've been wondering what it would be like. If the old spark is still there."

"Your ego is incredible."

"Along with other things."

She couldn't believe he would be so bold. "For the love of Mike, give it up," she said, but she didn't pull out of his arms and hated the fact that part of her thrilled to be held so tight, that the scent of his cologne caused her heart to race, that the heat of his body caused her blood to heat. She flicked a glance at his lips. Hard. Blade-thin. Nearly cruel.

"Come on, Jamie, admit it, you want to find out."

"I think it's you who wants to find out."

"Definitely." His face was so close she noticed the layers

of blue in his irises, saw that his thin scar was taut and white. "And we still have a few minutes left on my hour. We may as well make the best of them."

"By doing this?"

"Absolutely."

Before she could take a breath, his lips slanted over hers. Pressed hard. Touched her as no one else's ever had. She closed her eyes, gave in for the briefest of seconds, felt the play of his tongue against her teeth, remembered how much she'd loved him, that she would have given her life for his.

*Oh, please, no.* Pulling back, she said, "This can't happen, Slade. We both know it."

"Do we?" He was still holding her, his fingers splayed possessively over the small of her back.

Gritting her teeth, she slipped out of the embrace. "Yeah, we do. I'm not some silly schoolgirl with romantic fantasies about love any longer, and I don't believe in making the same mistakes I did in the past. You know the old expression, 'Once burned, twice shy'? Well, that's me." She leaned one shoulder against the wall and told herself it wasn't to steady her suddenly weak knees.

"And you think I'll burn you?"

"Damn straight." On legs more unsteady than they should have been, she strode into the kitchen, retrieved the damned hundred-dollar bills from the windowsill and marched back to the living room. "Our time is up," she said, stuffing the bills into the pocket of his jacket. "It has been for years."

He reached for the money as if to give it back to her, but she held up a palm to stop him. "Don't even think about it."

His smile was pure evil. "You're a hard woman, Counselor."

"And I pride myself on it."

Blue eyes mocked her and she realized she'd inadvertently

thrown him a challenge. "What's the quote? 'Pride goeth before a fall'? Something like that?"

"You are a bastard, you know."

"And *I* pride myself on that."

Folding her arms across her chest, she said, "Not only a bastard, but insufferable, as well."

"So I've been told." He winked at her as he walked to the door.

So cocky. As if he knew he was getting to her.

Grinning as if her discomfiture amused the hell out of him, he opened the door and drawled, "'Evenin', Counselor. Sleep well."

"I will."

"Alone?"

"That's the way I want it." Cold air seeped into the house.

"Is it?" He hesitated. "I wonder."

"Don't," she suggested, cutting the distance between them with quick steps. She wasn't going to let him get the best of her. "And for the record, it's Neanderthal."

"What?"

"You didn't know if you were Cro-Magnon or Neanderthal a little while earlier. I thought I'd clear it up for you."

"Much obliged," he mocked as he slipped through the door and closed it firmly behind him.

"And good riddance," she muttered, glancing through the blinds to watch him walk across the snow-crusted yard to the spot where his pickup was parked. He paused to light a cigarette, the flame from his lighter illuminating the bladed angles of his face in the encroaching night. What was it about him that was so damned unforgettable? So sexy?

Angrily she snapped the blinds shut but it didn't help because, as much as she'd argued against it, she knew as she heard the sound of his truck roaring away, that she'd lied to him. As well as to herself.

It wasn't over with Slade McCafferty. It probably never would be.

# Chapter 7

*So Jamie Parsons has a boyfriend.*

*So what?*

*What did you expect?*

*At least she's not married.*

"Damn!" Swearing under his breath as snowflakes drifted from a leaden sky, Slade gave the wrench one final twist, then dropped it into his open toolbox. What the hell did it matter to him if Jamie was married or not? She'd made it clear that she didn't want anything to do with him.

A gust of icy wind blasted around the corner of the stables where he'd been working on an exterior spigot. What had gotten into him? Why after fifteen years of hardly thinking of her, was she now lodged permanently in his mind?

Why couldn't he forget the conversation they'd had last night? Forget the fact that she was involved with another man?

Hell, hadn't he been through his share of women in the past decade and a half?

But he hadn't lied to her when he'd told her she'd scared him as a youth. She'd been so wild, unafraid to go toe-to-toe with him, that he'd worried they'd self-destruct.

In a way they had. He'd seen to it.

"Hell." Squinting against the wind and snow, he turned on the spigot enough to allow a thin stream of water to run onto the fresh snow and to see that the pipe didn't leak, then he replaced the insulating cap and straightened. He'd been checking all of the pipes running to and from the barns and stables, making sure none had frozen, just to keep himself busy. He couldn't spend every waking minute dogging after his sister even though he considered himself her bodyguard. Nor could he chase after Jamie, which he'd been considering. She'd lay him flat. And he couldn't go home to Boulder. Never would again. Because of Rebecca and the baby.

He glanced at the sky as if he could see God through the thick clouds. Why? Why take Rebecca and the baby? Guilt tore through him; raged as cold as this damned storm.

He straightened. He'd been checking the pipes for hours, all the while either worrying about his sister, wondering why Rebecca's image was fading, or thinking about his conversations with Jamie the past couple of days. He wondered about the man Jamie had been dating, the senior partner in the law firm, the older guy with kids. Last night Jamie had ducked the question about Chuck wanting to marry her.

Chuck. With a ready-made family and a secure law practice. A senior partner and probably stuffy as hell. But he could offer her a home, job, money…if that's what she really wanted.

Slade wasn't sure…there was a part of her that would rebel against the staid type. He'd seen the flash in her intriguing hazel eyes, felt it in the fever of her kiss… No, Jamie Parsons wouldn't be satisfied being a traditional corporate wife and stepmother.

But then, what the devil did Jamie Parsons's marital status have to do with him?

Nothing.

Absolutely nothing.

She'd made that abundantly clear. He turned up the collar of his jacket.

But she'd liked the kiss. Oh, yeah. She'd deny it from here to eternity, but the truth of the matter was that the lady, in the split second before she'd come to her senses, had kissed him back. Hard. Urgently. As if she'd been waiting for years. He'd felt it. That sizzling spark of warm, wet lips eager for more.

"Give it up, McCafferty," he growled under his breath as he snapped his toolbox closed. Even if Jamie was available, he didn't have time for a woman right now.

"Give what up?" Matt's voice stole upon him.

Slade turned to spy his brother, shoulders hunched, trudging through the snow toward him. Harold, paws slipping a bit, followed behind, keeping to the path Matt had broken through the icy powder.

"Never mind," Slade growled.

From somewhere in the nearby fields a calf bawled.

"Doesn't have anything to do with a certain good-lookin' attorney, now does it?"

Slade impaled his brother with his sharp gaze. "You've been talking to Randi."

"She swears you've…let's see, how did she put it?" He tapped a gloved finger to his lips as if in deep thought though Slade suspected better. His brother knew exactly what their sister had said. He was just enjoying needling his younger sibling. "Oh! That you've got it 'bad' for Ms. Parsons, that was it."

"What would Randi know about it?" Slade countered. "She can't remember anything about her own damned life."

"She remembers some things. And besides, she does write a column for singles. 'Solo' has a pretty big readership, so I imagine she knows a little about relationships."

"Then what about her own? Hmm? What about J.R., er, Josh's father? Who the hell is he? Why should Randi give two cents about my life when hers is a full-scale nightmare?"

"Ouch. Touchy, aren't you?"

"Yeah, well, yeah, I am. It's below freezin' out here and if you haven't noticed, someone's trying to kill my sister, and I've got to put up with you jawin' about my love life or lack thereof when it's none of yours or Randi's damned business." He pulled his hat lower on his head and picked up the tools.

Matt's dark eyes turned serious. "You've got a point there. Until we find the maniac who ran Randi off the road and tried to kill her when she was in the hospital, nothing else matters."

"Except your wedding," Slade reminded him as he glanced at the long drive and saw headlights cutting through the gloom of the afternoon. "It looks like your bride is here."

Matt's face visibly brightened and for the first time in his life, Slade felt a jolt of envy.

"See ya later." Matt was already plowing through the snow to Kelly Dillinger's little beat-up Nissan while Harold sniffed at the fence posts. As Kelly climbed out of the car, Matt scooped up a handful of snow and lobbed it in her direction.

The redhead laughed, hid behind her open car door and began furiously gathering snow, packing tight balls and flinging the frozen missiles in rapid succession at her fiancé. "You're in trouble now, McCafferty," she warned, firing yet another icy ball. It smacked hard against Matt's jacket, leaving a splat of white powder, proof of her dead-eye aim.

"Don't I know it?" Another snowball whizzed by his ear and

he ran forward, past the shield of the door, and grabbed her around the waist as Harold barked wildly at the excitement.

"Oh!" Kelly cried, but was laughing as Matt spun her off her feet and kissed her as if he never intended to stop.

Slade had seen enough. He turned away and carried the toolbox into the stables. It was good that Matt was finally settling down, that he'd found a woman who was strong enough to stand up to him, a tough, determined lady who, until a few weeks ago, had been with the sheriff's department.

Kelly Dillinger had given up her job to marry Matt. Now, she worked with Kurt Striker as a private investigator. Together they were tracking down Randi's would-be killer.

Slade thought of Jamie Parsons—Attorney-at-Law. Would she give up her career for Chuck Jansen? Did she care for the bastard, or was she just using him?

What does it matter? Slade thought, closing the door behind him. Inside, the familiar scents of horses, dung and leather mingled with the aroma of dusty hay. The General, an aging chestnut gelding, snorted at Slade's approach, then poked his head from his stall. "How're ya, old man?" Slade asked, rubbing the horse's crooked blaze.

Nickering softly, the gelding sniffed at Slade's pocket where oftentimes he hid a treat.

"Nothin' today," Slade said, hearing the sound of Kelly Dillinger's laughter seep through the cracks in the siding. With some effort, he tamped down his jealousy. He had no right to feel this way. He was glad Matt and Kelly were getting married. It was time for ex-lady-killer Matt to become a one-woman man.

*And what about you? Are you going to spend the rest of your life mourning Rebecca and the baby? Or are you going to get on with your life? Find yourself a wife?*

A wife. Man, he'd never considered himself the marry-

ing type, even with Rebecca and a baby on the way. He felt
another slash of guilt because he hadn't really loved her, not
the way Thorne adored Nicole or Matt idolized Kelly. He
and Rebecca had been better friends than lovers. They'd met
white-water rafting, had enjoyed extreme sports together and
had dated eight months when she'd found out she was pregnant. The accident that had taken her life had taken place less
than a month later.

*So what about Jamie?*

Yes, what? His eyes narrowed as he considered. His feelings
for Jamie had never even bordered on "even keel." No, he'd
been passionate for her. Wild. Out of his head with wanting to
make love to her over and over again…her appetite and curios-
ity had matched his own and never had another woman been
so uninhibited as she had. Every other woman had wanted
something from him. Including Sue Ellen and Rebecca.

"Fool," he grunted.

The General, as if in agreement, turned back to the manger.

Slade frowned when he thought of the other women he'd
been involved with, too many to think about. The only one
that mattered right now was Jamie Parsons. Even Rebecca's
image was fading.

Absently he fingered the scar on the side of his face and
listened as a mare whinnied softly in the darkness. *Rebecca.*
Pregnant and dead at twenty-six. He closed his eyes for a second, took a deep breath and told himself not to step into that
particular guilt trap, as it was laid open, waiting for him, always ready to spring.

Walking through the building, he reached for his pack of
cigarettes out of habit, his fingers scrabbling at the pocket and
coming up empty. He hadn't been with a woman since Rebecca's death. Hadn't wanted one.

Until now.

Until Jamie Parsons.

And he felt guilty as hell about it.

"You're coming to Grand Hope?" Jamie said into the receiver, her heart dropping as she twisted the cord of her grandmother's phone. The last thing she needed was Chuck Jansen showing up right now.

It would be complicated.

Messy.

And she didn't want to deal with him; not only personally but professionally, as well. Didn't he trust that she could handle the property transfer, name change and whatever other legal matters the McCaffertys wanted without him peering over her shoulder? "I thought you were too busy to get away right now," she added, shivering as the heat from the fireplace wasn't able to seep from the living room to the back of the house.

"I am, technically," Chuck conceded, "but then I realized that the McCafferty account is worth switching my schedule around, and besides…" His voice lowered and Jamie braced herself.

*Here it comes,* she thought with mounting dread.

"I miss you."

"Oh."

He paused. "'Oh'?" he repeated. "That's all you have to say? Just 'oh'?"

"You surprised me." *Liar! Come clean.*

"The proper response is, 'Oh, Chuck, I miss you, too. I can't wait to see you. When will you get into town?'"

"I guess I missed my cue," she countered, unwilling to go there.

That was one of the problems with Chuck. As her boss, he was a great one to laud her accomplishments in public, to extol her "sharp mind." But when they were alone, he was often quick to point out how she could have handled a situation with what he referred to as "a little more legal finesse." He'd often wink at her, rap his knuckles on her desk and say, "Don't worry, hon, you're getting it."

As if she were a fifteen-year-old girl instead of a grown woman with a law degree displayed on the wall of her office. Or as if she weren't quite as bright as she thought. It griped her. "So, when will you…get into town?" she asked, refusing to be baited or to mouth the words he wanted to hear.

"Day after tomorrow. I've already booked a night at the Mountain Inn. I'll give you a call once I get settled. Maybe we'll go out to dinner."

"Maybe," she said, trying to force a lilt into her voice. But she couldn't muster any enthusiasm at the prospect of seeing him again. Ever since returning to Grand Hope she'd realized just how little they had in common, how little she wanted to be with him.

For months she had talked herself into the relationship, reminding herself that he was successful, wealthy, smart, in great shape…but…the truth of the matter was her pulse never quickened at the sight of him, her heartbeat didn't accelerate. Not like it did whenever she was around Slade McCafferty. She'd told herself that she was too mature for those kinds of girlish feelings…but then she'd run into Slade McCafferty and realized she'd been lying to herself and all those things she'd thought were important—security, a man with a steady job, a responsible person with a stock portfolio—weren't enough… or maybe even important.

"Oh, I've got to run," he said. "Barry just walked into the office. See you soon."

He hung up before she had a chance to say anything else.

*You should have broken it off with him,* before *he showed up here. You've been meaning to end it for months.*

Getting involved with Chuck had been a mistake from the get-go. She'd started dating him out of convenience. He was older, yes, and she supposed he represented some kind of father figure to her. But they didn't want the same things in life and he expected her to change her dreams, to give up any thoughts of conceiving a child of her own, and that didn't sit well. Damn it, she wanted a baby, wanted to be a mother. Stepmother to nearly grown kids that were being raised by their biological mother in another state just didn't cut it.

She'd have to break it off with Chuck. And soon.

Before he met with the McCaffertys and figured out that she and Slade were...*what*? Ex-lovers? There was nothing between them anymore, no matter what Slade implied. So they'd shared a kiss, so what?

*So your knees turned liquid when he touched you... So looking into his eyes causes your heart to trip... So the sound of his voice, saying your name, gives you a thrill.*

All just stupid, leftover emotions from something that happened a lifetime ago. And yet those damned lingering feelings served to point out why it wasn't working with Chuck—why it would never work.

Rubbing her arms against the chill, she tried not to think about her reasons for accepting her first date with Chuck. She'd resisted for a few weeks, then agreed to meet him for dinner. She hadn't been seeing anyone at the time and he seemed like a perfect match. He was handsome, successful, and had a quick sense of humor. True, he was quite a bit older than she and in a different place in his life. Now, as she yanked her jacket off a peg near the door, she supposed Chuck Jansen represented everything that had been lacking in her life—specifically a responsible father figure.

"Shrink fodder," she muttered under her breath as she slipped her arms into the heavy jacket, then yanked on a pair of boots. After donning gloves, she grabbed the largest basket she could find and braved the elements. The snow hadn't stopped all day and she broke a path through several inches of white fluff to the little barn where she checked on Caesar who, tail to the wind, stood in the paddock near the stables. He greeted her with a whinny, and trotted inside, where she poured oats into his manger and scratched him between the ears.

Satisfied that he wasn't freezing, she made her way to the garage, then loaded her basket with kindling and firewood.

Her breath fogged in the air as she stamped the snow from her boots on the back porch.

Once inside she found Lazarus lazing on the back of the couch, close enough to the fire to keep warm. He yawned, showing needle-sharp teeth and a long pink tongue as she pushed aside the screen and tossed fresh wood onto the flames.

Sparks drifted up the flue and hungry flames licked the dry oak as she glanced at a picture on the mantel taken forty years earlier. Nana, Grandpa and their only son. Jamie's father.

She gritted her teeth as she picked up the photo in its tarnished silver frame. Leonard Parsons had been a promising athletic boy who had turned into a handsome, hard-drinking, womanizing man who had been unable or unwilling to hold a steady job. He'd pulled a disappearing act when Jamie was in elementary school and her mother had promptly gotten involved with an uptight older man who had never bonded with Jamie and as she'd entered high school, had had no use for a headstrong teenager. Eventually, after one too many run-ins, Jamie had landed here in Nana and Grandpa's loving, if strict, arms.

Nita Parsons had been bound and determined to not make the same mistakes with Jamie as she had with her son. Hence, her chores.

"Now, listen, you're my granddaughter, and Lord knows I love you more than life itself, but you need to learn about responsibility," she'd told her headstrong granddaughter. "The henhouse, that's yours. You be good to my little ladies. Gather the eggs, keep fresh straw in the nests, give them oyster shell and corn and feed, let 'em pick bugs in the yard and you'll clean the mess in the henhouse—every two weeks whether it needs it or not—mind you, it will. Then there's the garden..."

The list had never seemed to stop. But Nana had been fair and paid her granddaughter each Sunday evening, rationalizing that Jamie would spend the money more wisely if she was given her wages at the beginning of the week rather than near the weekend, where, Nana knew, trouble could tempt.

Jamie had resented her chores at the time, but now realized the hard work of keeping up the little farm—whether it had been learning to put up jam, taking care of the cackling hens or reshingling the garage—had not only taught her skills, but also kept her busy, tired, and walking the straight and narrow.

It hadn't worked entirely and Jamie's fascination with Slade McCafferty had been the result. A daredevil who defied convention, a rebel after her own rebellious heart, Jamie had stupidly fallen head over heels. When he'd kissed her, she'd melted. When he'd reached beneath her blouse into her bra, she'd been exhilarated. When he'd slid her jeans off her tanned legs, she hadn't resisted.

Oh, no, she thought now, pulling back the old gauze curtain and gazing at the blanket of snow on the bare branches of the aspens in the front yard. She'd given herself willingly, beneath a bright Montana sun in a field of tall grass and wildflowers. Slade's body had been tanned and taut, smooth skin tight over defined muscles, dark hair sprouting from a rock-hard chest. The day had been warm, his body hot, her virginity ripe for the taking.

They'd come close before, but she'd always resisted. That afternoon as a few lazy clouds drifted across a blue sky and the sounds of the creek echoed through the canyon nearby, she'd closed her ears to the voices of denial reverberating through her head. She'd drunk a little wine, just enough to lose what little inhibitions she'd had, and given in to the glorious sensations singing through her body. His hands against her sun-warmed skin were magical. His lips, sensual fire. His words, intoxicating.

"Goodness, you're something," he'd whispered, looking down at her breasts, pink-tipped against the white skin forever covered by the top of her swimsuit. He'd leaned down and slowly kissed each rosy bud, taking his time, gently pulling back his head and tugging until a throb of hunger made her achingly aware of that private spot between her legs. "Beautiful. So...so damned beautiful." He'd kissed her lips and his hands slid over her flat abdomen to the mound of curls where her legs came together. "I've never seen a girl as pretty as you."

Somewhere in the back of her mind she'd thought he might be lying, but she'd ignored that horrid little idea. His hand had slipped lower, found her, and she'd froze.

"Easy now," he'd whispered gently. "Just relax..." His lips, tasting of wine, were upon hers again and he'd kissed her long and slow, all the while his fingers explored, touched, gently probed, until she'd felt hot and moist and been aching for more. "That's it. That's my girl," he'd said as she'd started to move with his touch, her hips lifting, the ache in her intensifying. "Let me love you, Jamie."

The words had brought tears to her eyes.

"Please." His lips, against her ear, allowed his tongue to trace the shell. "I won't hurt you."

*Oh, but you might,* she remembered thinking vaguely as he'd begun to kiss her neck and the tops of her bare shoulders.

"I'll make you feel good." He'd rubbed against her, his hot, sun-drenched skin, causing friction with her. "So good."

She'd moaned softly and he'd rolled atop her, his weight a pleasant burden. He'd nudged her knees apart and she'd felt his arousal, hard and long, as he rubbed her with it. Deep inside she'd been on fire and, as he'd pressed against her, levering up on his elbows, leaning down to kiss her lips, she'd given in completely, her arms encircling his neck, her mouth molding over his, her tongue seeking its mate.

With a groan, he'd thrust into her. Deep. Hard. Pain had seared through her and she'd jolted, her eyes flying open as he'd begun to move. *No! It wasn't supposed to be like this!*

But he'd plunged into her again and she'd felt a tingle of something new. Pleasure and pain. But the pain faded and she'd moved with him, sweat breaking out on her body, desire flooding through her veins. Her mind had spun wildly; she'd gasped for air, wanting more, fingers digging into strident, straining shoulders as he'd shuddered and she'd convulsed.

He'd fallen against her, gathering her in his arms as if he'd never let go. Which, of course, he had. In a big way.

They'd spent the next three or four weeks together…then Sue Ellen Tisdale had decided she wanted him back.

And that had been that.

Until now. She heard the rumble of a truck engine and watched as a van emblazoned with *Grand Hope Electrical* slid to a stop in the drive.

The cavalry had arrived.

But she was disappointed. She'd half expected to see Slade's truck parked outside.

The paunchy repairman carrying a clipboard with a work order was a sorry replacement for the man she wanted.

"Oh, God," she whispered at the realization. No way. She couldn't—*wouldn't*—want Slade McCafferty.

Not unless she wanted her heart broken into a thousand pieces.

Again.

# Chapter 8

"I'll look into custody rights when the father isn't around," Felicia Reynolds promised from the offices of Jansen, Monteith and Stone, hundreds of miles away, "but it would make my job a lot easier if I knew the father's name and how to contact him. From the sounds of it, he may not know he has a child, and there's always the chance that if he gets wind of it later, he could petition the court."

"I figured that." Jamie cradled the telephone receiver between her shoulder and ear as she pushed one hand through the sleeve of her coat. "But I doubt if that will happen unless Randi McCafferty contacts him or someone else spills the beans—you know, either a friend or a friend of a friend. Grand Hope is still a small town. Anything the McCaffertys do is big news around here. If the father of Randi's baby is a local guy, he would have put two and two together by now."

"But no one's stepped forward."

"Right." Shifting the receiver to her other shoulder, she stuffed her free arm into its sleeve.

"So either he doesn't know or doesn't want anything to do with the kid."

"Looks that way." Jamie's heart twisted when she thought of Randi's baby. All dimpled smiles and playful gurgles, with big, curious eyes and fuzzy reddish hair, the newest member of the McCafferty family had already gotten to her.

What idiot of a man wouldn't want to claim the baby as his son?

"I'll check all the angles."

"I'd appreciate that."

"It's a weird deal, though, don't you think? I mean, the buzz here at the office is that someone's trying to kill her and maybe the baby, too. God, how awful! Do you think… I mean, some people around here think the killer could be the baby's father, or even one of her half brothers, since she's inheriting the lion's share of the property."

Jamie bristled. "I don't know about the baby's dad, but it's not one of her brothers. I've seen them with Randi and her son. Thorne, Matt and Slade are extremely protective."

"If you say so," Felicia agreed, but wasn't quite done fishing. "What's this I hear about Chuck coming to visit you in Grand Hope?"

"Business. He wants Thorne McCafferty to transfer all his legal work to the firm."

"I think it might be more than that," Felicia suggested, and Jamie could envision the petite blonde sitting at her desk, looking out the window and twiddling her pen as she usually did when the gears were turning in her mind. "Chuck's got it bad."

"Bad?"

"For you. Don't play dumb with me, Jamie, because I know

better, okay? I wouldn't be surprised if he popped the question when he got there."

Inwardly Jamie groaned. "You think?"

"He's been walking around the office whistling, for God's sake. Can you imagine that? Chuck Jansen *whistling?*"

"That is a little out of character."

"A lot. It's a lot out of character, so I expect you to come clean with me and tell me *all* about it, every minute detail! You know I get all my thrills vicariously through you."

"Of course you do," Jamie mocked. Who was kidding whom? In the three years that Jamie had known her, Felicia had been through half a dozen boyfriends and dated men in between. Gorgeous and clever, with a wicked tongue, Felicia Reynolds was never at risk of spending a Friday or Saturday night at home.

"Talk to you in a few days."

"Promise?"

"Absolutely." Jamie hung up and snagged her briefcase. Thorne McCafferty had called earlier, requesting a meeting, so she was on her way. Back to the Flying M. And probably Slade McCafferty.

"If you break him, you can have him," Matt said, nodding toward Diablo Rojo, the orneriest horse on the spread.

Two and a half years old and full of fire, the Appaloosa snorted as if he'd heard his name; then, tail hoisted high, he ran lickety-split from one end of the paddock to the other. Snow churned from beneath his hooves and he whistled loudly, searching for the rest of the herd, and, Slade suspected, showing off. The colt knew he had an audience.

"Red Devil. Never was there a horse more aptly named," Slade said. "I thought you'd already broken him."

Beneath the brim of his Stetson, Matt's dark eyebrows

slammed together. "I tried everything. I've never seen a horse so damned stubborn."

"More stubborn than you?"

Dark eyes flashed. "Maybe."

"I didn't think a horse existed that you couldn't break." Propping a boot on the lowest rail, Slade leaned over the top of the fence. He eyed the colt who was prancing and bucking, tossing its head and snorting proudly.

"Fine. I take it back. You can't have him. I'll finish the job." Matt slapped the top rail of the fence with a gloved hand, then pointed a damning finger at the horse. "You and I, Devil, we aren't finished."

The wide-eyed colt pawed the snow and stared at Matt as if he'd understood, as if he couldn't wait for another showdown with the man who was determined to be his master.

"Yeah, he's scared to death, isn't he?" Slade said as they turned toward the house, where, though there was still some daylight left, interior lamps glowed through the windows. Smoke curled skyward from the chimney and as they watched, strings of Christmas lights blazed to life, only to quickly die. A second later the eaves flashed with pinpoints of light again, then snapped off. Again the lights blinked.

The brothers glanced at each other as the door flew open and one of the twins barreled out of the house, down the steps, and plowed through the snow as fast as her tiny legs would propel her. She beelined straight at her uncles and as she closed the distance in her stockinged feet, Slade recognized Molly— the bolder of Nicole's girls.

"Dumb Buandita won't let me turn on the lights," Molly cried, throwing herself on the mercy of her uncles. Her lower lip protruded and she had to blink rapidly to keep snowflakes from catching on her eyelashes.

Slade lifted the little girl into his arms. "*Juanita* is giving you a hard time? I find that hard to believe."

"It's true!" Molly insisted, scrunching up all her features and folding her chubby little arms over her chest. "She's mean!"

"Mean? Juanita? Nah!" He touched his nose to hers. "But when she figures out you ran out of the house in the snow in just your socks, she'll probably skin you al—er, she won't be happy."

"She yelled at me." Molly's face was suddenly angelic, the picture of four-year-old innocence.

Slade hugged her more fiercely to his chest as he carried her up the rise toward the house, Matt close behind. "Why do I have the feeling that you yanked Juanita's chain?"

"She's got no chain!" Molly insisted as Juanita, eyes round, lips pursed, gray hair springing from its usually neat coil, appeared in the open front door.

"There you are! *Dios, muchacha,* it's freezing out here and you without a coat. Or shoes!" She made the sign of the cross over her ample chest. "You'll catch your death."

Molly squirmed ever tighter to Slade.

"She seems to think you're abusing her by not letting her turn on the Christmas lights," he explained.

"Forever she is with the switch. On, off. On, off. The fuse will blow, and then Thorne, he will be upset because of his computer. You, little one," she said, wagging a finger at Molly, "will leave the lights alone. And you will not go out without boots and a coat." She looked pointedly at the four-year-old before a timer started chiming from deep inside the house. "My pies!" Turning quickly and muttering under her breath in Spanish, Juanita hurried down the hallway toward the kitchen.

"She's an old crab," Molly stated.

"I don't think so."

"I want Mommy."

"She's at work."

"Then I want Daddy!" As they walked up the steps to the front porch, Molly pushed herself out of Slade's arms, slid onto the worn floorboards and scampered inside, off to look for Thorne. Though he was legally only their stepfather, both girls had dubbed him "Daddy" since their biological father, Paul Stevenson, an attorney in San Francisco, was out of the picture. Paul and his new wife just didn't have time for two rambunctious four-year-olds. In Slade's opinion the guy was a first-class jerk, but then, most lawyers were.

His jaw tightened as he thought of Jamie, an attorney in her own right. She, he believed, was different. Though she tried to don the icy, all-business veneer of a corporate lawyer, he knew better.

He stepped into the entry as Juanita's voice rang clearly from the back of the house. "Leave your boots on the porch. I just cleaned the floors."

The brothers exchanged glances, then, grudgingly, used the bootjack before walking inside where the house smelled of roasting beef, fragrant pine boughs and cinnamon.

Nicole, with the questionable help of the twins, had spent the past few days decorating the house. Garlands of greenery had been woven with silver and gold ribbons and punctuated with sprigs of holly before being draped along the railing of the staircase and across the mantel. Colored lights glittered around all the windows and the living room furniture had been arranged to make room for a Christmas tree that had yet to be cut.

As Matt and Slade hung up their jackets, Thorne, limping slightly, ambled down the hallway. He was carrying Molly, and Mindy, the shyer twin, tagged behind them. "Striker called," he announced. "He's on his way over."

"Just Striker?" Matt asked.

"I think so. Kelly will be here later. She's over at the sheriff's department talking to Espinoza."

Roberto Espinoza had been Kelly's boss and was still in charge of the investigation into Randi's accident.

The front door opened, and Jenny Riley, a college student who looked after the girls, entered, causing Molly to scramble from Thorne's arms and both twins to demand her attention. "Just in time?" Jenny asked with an arch of one eyebrow at the uncles. "These little angels haven't been giving you any trouble, have they?"

"Not a second," Thorne lied, and Jenny laughed knowingly. "Come on, girls, I've got a surprise."

"What? What?" Molly asked, jumping up and down while Mindy tugged on the hem of Jenny's jacket.

"It wouldn't be a surprise if I told you, would it?"

"What *is* it?" Molly demanded.

"I'll tell the both of you when we're alone, but it's a secret. A Christmas secret!"

"Oh." Mindy held a finger to her lips.

"That's right." Glancing pointedly at the McCafferty brothers, Jenny whispered, "We can't tell your uncles. It'll spoil the surprise." She hung her jacket on a peg near the door, then, carrying a suspiciously large oversize bag slung over one shoulder, shepherded the girls upstairs. "Come on, now, but don't say a word…"

For the next fifteen minutes the brothers discussed the ranch, Matt's upcoming wedding and, of course, the investigation into Randi's accident.

Kurt Striker, looking like a Hollywood interpretation of a rugged, lantern-jawed private detective, arrived half an hour later with the news that he'd located two maroon Fords that had been involved in accidents and had subsequently been repaired.

"Unfortunately, neither vehicle was anywhere near Glacier Park on the day of Randi's accident. The pickup was involved in a three-car pileup west of here—an old farmer was driving it on his way fishing. The other one, a minivan, hit a telephone pole when the owner's fifteen-year-old took it out for a joyride behind his parents' back."

"So we're back to square one," Thorne declared from his position on the couch.

"We'll keep looking," Striker said, his jaw set in determination. "Either the car wasn't repaired, we haven't found the right shop yet, or the work was done under the table, in a shop where they don't keep records. But we'll find it."

"If it exists," Matt said, as Randi, carrying the baby, walked into the room.

"You don't remember another vehicle?" Striker turned his attention to Randi and the baby, and if possible, his features hardened.

"No, and I think I've told you that before. If and when I do, you'll be the first to know," she said, sarcasm lacing her words. She sat in the old rocker, the bottom of her foot resting against the coffee table as she cradled her son to her shoulder.

"What about the guy Nicole saw at the hospital? The one dressed as a doctor, any news there?" Randi asked, as if to prove to her brothers that she was trying to be helpful. Matt propped himself against the windowsill and Slade sat on the end of the piano bench. Kurt sat in the recliner, but he was leaning forward, his hands clasped between his knees, his eyes focused hard on Randi. She returned his stare and Slade thought, for just a second, that he saw more than anger in Randi's eyes…it was almost as if…nah! She wouldn't be interested in Striker, wouldn't find him attractive…

"Kelly and I have been talking to some of your acquaintances in Seattle," Striker said.

"I thought you already did that."

"We widened the circle."

"To include?"

"Anyone you had any dealing with in the past couple of years."

"That's quite a task, considering how many people I come in contact with in my job." Gently she pushed the rocker, her hand rubbing her baby's back.

"We even got hold of your agent in New York. He said you were working on a book about relationships, that you were using information you'd gathered while working at the *Clarion,* maybe some actual case histories, that kind of thing."

"I don't remember authorizing you to contact my agent."

"You didn't. *I* did," Slade volunteered. "Since your memory is so iffy, I figured it would be the only way to piece what happened together."

"You could have told me."

"I did. But you were in a coma. And I asked Kurt to dig deep, Randi, to turn your life upside down. I figured you'd be upset, but I decided that was just tough. It's time to nail the bastard."

"But my book has nothing to do with it. Or my job…"

"Then what?" Slade demanded. "What does have something to do with it?"

"I don't know," she admitted, and some of the starch left her spine. Slade was reminded of her as a little girl, trying to gain approval from older brothers who didn't want anything to do with her. Now, it seemed, the tables had turned.

From his spot at the window, Matt shot Slade a glance. "Jamie Parsons is here." He couldn't help but grin widely, which irritated the hell out of Slade.

"Good." Thorne straightened. "I asked her over."

"Now what?" Randi mumbled suspiciously.

"Actually, it's not about you this time. I'm going to contract the law firm to work on another property transfer here in Montana, but I'm sure your name might come up."

"Perfect, just what I need, all my brothers trying to run my life."

"Maybe that's a good idea," Slade suggested, pushing himself upright as the doorbell chimed. "'Cause from where I stand, it looks like you could use all the help you can get." He walked to the door and cursed himself for wanting to see Jamie again. Tiny footsteps pounded, and the twins careened down the stairs.

Jamie was standing, briefcase in hand, on the porch. God, she was beautiful, her cheeks tinged pink from the cold, some strands of sunstreaked hair escaping from the knot at the back of her neck. "Come on in," he invited, offering her an easy smile and noticing the wariness in her hazel eyes.

Because of the kiss.

"Thanks."

"Get the furnace going?"

A smile touched her lips. "Finally. The thermostat was shot."

"Are we getting a Christmas tree today?" one of the girls asked, tugging on Slade's sleeve.

"Maybe later."

"You promised!" Molly charged.

"I know, but we have company now."

Molly glared pointedly at Jamie as if wishing her to evaporate.

"You said we could get one today," Mindy, the shyer girl, reminded her uncle.

"Okay, then we will." Squatting to be at eye level with the girls, he said, "As soon as I'm finished. Now you get bundled up, okay? No more running outside in stockings!" He looked up at Jamie. "Don't ask." Then he touched Molly's dark curls. "We'll take General out with the sleigh and get the tree."

"Promise?" Molly asked, her little face screwed up in disbelief.

Slade lifted a hand. Held up two fingers. "On my honor. Now, have Juanita pack us a thermos of hot chocolate and maybe some cookies, then get Jenny to find your snowsuits. And boots. But don't bug me anymore. When I'm done here, I'll take you. We'll find the best Christmas tree on the ranch!"

Molly's face burst into a wide grin and Mindy glanced up at Slade through her eyelashes.

"Go on!" he said, and they took off, running down the hallway toward the kitchen.

Straightening, Slade found Jamie staring at him as if he'd lost his mind. "I never thought I'd see the day," she said. "You? Going out for a Christmas tree with two little girls? *In a sleigh?*"

"Well, Counselor, maybe there are a few things you don't know about me."

"Maybe."

"You could come along if you want." The thought of her bundled up next to him in the sleigh held more than a little appeal.

"I—I'm here on business."

"After business."

"I don't know. I'm not really dressed for it..."

"All you have to do is ride. I'll handle the horse and hauling the tree. Come on, you know what they say about 'all work and no play.'"

"It pays the bills?"

"Yeah, that's it," he remarked as Kurt, zipping his jacket walked through the hallway and out the front door.

"I'll call you later," he promised, then hitched a thumb toward the living room. "It would help a helluva lot if your sister cooperated."

"She's trying."

"Like hell. Talk some sense into her. Before she gets herself killed." Without pausing for an introduction, Striker stormed out of the house.

"Nice guy," Jamie observed, and it wasn't just her opinion. Randi was beside herself in the living room.

"What an A number-one jerk," she raved, carrying the baby and, limping, making her way to the window as if to make sure that Kurt Striker was actually leaving.

"He's just what we need," Slade countered.

"Since when do we need a rude, obnoxious jerk poking around?" Randi demanded.

"Since someone tried to kill you and you can't or won't tell us what happened."

"Don't you think I'd be the first one to go to the police and explain who was doing this if I knew?"

"I don't know, Randi," Slade admitted. "I honestly don't know."

"You miserable..." Randi glanced over at Thorne and met an expression as hard and determined as Slade's, and when she turned to Matt, she swallowed back any further argument because from the determination in his dark eyes it was clear that even he was taking a hard line with her.

"This is serious stuff, kiddo," Slade pointed out. "I was willing to believe that maybe you were in just some kind of odd, single-car accident, but then someone tried to kill you in the hospital. You don't remember it, but I do. Damn, it was scary, so don't argue with us, okay? The police are fine, but we need more. I've known Striker for years. He's good. He'll find out who's behind all this, but you've got to help him."

She gritted her teeth, looked down at her baby and then

sighed as she saw little Joshua move his tiny lips. "Okay, I'll try," she vowed. "Really, I will, but there's something about that guy I don't trust."

The baby opened his eyes and suddenly began to fuss. All of Randi's attention was riveted on her son. "Uh-oh. Look who's getting cranky." She dropped a kiss onto his forehead, then nuzzled his cheek. "Bedtime for you, I think," she said, and winked at her baby. The transformation was remarkable. Ready to take on Kurt Striker and the whole damned world one minute, Randi became a doting mother whose only concern was her baby the next. She breezed out of the room, and Slade watched her climb the stairs. Once she'd disappeared, he looked at Thorne. "It would help if she would cooperate a little more."

"Oh, give her a break." Matt eased away from the window and tossed a log onto the dying fire. "She can't remember much."

Slade's gaze lingered on the stairway. "So she says."

"You're not buying it?"

"Nope," Slade admitted. "Not in a million years. I think our sister is hiding something."

"What?"

"Now that's the million-dollar question, isn't it?"

"What are we gonna do?" Randi asked as she tucked Joshua's blanket to his neck. His eyes were already closed and he let out a soft little sigh that nearly broke her heart. Lord, how she loved him. She hadn't known that kind of love was possible, though her father had warned her enough. "Wait till you have yourself a little one," John Randall had told her one day before he'd died. "Then you'll understand what it's like to love something more than life itself."

It had been early spring and he'd been sitting on the porch

and watching the spindly legged foals scamper in the field they called Big Meadow. While the mares had lazily plucked grass, their tails switching at flies, the rambunctious fillies and colts had bucked and galloped through the long grass. Her father had nodded to himself, approving of his wisdom. He'd grabbed her hand with long fingers and a surprisingly strong grip. "You think you're invincible, you think nothing can hurt you, but once you have a child, that's when you're vulnerable, when you experience real fear for the first time."

She hadn't really understood him at the time, but now, looking down at her baby, realizing that if she didn't stop whoever was trying to harm her, her son could be injured. John Randall's words had new meaning.

She thought of the baby's father...yes, no matter what she said to her brothers, she knew darned well who had sired her baby. And the bastard didn't deserve to know about him.

"I'm sorry," she whispered to little Joshua. So innocent. Someday he would have to know the truth, hard as it was. "I'll take care of you," she promised, smoothing his downy red hair. "I promise. I won't let anyone hurt you."

She turned and found Slade standing in the doorway of the nursery. His arms were folded over his chest, a shoulder propped on the door frame. "You got something you want to tell me?" he asked, and she felt a second's hesitation. Could she confide in him? Slade and she were the closest, not only in age, but temperament. And that was the problem. If Slade knew the circumstances behind Josh's conception and birth, he'd go ballistic.

"What would that be?" she asked, offering him a smile as she pressed a finger to her lips and turned off the light. She grabbed Slade's arm and propelled him into the hallway where she left the door to the nursery slightly ajar.

His lips pulled into a tight, unyielding frown. "I think

you're holding out," he said, resting his hips on the railing of the upper landing.

"How's that?"

"Something's up with you, Randi, and don't try to deny it. You're talking to me, remember? I know you. This amnesia thing is all a blind. Smoke and mirrors. I think you've got yourself into some kind of big trouble and you're pretending not to remember it in the hope that it'll conveniently disappear." His eyes narrowed slightly. "I'm thinking that you've manipulated all of us—Thorne, Matt and me—even the doctors—so that word will leak out to the street via the press. You're a reporter, and you know how that works. You're hoping that you can buy yourself some time with the amnesia bit."

"Why would I do that?"

"My guess is because you're scared. Either you're protecting someone or you need some time in order to..." He snapped his fingers. "Is it about the book? Have you got yourself into some hot water over the book? Striker and the police have already questioned everyone at the paper and gone through all your old articles, even the ones written under the name of R.J. McKay."

"R.J.?" she repeated.

"The freelance articles..."

The name did ring a bell—a far-distant bell.

"Your editor thought you probably wrote them for some extra cash."

"I...I suppose."

"But they weren't anything that would get you into any trouble, nor were your columns, not that we could figure. So either what's got you on the run is—"

"I'm *not* on the run," she clarified. "I'm recuperating. As soon as I can, I intend to reclaim my life, pack up Joshua—" she hitched a thumb to the cracked nursery door "—and return to Seattle. I've already talked to my boss. Bill wants me back as soon as I can get there, so I'm not on the run."

"Fine, but you're scared. And you're involved in something dangerous. Is it the book? What could that be? Are you writing some kind of exposé on political crime or the Mob or…what? Or is it J.R., er, Josh's dad?" He stared at her and she saw that he cared, really cared. Slade, for all his bluster and bravado and macho attitude, had a soft side, a soul that could be hurt.

"Tell ya what," she said, fighting the urge to tell him everything. "As soon as I remember anything important, I'll let you know."

He eyed her suspiciously. "Why do I think you're lying?"

"Because you have trust issues," she said, and he rolled his eyes. "Things are getting clearer." That much was true. "Just be patient, okay?"

"It's not, and patience isn't my long suit. But I'll give you some space, not much, but a little, and when you have a breakthrough or whatever it is, you'd better talk to me."

"Scout's honor," she promised, cringing a little at the lie. She would tell him. Soon. But she wasn't sure when. Or how. There were things in her memory that were fuzzy, some seemed to have disappeared entirely, but day by day, bit by bit, her past was returning. It was just a matter of time.

"You'd better not be yanking my chain."

"Why don't you forget about me for a minute? There are other things we've got to work out." When he lifted a dark brow, she said, "Let's start with the transfer of property. When Matt buys you out, what're you going to do with the rest of your life?"

"I haven't decided yet."

"Well, you'd better figure it out, and while you're at it," she advised, starting for the stairs, "you'd better pencil Jamie Parsons into the equation."

# Chapter 9

"So what you're suggesting," Jamie said, leveling her gaze across the desk, "is that the firm use all its resources to try to find out everything we can about your sister, pry into her personal life, dig deep, use private investigators, snitches—whatever it takes—to find out who's the father of her child. And in return, you'll throw us a bone, a little more business our way. Is that what you want to do?"

"Absolutely." Thorne leaned his elbows on the scarred wooden desk. The den was small and had never been intended to house computers, a fax machine, printers, scanners, copiers and a phone with several lines, yet it didn't seem cluttered—just compact and efficient. Like the man trying to convince Jamie that what he was doing was somehow benign. Thorne wasn't giving an inch. "The police are too slow. Striker's frustrated. Randi can't or won't remember anything that might help, and

I have the feeling we're running out of time. Whoever wants to harm her won't wait to strike again."

"Isn't that her business?"

"I'm just taking care of my sister," Thorne insisted, his gray eyes steely with determination. "I would never forgive myself if I let her bully me into backing off and something happened to her or the baby. Don't worry, this isn't going to be behind her back. I'll tell her."

"That you bargained for her. Offered more business to Jansen, Monteith and Stone *if* they were able to unearth her deepest secrets? *That's* what you're going to tell her?" Jamie stared at the man in disbelief. "I'm just glad you're not my brother."

"She'll appreciate it."

"I met her. I don't think so."

Thorne's jaw hardened. "You don't have to second-guess me, just pass the information along. We're talking a lot of business to the firm. I've already got my eye on two potential developments in this county, one outside of Grand Hope, another on the way to Carver…and that's just a start. I've got drilling rights in Colorado and…" His face fell away as he leaned back in his desk chair and it squeaked. "Just have Chuck give me a call."

"I will," she promised, standing briskly.

He must have read the censure in her eyes, because his expression was suddenly not set in granite. "I really am looking out for my sister and her son's best interests. How would any of us feel if we hadn't done everything possible to ensure their safety and something tragic happened? Not only has someone tried to kill my sister twice, but the baby nearly died in the hospital from complications surrounding his birth. Bacterial meningitis."

Lines of worry creased Thorne's face and Jamie realized that be he right or wrong, he really was doing what he thought best, that he cared. Even if she thought he was going about it all wrong. He hadn't suggested anything illegal.

"I'll talk to Chuck," she promised, leaving the small office. What the devil was she getting herself into? The McCafferty brothers were all hardheaded and extremely protective when it came to their sister.

*You're not getting yourself into anything. This is just business. Try to remember that.*

But it seemed impossible. Especially with Slade. The other brothers were handsome, intriguing men, but even if they were both single, she could have resisted their charms. Not so with the youngest brother, even though he'd nearly destroyed her once before. Well, never again, she thought, squaring her shoulders as she walked to the front of the house.

Slade was waiting for her.

Leaning against a post near the stairs, arms crossed over his chest, amused smile curving his lips, as if he knew her recent thoughts and was hell-bent to prove her wrong.

"Have fun with Thorne?" he drawled.

"It was business."

"Business is his fun."

She arched a brow. "Is it?"

"Well, it was. For years, it was all he talked about. Hooking up with Nicole mellowed him out."

"I don't know if I'd call him 'mellow.'"

"Yeah, well, you should've seen him before. So." He straightened and hitched his chin toward the door. "Ready?"

"For what?"

Before he could answer, tiny feet pounded, and the twins raced down the hall. One wore a pink snowsuit, the other was dressed in yellow. Both wore boots and mittens. Eager, rosy faces turned upward in anticipation.

"Can we go now?" one cherub asked. She was jumping up

and down, unable to contain an iota of her excitement, while the other one was all shy smiles that she cast up at her uncle.

"I think so," Slade said, winking at the girls. "I was just trying to talk Ms. Parsons into joining us."

Two sets of bright eyes focused on Jamie.

"Hurry!" the liveliest twin—was it Molly?—ordered as if she were a little drill sergeant. "We gots to go. Now!"

"Oh, I don't know. I don't have a snowsuit like you girls and—"

"And you'll be fine," Slade insisted, opening the door.

Crisp winter air slid inside. Snow was falling in lazy flakes and a tall chestnut-colored horse stood in the drive, harnessed to what had once been a sleek red sleigh. "It'll be fun," Slade insisted.

Fun? With Slade McCafferty?

Jamie didn't think so.

The horse shook his great head and bells attached to his harness jingled in the snowfall.

"Oo-oh!" one little girl cried, placing her hands over her cheeks. The other one was out of the door like a rocket, black boots flashing against the white snow.

"Come on, Counselor," he insisted, touching her arm. "What would it hurt?"

She thought of her heart, once so bitterly wounded by this man, considered her pride, how it had been battered, her self-esteem that had been pounded into nearly nothing. It had taken her years to get over the ache, and now...now she should risk it all again? "I'll let you drive." His blue eyes flashed with a dare and a crooked smile slashed across a square jaw dark with beard shadow.

She couldn't resist. "All right, McCafferty, you're on," she agreed. "But only if I can use the whip on you if you get out of line."

The smile stretched wider. "It's a deal. I'll try to be on my worst behavior."

He took her hand, and with the shy twin following, they walked briskly down the broken snow path to the sleigh. The impetuous twin was trying and failing to climb into the old sleigh. "Here ya go, pumpkin," Slade said, hoisting her into the backseat where thick coverlets had been tucked around the cold leather.

"What's in here?" Molly asked, pointing to an insulated pack as Slade plopped her sister next to her.

"Hot chocolate and cookies for *after* we cut the tree."

"But I'm thirsty now."

"Then you'll have to wait to cut the tree."

"No!"

"Patience is a virtue, Molly," Slade said as he helped Jamie climb into the front seat, then swung into the rig and settled next to her. With a wink at Jamie, he cracked the whip over the horse's head and the chestnut stepped forward. The sleigh slid easily over the thick snow and through the gates Slade had already opened. Both girls giggled from the back.

"I hadn't planned on this," Jamie said.

"I know." He slid a glance her way, taking in her wool slacks, sweater and overcoat. She wore boots, but they weren't meant for trudging through the snow, nor were her gloves insulated. He placed an arm around her shoulders and, breath fogging in the air, whispered, "Trust me, darlin'. I won't let you freeze." Her breath caught in her lungs for a second, then she looked away, refusing to be seduced by the kind gesture or the care in his voice.

"Here, you drive for a while." He placed the reins in her gloved fingers, then reached beneath the seat and pulled out a sheepskin blanket. As the bells jingled and the sled skimmed across the snow, Slade unfolded the short blanket and tucked it over her lap. As if he cared. Her heart twisted.

*He used me,* she reminded herself, the old pain returning as she thought of the baby she'd lost, the child she'd mourned alone.

She'd never confided in her grandmother, but Nana had suspected something was wrong. She'd caught Jamie crying behind the barn where Caesar had been grazing, swatting flies with his tail as he nipped at the dry stubble near the fence. Wearing her floppy straw hat and gardening gloves, Nana had rounded the corner with a basket of weeds she'd pulled out of the garden and stopped short when she caught sight of Jamie. "It's that McCafferty boy, isn't it?" she'd guessed, and when Jamie hadn't answered, Nita Parsons had become very serious and placed a gloved hand on Jamie's bare arm. "You would tell me if you needed help, wouldn't you?"

Jamie had nodded and sniffed but hadn't forced the painful words over her tongue.

"Sometimes...sometimes a girl gets herself into trouble before she even really thinks about it."

Worried eyes had peered through rimless glasses. "I'm here for you, honey, I always will be, and if that boy has done anything to you, anything at all, I'll take it up with his father. There are laws concerning what can happen between a boy and a girl your age."

"I—I'm fine, Nana," she'd lied, shifting her gaze away from the doubts in her grandmother's eyes.

"You're sure?"

"Absolutely." She'd swallowed back her tears. "I'm just kind of emotional, you know, that time of the month."

Nana's lips had pinched in disbelief, but she hadn't called Jamie on the lie. "Just know that I'm here for you. No matter what." Then she'd dumped her weeds into the growing pile near the barn and walked slowly back to the garden. Jamie had wanted desperately to confide in Nana, but knew it would serve no purpose. Slade had left, was engaged to Sue Ellen, and Jamie had lost the baby. She'd been to see a doctor in a neighboring town who had confirmed the miscarriage. She'd been certain that a part of her had died with her child.

Now, she shivered in the sleigh.

Next to the man who had so callously turned his back on her.

Slade took the reins from her fingers and snapped them. The horse picked up speed across Big Meadow toward the far side where the foothills sloped upward and thick stands of pine and aspen crowded around a creek bed.

In the backseat, the girls giggled and refused to sit still no matter how many times Slade reminded them to stay put. They were excited, pointing and laughing, chattering about Christmas and Santa and what they wanted.

The horse shied as a rabbit, as white as the snow drifting from the heavens, jumped out of the way and into the safety of skeletal, icy brambles.

"There. That one, that one!" Molly cried, standing quickly and pointing a mittened hand straight ahead, over the horse's ears to a huge tree in the distance.

"I think it's a little big," Slade said, and chuckled to himself as he glanced at the thirty-foot tree. "The General would probably have a heart attack if he had to pull that one back to the house. Then there's me. More than likely, I'd keel over if I had to cut it down. Let's try to find something that will fit *inside* the house."

"Spoilsport," Jamie muttered, caught up in the magic of the moment. He slid her a glance, then clucked to the gelding and snapped the reins. Snowflakes danced and swirled. Frigid air caressed her cheeks.

The acres sped by in a cold, wintry rush as Slade guided General through the foothills until they came to a thick stand of smaller trees. The girls couldn't sit still a moment longer and as Slade reined the horse to a stop, they tumbled out of the sleigh, running pell-mell through the unbroken snow. "I think we'll find one here," he said, climbing out and offering Jamie his arm.

She should ignore it, but looking down into his upturned face, staring into eyes as clear and blue as the summer sky, she grabbed his hand. Something inside her caught. Her heart gave a quick little leap, but she refused to recognize the glimmer in his eyes. She hopped off the sleigh. He tugged on her arm, dragging her close. Before she could so much as catch her breath, he kissed her. Hard. As if he'd been waiting for just the right moment. Chilled lips fastened to hers for an electric instant that caused her heart to kick. Oh, God, her knees turned to water.

The kiss deepened for a second and her blood ran hot. Why was it always like this? Why couldn't she turn away from this one man who seemed determined to break her heart over and over? *Fool me once, shame on you, fool me twice, shame on me...*

He lifted his head, then, still holding her, slowly winked at her. "Let's play lumberjack," he suggested, and she arched a brow. He whispered, "I'd prefer doctor, of course, but with the kids around—"

"It wouldn't be proper."

"And you know how dead-set I am about propriety."

She laughed and shook her head as he released her. "You don't give up, do you?"

"Never." He flipped open a compartment in the back of the sleigh and pulled out his tools. Packing a small chain saw in one hand and a coil of nylon rope on his shoulder, he plowed through the snow, following the trails made by tiny little boots.

"Over here! Over here!"

Jamie saw a flash of a pink snowsuit between the saplings.

"Uncle Slade!" Molly was yelling and pointing to a crooked pine tree about ten feet tall. "This one. This one."

"It's not straight, darlin'," he said, eyeing the listing pine.

"It's perfect," Molly insisted, jumping up and down.

"Yeth," her sister said. "This one, Unca Slade."

"She's right, it's...perfect," Jamie agreed.

A wry smile twisted Slade's lips. "Outvoted by the females," he mused under his breath. "Well, if you two, er, three, are sure."

"Yeth!" Even Mindy was jumping up and down.

"Cut it down!" Molly demanded.

"Vicious little thing, aren't you? Now, stand back. Both of you." He bent on one knee and looked back at Jamie, who got the message.

"Come on, girls, over here," she said. "Let's give...uh, Uncle Slade, some room."

With a growl and plume of smoke, the chain saw roared to life, bucking as the blade bit into the base of the pine. Sawdust plumed and littered the snow. A few seconds later the tree tumbled to the ground, sending up a burst of white powder.

The girls sprang forward. Insisting upon helping their uncle, they unlooped the coil of rope as he baled the tree.

"Good job," he said, carrying the tree back to the sleigh and tying it to one side, above the runners. "I'll recommend you both to the Lumberjack Hall of Fame."

"Can we gets another one?" Molly asked, her eyes bright as she spied another tree.

"I think one's enough, sprite." He rubbed the top of her head and she grinned widely. "We'll take this one back and maybe make some snow angels or a snowman while the tree dries out, then we'll take it inside and you can get your aunt Randi to help you decorate it."

Mindy's mittened hands clasped together at the thought. "With candy canes?"

"If that's what you want." Slade tested the ropes lashing the tree to the sleigh. The bundled pine didn't move. "Okay, how about cookies and cocoa?"

They ate in the sleigh, the twins chattering in the still afternoon air, the warm smells of hot chocolate and coffee drifting through the snowflakes that swirled around them. It felt so natural, so right, with thick blankets and sheepskin tossed over their laps, noses red with the cold, laughter coming easy. As if they were a family, Jamie thought. The family she'd never really known.

Except that the children weren't hers.

Except that she wasn't married to Slade.

Except that he'd left her years ago.

Except that the baby they'd created hadn't survived long enough to be born.

Hot tears burned the backs of her eyes and Slade reached forward to touch her cheek. "Somethin' wrong?"

*If you only knew,* she thought, but shook her head. "Nah. Just a little nostalgia."

"For?"

"Things that could have been." That was vague enough. She sipped her coffee and felt its heat burn a path down her throat. But it couldn't warm that icy spot in her heart, the part that had died when Slade had left her and she'd lost their child.

"Maybe you should start lookin' forward, instead of lookin' back," he suggested, as if he could read her mind.

"You're a great one to give that kind of advice." She'd seen the torment in his expression when he'd mentioned the accident that had taken the life of someone close to him. It was her turn to touch, the finger of one kidskin glove tracing his scar. "You still beat yourself up for this."

His expression changed. Darkened. As if the demons he'd so recently put to rest had awakened. His lips pursed for a second and he tossed the dregs from his cup into the snow. "I don't think we should go there."

"You said—"

"Go where?" Molly asked, leaning forward, breaking into the tense conversation. "Where should we go?"

"Never mind." Slade half turned in the seat. "Let's pack up our things and head back before it gets dark. Hiya!" He slapped the reins over General's rump and the sleigh eased forward.

Twisting over the seat back, Jamie wiped smudged faces and tucked the two uneaten cookies and empty cups into the insulated pack, then settled into the front seat as the girls snuggled under their blankets.

Slade stared straight ahead, his jaw set, pain etching his features as darkness crept through the trees and into the gullies. Rudders gliding, the sleigh slid over the smooth snow. Snowflakes swirled and caught in Jamie's hair and eyelashes as the words to "Winter Wonderland" rolled through her mind. She cast a glance at Slade, his lips compressed. Dear God, how she'd loved him all those years ago. If things had been different, perhaps they would have...

*Stop it! What would have been better? That he found out you were pregnant and married you because he felt obligated? That you gave up your dreams of college and career to be what? Slade McCafferty's wife? That's not what you wanted.*

No, Jamie thought as the night closed in around them. But the baby, oh, how she'd wanted the baby. And there was more. Whether she wanted to admit it or not, she'd wanted Slade to love her.

# Chapter 10

"Did you see that?" Slade's eyes narrowed on the stables. He reined General to a stop near the front porch of the ranch house. Was it his imagination, or had he seen someone's face in the darkened window of the horse barn?

"What?" Jamie asked.

"Someone inside the stables...not Larry Todd, our foreman, or Adam Zollander, our ranch hand, or one of my brothers." His voice sounded tight, even to his own ears, and every muscle in his body tensed. He dropped the reins as Jamie swung her head, surveying the outbuildings surrounding the yard.

"I don't see anyone," she said.

"Neither do I. Now." But he had.

Or was he just jumping at shadows? Edgy because of the attempts on Randi's life? He wasn't willing to take any chances, and the gut feeling he had—that something wasn't right—stuck with him. "You take the kids inside. I'll go check it out." He was out of the sleigh in an instant.

"What about the tree?" Molly demanded as she flung herself into a thick, soft, drift.

"I'll get it later."

"But—"

He focused hard on his niece. "I said I'll bring it in. Later. Or you can have Uncle Matt or Thorne do it now. But you two—" he motioned to both of his nieces "—go inside and warm up."

"I wants to do snow angels!" Molly was as stubborn as he was, but this wasn't the time to back down, not when the hairs on the back of his neck were rising. He glanced at Jamie, sending her a silent message that she picked up.

"Come on, girls," Jamie said, ushering both rambunctious twins toward the front door. "Maybe Juanita has something for you in the kitchen."

"Dumb Buandita," Molly muttered, but as Mindy climbed onto the first step, the door swept open and the twins shrieked in glee at the sight of their mother.

"Mommy, Mommy, we gots the tree! Look! Uncle Slade, he sawed it down—" Mindy was pointing frantically at the sleigh, but Slade ignored the little girl and, jabbing his fists into the pockets of his jacket, trudged through the snow to the stables. He considered a weapon, but figured he'd grab a pitchfork once he was inside the barn.

*It's probably nothing,* his mind nagged. But he wasn't willing to take a chance. Not on his sister's life. Not on the baby's. Not on anyone in his family's. And not on Jamie's. He stopped short. Jamie wasn't part of his family.

Whoa.

He was getting ahead of himself. Way ahead. He made it to the barn door, swung it open and reached inside, but didn't flip the switch. If someone was lurking in the shadows with a gun, he didn't want to give the guy an open shot at him.

Instead, he grabbed a pitchfork as he slipped inside. Horses snorted and shifted in their stalls. One gave out a nervous nicker as Slade waited in the darkness, ears straining, listening for the slightest noise. His fingers grasped the smooth wooden handle of the pitchfork and he crouched, keeping his back to the wall. Did he hear the scrape of a boot or was his mind playing tricks on him? Was there a change in the atmosphere inside the old building or was he jumping at shadows?

His eyes adjusted to the blue light shining through the windows, a watery illumination from the exterior security lamps. Slade made out the familiar shapes of the horses as they dozed in their stalls. Nothing appeared out of place. Silently he crept along the walk between the stalls, his pitchfork ready. He peeked cautiously into each box, expecting a figure to leap out of the shadows at any second. A few of the horses snorted. One pawed the straw, and despite the chill in the air, Slade felt a trickle of nervous sweat slide down his spine.

Did he smell something...the hint of some aftershave still hanging on the air, or was he, again, conjuring up a sinister scenario that didn't exist?

A mouse scurried across the floor and he jumped, landing on the balls of his feet. But there was nothing but the sound of frantic little claws on concrete.

Slade paused at Diablo Rojo's stall, the very end box. The colt tossed his head and huffed out a disgusted blast of air, as if he knew the folly of it all.

Silently, Slade slipped around the last box to the next aisle and as he walked between the set of stalls, he saw no one. Heard nothing out of place. Maybe he'd imagined the face in the window. Unconvinced, he searched the tack room, again, without bothering with the lights. Nothing seemed out of place. He stepped on the lowest rung of the ladder to the hayloft.

The door burst open. Slade spun, his weapon ready. The lights blazed on.

"What the devil's got into you?" Matt stood in the doorway, his eyes focused on the sharp tines of the pitchfork aimed in his direction.

The knots in Slade's shoulders relaxed a little. "I thought I saw someone here when I brought the twins back to the house."

"So what...you thought you'd surprise him and prong him to death? Like somethin' you were going to put on the barbecue? Hell, why didn't you grab Dad's rifle?"

"I wasn't sure."

"But you thought you'd grab the pitchfork just in case."

"Yeah."

"Damn." Matt's smile twisted in open amusement. "Sometimes I don't know what the hell you're thinkin'." Matt walked to a shelf where a pair of leather gloves was tucked between the curry combs and brushes. "Seems to me you've been jumping out of your skin ever since a certain lady lawyer showed up in town." He picked up the gloves and pulled them on.

"Meaning?"

"Meaning anything you want it to." Chuckling under his breath, Matt headed for the door. "I guess I'll leave you and the bogeyman alone. But I will haul the Christmas tree into the house. The girls can't wait."

"Do that," Slade growled irritably.

"Then I'll put the sleigh away and take care of General."

"Thanks."

"No problem." Still chuckling to himself, Matt yanked on the gloves and disappeared through the door. Slade felt like a fool. But he couldn't shake the feeling that something was wrong, so, with the interior lights burning bright, he climbed the ladder to the hayloft where the air barely moved. The smells of hay and horses, dust and dung filtered upward. The lights were dimmer here, the shadows murkier. Bales were stacked to the high, pitched ceiling and loose straw was several inches thick across the old plank floor. But there wasn't a sound up here. Nothing looked out of place. Nothing moved.

*Fool. You're starting to be paranoid.*

Downstairs, the door creaked open.

Slade nearly jumped out of his skin.

"Slade?"

Jamie's voice. He relaxed a little.

"Up here." Looking down the ladder, he found her craning her neck and staring up at the hole cut into the floor.

"Find anything?"

"Just Matt. And that was pretty scary."

She smiled and shook her head. "You can be funny when you're not a pain in the backside."

"I'll take that as a compliment, Counselor. Come on up."

She hesitated. Frowned enough to create little furrows between her eyebrows. "What about the twins? They're waiting for you. When it comes to promises about Christmas trees and snow angels, kids have incredible memories."

"They can wait a little longer. It's the anticipation that's the fun part." He crooked a finger at her. "Come on up."

"Well, I don't think I should—"

"Afraid?"

"What? Afraid? Of you?" Her eyes sparked. She couldn't resist a dare.

"Of us."

"I told you—"

"Yeah, yeah, I know." God she was beautiful. Staring up at him with wide hazel eyes filled with indecision. "Come on,

Jamie, it's time to drop the sword. I won't hurt you. I don't bite...well, not hard and only if the lady asks for—"

"Oh, save it, McCafferty." He saw it then, that little shadow of pain that he'd witnessed before, but she quickly disguised it with a determined thrust of her chin. She grabbed the metal rung and stepped onto the ladder. Within seconds she was up in the hayloft, looking out of place in her wool slacks, sweater and overcoat.

"Sit," he suggested, kicking a bale toward her.

"You've got something you want to say," she guessed, smoothing her coat before perching on the edge of the bale.

"Yeah. I do." He sat next to her, his hands clasped between his knees. "I enjoyed myself this afternoon."

Worry clouded her eyes. "Oh."

"Didn't you?"

"Well, yes. The girls were so excited, and it's been years since I was out in the wilderness to cut a tree. I usually get a small one from a lot in town."

"That wasn't what I was talking about, and you know it."

She glanced up at him, then let her gaze slide away as if she were suddenly interested in the rafters and the feathers and droppings from an owl that had once roosted near the small round window high above.

The barest hint of her perfume tickled his nostrils, and he couldn't help but notice the slope of her cheek and the way her lips folded in on themselves.

"I was talking about being with you," he admitted when she didn't say a word. "Yes, I know it sounds corny."

"Like a line out of a sappy romantic movie," she said, but her voice had changed, deepened.

"Yeah, maybe." He snorted a laugh, his fingers laced with hers. "But I meant it." He tipped her chin up with one gloved finger, gazed into her incredible eyes for just a second, then pressed his lips to hers. She uttered the tiniest moan of protest, then sighed against him. His blood heated. He wrapped one arm around her, pushing closer, feeling her mouth part slightly as his tongue touched the sexy seam of her lips.

*Don't do this,* his mind screamed. But he didn't listen. Wouldn't. He'd spent the past week waking up in the middle of the night so hard he couldn't think straight, drenched in sweat from the vivid dreams he'd had of kissing her, touching her, making love to her, and now they were alone and he felt the heat throb between them, the passion she denied just beneath the surface. He pressed harder, his tongue sliding along the slick ridges of the roof of her mouth, her tongue playing with his, her breathing shallow. Rapid. Warm. "Slade," she whispered as he pulled back to look at her flushed face and to smooth a lock of hair from her cheek.

"What, darlin'?"

"This isn't a good idea."

"You got that right."

"I mean...I think it's a bad idea."

"Probably."

"We're going to regret this."

"Never." He nuzzled her cheek and she quivered, her fingers tracing the slopes of his shoulders. Horses moved and nickered beneath them and in the muted light Slade worked at the buttons of her coat, pressed her down until they tumbled off the bale onto the loose hay.

"Please, listen..." She looked up at him and he was lost in that troubled hazel gaze.

He levered himself on one elbow. "I'm listening."

"This...you and me...it's dangerous...we'd better leave it alone."

"Because of the other guy."

"'Other guy'?" she repeated, and those two sexy little lines appeared between her eyebrows again.

"Your boss."

"Oh. Chuck."

"Yeah. Chuck." The guy's name even tasted bad.

"It's not about Chuck," she admitted honestly as he plucked a piece of straw from her hair.

"Well, to tell the truth, I don't give a damn. Right now, Jamie, it's just you and me," he said, and kissed her again, his mouth slanting over hers as a wave of possession washed over him. He didn't want to talk about the past or her boyfriend or anything else. They were here. Together. Alone. A man and woman. He wanted her. More than he'd wanted a woman in a long, long time. For the first time since Rebecca...squeezing his eyes shut, he concentrated on Jamie. The touch and feel of her. Old memories reawakened, long-forgotten emotions surfaced. He heard her sigh, felt the sweet pressure of her lips on his, sensed her shift from denial to need.

His jeans were suddenly too restricting, the thickness in his crotch beginning to ache as he tossed off his jacket. He stretched out over her, unbuttoned her coat and reached beneath the hem of her sweater. Her skin was warm and smooth to his touch. She gasped as his hands scaled her ribs to dip inside her bra.

"I don't... I don't know..."

"Shh," he breathed into her mouth, kissing her, his tongue mating with hers as he stroked her breast.

"Oo-oh," she moaned as the tip of his finger scraped her nipple. She bucked beneath him, held on tight, kissed him back. Her fingers dug into his shoulders as he kissed the side of her neck, then, lifting the sweater over her head, pressed urgent lips to that warm, dusky hollow of her throat. Her pulse jumped beneath the ministrations of his tongue and her fingernails dug deep into his muscles.

Slowly he lowered himself, kissing the tops of her breasts, touching the lacy edge of her bra with his tongue. Her fingers curled in his hair and she guided him to one nipple. Gently he lifted the breast from its bonds and tentatively tasted of her, his tongue tickling the very tip of her nipple, his lips just brushing that puckering little bud.

"Slade," she moaned insistently, pulling his head closer.

"Oh, darlin', there's no need to rush," he breathed across her wet skin. But she was ready. Hot. Anxious. He saw it in her eyes. She wanted him, damn it.

He slipped a hand beneath the waistband of her slacks and she sucked in her stomach and began working at the buttons of his shirt. "You want me," he said, and she didn't answer. "Come on, Counselor, admit it."

"*You* want *me*," she said, telling herself that she was about to make a mistake of epic proportions.

"Oh, baby, yes." He unbuttoned her slacks, pulled them down over her hips and kissed his way along her abdomen. His tongue was moist and warm in the cold air. Tantalizing. Tempting.

She told herself she couldn't do this, not again. Yet the words of denial slipped away from her as he slowly slid her panty hose down her legs, the tips of his fingers tickling her, his lips following the same sensual path.

*No! No! No!* What was she thinking? This was a mistake of epic proportions. His hands were kneading her buttocks and the stubble of his beard grazed the skin of her inner thighs. She wiggled. He held her fast. Hot fingers dug into her flesh. Warm breath steamed against her skin. Inside she throbbed, felt moist. Wet. His lips and tongue skimmed closer.

Skilled hands massaged her hips.

*This is so dangerous…a big mistake…remember how he hurt you,* her mind screamed from some distant, far-off shore. But her bones were melting, her breathing difficult, and her entire being seemed to center where he touched her, at that private place where her legs joined. They parted of their own accord.

"That's a girl," he said as she arched upward and felt air from his lungs whisper over the curls down below. "Let me in, Jamie."

She wriggled, desire beating through her, need burning in her blood. She closed her eyes, felt the warmth of her coat beneath her and the cool air above. And Slade, she felt Slade kiss her, his lips caressing her so gently tears burned behind her eyelids and her throat caught. She couldn't stop, didn't want to. She craved more of him. She thought she'd go mad with his slow, deliberate ministrations. "Slade," she cried, lifting her eager hips to meet him, arching as she felt the slick penetration of his tongue.

"Oh," she cried, her fingers curling in the loose straw. "Oh, oh, oooooohhhh." She shuddered, her eyes opening to see the timbers of the hayloft swirl above her. The hayloft spun and she convulsed, sweat running down her body.

Then he was upon her, kicking off his jeans, stretching his long, lean body against hers, rubbing his flesh against her fevered skin. He kissed her hard. With purpose. His hands were no longer gentle, but firm as they kneaded her flesh. He pressed his hungry mouth to hers and kissed her as if he would never stop.

Her arms wound around his neck. She felt his hard, sinewy muscles as she kissed him wildly. Madly.

She threw all her inhibitions to the raw Montana wind. This is all that mattered. Here. Now. Slade McCafferty.

"You're so incredible," he breathed, voice raspy, face flushed.

He prodded her legs apart, used his hands to lift her buttocks and, thrusting hard, stared straight into her eyes. She gasped.

He slid out, then drove forward again.

"Oh...Slade..."

Again.

She clung to him, her neck bowed as she met each hard stroke. Again and again, faster and faster, until the center of the universe seemed to spin within that sensual spot where their bodies joined, until she could think of nothing but the pure animal pleasure of his body melding with hers, until sweat drizzled down their fused bodies despite the cold winter air. He kissed her. Hard. Desperately.

"Jamie," he whispered in a rush. "Jamie, oh...woman... Oh..."

She spasmed. Cried out. The stables whirled around them, the sound of horses far off as he collapsed against her, breathing hard, his body dripping with sweat, his arms surrounding her.

Tears threatened her eyes as he held her. How many times had she thought of making love to him, of feeling his hard body pressed against hers, or kissing him until her lips were raw? It had been her dream, long ago, one she'd tried determinedly to forget.

And here she was. In the hayloft of the Flying M ranch, feeling Slade's warm breath ruffle her hair and knowing she'd probably made the second worst mistake of her life. The first had been falling in love with him all those years ago.

Oh, what had she done?

She blinked hard. She wouldn't break down. No...what was done, was done...she would have to live with it.

He levered himself up on one elbow and, grinning widely, looked down at her. "Well, well, well."

"My thoughts exactly," she lied, trying to slide away from

him, embarrassment coloring her cheeks. "I...I don't know what got into me—"

"I do."

"I wasn't talking about *that*."

"Neither was I."

"Right. Look, this has been fun and all—" Oh, dear, listen to her ramble on. "But I really should be going."

His blue eyes gleamed wickedly. "So soon?"

"You know my motto—'Love 'em and leave 'em.' Oh, no, wait, that was yours." She regretted the words the second they tripped over her tongue.

His eyes darkened. His smile disappeared. "I tried to explain—"

"And I wouldn't let you." She held up a hand and reached for her panties. "I know."

"That's right. You wouldn't." Quickly he lunged, his hands grabbing her wrists, his weight pinning her down.

"Okay, okay, I give," she said, regretting the bad joke. "I made a mistake."

"No. I did. When I left you."

Her throat thickened. A lump formed. Oh, for the love of Pete, she couldn't break down. Not now. Not after all the years of bearing the pain alone. "You don't have to—"

"I know I don't. I'm just tellin' you what I feel. Isn't that what women always complain about men? That they aren't in touch with their feelings? That they never say what's on their mind? Well, I'm tellin' you. I made a mistake. I didn't know it at the time. Hell, I didn't know it for years. But I know it now, okay?" Intense eyes stared down at her and not a trace of the amusement she'd seen in his expression only seconds before lingered. "Jamie, do you hear me?"

"Yes." She couldn't breathe. Her eyes filled and she blinked hard. This couldn't be happening. She thought of the summer they'd been together, the lovemaking…their baby.

"What?"

"It's…it's nothing."

"The hell it is." He released one wrist and wiped a tear that had begun to drizzle from her eye.

"Damn."

"What's this all about?" he demanded, glaring at her. "You're holding back."

"It doesn't matter." She brushed the tears quickly aside with her free hand.

"It sure as hell matters to you."

"It was a long time ago."

His eyes narrowed thoughtfully as he stared down at her and she bit her lower lip, refusing to break down. "What is it? There's something else, isn't there? Something I don't know about."

She tried to wriggle free, but his hands were like manacles, his weight immovable.

"What?"

*Why not tell him the truth? Let him deal with it?*

Because it would serve no purpose. Only open old wounds.

"Come on, there's something, Counselor, some deep dark secret that you're hiding from me."

Taking a deep breath, certain that her voice would fail her, she braced herself. "All right," she finally acquiesced. "If you want to know the truth, it's pretty simple. When you left me, I was pregnant."

"What?" The color seeped from his face in one instant. He released her wrists. "Pregnant?" he repeated in a hoarse whisper.

"That's right."

"But the baby? Where is…"

In for a penny, in for a pound. There was no turning back now. "I miscarried, Slade. Right off the bat. One month it was confirmed I was pregnant, the next…" Her throat closed and she felt another tear slide down her face before she was able to pull herself together. "The next month…I wasn't."

"Why?" His eyes were dark as the night.

"I don't know," she said, then saw the hardness of his jaw, the anger in the lines of his face. "Don't you even suggest that it was anything other than natural," she said, reading the unspoken message in his gaze, "because that's just what happened, okay? And it really isn't any of your business."

"My child isn't my business?"

"You were already gone, remember? You'd walked out on me and so it wasn't your concern. Did you ever call? Ever stop by? Ever write?" she challenged, her chin trembling as he rolled off her and stared in disbelief. She scooped up her clothes and started struggling into them, her fingernails ripping through her panty hose in her haste. "No. You didn't. Why? Because you didn't give a damn."

"That's not how it was." But his words lacked conviction, and her stupid heart tore again.

"No?" She yanked her slacks over her hips. "Then tell me, how was it? Hmm? Because from where I sat, alone, pregnant, not knowing what to do, it sure felt like you left me for another woman."

His face flushed a deep, angry scarlet as he reached for his clothes. "If you had told me—"

"About the baby? Would that have made a difference in how you felt? Is that what you're trying to say? I wasn't good enough, but, gee, if I had your baby, then suddenly I was?" she stormed, tossing on her sweater and stuffing her arms angrily down the sleeves.

Slade had pulled on his jeans as she reached for her coat. "I made a mistake."

"That makes two of us, and now…now we've made another, but let's just forget it, okay? We've literally had our roll in the hay, and now we can go back to our normal, regular lives." She cast a glance down at the mussed straw, then rolled her eyes at her own stupidity and marched to the ladder. She was down the rungs and out the door of the stables in less than a minute.

The cold air hit her with the force of a northern gale. What was she thinking, confiding in Slade? She'd read the accusations in his eyes. Damn it all, she should never have told him. Never.

She strode through the snow as best she could, made her way to the car, reached for the handle and realized her purse and briefcase were at the house. Well, fine. Turning on her heel she started for the snow-covered walk. In the living room window stood the Christmas tree. The two little girls were dancing around it, holding up tinsel and glittering decorations, laughing and giggling as Nicole and Randi strung lights around the branches. Through the panes, she saw Thorne. His face was relaxed, a wide, adoring smile on his face as he gazed at his wife.

Jamie's heart shattered into a million pieces. The scene through the frosted windowpanes was something right out of Currier and Ives, everything she'd once hoped for, everything she'd thought, naively, that she might have with Slade and their child… She bit her lip, fought tears. From the corner of her eye she saw Matt walking General to the stables. He and Kelly were about to be married, to increase the McCafferty family.

Jamie had to leave. Now. She couldn't take another minute of this perfect family holiday scene.

Slade burst out of the stables. Furious eyes focused on Jamie, he hitched his way through the drifts. Great. Just what she didn't need. She couldn't face another showdown, not now. She was too raw.

She started for the house.

"Jamie! Wait!"

No way in hell.

She marched up the steps to the front door and without knocking and disturbing the decorating party, eased into the front hallway. Music and the smells of apples and cinnamon greeted her. Burl Ives was singing some lighthearted Christmas carol from the CD player and the twins' high-pitched voices chirped above the song.

"I want to puts it on," one little voice insisted on the other side of the wall in the living room.

"You can, honey, just let me get the lights in place." Nicole seemed always the voice of reason.

Thorne said, "That's right...here ya go. Why don't you try the switch, now, then put the ornament on? Here let me get the main lights."

Jamie thought of the baby she'd lost and fought tears. She slung the strap of her purse over her shoulder and reached for her briefcase. She cast a final glance to the archway separating the landing at the base of the stairs and the living room.

"Okay, now," Thorne said as the house lights dimmed.

"Ohhh," one of the girls said.

"Ith's be-you-ti-ful," the other agreed, and Jamie saw the reflection of colored Christmas lights on the wall. They'd turned on the tree.

Jamie couldn't listen a minute longer.

Armed with her briefcase, she turned.

The door burst open.

Slade McCafferty, all six feet of glorious anger, filled the door frame.

"Excuse me," she said, trying to dodge past him.

"Not yet." He grabbed her arm roughly and she sent him a glare as icy as the day.

"Let go of me, McCafferty," she warned as the sound of a car, tires spinning in the snow, engine purring, reached her ears.

"Now what?" Slade looked over his shoulder, and Jamie caught a glimpse of the new visitor as he climbed out of his silver Mercedes. Her heart nose-dived as she recognized the driver.

Chuck Jansen had arrived.

# Chapter 11

"I thought I might find you here." Chuck's affable grin was wide as he walked up the steps to the front porch where Jamie and Slade were standing. Tall, lean, tanned from skiing in the winter and golf in the summer, Chuck leaned forward to hug Jamie, but stopped short. His smile faded, and the arms that he'd opened fell to his side when he saw Slade's hand upon the sleeve of her coat.

"I was just leaving," she said awkwardly. Of all the times for him to show up. She yanked her arm away from Slade's hand. "Chuck Jansen, this is Slade McCafferty."

Eyeing each other warily, the two men shook hands as Randi, holding her sleeping baby to her shoulder, stepped into the foyer through the archway from the living room. "I thought I felt a draft. For Pete's sake, Slade, close the door—" Her expression changed from mild irritation to concern, her eyebrows pulling together, her arms inadvertently tightening over her child as she saw the stranger.

"Randi, I'd like you to meet my boss and a senior partner for Jansen, Monteith and Stone," Jamie said, recovering quickly as Slade pulled the door shut and little Joshua Ray let out a soft, sleepy gurgle.

More introductions were made as they eased into the living room, and Jamie realized her escape from the Flying M would have to be delayed.

"Chuck!" Thorne, looping a strand of tiny gold beads over the tree's sagging branches, peered through the uneven boughs as Randi carried her son upstairs.

The attorney grinned. "I never thought I'd see the day," Chuck observed as the twins clustered glittering ornaments on the lower branches.

Nicole, after a quick "Nice to meet you" and perfunctory handshake, continued sorting through dozens of boxes of decorations.

Jamie wanted to vaporize.

Chuck had recovered from the shock of seeing Jamie with another man. "I just didn't think domesticity was ever your thing," he said, needling Thorne.

"I'm a changed person these days." Thorne cast a loving glance at his wife and stepdaughters. "A family man."

"I see." Was there amusement in Chuck's voice, or just disbelief? As if a McCafferty could never settle down.

"Let me get your coat," Nicole suggested, and Jamie, wishing she were anyplace else on earth, suffered through the small talk and offer of refreshments, all the while aware of Slade's gaze upon her.

She realized that tiny pieces of straw were sticking to her coat and that her hair was a mess, probably punctuated with hay, as well, her clothes askew. She just wanted to leave, but

Chuck had different plans and had her sit in as he asked for an update on the transfer of the property. He and Thorne cradled drinks and traded stories about practicing law together for a brief but obviously memorable time, then they moved to the dining room table and a pot of coffee.

Jamie felt like the underling she was. Worse yet, she sensed that Chuck was making a point about who was in charge of the McCaffertys as clients. Chuck and Thorne had worked together, and the intimation was that they were part of the same "good ol' boys club," an idea as antiquated as some of the furniture that still graced the law offices at Jansen, Monteith and Stone.

Jamie didn't make too many waves, but did explain what was happening with the deed transfer and sale of the acreage. She didn't mention calling Felicia Reynolds about the baby's custody, nor did she bring up Thorne wanting the firm to use any means possible to locate Joshua's father. Chuck was in error on a couple of points concerning the title transfer, and Jamie gently straightened him out. She wondered about that. Chuck was pretty sharp. Was he testing her?

While sipping coffee, they discussed every aspect of current legal concerns, and Chuck, good-naturedly, pitched the firm again, suggesting that "J.M.S.," as he liked to refer to the law firm, could do a lot more for Thorne and his siblings.

It was after seven by the time Jamie left. Chuck promised to stop by her place. He suggested they go to dinner so that he could catch up on all she'd been up to. Slade, seated insolently across the table from Jamie, had listened to the exchange silently. He'd kicked out his chair and rested on the small of his back as he witnessed the interplay between Jamie, Chuck and Thorne, but he hadn't said a word.

It was the longest hour of Jamie's life. When Thorne offered drinks and cigars, Chuck accepted, and she made a quick excuse of having to get back to her house. No one argued, least of all Slade. She made her way to her car and was surprised when she heard footsteps behind her.

"You're not seriously considering marrying that pompous ass, are you?" Slade asked, and Jamie gnashed her teeth as she opened the car door and turned to face him. Snow was falling again, creating a soft, shifting curtain between the parking area and the house where the windows glowed warmly, yellow patches of light in the coming night.

"I was thinking about it, yes," she admitted.

Slade's face was serious. "You'd be bored inside of a month."

"You don't know Chuck."

"That's right. And I'm not sure I want to. That guy's dry as a bone on a desert carcass."

"Thanks for the advice," she said sarcastically. "I'll keep it in mind."

"Do."

She tossed her briefcase onto the passenger seat.

"There's something else you should keep in mind, as well."

"Oh? What's that?" she asked, turning as his arms surrounded her and he pinned her to the car. "Now, wait a second."

"Nope." His lips crashed down on hers, reminding her of their recent lovemaking. He kissed her hard. Long. To the point that her knees threatened to give way and her heart pounded a thousand times a minute. The memory of making love with him was fresh, the scent of his skin tantalizing... Why did she feel this way about him? Why? Chemistry? Forbidden fruit? Flirting with the devil?

Or was she just plain nuts? A masochist who wanted her heart broken a dozen times over?

Slade lifted his head and looked at her with smoky-blue eyes. "That, Jamie. That's what I want you to keep in mind," he said as he released her and started for the stables in his long, easy stride. Breathless, she slumped against the car. Then she smelled a trace of cigar smoke and noticed three men on the front porch. Thorne and Matt McCafferty were cradling drinks, smoking big cigars and talking with Chuck Jansen.

"Wonderful," she muttered under her breath as she slid behind the wheel and twisted her key in the ignition. Her little car sparked to life. She rammed it into Reverse and caught a glimpse of Slade in the rearview mirror. She threw the compact into first. With a spray of snow she was heading down the long lane of Flying M and wondering how in the world she was going to break it off with her boss.

"...so you and Slade McCafferty," Chuck said as they sat across the table in a booth at a small restaurant in Grand Hope.

They'd spent the meal talking about what was going on at the office, how the repairs to Jamie's grandmother's house were coming along and the legal work the firm was handling for the McCaffertys, including discussion of Randi's baby, custody rights and the identity of the missing father. But the conversation had steered clear of her involvement with Slade. Until now.

"Slade and I have a history." She pushed her plate aside, half her fillet untouched.

"Do you? You never mentioned it."

"Didn't see the need."

A slim, blond waitress swept by and cleared off the plates. Bland music drifted around the cavernous room split by half walls and booths.

"So what're you going to do about it? A history is one thing, a future another." Chuck reached across the table and took her hand in his. "You know how I feel about you, Jamie. I was hoping you and I could work things out." Gently he stroked the backs of her knuckles with the pad of his thumb.

"I don't think that will happen," she said, and withdrew her hand. "We want different things."

"And you and McCafferty don't?"

"This isn't about Slade," she insisted, holding his gaze. "It's about you and me."

"I love you."

She shook her head. "But you ridicule me."

"No, I—"

"Sure you do, Chuck. You did so a couple of hours ago with that tired old song and dance with Thorne at the Flying M. You tried to show me up, all under the guise of being my boss, of caring for me, of mentoring me, when we both know you did it because I'm a woman."

"What?" His face showed sincere shock. "What the devil are you talking about?"

"You should have backed me up, Chuck. Instead, you tried to show me up by pointing out where I could have made a mistake, and you were grinning while you were doing it. That was the worst part. As if Thorne and you were in on some private joke over the poor dumb woman."

"That's ridiculous, Jamie. Paranoid. I never hire by race or creed or sex, you know that."

Jamie barreled on. "The point you were trying to make was that, 'Hey, I've got this young woman handling the case and she's pretty good, but you know—' and this is where you wanted to insert a wink, wink, just to make sure that Thorne was on the same wavelength '—she's just a pretty underling.'"

"I didn't do anything of the sort!"

"Sure you did. If Frank Kepler or Morty Freeman or Scott Chavez had been in the room and you'd thought they'd made a mistake, you would have taken a firm line with them, pointed to the error and cleared it up one way or another. There wouldn't have been any of this patronizing, I'm-such-a-good-guy-helping-out-this-poor-little-woman attitude."

"I didn't."

"Hogwash. I was there, Chuck." She hooked her thumb at her chest. "And it made me feel small."

He was actually horrified. Didn't believe a word she was telling him. "Maybe you were overly sensitive. Maybe you were trying to make a big splash, impress the McCafferty brothers. Especially the hellion."

"Low blow, Chuck."

"But true."

She couldn't argue that point. Because some of his argument was true. There was a part of her, a small, petty part, that wanted to rub Slade's nose in the fact that she'd grown into a successful attorney, that she'd become the kind of woman good enough for him, the kind of woman he'd thrown her over for years ago. She had money, looks, charm and success.

*So what?*

*Big deal.*

Right now it seemed trivial and vain. She poured cream into her coffee. Chuck was smart, was used to reading human emotion for the witness stand, so he probably understood the emotions she tried vainly to hide. Her need to prove herself to Slade was just wounded pride talking. Deep down, she knew that dealing with Slade was only asking—no, make that *begging*—for trouble. The kind of trouble she didn't need.

*And yet you made love to him. Wild, crazy, cast-all-your-worries-to-the-wind love. You haven't gotten over him. All those years and all the pain, and you're still a foolish, lonely girl who finds him sexy as hell. Which is just plain stupid.*

*His devil-may-care attitude may have matured a bit, but he's still a wild man, one who isn't putting down any roots, one to whom home is the open highway. And that's not what you want. Or is it?*

She took a sip from her cup, then set it down and stared at Chuck. "Regardless of what I do or don't feel for Slade Mc-Cafferty, it's not working for us. You and me. It hasn't been for a long time and we both know it."

A silver eyebrow lifted, begging her to continue.

"We want different things in life, Chuck. We're at different places in our lives."

"And I'm a supercilious prick."

She nearly choked on a swallow of coffee, then dabbed at her lips with a napkin and nodded. "Well…yeah…sometimes."

"Maybe I need a strong woman to keep me in line."

"Definitely. But not me."

Sighing, he folded his arms across his chest and leaned back against the booth. "I guess you don't realize how much I love you and, yes, how much I like you. And that's important. Whether you know it or not. You've never been married. Sure the passion, the spark, is important, but you've got to be compatible with the person you choose. You've got to like him."

She didn't disagree.

"And you're right in the respect that I don't want to have more children. Three is enough, if not just financially, then emotionally, personally and globally, as well. I've already done my share of leaving my genetic imprint, if you will, and, also, I've suffered through diaper changing, scraped knees, broken hearts and car wrecks—none of which is easy, all of which, I know, is important.

"But now I'm paying through the nose for college. By the time the last one is finished—and this isn't including grad school—I'll be almost ready to retire. I'm just not willing to start over and do it again. I want some time for me. What's left over I need to give to the kids I've already got and the grandkids that will inevitably come along. My children deserve that."

"And what about your new wife? Would she get any of that precious time of yours?"

"That goes without saying."

"Does it?" She shook her head. It wasn't that she didn't believe him. Chuck was baring his soul; she knew that. But it still wouldn't work. Not for them. "I can't give up the dream, Chuck. I won't. Call me old-fashioned, or even a dreamer, but I want it all—a career, a husband, babies, station wagon—no, make that a minivan—and a cute little house with a garden, swing set and white picket fence."

"And you think Slade McCafferty can give you those things?"

"I doubt it. I'm not talking about Slade or what he wants. I'm talking about me." She opened her purse, withdrew her wallet and flipped it open.

"What are you doing?" He was aghast.

"Paying for my dinner." She slid out her credit card.

"No way. This is on me. On J.M.S." He was already reaching into his jacket pocket.

"Not this time."

"I insist."

"Of course you do." She caught the waitress's eye. "Would you ring this up for me?" she asked when the girl stepped to the table.

"Bring me the bill," Chuck ordered the blonde.

"I—"

"I don't want to hear another word about it."

Jamie's temper flared. "That's just what I'm talking about."

"I asked you to dinner."

"Should I split the bill?" the waitress, her face anxious, offered.

"No!" Chuck was adamant, his male pride shredded.

"No, I'll get it." Jamie slapped her card into the startled woman's hand and she glared directly at her boss. "And I don't want to hear another word about it."

"This is ridiculous," Chuck snapped.

"Beyond ridiculous."

They waited in tense silence. When the waitress returned, Jamie added a healthy tip to the tab and signed her name to the receipt. She felt freer than she had in years.

On the other hand, Chuck stewed. He tried not to be churlish, but he was steamed. Deep furrows lined his brow.

As the waitress turned her attention to another booth, Jamie hauled her purse from the bench beside her.

"You can expense out the meal," Chuck finally said, as if he was trying to find some way to deal with her erratic behavior.

"I know I can, but I won't." Jamie stood and looked down at the man she had nearly married. Oh, God, what a mistake that would have been. Impulsively she added, "I quit, Chuck. Not just this relationship, but the firm, as well."

"Wait a minute, Jamie. Quit? No. *Now* you're acting like an emotional female."

"Well, good. Because that's what I am. But I'm also a damned good attorney and you know it. I'll be faxing my resignation to the office in the morning." She left him gaping, looking like a landed fish gasping for air. And it wasn't until she'd unlocked her car, started it and began driving through the snowy streets to her grandmother's house that she realized what she'd done.

"So be it," she said to her reflection in the rearview mirror. It was time to start over. With or without Slade McCafferty.

"So what're you going to do about Jamie?" Randi asked as she padded into the living room. The house was dark, everyone having gone to bed, except Slade. He sat near the dying fire, glowering at the lopsided Christmas tree and remembering making love to Jamie in the hayloft. A drink sat on the table beside him but he didn't really want it. Randi, in a worn robe and fluffy slippers, settled into the rocker, cradled her son and smiled down at his little face. She cooed at him as she offered him a bottle. The baby played with the nipple and stared straight into his mother's face as if mesmerized.

"What do you mean, what am I going to do about her?"

Randi yawned. Her short hair stuck up at weird angles but her face, devoid of makeup looked healthy and fresh, no bruises or scars visible from the accident that had maimed her. "Let's not go over this again, okay? We both know that you've got it bad for the lady lawyer, and if you don't do something about it soon, you're going to lose her to the likes of Chuck Jansen."

"How can I lose what I haven't got?"

"Oh, give me a break. This is how I make my living, remember? I'm a professional."

"A professional who self-admittedly doesn't have all of her faculties."

She grinned, placing a foot on the hearth and gently rocking as the baby cooed and gurgled and continued to stare up at her as he suckled. "I know what I see. You love her. She loves you. End of story. It's simple." Before he could argue she pointed a long finger in his direction. "But she's not going to make the mistake of waiting around for you again. She did that once, and a woman like Jamie's got too much on the ball to make the same mistake twice."

He frowned, thought about their brief love affair and the baby he hadn't known existed. That was twice now that he'd lost an unborn child, and it hurt. It hurt like hell. Guilt, for living when his progeny had not, twisted his guts. He watched

Randi play with her newborn and felt a pang. Would he ever have a son of his own? A daughter?

*Not if you don't settle down, Slade. It's time. Randi's right.*

And his father—what was it John Randall had said to him? *Don't waste your life, son. It's shorter than you think. Now, it's time for you to move on. Settle down. Start a family.* He'd given that advice on the front porch, in the very rocker Randi was now seated in, on the day he'd tried to give Slade his watch. Slade had been angry. Mad at the world. Sick of his old man trying to manipulate him. In utter disdain, he'd dropped the damned timepiece into the old man's lap. He'd refused to take it; hadn't accepted it until John Randall had died. And then it was too late. He reached into his pocket for the watch and realized it was gone...but where? Then he remembered. In the hayloft, when he'd kicked off his jeans...it must've dropped into the loose straw when he'd been making love to Jamie... Hell.

As Randi swayed in the old rocking chair, Slade picked up his drink and tossed back the watered-down whiskey. It was smooth against his throat, but didn't quiet the rage in his soul.

"I don't know what she sees in Jansen," Randi said out loud. "He's too old for her and so...nothing. But maybe she's not looking for a spark, maybe she's looking for security, maybe she's tired of being alone."

"Are you talking about Jamie or you?" Slade asked, wiping the back of his hand over his lips and setting the glass on the table. "I know you're used to being the one handing out advice, but I think it's a waste of time with me. I know what I want."

"I beg to differ, little brother." She lifted the baby to her shoulder and rubbed his back.

"I'm *not* your little brother," he reminded her.

"You're my youngest brother...you just happen to be older than me and bigger than me but surely not wiser."

"Tell me about it," he mocked. "I don't see that you've got everything all planned out."

"What do you mean?"

"Let's start with your son."

"Let's not."

"But, you have to admit, great as he is, it wasn't exactly perfect family planning on your part."

"You don't know what you're talking about."

Joshua gave up a loud burp. His little head bobbed, reddish hair glinting in the remaining firelight.

"There ya go," Randi said to her son, before settling him into her arms again. "You know, Slade, we weren't talking about me, so don't turn this around. Let's talk about you. And our brothers. Look at Thorne. I always thought he was the ultimate bachelor. But he's married now. Happy. He and Nicole and the girls are a complete family, even though technically the twins have another biological father."

At the thought of Paul Stevenson, Slade snorted and considered another drink. What a jerk. Paul had remarried, still lived in San Francisco, and aside from sending an occasional check that Nicole deposited for the twins' college account, he never acknowledged his daughters. He didn't call, he didn't visit, he didn't ever have them come to spend time with him. Nicole had once called him a sperm donor and Slade agreed with her.

"Yeah, so Thorne's married, so what?"

"And Matt will be soon. He and Kelly are so happy—"

"So happy they're sickening."

Randi chuckled. "They're in love."

"I guess."

"I *know.* So, that leaves you."

"And you," he reminded her, and saw her bristle.

"I've got the baby. I don't need a man, and don't argue with me. I see it in your eyes. You're one of those guys who thinks every woman needs a man. Or wants one. Or can't get by without one. But I don't. I can take care of myself."

"Well, you're doin' a helluva job of it. So far someone's tried to kill you twice." He pushed out of his chair and crossed the room to the rocker. Smiling, he reached down and patted the baby's downy little head. "The next time the creep, whoever he is, tries to nail you, you might not be so lucky. And, whether you want to admit it or not, you're not as independent as you like to claim. You've always depended on men.

"First there was Dad and now, when you're in trouble, you've got the three of us—half brothers—who think we need to do what we can to keep you safe." She looked up, her eyes glistening, then turned to the fire. "Contrary to what you think, *little* sister, you're not so tough, and maybe not every woman needs a man or vice versa, but sometimes it's nice to have one around."

"That's just what I was getting at." Her voice was a little gruffer than usual. "You could have that same love that our brothers have found. With Jamie. If you're not too stupid and bullheaded to throw it away again."

"Thanks for the advice," he muttered, unable to hide the derision in his voice as she sniffed back the unwanted tears. "I'll think about it."

His bad leg ached a little as he walked to the front door and snagged his jacket from a hook. Randi's advice chased after him as he stepped outside and a gust of raw Montana wind slapped him. Ice dripped from the eaves and snow continued to fall and swirl, the wind blowing it around. Drifts piled against the barns and fence.

Harold, the crippled old dog, trooped after Slade as he headed for the stables. He found his last cigarette in the crumpled pack; he swore it would be his last. No reason to let the filter tip go to waste.

Pausing near the machine shed, he turned his back to the wind, cupped his hands around the tip of the cigarette, and clicked his lighter about five times before a flame sparked. He inhaled and felt the warm smoke curl deep inside his lungs as he and the dog slogged through the unbroken snow to the stables. He'd finish his last smoke, then go inside and find his father's watch.

As he smoked and looked at the vast acres of the ranch, the fields and paddocks, ranch house and sheds, he understood why his father had loved it here. Maybe John Randall had been right about other things, as well. Maybe it was time to settle down. He thought of Jamie. Damned if she wasn't the right woman. If he hadn't blown it with her.

He took a final drag, tossed his cigarette into the snow and reached for the door.

First thing tomorrow, he'd find her and tell her how he felt. He yanked on the door handle.

Lightning flashed before his eyes.

*Bam!*

Slade flew backward. Landed hard on the snow.

A ball of flames roared to life. Hot. Bright. Blinding.

Horses squealed in terror.

Flames burst upward, crackling hungrily through the old timbers and dry hay. Smoke billowed into the cold night air.

Slade scrambled to his feet. Panicked horses kicked and shrieked. The entire building was ablaze.

He didn't have time to think.

He catapulted through the doorway.

And straight into hell.

# Chapter 12

*Bam!*

The sound was like a shock wave.

Randi bolted from the bed, picked up Joshua Ray and hauled him to the hallway.

"For God's sake, call 9-1-1! Use the damned cell phone, we've got to get out of here!" Thorne burst from the master bedroom. He packed a groggy twin in each arm. Frantic, he yelled over his shoulder, "Nicole! Come on!"

Randi struggled into shoes, her heart drumming a thousand times a minute. "What was that? Did you hear it? An explosion."

"I don't know what it was, but it's not good. Everyone outside!" Thorne screamed. "Nicole! Come on!"

His wife burst out of the bedroom. Her blond hair fell around her face as she struggled with the tie of her bathrobe with one hand. A cell phone was pinned to her ear with the other.

They trampled down the stairs.

"Where's Slade?" Thorne said as they reached the first floor.

"He was outside a few minutes ago. I just came upstairs," Randi said. Where the devil was he? The interior of the house began to turn a bright, vibrant orange. "What's going on?"

"Oh, God." Ushering everyone to the foyer, Thorne paused long enough to stare through the window. "It's the stables!" He shouldered open the door and they all streamed onto the porch. The old building was ablaze, orange and gold reflecting on the snow. Smoke poured from the roof where flames ate the old shingles and shot skyward.

"No!" Randi cried.

"Oh, my God..." Nicole's eyes were round.

"Get away from the house!" Thorne ordered. "Everyone!" He reached back through the doorway and yanked every coat from the rack, then, still carrying the girls, kicked boots and shoes onto the porch. "Hurry!"

The twins were crying now, clinging to his neck as Randi found a coat and dashed away from the house. Where was Slade? Where the devil was Slade? Not in the stables. No...it couldn't be... And yet she'd seen him leave the house... Oh, God, oh, God, oh, God...

"—That's right, at the Flying M ranch, twenty miles north of Grand Hope," Nicole was screaming into her cell phone. "We'll need firemen and rescue workers and...and a veterinarian and God knows what else! This is an emergency! I repeat, an emergency at the McCaffertys' Flying M ranch!"

The twins, ashen-faced and wide eyes, wailed. They buried their little faces into Thorne's shoulders and clung to his neck as if they would never let go.

"Was Slade in the stables?" Thorne demanded, his harsh

gaze centering on Randi as they hurried toward the parking lot, away from the buildings.

"I don't know..." Randi stared at the inferno as the first horse burst out of the flaming building. White-eyed and sweating, the gray galloped crazily through the snow. A bay followed after, whistling, hooves flinging up white powder as she tried to escape the blaze. "I don't know where he went. We were talking in the living room, then, then...he went outside for a smoke." She stared in horror at the burning building.

"Well, someone's letting the stock out. Idiot!" Grim-faced, Thorne shoved both twins at Nicole as she flew out the door. The girls screamed their protests.

"No! Daddy! No."

"Here. Take the girls and don't go inside any of the buildings. None of them. The stables might just be the first. And—oh, damn!" He glanced at the cars and trucks. "Keep away from the vehicles in case there's some sort of chain reaction." His jaw tightened as he herded them to relative safety.

"I've got 'em," Nicole said, peeling each girl from their father's body.

"Chain reaction?" Randi asked.

His face was stretched taut. "You don't think this is an accident, do you?" He yelled over the screams of the horses and roar of the fire. Timbers creaked eerily and thick smoke bilged outward. Thorne started for the stables.

"Wait a minute. You can't go inside there," Randi cried. "It's too late."

"Thorne!" Nicole was running after him. Packing her girls, frantic, she stumbled forward. "Thorne! No! No!"

"Get back. Take care of the kids and call Matt!"

"No! Oh, God no! Wait for the firemen!" she pleaded, distraught as she clung to her children. "You can't—"

"It'll take too long." Thorne took a second to turn to stare at her horrified face. As if to memorize her features. "I'll be all right. You take care of the girls. Now!" Nicole took a step toward him, and Randi wanted to help. To hand the baby off to Nicole and brave the fire herself. Oh, God, was this her fault? Could this be because of her? Was it a freak accident… or a planned execution of some of the stock…and maybe a McCafferty or two?

Thorne spun again and a few seconds later nearly collided with a wild-eyed horse galloping out of the open doorway. Other animals burst from a door on the west end of the building, a mare and two foals, their tails singed, their screams blood-chilling.

The baby was crying, the girls screaming, and Randi tried to herd them all together. "It'll be all right," she said, though she didn't believe it.

"Daddy. Daddy! No-oo." Molly was sobbing; Mindy ashen-faced as she stared after her father.

Thorne disappeared into the doorway. Into the smoke and flames. Randi was shaking, but she said, "He's going to be fine."

Nicole's face was as pale as death, her eyes round with fear, but she visibly pulled herself together and held her daughters tight. "Daddy's gonna be just fine. He has to help Uncle Slade and the horses…see there…some of them are getting out now." She kissed each crown as Molly and Mindy cried all the more loudly. Nicole managed to hold on to her shivering children while punching the numbers of her cell phone frantically. "Matt? It's Nicole." Her voice was surprisingly steady. Probably from years of working in emergency rooms. Eyes fixed on the blaze, she said, "You'd better get over here. And bring help. There's been an explosion in the stables. It's on fire and it's bad. Some of the stock might be injured. I've called

9-1-1, rescue crews are on their way, but the building's in flames and…and both of your brothers are inside."

Slade coughed, stumbled through the smoke. He'd opened the main door and was going down the aisles, unlocking stalls, forcing panicked horses from their boxes. "Go! Out! Hiya!" he yelled, his eyes burning, the cloth he used to cover his nose and mouth no insulation against the blast of heat that singed his skin.

"Slade!" Thorne's voice screamed from somewhere through the smoke. "Slade!"

"You, out!" He held open a door but the frightened mare reared, her hooves flashing, her coat soaked in lather. "Now!" Slade bellowed, and pushed at her. She kicked wildly, her muscles quivering. He slapped her rear and a leg shot out, narrowly missing him as she bolted. He fell against the rail.

Two more stalls. He flung himself down the aisle, aware of the creak of timbers, the crackle of flames, the roar of the fire itself. Moving blind, he made it to the next stall where Mrs. Brown, a spunky mare was shivering, the whites of her eyes visible. "It's okay, girl…" he said, his lungs on fire.

Timbers creaked ominously and the smoke…God, the smoke. He hacked and forced himself out of the stall.

"Slade! Damn it, where are you?" Thorne's voice was farther away. Slade tried to respond but his throat, filled with smoke and soot, wouldn't work. He kicked open the door, flailed at the horse and she shot through the stall door like a bullet.

One more. He stumbled forward. Saw the terrified animal. Diablo Rojo. Pacing. Rearing. Neighing in terror as flames crawled through the straw at his hooves. "Come on, boy," Slade tried to say, but the words stuck. Coughing, he threw open the door to the box and Red Devil lunged through the opening, a huge shoulder knocking Slade off his feet. Crack. His head hit the floor.

"Slade! Oh, damn—*Slaaaaade!*"

He tried to pull himself to his feet. A spray of sparks showered from above. Rafters groaned and he thought of all the tons of hay overhead. He glanced up. A huge blackened beam began to crumble. Ah, hell!

Slade dived toward the window.

With a tremendous wrenching moan, the beam snapped.

All hell rained down.

"A fire. What do you mean, there's a fire?" Kelly demanded as Matt rolled out of the bed in her condo.

"In the stables at the ranch. Thorne and Slade might be trapped inside."

"No." Kelly couldn't believe it. She shook off sleep. "But… why? How?"

He was already throwing on clothes. "Nicole didn't say. Probably doesn't know, but I gotta get over there."

"I'm coming with you." She grabbed her sweatpants and a sweatshirt, then reached into a drawer for her .38.

"You don't need that."

"I hope not."

Matt didn't bother with a belt. "It might be safer for you to stay here."

"No way." She pulled on work boots, then followed him out the door of the bedroom and down the stairs to the garage. They both grabbed jackets and climbed into his truck.

Kelly hit the electronic opener. Matt twisted on the ignition. As the garage door opened, the wail of sirens split the cold winter air.

"Fire trucks," Matt said.

"And an ambulance." Before she could buckle her seat belt

he'd thrown the pickup into Reverse. Cranking hard on the wheel, he backed into the parking space, then gunned it. Spraying snow and gravel, the pickup shot forward. Kelly grabbed her cell phone. "I'm calling Striker," she said. "And Espinoza."

On the third ring, a clear voice answered. "Striker."

"There's a fire at the McCafferty ranch. No one knows the cause, at least not that I'm aware of. Slade and Thorne could be trapped in the building. Emergency services have been called."

"I'm already on my way," Striker said. "I was on my way over there when I heard the call on the police band."

Kelly hung up as the wipers slapped snow from the windshield and Matt glowered at the road. He drove as if his life depended on it. As if his brothers' lives depended on it. "I should have stayed at the ranch."

"Oh, right. Then maybe you could be trapped in there, too."

"Maybe I could have prevented it."

Kelly checked to see that her pistol was loaded. "I don't know, Matt. I'm starting to think no one can prevent what's happening with your family."

"And you want to marry into it." He slid her a questioning glance.

"It takes more than this to scare me off." She flipped on the radio to a local news program. "Striker will be there in a few minutes."

"Not soon enough." Matt drove like a madman but Kelly didn't comment, just punched out the number for Detective Espinoza's home. Her heart felt like lead, her throat tight. Despite all her years of training on the force, she couldn't maintain a professional veneer of calm. Not when two men she'd grown to love, Matt's brothers, the men who would soon be a part of her family, were in danger.

*Please let them be safe,* she thought, reaching over and placing her hand on Matt's thigh. She needed to touch him, to be reassured, to believe that they would be safe.

"Yeah?"

"Bob. It's Kelly. I don't know if you've heard but there's been more trouble at the McCafferty ranch. The stables are on fire. According to Nicole McCafferty, her husband and brother-in-law Slade are trapped inside. She's already called 9-1-1. We're driving over there now and emergency crews are on the way."

"I'll be there...oh, I'm just getting a page. That must be the call." He clicked off.

"I don't suppose you know Jamie Parsons's number?" Kelly asked.

Matt frowned and shook his head.

"She'll want to know," Kelly added as the weather report reverberated through the speakers. "According to Nicole, Jamie's in love with Slade. Nicole's seen the way she looks at him."

Matt's fingers tightened on the wheel. He took a corner too fast and the truck skidded before its wide tires grabbed the road. "You could probably get hold of her through her grandmother's old number...well, unless they interrupted service. It would be under Nita Parsons, I think, or Anita."

Kelly dialed again, this time to directory assistance. After a few false starts, she located the number of Jamie's grandmother. Punching the numbers quickly, she watched through the windshield as the town of Grand Hope sped by. Christmas lights reflected on the snow-blanketed streets, very little traffic disturbed the quietude, the peace and tranquility that accompanied the Christmas season.

Not far away, the sounds of sirens shrieked of impending doom.

The phone jangled. It sounded as if it came from a distance. Jamie stretched and frowned, pulled the covers over her head, then, finally, when the ringing didn't stop, realized where she was. The digital readout of her travel clock showed that it was after one in the morning. Above the soft hum of the furnace, she heard the sound of sirens wailing. Groggy, she rolled out of bed, banged her head and didn't bother with slippers as she made her way down the stairs to the kitchen.

Lazarus meowed and hurried after her as she finally picked up. "Hullo?" she mumbled, catching sight of her reflection in one of the panes above the sink. Her hair was tossed and wild, and she could detect smudges under her eyes from lack of sleep.

"Jamie? This is Kelly Dillinger. Matt's fiancée."

Jamie's heart stopped. *Slade!* Something had happened to him. She knew it.

"There's a fire at the ranch. The stables."

"What?" Her legs gave out and she slumped against the counter as her mind cleared.

"I don't want to alarm you, but there's a chance that Slade and Thorne might be inside." Jamie's knees gave way. She slid down the cabinets to sit on the floor. A million questions raced through her mind. This had to be a dream—a horrid nightmare…that was it. "Emergency crews are on their way."

"Wait a minute…there must be some mistake," Jamie said, almost pleading.

"I wish there were." There was a pause and Jamie started to shake. The sirens sounded farther away. Oh, God. It couldn't be.

"No," she whispered.

"I just thought you'd want to know," Kelly said.

"I can't believe it."

"I know…and…Slade's probably safe. I haven't tried calling the ranch again. We got the call about ten minutes ago, so things could've changed by now."

But Jamie heard the doubt in Kelly's voice. "I—I'll be there."

"That's probably not a good idea. It'll be chaos. I just thought you'd want to know. So why don't you wait there? We'll call you. Really. Stay put. I'll keep you informed. Will you be okay?"

Jamie didn't answer. She hung up and took the stairs two at a time. She threw on the first clothes she found, grabbed her keys, then raced down the stairs again. She was out the door and in her car within seconds.

This couldn't be happening. Not to Slade. No, no, no! Her fingers shook as she jammed the key into the ignition and cranked the defroster to high. She didn't wait for the window to clear, just twisted on the wipers and with her head hanging out the driver's window, drove like crazy. Her car slid and skidded. She didn't care. She blinked against the snow, swore as she slid on the bridge, then floored it. Tires spun. The wind slapped her face and she blinked as the defroster and wipers cleared the windshield.

She nosed her little car north toward the Flying M, toward a glimmer of light, a bright orange glow that cut through the snowstorm. "God help us," she whispered, then drove as if Satan himself were following.

"Slade! For God's sake, where the hell are you?"

Slade heard Thorne's voice, tried to shout but could only moan and cough. The timber that pinned him down singed his back and fire danced in front of his eyes. He tried to drag himself out from under the heavy weight, his hands clawing at the hot cement. He didn't so much as budge. It was too late. "Get out," he tried to scream to his brother. Heat as intense as a blast furnace poured over him. The fire raged, flames crawling everywhere.

He thought of Jamie. "I love you," he mouthed, envisioning her face. Would he ever see her again?

A window splintered. Shards of glass spattered. Somewhere too far away, over the roar of the blaze, sirens screamed. Help was on the way. Too little. Too late.

*Get out, Slade. Don't give up!* The voice in his head nagged him as the fire stormed. With all his effort he reached forward, straining, stretching, until he heard his tendons pop. Pain shrieked up his spine. He grabbed hold of the lowest rail of a stall. Inside the box the straw ignited. Gritting his teeth, he pulled. Hard. His muscles rebelled. Agony ripped through him. The heat was unbearable, the smoke thick. He began to pass out, his vision blurring from the outside in...

"Hang on!" Thorne yelled.

"Get the hell out of here," he croaked.

"Not without you."

The building shuddered and another flaming beam crash-landed two feet from Slade's head. Burning splinters flew crazily. Bales tumbled down. Dust exploded. Smoke billowed. From somewhere nearby, choking and gasping, Thorne appeared.

His face was covered in soot, his eyes searching the inferno until his gaze landed on his brother.

"Let's go."

Sirens shrieked. The rumble of huge engines—fire trucks—was barely audible over the blaze.

"Come on—" Thorne grabbed hold of Slade's shoulders, tried to pull, got nowhere. "Slade, come on..." Choking and gasping, Thorne let go, yanked an ax from the wall and while Slade barely hung on to consciousness, threw his weight into a swing. The beam shuddered. Pain screeched through Slade. The world swam in darkness.

Thorne swung again, coughing, nearly doubling over, then threw his weight into it again, jarring Slade, hacking at the beam. "Hang in there!" Thorne yelled as the flames hissed. *Cra-a-ack.* The timber split. Thorne threw down the ax, grabbed Slade by the arms and dragged him toward the open double doors.

Another window burst. Glass sprayed. Air rushed. Flames licked around them. Slade tried to move his legs, but they were dead weights, wouldn't so much as flinch.

"Help out here," Thorne demanded as he pulled Slade outside. Cold air swept over him and in his blurry vision he saw the flash of red and blue lights strobe the night. Firemen in slick suits carried hoses, aimed huge nozzles at the stables and shouted orders. Horses galloped madly throughout the property, generally getting in the way. A group of people, his family, was gathered on the front lawn. Safe. Thank God.

"Is he the last one?" a fireman asked.

"I—I think so," Thorne said as Slade fought the urge to pass out. He willed his eyes open, but the pain in his back brought the blackness again. Coughing, feeling as if his lungs were charred, Slade looked toward the ranch house and saw Jamie.

Running through the snow toward him, tears streaming down her face, her hair wild and streaming behind her, she ignored the shouts of firemen and police to stay back.

"Slade," she cried, her voice dim in the cacophony. "Slade... oh, God!" Two ranch hands chased after her. But she was determined and as she reached him she fell to her knees, her tears raining upon him. He tried to smile, to form her name, but he couldn't move and the blackness, sweet and enticing, promising freedom from pain, finally closed over him.

"Help him!" Jamie cried as she witnessed Slade drifting away. One minute he was staring up at her, alive, breathing. The next, his eyes closed. "Oh, God, no..."

"Excuse us, ma'am." Big arms pulled her back as a team of rescue workers, EMTs, worked over Slade and Thorne, who, after the supreme effort of pulling his brother to safety had fallen in a heap in the snow. Like Slade's, Thorne's jacket and hair were singed, his face lacerated and blackened, but he was awake, barking orders while Slade... Oh, Lord...Slade was immobile, unresponsive and as a team of rescue workers and Nicole began to tend to him, they pushed her further to the background.

Jamie heard pieces of the conversation, his blood pressure, heart rate...other statistics as they hooked him to tubes and carried him on a stretcher to the waiting ambulance. Nicole was helping Thorne to his feet and he was limping, but insisting that he didn't need a stretcher as they made their way across the snowy yard. The sheriff's department had arrived and deputies, the firemen and ambulance workers were trying to contain the blaze, the horses, and keep everyone safe.

"Are you all right?"

Jamie turned and stared at Kurt Striker, not immediately recognizing the private detective in his hooded ski jacket.

"Yes...I guess... But, Slade..." She swallowed hard as she watched the EMTs load him into the ambulance.

"They're taking him to St. James Hospital."

"Then I have to go." She started for her car, but he held on to her arm.

"Why don't you ride with Nicole? She's driving Thorne." Striker motioned to one of the trucks owned by the Flying M. Nicole was helping Thorne into the cab.

*Pull yourself together, Jamie. Obviously this man thinks you're out of it.* A horse raced by, galloping to join some of the herd. Randi was holding her baby and talking to Kelly Dillinger who was shepherding the twins as they cried and pointed to the pickup.

"I'm not sure you should drive," Striker was saying.

Jamie glanced back to the truck. Nicole was already at the wheel. With a roar, the engine sparked to life and wipers tackled the snow on the windshield. "I can drive myself." She pulled open her car door, determined to follow the ambulance to the hospital. To be near Slade.

"Are you sure you're okay?" Matt was asking this time, his dark eyes penetrating from beneath the brim of his Stetson. "There's plenty of room in Thorne's truck. I'd drive you myself, but I've got to stay here awhile until the bomb squad has searched the place." He looked at Striker. "The police think the fire might have been arson and want to know that the house isn't booby-trapped."

"What? Bomb squad? Booby-trapped? It wasn't an accident?" Jamie asked, stunned.

"Probably not," Kurt said.

"Someone intentionally did this?" She swept an arm to include the stables, now soaked with water, the flames sizzling and sending up deep clouds of steam with the smoke. "How do you know so soon? I mean..." She stared at what was left of the charred, gutted building and the fire that was slowly beginning to die.

"Gut instinct," Striker said, pushing gloved hands deep into his pockets as he eyed the house. His gaze dropped to Randi and the girls, and his jaw visibly tightened. "I think this is another attempt to warn the McCaffertys, especially Randi."

"By killing horses?" That didn't make sense.

"*Her* horses. She owns half the ranch."

The ambulance, lights flashing angrily, took off.

"Matt owns half the ranch, as well," Jamie said. "Or will soon." She wasn't letting out any information that Striker didn't already have.

"I know, but no one's made an attempt on my life before and Randi's seems to be a target for some nutcase." Matt glowered into the night.

"So you think that whoever started this fire was warning Randi to back off of something?"

"Could be," Striker said.

"I think he's right." Matt looked over at his nieces and fiancée. "I'd better help out with the girls." He looked over at Randi, who was clutching J.R. With Kelly's help, Randi was to ride herd over the twins who continued to sob and cry even after their parents had driven off. Snow swirled around them. Kelly leaned down and picked up one little girl while Matt ran through the trampled yard and snagged the other off her feet. Jamie felt cold to the bottom of her soul. Who would want to harm this family? "What could Randi be doing that would make someone want to kill her or her child or the livestock?"

"That's what I have to find out," Striker admitted as he gazed at the horses, calmer now, ears flicking as they huddled together on the far side of the house. "Before anyone else gets hurt."

Jamie stared down the lane. The ambulance lights flashed through the trees and her heart twisted. Slade was inside…but surely he would pull through. She slid behind the wheel of her compact and twisted the key in the ignition. She'd always thought of Slade McCafferty as indestructible.

Now she prayed that she was right.

# Chapter 13

Dawn was still a few hours off. Through the windows of St. James Hospital, Jamie stared into the darkness, to the parking lot of the hospital. The snow had stopped falling.

And not a word about Slade.

Her stomach in knots, Jamie leaned against the windowsill and swirled powdered cream into her tepid coffee. She knew he was alive. Certainly someone would have told her if he wasn't okay. But how long could it take?

Glancing at the double doors of the hospital emergency room for the zillionth time, she willed someone, anyone—doctor, nurse aide—to appear and give her a sliver of information. All she knew was that aside from the smoke inhalation and burns, his back was involved.

Broken?

God, no. She couldn't think that way. She looked at the clock for the tenth time in as many minutes. What was taking so long? She hadn't heard a word on Thorne, either. Where was Nicole? Why didn't she appear with some kind of information?

*Because she's with her husband. Standing by the man she loves. Where you should be, if you could.*

Jamie paced from one end of the small waiting room to the other, then rested a hip against the wide ledge of a window again. She'd arrived five minutes later than the ambulance, hadn't gotten so much as a peek at Slade, and the hospital staff was being tight-lipped. She wasn't family.

She sipped the horrible sludge in her cup without really tasting it. She'd been up for hours, was bone-weary, but knew that if she went home, she wouldn't be able to sleep. Not with Slade here. Not without knowing about his condition.

Surely he would pull through. He was a McCafferty; they were all tough as old leather and had more lives than the proverbial cat. Right? Then why did she have a cold feeling in the middle of her stomach, a knot of fear that wouldn't go away?

She remembered him swinging the ax and splitting kindling for her that first night they were alone together. Then there were images of him cutting down the Christmas tree and driving the sleigh, mental pictures of him holding Randi's baby or playing with his nieces. And, of course, the more recent memory of being with him, of gazing into his eyes as he'd peeled off her clothes and made love to her in the very building where he'd been nearly crushed to death and burned alive.

Her throat ached. She wanted to break down, but wouldn't. Couldn't. He might need her.

*When pigs fly, Jamie. When has he ever needed you?*

*Now,* she thought determinedly. *He needs me now!*

He would be all right.

He had to be.

She dropped into one of the chairs.

"Jamie!" Chuck's voice rang down the empty corridor and

she looked up to see him breezing toward the waiting room. Four-seventeen in the morning and he was clean shaven, not a hair out of place, dressed in pressed khakis, the sweater she'd given him last Christmas and a wool overcoat. As if he were going to the damned golf course. All he needed was one of those funny little caps. "I just heard what happened."

"How?" she asked. Why hadn't he been sleeping?

"Cell phone. Matt called from the ranch. Thought I'd want to know what was going on." His smile seemed genuine, his eyes kind. "Thorne McCafferty is a friend of mine, you know."

That's right. All of Chuck's friends were business associates in one way or another. She closed her eyes for a second, hated to be so cynical. "And Matt was concerned about you. He and...oh, what's her name?" Chuck asked.

"Kelly?"

"Yeah, the wife-to-be will be here as soon as they've got things handled at the ranch. I think the sister will be here, too. Something about waiting for a babysitter or the housekeeper, or someone to look after the kids."

"Good."

"Are you all right?" Was there genuine concern in Chuck's voice?

"Holding my own," Jamie said, though she knew she must look a wreck. Not that she cared. She shoved her hair from her eyes and glanced at the clock again.

"And Thorne?" Chuck's expression grew more serious.

"He'll be all right, I think, though I haven't heard... I expected Nicole to come out and explain what was going on."

"From what Matt said, Slade was injured more seriously. Thorne went in to save him."

"That's what I've heard... Slade ran into the stables to save the stock, so he was in there the longest... I really don't know what happened, just that Thorne dragged him out of the fire and Slade lost consciousness."

Chuck took a seat on the arm of her chair. His hands were clasped between his knees. "You're in love with him, aren't you?"

Jamie nodded, shook her head, then sighed. "I think so... yes. I mean—"

"I get the picture. Oh, Jamie." There was pain in Chuck's voice as he gazed at her for a minute, touched her shoulder, then, as if aware of the tenderness of the gesture, stood suddenly. "I always knew it wasn't quite right between us. I wasn't what you wanted, but I was hoping..." He lifted a hand, then let it drop. "Well, I just hope you know what you're doing."

"I do, Chuck."

"Then good luck." He seemed as if he was about to say something more when the double doors swung open.

Jamie shot to her feet. Nicole, disheveled, her expression grim, swept through the opening. "Sorry I didn't get to you any earlier," she said as Jamie met her halfway across the waiting area.

"Slade?"

"He's going to live," she said, her amber eyes dark with pain. Then, as if quickly donning her professional persona, she squared her shoulders and added, "The surface stuff, cuts and bruises, will heal quickly. He's got some second-degree burns on his hands and face, but, that, too, isn't what's of the most concern."

"What?" Jamie asked.

"It's his back, Jamie. One vertebra is cracked and there could be some damage to his spinal cord." Jamie's knees threatened to give way.

Chuck grabbed her arm, but she made herself stand and forced the hated words over her tongue. "How much damage?" she asked, not daring to think about the possibility that Slade might be paralyzed.

"We don't know. Bruised for certain, maybe just pinched, probably not severed." She began talking in medical terms that Jamie, had she not been fighting the buzz of fear thrumming through her brain, or the denial that threatened to rise in her throat, might have understood. But all she could think about was seeing Slade again. Touching him. Telling him that she loved him.

"Is he conscious?"

"Not yet."

"And the prognosis?" Chuck asked as a cart, wheeled by a balding male aide, rattled past.

"It's too early to tell. But Dr. Nimmo is an excellent neuro-surgeon and he's linked via computer to the best in the country. I can assure you that Slade is getting the best possible care."

"When can I see him?" Jamie asked.

"Not until the doctors have finished. That might be a while." Nicole placed a hand on Jamie's sleeve. "Why don't you go home for a while? Rest. There's nothing to be done here and I promise I'll call you myself if there's any change."

"I want to stay," Jamie insisted.

"Why? It serves no purpose. Won't help." Chuck gave her one of his now-let's-be-reasonable looks, the one where one of his silver eyebrows raised slightly as he looked at her from the tops of his eyes.

"I'll feel better about it if I'm close by."

Chuck sighed. "He doesn't even know you're here."

"That's right," Nicole said. "It would be best if you got some sleep."

"I'll doze here." Jamie was adamant. Her gaze touched the other woman's and she saw a spark of understanding in Nicole's eyes. She didn't have to say, *If things were reversed and it was Thorne battling for his life, where would you be?* "If there's any change, you'll let me know."

"Yes." Nicole nodded and offered an encouraging smile. "The second it occurs."

"Thanks."

"Now wait a minute..." Chuck tried to talk her into going back to Nana's place, but Jamie was determined to stay.

"You can't change my mind and that's that," she finally said, and rested her hips on the window ledge again. Chuck gave up, said something about going down to the cafeteria to try to scrounge up breakfast. Jamie wasn't hungry. She glanced at the clock again, saw the precious seconds sweeping by and realized she'd spent too many years running away from the truth that she loved Slade McCafferty. She always had. She probably always would.

"You have to face it, Randi, someone's sending you one helluva message." Kurt Striker's voice was harsh, his green eyes jade-cold as he watched her descend the stairs.

Damn the man, why was he hounding her now—when all hell had broken loose? She brushed past him on her way to the living room. The bomb squad had dispersed, declaring the house safe. The fire in the stables had been extinguished, leaving charred, soggy remains. The police vehicles and fire trucks had departed, but yellow crime scene tape now roped off the still smoldering building. Matt had called Larry Todd and the foreman had rushed over. The two men and Kelly had dealt with the frightened livestock, rounding up the crazed horses and finding shelter for them in the barn.

It was such a nightmare. Slade and Thorne were in the hospital, two of the horses had died, the ranch was a shambles, the children distraught.

While Kelly Dillinger should have been planning her wedding to Matt, she'd been chasing after terrorized livestock in the middle of the night and worrying herself sick over the men who were to become her brothers-in-law.

And the kids... It had taken hours but Randi had finally gotten the children into bed.

"Did you hear me? This is about you, you know." Striker wasn't giving up. But then, from what she'd heard of him, he never did. Dressed in Levis and a sheepskin-lined denim jacket, he was standing near the fireplace where he'd managed to stoke the dying embers into flames. The familiar room looked cozy and secure, yet all she had to do was glance past the Christmas tree, through the window, to the destruction beyond.

"I'm not convinced it has anything to do with me. It could have been an accident."

"I talked with the fire chief. They're about ninety percent certain it was arson. They even think there was a trip wire to the door. When Slade opened it, he didn't have a chance."

"Oh, God."

Kurt crossed the room so that he was standing toe to toe with her. "You could be right. Even if the fire was arson, maybe it had nothing to do with you. Maybe the Flying M was a random target, maybe the arsonist has a grudge against someone else in your family, but, given what else has been happening in your life, I think the odds are against it." He rubbed the back of his neck, but his gaze never left hers. "I don't think you're willing to play God with your brothers' lives, with your nieces' lives or with your son's life."

"Of course not!" Her nerves were strung tight, her emotions raw, her brain running in circles so fast that she couldn't sleep though she was exhausted. She didn't need Striker with his accusations and suspicions. Not right now.

"All I'm asking is that you help us nail the bastard who's behind all this."

"Don't you think I would if I could?"

He didn't answer and she tipped her chin up so that she could impale him with her self-righteous glare. "I'll do everything possible. Of course I will." She was angry now, tired of the silent stares, the accusations. "What is it you want to know?"

"Everything, Randi. Everything you can remember about your life before your accident. I want to know what you were working on for the Seattle *Clarion*. I want to know if you were writing a book and what it was about. I want to know why you fired Larry Todd. I want to know why you were on that road in Glacier Park. And I want to know the name of the father of your child."

She swallowed hard and, as if he sensed resistance, he grabbed her arm with unforgiving fingers.

"No more lies, okay? No more half-truths. No more faked amnesia. We don't have time for any of that bull. Slade and Thorne are lucky to have gotten out of the fire alive. You and your son are lucky you survived the accident. It's probably a miracle of God you weren't killed in the hospital. But your luck might not hold. The next time someone might die."

Someone had taken a sledgehammer and was pounding it against his brain. And that same someone had decided that his lungs would feel better if they were on fire. Then Slade remembered. In terrifying Technicolor.

The fire. The horses. Thorne's voice and the beam splitting to pin him against the floor. The expression on Jamie Parsons's face when she'd seen him being dragged from the burning building.

He opened a bleary eye and saw metal rails. Beyond that were curtains—no, privacy drapes that sufficed as walls, and monitors surrounding him. He was in St. James Hospital, ICU, if he had to guess. Where Randi had recently been.

"Mr. McCafferty?"

He focused on a round-faced nurse who was staring down at him. She smiled benignly as she touched his arm. "How're you feeling?"

"Like hell," he rasped, but his throat was raw and the words barely passed his lips. His face felt cracked, dry, his arms like dead weights. There was a pain in the center of his back and his legs...what the hell? He tried to sit up.

"Whoa, there, we'll adjust the medication for your pain," she advised. "I've already called the doctor. He should be in to see you very shortly."

But there was something in her eyes, something he didn't trust. He tried to move his leg, but nothing happened. He attempted again. "My legs..." He looked down, saw them stretched out beneath the sheets.

"You've had some trauma to your back. As I said, the doctor will be in to talk to you about it."

"Trauma?" He gritted his teeth, tried to budge his damned legs, felt sweat bead on his skin. What was the issue she was dancing around? Trauma to his back. "You mean, to my spinal cord?"

"The doctor will be in—"

"Like hell. Are you telling me I'm paralyzed?" he demanded, the rest of his life flashing ahead of him. He saw wheelchairs, aides to help him do everything from bathe to urinate, to help him dress. No. He wouldn't believe it.

The nurse's lips pursed.

"Get me the doctor. Now!" he bellowed, though the words came out in a harsh, damning whisper. "And get my sister-in-law, Dr. Nicole Stevenson, er, McCafferty."

Another nurse appeared at the foot of his bed as he pushed himself upright. "Doctor ordered a sedative."

"I don't want a damned sedative. Hell's bells, you're telling me that I'm paralyzed, and now you want to knock me out?" He forced himself to a full sitting position, bracing himself with his hands, staring down at the useless limbs hidden by the crisp bed sheets and thin coverlet.

"Mr. McCafferty, please—just calm down and—"

Gritting his teeth he glared at his legs and willed them to move. Nothing. As the nurses adjusted his IV, he yanked off the coverings and saw beneath the short gown nothing out of the ordinary—two somewhat hairy legs that just wouldn't move. He panicked, then calmed. This was a nightmare, that was it. He was dreaming. He'd wake in his own bed and find out that everything was the same. The stables would be standing, all the horses, including Diablo Rojo waiting impatiently to be fed...so why the hell wouldn't his legs move?

"Where the hell is the doctor?" He glared at the nurse. "You call him now and...and..."

He felt suddenly drowsy. The words died in his throat. His arms gave out and he flopped against the pillows as a door flew open and Nicole appeared.

"Slade? How are you?"

"You tell me," he said, though he had trouble wrapping his tongue around the words. God, he was tired. He wanted to close his eyes, to sink back into black oblivion and know that when he awoke everything would be the same. "Am... am I paralyzed?"

Gold eyes held his for a second. "We don't know the extent of damage to your spinal cord just yet," she said, and he felt as if a thousand-pound weight had been dropped on his chest. "It's too early to tell. Dr. Nimmo is doing everything he can. He's consulting with other specialists."

"But...there's chance..." He couldn't stay awake. Cool fingers surrounded his wrist.

"Let's not borrow trouble," Nicole said as his eyelids lowered and he envisioned for a second what his life would be like as a cripple...no that wasn't politically correct...a handicapped person...physically challenged... For a second Jamie's face came to mind. Beautiful. Smart. Successful. An attorney, for God's sake. A woman who had once been pregnant with his child...but if he was paralyzed, he wouldn't be able to father children, to make love...he remembered the feel of her beneath him, the way her eyes had shone as she'd looked up at him...and as the blackness overcame him he realized he'd never make love to her again.

"I want to see him." No longer tired, adrenaline shooting through her veins as she heard Slade had been conscious, she was on her feet and squaring off with Nicole. Chuck had taken Thorne back to the ranch but Nicole had stayed to consult with the neurologist and to keep Jamie informed about Slade's condition. "If he's awake and can have a visitor, I want to see him."

Nicole frowned slightly. "Slade's sleeping now, he was only conscious for a few minutes. He's in a lot of pain so the doctor had standing orders for a sedative."

"I don't care," Jamie said, refusing to back down an inch. She'd spent the past five hours waiting for a glimpse of him, to know that he'd recover, praying that he'd survive, and she wasn't about to leave now. "Look, Nicole, please try to understand. I need to see him. I know I'm not family, but I thought you could see that I got inside."

"I could," Nicole hedged. She was wearing a lab coat and a worried expression that caused tiny lines to appear between her eyebrows.

"Then let's go."

"Are you sure you're ready for this?"

"Absolutely."

"You can't stay more than a couple of minutes."

Jamie took in a deep breath. "I understand."

"Okay, I'll do it, but only on one condition. You see Slade for a couple of minutes, then I want you to go home and get some rest." Nicole offered a tentative smile. "Doctor's orders."

"Fine. Anything. Just get me into his room."

Nicole hitched her chin toward the elevator. "ICU's on three. His 'room' is part of the ward, divided by curtains. I'll take you up there, make sure no one hassles you."

"Thanks." They rode up in the elevator in silence and Jamie, desperate to see for herself that Slade was alive, that he would make it, braced herself.

Still, she wasn't prepared for the sight of him.

Slade, bandaged, was lying immobile in a bed while tubes and wires ran into and out of his body. A shock of singed black hair fell over his forehead and cuts and abrasions sliced through his skin, some crossing the scar running down the side of his face. Burn marks—probably from cinders and sparks—were visible. "Oh, God," she whispered, her hand flying to her lips before she grabbed hold of herself.

"Are you okay? Sure you can handle this?" Nicole asked.

Jamie nodded mutely, steeled herself.

"Then I'll give you a minute alone with him." Nicole wandered a few feet to the nurse's station, the hub from which all the sectioned, curtained "rooms" spoked.

Biting her lower lip, Jamie walked to the edge of the bed, to a spot near his head, her fingers curling over the cold steel rails. "Slade," she said, her voice catching as she looked down at the strong angles of his face. Eyelashes curved against his cheekbones, his breathing was slow, but sure. "It's Jamie. I came to see how you were doing." Tears filled her eyes and her throat caught. She'd thought him indestructible with his sexy smile, devil-may-care attitude, and damned independent streak. Now, here he lay. Broken. Unconscious. Maybe never able to walk again. She picked up his hand, laced her fingers through his, and fought the urge to cry.

"You're gonna be okay," she said roughly, inwardly cringing as she heard the platitude in her voice, knowing she might be lying.

She couldn't see Slade confined to a wheelchair; this man who'd spent his life helicopter skiing, mountain climbing, bronc busting or white-water rafting. He'd been a hunting guide, raced cars, even been a stuntman. How could he adapt?

*Don't give up on him. He'll be able to handle it. He's a McCafferty. Lord knows they're resilient. In no time he'd find a way to whip his wheelchair around the Flying M, to ride a horse, to shoot the rapids. He wouldn't let a disability beat him. This is Slade you're talking to. For God's sake, don't write him off.*

Her voice was a little stronger. "You know, cowboy, there's something I've been meaning to tell you." The words formed in her heart but lodged in her throat. Giving his hand a squeeze, she forced them out. "I love you, Slade. I think...I know this sounds crazy, but I do think that a part of me has always loved you." She studied his face, so peaceful as he slept, so handsome and still, his jaw dark with beard shadow, bruises forming under his eyes. "I'll be here, when you wake up."

He didn't so much as twitch. No rapid eye movement behind his lids, no tentative squeeze of his fingers, no quick intake of breath. No flutter of his eyelids and, because of her words, no miraculous healing.

She saw Nicole looking in her direction. Knew her time was up. "I'll be back," she promised as she blinked away tears. "Don't go anywhere." Gently she dropped his hand onto the bedsheet. Wiping her eyes with the back of her hand, she met Nicole's gaze, then, fearing she'd break down all together, strode swiftly to the door.

"He'll get better," Nicole said as she caught up with her in the hallway.

"When?" Jamie snapped, then bit her tongue. Before Nicole could respond, Jamie held up a hand. "I'm sorry. I—you were right. It's hard to deal with. Thanks for letting me see him."

Nicole smiled, but her eyes were glassy with unshed tears. "Go home and get some sleep. Maybe when you wake up, Slade will be back to his normal cantankerous self and we'll have figured out who torched the stables. I'll call you if anything changes."

"Thanks again." They walked to the elevator and Jamie pushed the call button. She had to ask the question burning in her mind. "So, in your opinion as a doctor, what are the chances that Slade will walk again?"

"That I don't know," Nicole said, honesty showing in her weary features, "but I'm certain he's getting the best care available. I would trust my life and my daughters' lives to Dr. Nimmo." She offered Jamie a tiny, tired smile. "Besides that, Slade's a McCafferty. If anyone was going to pull through this, it would be Slade." She tucked a stray strand of hair behind her ear. "He's suffered worse. He was almost killed once before, just last winter in the skiing accident. You know about that, don't you?"

Jamie nodded. "He told me."

"I wasn't in the family then, of course, but Thorne told me about it later. It wasn't so much his injuries, though they were bad enough, but when Rebecca and the baby didn't make it, he was lost. Despondent. He kind of dropped out of sight for a while. He blamed himself though no one could have talked Rebecca out of skiing that day."

Jamie froze. Slade had been a father? His child had died? Her heart crumbled. "They took the baby skiing?" she whispered, suddenly cold to the marrow of her bones.

"No...Rebecca was pregnant, somewhere between four and five months along, I think..." Nicole winced as if she'd realized she'd given away a confidence. "I thought he told you about this."

"I didn't know about the baby." Dear God, Slade had lost another unborn child? No wonder his reaction had been so violent when she'd told him about her own pregnancy. "I only knew that he'd lost someone dear to him, someone he loved." No wonder he'd been so upset in the hayloft. Dear God, had that been just yesterday? It seemed a lifetime ago.

The elevator arrived with a soft chime. The doors slid open. Her mind spinning, Jamie stepped inside.

"I'll keep you posted," Nicole assured her. "I promise." She lifted a hand as the doors whispered shut and Jamie sagged against the handrail. *Another baby. He'd lost another baby.* What were the odds of that? Her heart ached for him and for the child he'd never met—the two children.

The elevator stopped on the first floor and she walked on wooden legs toward the front door. As she stepped into the parking lot, she looked upward to the third floor and the windows she thought might be a part of ICU. Shivering and wrapping her coat more tightly around her, she noticed a stray piece of straw...a remnant from their lovemaking. A few flakes of snow began to fall in the early morning light. Jamie unlocked her car and slid inside. As she switched on the ignition, she prayed that Slade McCafferty would walk again.

# Chapter 14

*You know, cowboy, there's something I've been meaning to tell you...*
*I love you, Slade. I think... I know this sounds crazy, but I do think*
*that a part of me has always loved you. I'll be here, when you wake up.*

Jamie? Had Jamie been here? In his room? Or...where?
Where the devil was he? He moaned, felt a shooting pain in
his back and opened an eye.

It all came crashing back. He was in the hospital. There had
been a fire. The horses...yeah, that was it, and he'd woken up
earlier... Oh, God.

No! He tried to roll over, tried to lift a leg and...nothing.
His mind was instantly clear. Pain screamed from the base of
his skull, down his back and then just stopped. "Get me a doctor," he roared, his voice booming through the drapes to the
station where a slim woman was bending over a chart. She
looked up, her short brown hair neat, a patient smile tacked to
her face. "Mr. McCafferty," she said, rounding the desk that

looked as if it belonged at the helm of something out of *Star Wars*. "I wondered when you'd wake up."

"I want a doctor."

"Dr. Nimmo will be in this morning. How're you feeling?"

"How do you think I'm feeling?" he snarled, frustrated. "My damned legs won't move."

"I thought the nurse from the night shift explained that you've been in some trauma."

"I know that. What I don't know is how much damage there is. Am I going to be a cripple?"

She looked at him with kind eyes. "Let's not think that way, okay? Positive thoughts."

"I don't feel very positive," he rasped, his throat burning with the effort.

"Try." With the efficiency of years on the job, Slade watched her as she checked his temperature, blood pressure and pulse… which seemed overkill as there were half a dozen machines monitoring every bodily function known to man.

"Get my sister-in-law. Nic—Dr. Nicole McCafferty." God, his throat ached.

"I already paged her when I noticed you were rousing."

"Has anyone been in here? To see me?" he asked, wanting to know if Jamie had actually been at his bedside or if he'd dreamed it. The thought of her standing over him, knowing that his spine was injured…

"Dr. McCafferty's been in three times and your brother, Thorne, and someone Dr. McCafferty introduced as a family friend. A woman."

So it was true. Hell. She had been standing over him, knowing that he might never use his legs again, seeing him as half the man he was. His jaw tightened. He remembered making love to her in the hayloft. No wonder she'd said what she did. That she loved him. Bull. She felt obligated, as if in being with him in the stables she'd sealed her fate and now had to tie herself to a cripple. Which was ridiculous. And downright pathetic. He didn't want her feeling any sort of debt to him and he certainly didn't want her pity. God, he couldn't stand that.

The doors to ICU opened and he saw Nicole, looking as if she hadn't slept in days, sweep into the room. "Look who woke up," she chirped, offering him a smile that warmed her eyes. "Sleeping Beauty."

"Yeah, right," he grunted around the pain in his throat. "How's Thorne?"

"Fine. No serious damage. Minor burns and cuts. He'll live... Now, about you..."

"Yeah, about me. I can't move my damned legs. I've tried. Everyone is trying to placate me and pretend that everything's just hunky-dory and all the while they're mentioning things like cracked vertebrae, spinal trauma or spinal distress or even spinal bruising... I've heard them talking when I surfaced a time or two." He saw the darkness in his sister-in-law's gaze and her smile slid quietly from her face. "Tell it to me straight, Nicole. Am I going to be a cripple for the rest of my life?"

"I don't know." She sighed and met his gaze. "I won't lie to you. There's always that possibility, but the extent of the damage to your spine hasn't been established. Dr. Nimmo will be in soon. He's been consulting with his colleagues, and he's kept me apprised of your condition. He thinks you'll recover, at least partially, but I think it would be best if he talked to you himself."

"Then get him the hell in here."

"I will...the nurse has already called him and told him you were awake, but there's someone else who wants to see you. I promised Jamie I'd call her the minute you woke up. She's on her way. I'm meeting her in my office in fifteen minutes."

Slade's heart soared for a second, then he remembered her

vows of love, whispered to a man near death, a man who might never be able to love her physically, a man to whom she felt indebted. Before the accident she'd insisted that what they'd shared all those years ago was nothing more than a quick fling, a "blip," sexual experimentation by two wild kids, nothing more. But then she made love to him and told him about the baby; he'd felt something change. Had it been love? Nah. No way. During their last conversation, they'd been standing in the snow by her car, spewing words of anger.

*You're not seriously considering marrying that pompous ass, are you?* Slade had asked and her response still rang through his head. *I was thinking about it, yes.*

The guy was a condescending jerk.

So now Slade was supposed to believe that she loved him? Damn it all to hell, he wasn't that much of a fool. He wouldn't let her guilt or pity or whatever the hell damned misguided emotion was driving her tie to him.

Not until hell froze over.

Nicole was still observing him. Waiting.

"Tell Jamie to go home," he muttered. "I don't want to see her."

Jamie wanted to scream in frustration. "What do you mean, he won't see me?" she demanded as she plopped into the visitor's chair in Nicole's office. She hadn't bothered to take off her coat and was stuffing her gloves into her pockets.

"Slade wasn't into elaborating. In fact, he was pretty angry about what has happened to him. But he was firm. Maybe he'll change his mind once he talks to the neurologist."

"And if he doesn't?"

"Then there's nothing I can do. I have to honor his wishes. He's a patient here at St. James. And even though he's my brother-in-law and I think he's making a helluva mistake, as a doctor, I have to do what he asks."

"Damn." Jamie leaned back in the chair and looked at the tiles in the ceiling. "He's just being stubborn...or thinks he's being noble...right now he needs all the support he can get."

*Or maybe he really doesn't want to see you.*

No, she wouldn't believe that. Not after the way he'd made love to her, after the way he'd kissed her at the car in the snow despite the fact that she told him she might marry Chuck.

"I agree about the support," Nicole said. She leaned back in her chair and nervously toyed with a pen. "But, unfortunately, he doesn't see it that way. Let's just give him some time to come to grips with his situation."

"I don't think it would help."

"It might."

Jamie was on her feet and it was all she could do not to rush out of the office, run up the stairs to the third floor and find a way to get through the locked doors of ICU. "I don't care what Slade says, I want to see him, I *need* to see him, and whether he admits it or not, he needs me. Right now."

Nicole looked bone-weary. And in no mood to take on an argument. "I told him I thought it was a mistake, but he was adamant. I don't know what went on between the two of you and I really don't need to know. It's your business. But, for the time being, I think, you should give it a rest. After he's talked with the neurologist and been moved to his own room and had some time to think things over, then he might change his mind, but for now, it would be best to let him have his way. He's going through a lot."

"He needs family around him. Friends. People who care."

"Meaning you."

"Yes!" She clenched her fists at the impossibility of the situation.

"That may be so," Nicole said as her pager beeped. "But, speaking as a professional, I really do think the best way to do that is to leave him be. Let him work things out." She leaned across the desk where a cup of coffee sat untouched, papers were piled in an overflowing In basket and a bifold picture frame displayed glossy prints of her twins. "Now, speaking as a woman, one who herself couldn't resist the charms of a Mc-Cafferty brother, let me give you some advice. Let Slade come to you. That's the only way it'll work between you."

Jamie wanted to argue, to pull out all the ammunition in her arsenal to convince Nicole that she should see him, but the honesty in the doctor's face, the concern in the curve of her mouth, and the clearness of her eyes convinced Jamie to let it go.

"I really have to go," Nicole said, standing as her pager bleated again. "But I'll be in touch. I promise." Rounding the desk, she gave Jamie a hug, as if they were sisters, part of a family.

Which was ludicrous.

Slade had rejected her once before.

And he was doing it again.

Whatever his reasons, he was letting her know that he didn't want Jamie Parsons a part of his life. If she had any brains at all, she'd sell her grandmother's house to the first person who was interested, wrap up the title transfer of the Flying M, turn on her high heels and head out of town, to Seattle, or to San Francisco, or even to L.A. and find herself another job. One thousands of miles away from Slade McCafferty, the one man guaranteed to break her heart over and over again.

Kurt sat in his motel room, a beer on the scarred wooden table, the television flickering at the foot of his too soft bed. Barely a week before Christmas and he was stuck in Mon-

tana trying to figure out why Randi McCafferty was holding out on him and her family. He glanced at the TV screen.
The local news had moved away from the recent McCafferty
family tragedy that had taken the lives of two horses and had
landed one of the brothers in the hospital. Now the anchor-
woman was talking about the Christmas season.

Well, fa-la-la-la-la-the damned-la. The holidays were always
a pain...or had been in the past few years. He didn't want to
go there. Didn't want to think of the time before. Right now
he had to concentrate on the McCaffertys.

It had been three days since the stables had burned, and
the preliminary reports were in, reports that Kelly Dillinger,
through her connections with the sheriff's department, had
been able to peruse.

As was suspected, the fire had been intentionally set. Arson.
Probably attempted murder. The press had had a field day
with that turn of events and still the rumors around town
persisted that one of the brothers was behind all the trouble
at the Flying M.

Worse yet, the insurance company, Mountain Fire and Casualty, was balking at paying the claim because of the suspected
arson. A claims adjuster had already been out and a private
investigator, a guy Kurt knew, had been hired by the insurance company. It was Mountain Fire and Casualty's position
that the fire could have been set by anyone on the ranch, especially the owners.

All in all, it was a helluva mess.

And it had all started with Randi McCafferty and her
baby. Why was she so reticent to name the kid's father? It had
crossed his mind that she didn't know the paternity of her own
child, but he'd checked her out through friends, coworkers,
landlords—everyone she'd come into contact with in Seattle.
Though she'd been in several relationships over the past ten

years, she wasn't into the bar scene, nor did it seem that she was likely to participate in one-night stands. He'd bet a year's retainer that she knew damned well who the little boy's dad was.

Amnesia, *sham*nesia.

She remembered.

She just wasn't talking.

He thought before that she might open up to him, had seen the hesitation in those brown eyes of hers. But she'd held back. Why? Didn't she trust him? What did she think would happen?

He flipped through the photographs he'd taken, snapshots of the original car accident and the ranch and the charred remains of the stables. There were other pictures, as well—photos of the men with whom she'd been involved. Kurt stacked them in a pile and studied each one.

Brodie Clanton, about five-ten, with a physique honed at a private gym, was a lawyer and connected to big money in Seattle. His grandfather had been a judge. Brodie, with dark hair, an aquiline nose, a Ferrari he only used on weekends, and multiple degrees from Stanford, had dated Randi last year. Rich, smart, running in the correct social circles, Brodie wouldn't want the taint of any kind of scandal. He had his own political aspirations.

In Kurt's opinion, Clanton was about as warm as the Northern Pacific. Potential Dad Number One.

Randi had also kept company with Sam Donahue, a big, blond, tough-as-nails cowpoke who was a part of the rodeo circuit. Rough and tumble in denim and leather, Donahue was the diametric opposite of Brooks Brothers'–dressed Clanton. Number Two.

The third man Randi had been romantically linked to and, in Striker's opinion, Potential Dad Number Three, was Joe Paterno, a photojournalist who did freelance work for the *Clarion* and who had probably done the headshot of Randi in Striker's file. It was a great picture of Randi looking over a bare shoulder, her mahogany curls wild, her eyebrows arched, her brown eyes shining with mischief, as if she couldn't believe her own vampy pose. With cheekbones a runway model would kill for and a playful intelligence that had been captured on camera, Randi McCafferty was too damned sexy for her own good.

Paterno was an intellectual, who flew all over the world to take pictures of newsworthy incidents. Kurt had seen his work, and it was impressive. Paterno had an eye for the dramatic, the tragic and the humorous. In Striker's estimation, Paterno was the only one of those men who'd dated Randi who was good enough for her.

That thought surprised him. He'd better keep his feelings for the hot-headed McCafferty sister back where they belonged—at a level of suspicion and distrust unmixed with other, warmer emotions.

So, he wondered, tipping his bottle of Coors, had one of the men she'd been linked to held a grudge against her and the baby? Did any of these guys know about the kid? Maybe Kurt was barking up the wrong tree altogether. Maybe there was another reason someone was trying to scare Randi off. The housemaid, Juanita, had mentioned that Randi had been working on a book. Randi, under questioning, wasn't sure. Now what the hell was that all about? Where was it?

He made a couple of mental notes. Nicole had seen someone coming out of Randi's hospital room, someone dressed as a doctor, right before she'd stopped breathing, and they'd determined that whoever it had been—man or woman—it wasn't anyone on the hospital staff. So the would-be killer was an imposter; that wasn't a surprise.

As for the maroon paint on Randi's vehicle, potential evidence of her being run off the road, there had been no leads. Kurt had nearly exhausted his list of automobile repair companies. Either the vehicle had been driven out of state and repaired, hadn't been fixed or someone in a local auto body shop was lying.

Back to the kid's daddy.

If Randi was being reticent about the name of Joshua's father, there were other ways to narrow the field. The baby had been in the hospital, his blood typed. Now it was just a matter of determining if Clanton, Donahue or Paterno could have been the sperm donor.

If not, he'd be back at square one.

As for that damned phantom book, Striker would just have to keep looking.

He slid the photographs back into the file, pausing for one last glimpse of Randi. Man, she was sexy...probably too sexy for her own damned good.

"So, all in all, you were lucky." Dr. Nimmo peered at Slade through wire-rimmed glasses. A short man in a too long lab coat and loosened tie, he'd finished examining Slade and had talked in medical terms about tests, X-rays, MRIs—all of which Slade had endured in the past two days.

"Funny, but I don't feel particularly lucky."

"I suppose not, but it could have been so much worse. You have a cracked vertebra, L-3 or lumbar three, and there was some pressure on your spinal cord, but the cord's intact."

"No damage?"

"Nothing serious to the cord. You'll be fine and soon. As I said, lucky."

"So I'll walk again?"

"Yes."

A two-ton weight lifted from Slade's shoulders. "When?"

"I can't say. It may take some time, but, unless something unforeseen happens, you should be on your feet again. You might need some physical therapy, but no surgery…now we just have to wait."

"When can I go home?"

"We'll see," Nimmo said, marking Slade's chart. "I'll have a better idea in a day or two." He exited the room with a clipped-heel march and Slade stared out the window to the parking lot. The snow had stopped falling, but all the cars in the lot were covered with a blanket of white, the shrubbery hidden, the asphalt visible in black patches where the heat from exhaust and tread from tires had worn through the icy mantle.

He glanced at the clock and thought he'd go out of his mind. His family had visited and Nicole, it seemed, at least for the first thirty-six hours, had kept a vigil. A couple of times she'd mentioned Jamie, but Slade had refused to be pulled into that conversation. He thought of her nearly every waking moment, remembering what she'd said while he was drifting in and out of unconsciousness, recalling in vivid detail their lovemaking in the barns, fields and backseat of his Chevy that hot summer so many years ago. Then there was their recent encounter in the hayloft a few days ago. While the snow had drifted down and some jerk had trip-wired the door, they'd made love the way it was supposed to be. Hot, passionate… Her image came to mind and for the first time in days he felt a twitch…the hint of feeling…below his waist.

Was it possible? He tried to move his legs and failed, so he closed his eyes, conjured up Jamie's face—white skin softly dusted with freckles across the bridge of her straight nose. Lips that were full and stretched across the sexiest set of teeth he'd ever seen. And her eyes…an interesting shade of hazel that had darkened with desire when they'd been in the hayloft. Her kiss had sizzled, her hands, skimming down his body, touching and exploring, had caused his skin to fire and her tongue, wet, slick, agile…

There it was again.

The sensation in his crotch was familiar. And oh, so welcome. He felt himself thicken for a second...just enough time to give him a sliver of hope.

"I'm sorry, Jamie, but Slade doesn't want to see you." Nicole's voice was firm, but she couldn't hide the edge of concern in her words. "He's been moved to a private room, but he's been very insistent."

"Why?" Jamie asked, her heart breaking.

"I don't know."

"Is he walking?"

"He's trying."

"But he has feeling in his legs?"

"Yes. Look, technically I can't give out this kind of information. You know that."

"Of course I do. I'm a lawyer. I've had the classes, but I need to know, damn it."

"Please...just be patient."

"I'll try," Jamie lied, but the minute she hung up the phone, she grabbed her jacket and threw it over her jeans and sweater. She pulled on her boots and took the time to pet Lazarus and feed Caesar, then climbed into her car. She tore out of her grandmother's driveway and caught a glimpse of the For Sale sign at the end of the lane. Snow clung to the post supporting the sign, and her grandmother's advice to never sell the place echoed through her mind.

She felt a moment's regret and considered staying in Grand Hope. She was at home here. The house was paid for. She could start her own firm, hang up her shingle, maybe find another attorney who wanted a partner and someone to share expenses. She had a home complete with cat, horse and vintage car. What more could she want?

The answer was blindingly simple. She wanted Slade. And she'd always gone after what she wanted with a vengeance. She snapped on the radio.

Jamie turned toward town. Toward the hospital. Toward Slade McCafferty.

Slade fell onto the bed. Drenched in sweat from the effort of trying to force his damned legs to move as the physical therapist had urged him along a contraption that looked like parallel bars straight out of the Olympics from hell, he'd trudged slowly, the length of the contraption looking a hundred miles long rather than a mere eight or ten feet.

From physical therapy he'd been wheeled back to his room and now the damned wheelchair was parked in a corner, wedged between a tiny closet and the bed, mocking him for his dismal effort today.

*It's going to take time,* he'd been warned by his doctors and Thorne who had handed him a burned piece of metal…the pocket watch his father had given him. It sat on the rolling stand next to a box of tissue and a water pitcher. Slade reached for the timepiece and remembered his father's insistence that it was time for his youngest son to settle down, to get married, to start a family. Well, he'd tried that. And failed. Twice.

Pain started rolling down his legs and he winced, but was grateful for the sensation, for the misery. With pain came hope that he would be whole again.

He'd just closed his eyes when he heard someone enter. *Don't bother me,* he thought, then got a whiff of perfume…a scent he recognized. His heart jumped into overdrive.

"Slade?"

"I thought I told everyone I didn't want to see you." He didn't open his eyes. Didn't think he could bear the sight of Jamie.

"But I thought it was a crock. So I sneaked past security. It wasn't that tough. You know the nurses, doctors and aides, they have other patients to deal with. I know sometimes you think you're the center of the universe, but not everyone feels the same."

He almost laughed. Almost.

"I think you said you didn't want to see me because it's some kind of macho thing with you, because of the accident. Face it, McCafferty, you're in denial."

"So now you're a shrink."

She hesitated. Taking a quick breath, she said slowly, "Just someone who cares."

Oh, God, did he dare believe her? No way. She was doing the noble thing, being the doting woman, playing a part. He remembered what she'd said to him, the vehemence of her words.

"Go away."

"No."

"I'll call the nurse."

"Then I'll be back."

"I could have you arrested."

"Go ahead."

He couldn't stop himself. His eyes flew open, and he found himself staring into the most beautiful face he'd ever seen. Her hair was pinned haphazardly to the top of her head, some of the strands falling in disarray, she wasn't wearing any makeup that he could discern and yet she was drop-dead gorgeous.

"I thought you were marrying Chuck."

"Nope. Never. He knew it. I knew it."

"But you told me..."

"You were being a jerk, if I recall." She grabbed his hand. "We've been through this once before—a long time ago when you left me and I never had the chance to say what I felt. This time I'm not going to blow it, okay? This time I want you to understand. I love you. It's that simple. It might not make any sense—in fact, it might not be the smartest emotion I've ever embraced, but it's true. I love you. And it doesn't matter that you're injured. It doesn't even matter if you don't completely heal. I love you."

His throat felt thick. He wanted to argue with her, to tell her that she was wrong, but he saw the conviction in her gaze, felt her take his hand and squeeze, noticed that tears had formed in the corners of her eyes.

"I'm…I'm really sorry about the baby." He forced the words out.

"Me, too…both of them…" A tear slid down her face. "Why didn't you tell me?" she asked.

"Why didn't *you* tell *me?*" He saw her pain, understood.

"Two children… Oh, God, Slade, you've lost two. I wish there was something I could say or something I could do…"

His jaw was so tight it ached. How many times had he looked at Thorne's stepdaughters or little J.R. and thought of the children he'd never met? And now… He cleared his throat, fought his own tears. "Life goes on."

"And there will be more."

"Maybe not." He found that hard to believe, because even just looking at her he felt a twitch, a heating in his groin…. Oh, yeah, staring at her he began to grow hard. He smiled despite the pain. "There's no guarantee that this isn't permanent," he said.

"I know."

"You could—"

She pressed a finger to his lips. "There's no guarantees in life period, Slade. We both know that. We've both suffered enough. But…and this is a big point, I want to spend the rest of my life facing those challenges with you."

She withdrew her hand and he stared up at her. "That sounds damned close to a proposal."

One side of her mouth lifted. "See...you're smarter than you look."

"What about your job?"

"I've already quit. What about yours?"

"That's kinda up in the air right now. I had thought about..." His voice drifted away again. He didn't want to think about what he might not be able to do.

"What?"

He let his gaze slide away.

"What, damn it?"

"Before this, I'd thought...well, I figured I might take my share of the proceeds from the ranch and start a business. Tours. White-water cruises. Hiking expeditions. Skiing vacations, maybe even start my own dude ranch, advertise to city people...that sort of thing. But that was before the accident."

"So everything's changed?"

"Yes," he said. "Until I walk again."

"Well, you're right. Things have changed. But whether you walk again or not—and the way I hear it, you will—you could still run the business, maybe not be the guide per se, but you could still organize the trips, go out and explore. And you'd have me. I could help...well, in between making a fortune as the primary partner in the law firm of Jamie Parsons, Attorney-at-Law."

"It would never work."

"You're right. With that attitude." She leaned over the bed rail. "Come on, Slade. Don't give up. We lost each other once. Let's not do it again. What do you say?"

Nearly ripping out his IV, he wrapped a hand around the back of her head and pulled her face to his. His lips found hers and it felt so right, so natural. The hospital room seemed to fade away, and in his mind's eye, he saw the future with Jamie as his wife and kids surrounding them. They were all running through a field of tall grass, one little girl on Slade's shoulders, Jamie holding the hands of two older boys. Their kids. The sun was bright, reflecting on the waters of a clear creek that ran through the field....

"What do I say?" he repeated into her open mouth, his nose touching hers. "Haven't I been saying it ever since I saw you again? I love you. I always have. You're the one who wouldn't listen. I've spent every waking hour of the past few weeks trying to convince you that we should start over, because you're the one woman in the world for me. The one. Do you hear me, Jamie Parsons, Attorney-at-Law?"

She gave out a soft little moan as he released her. "I hear you, cowboy. Loud and clear."

Slade's throat tightened, and he felt her tears falling against his face.

"All right, Counselor, you win. I'll marry you."

She laughed and wiped at her eyes. "How romantic."

"It will be," he promised, pulling her face to his again, heat racing through his veins. From the corner of his eye he caught a glimpse of the charred pocket watch. *Yeah, old man,* he thought, feeling as if his father could see him. *You were right. It is time for me to settle down. With this woman. Forever.*

# Epilogue

The wedding was perfect. Half the town of Grand Hope had been packed into a tiny church near the old railway station and now the ranch house, bedecked with holly, candles, fir boughs and hundreds of tiny lights, was jam-packed. It was two weeks after Christmas but the ceremony, like the Christmas festivities at the Flying M, had been postponed until Slade had been released from the hospital.

Jamie had held her breath, half expecting another tragedy to befall the McCafferty clan, but in the three weeks since the fire at the stables, things had been quiet. And Slade was healing. Slowly, but surely.

Music played from speakers throughout the house and most of the guests wandered through the living room, dining room and kitchen as well as the back porch that had been draped with insulated tenting material and festooned with billowing lace and warmed by dozens of space heaters.

Matt, dressed in a black Western-cut suit, and Kelly, in a sparkling wedding dress, danced and kissed, laughing with the guests and, it seemed, paying particular attention to Kelly's parents.

Jamie had heard there had been bad feelings when Matt had started dating Kelly, as her mother, Eva, had once worked for John Randall and somehow gotten the shaft financially. Though no one was saying too much, Jamie had come to the conclusion that John Randall's heirs had made it up to the Dillingers. Even Karla, Kelly's sister, who, Kelly had insisted, had sworn off men, was dancing and drinking champagne and flirting with some of the unattached male guests. She'd streaked her hair a dozen shades of blond for the event and was an interesting, if unconventional maid of honor.

Randi, too, was mingling with the single men and dancing. To Jamie's amusement, Kurt Striker watched her every move. Was he acting as her bodyguard or a potential lover? The twins were having a ball. Dressed in matching red velvet dresses, white tights and black shoes, they tore through the guests, only to be picked up by this uncle or that and swept around the dance floor.

Even the baby, in a tiny tuxedo complete with bright red bow tie, little cummerbund and snap crotch, made an appearance. Jamie's heart filled...to be a part of this family was overwhelming. She'd watched as Thorne had toasted the couple, then cast his own wife a sexy smile.

But as she glanced outside, Jamie saw the stables, barely more than a patch of rubble, with a few remaining blackened posts visible. Throughout the service and reception, she'd noticed the ever-vigilant bodyguards and undercover police, half expecting another attack.

She heard movement behind her. "Care to dance?" Slade said from his wheelchair.

She grinned down at him. "With a scoundrel like you?"

The gleam in his eye was wicked. "A guy can hope."

"I would love to."

"Good." He pushed himself out of the chair and teetered a bit.

"Oh! I thought you were kidding!" He'd improved with the physical therapy, of course, could sometimes walk with a crutch, but this...

"Come on..." He winked at her. "You won't let me fall, will you?"

"Never."

He swept her into his arms and listed a bit, then when she gasped, grinned down at her. "Gotcha."

"You miserable..." His arms surrounded her. "You're right. You do have me, Slade McCafferty," she admitted, "and I'm here to tell you, you'll never get rid of me."

"Even if I try?"

"Especially then." She winked at him and thought of the nights they'd spent together since he'd been released from the hospital, the lovemaking, gentle at first, but intense as he'd healed.

They danced a few bars and then she saw the beads of perspiration dotting his brow. "Whoa...cowboy. I think you've had enough for one day. Besides, you've got to save your strength."

"Do I? What have you got in mind?"

"A special little dinner...just you and me...in bed." They'd converted the dining room in her grandmother's house to a living room and Slade had been staying with her. "I think we need to celebrate."

"Because Matt's no longer a bachelor."

"Hmm. That, too."

"And because you've agreed to marry me."

"Yes, that, and it was *you* who agreed to marry *me*. But there's something else."

"No one's ruined the wedding."

She helped him off the dance floor and they stood, propped against the staircase. "I guess that could be part of it."

"There's something else?"

"Oh, yeah." Her eyes twinkled. "I have a surprise for you."

"What is it?"

"Something special. But it won't be delivered until late next summer."

"Can I wait that long?"

"You'd better." She saw a spark of understanding in his eyes. "Because then, cowboy, you're gonna be a daddy."

She saw the emotion in his eyes, the way his throat worked. "Jamie...I... You don't know what this means to me. I've lost two children already. Nothing...nothing could make me happier!" Without another word, he kissed her hard. As if he would never let her go.

"Let's elope," he finally whispered into her ear, and she grinned widely. "Tonight."

"I...I...but..."

"Come on, Counselor, where's your sense of adventure?"

"It's with you," she said.

"Then let's go. Time's awastin', and there's been enough of that already." He took her hand and, walking unsteadily, wended his way through the crowd, only stopping long enough to whisper something to his sister. "Don't tell a soul until tomorrow," he warned, then pressed a kiss to his nephew's head.

"For the record, I think you're crazy," Randi said.

"You always have."

With a laugh, Slade guided Jamie to the front door.

Outside, snow was falling, the January wind bitter and cold. For the first time in her life, Jamie didn't notice. Her heart was warm and she glowed from the inside out. In a few short hours, she'd become Mrs. Slade McCafferty.

The adventure was just about to begin.

★ ★ ★ ★ ★

# Book Two:
# RANDI

# Prologue

"I'm dyin', Randi-girl, and there ain't no two ways about it."

Randi McCafferty stopped short. She'd been hurrying down the stairs, her new boots pinching and ringing on the old wooden steps of the house she'd grown up in—a rambling old ranch house set on a slight rise in the middle of No-Damn-Where, Montana. She'd been thinking of her own situation, hadn't realized her father was half lying in his recliner, staring at the blackened grate of the rock fireplace in the living room. John Randall McCafferty was still a big man, but time had taken its toll on his once commanding stature and had ravaged features that had been too handsome for his own good. "What're you talkin' about?" she asked. "You're going to live forever."

"No one does." He glanced up at her and his eyes held hers. "I just want you to know that I'm leavin' you half the place.

The boys, they can fight over the rest of it. The Flying M is gonna be yours. Soon."

"Don't even talk that way," she said, walking into the dark room where the afternoon heat had collected. She glanced through a dusty window, past the porch to the vast acres of the ranch that stretched beneath a wide Montana sky. Cattle and horses grazed in the fields past the stable and barn, moving as restlessly as the wind that made the grass undulate.

"You may as well face it. Come over here. Come on, come on, y'know my bark is worse'n my bite."

"Of course I know it." She'd never seen the bad side of her father's temper, though her half brothers had brought it up time and time again.

"I just want to look at ya. My eyes ain't what they used to be." He chuckled, then coughed so violently his lungs rattled.

"Dad, I think I should call Matt. You should be in a hospital."

"Hell, no." As she crossed the room, he waved a bony hand as if he was swatting a fly. "No damn doctor is gonna do me any good now."

"But—"

"Hush, would ya? For once you listen to me." Incredibly clear eyes glared up at her. He placed a yellowed envelope in her palm. "This here is the deed. Thorne, Matt and Slade, they own the other half together and that should be interestin'," he said with a morbid chuckle. "They'll probably fight over it like cougars at a kill…but don't you worry none. You own the lion's share." He smiled at his own little joke. "You and your baby."

"My what?" She didn't move a muscle.

"My grandson. You're carryin' him, ain't ya?" he asked, his eyes narrowing.

A hot blush burned up the back of her neck. She hadn't

told a soul about the baby. No one knew. Except, it seemed, her father.

"You know, I would have rather had you get married before you got pregnant, but that's over and done with and I won't be around long enough to see the boy. But you and he are taken care of. The ranch will see to that."

"I don't need anyone to take care of me."

Her father's smile disappeared. "Sure you do, Randi. Someone needs to look after you."

"I can take care of myself and…and a baby. I've got a condo in Seattle, a good job and—"

"And no man. Leastwise none worth his salt. You gonna name the guy who knocked you up?"

"This conversation is archaic—"

"Every kid deserves to know his pa," the old man said. "Even if the guy's a miserable son of a bitch who left a woman carrying his child."

"If you say so," she replied, her fingers curling over the edge of the envelope. She felt more than paper inside.

As if he guessed her question, he said, "There's a necklace in there, too. A locket. Belonged to your ma."

Randi's throat closed for a second. She remembered the locket, had played with it as a child, reaching for the shiny gold heart with its glittering diamonds as it had hung from her mother's neck. "I remember. You gave it to her on your wedding day."

"Yep." He nodded curtly and his eyes grew soft. "The ring is in there, too. If ya want it."

Her eyes were suddenly damp. "Thanks."

"You can thank me by namin' the son of a bitch who did this to you."

She inched her chin up a notch and frowned.

"You're not gonna tell me, are you?"

Randi looked her father steadily in the eye. McCafferty to McCafferty, she said, "Hell would have to freeze over first."

"Damn it, girl, you're a stubborn thing."

"Guess I inherited it."

"And it'll be your undoin', mark my words."

Randi felt a shadow steal through her heart, a cold premonition that settled deep inside, but she didn't budge. For her unborn child's protection, she sealed her lips.

No one would ever know who fathered her child.

Not even her son.

# Chapter 1

"Hell's bells," Kurt Striker grumbled under his breath.

He didn't like the job that was set before him. Not one little bit. But he couldn't say no. And it wasn't just because of the substantial fee attached to the assignment, no, the money was good enough. Tempting. He could use an extra twenty-five grand right now. Who couldn't? A check for half the amount sat on the coffee table. Untouched.

Because of the night before. Because of his secret.

He stood in the living room, a fire crackling and warming the backs of his legs, the sprawling snow-covered acres of the Flying M Ranch visible through frosted windows.

"So, what do you say, Striker?" Thorne McCafferty demanded. The oldest of three brothers, he was a businessman by nature and always took charge. "Have we got a deal? Will you see that our sister is safe?"

The job was complicated. Striker was to become Randi

McCafferty's personal bodyguard whether she liked it or not. Which she wouldn't. Kurt would lay odds on it. He'd spent enough time with the only daughter of the late John Randall McCafferty to know that when she made up her mind, it wasn't likely to be changed, not by him, nor by her three half brothers who all seemed to have developed a latent sense of responsibility for their headstrong sibling.

She was trouble. No two ways about it. The way she'd hightailed it out of here only a few hours earlier had clearly indicated her mind was set. She was returning to Seattle. With her child. To her home. To her job. To her old life, and the consequences be damned.

And she was running away.

From her three overbearing half brothers.

And from him.

Striker didn't like the situation one bit, but he couldn't very well confide in these three men, now, could he? As he glanced from one anxious McCafferty brother to the next, he didn't examine his own emotions too closely, didn't want to admit that the reason he was balking at the job was because he didn't want to get tangled up with a woman. Any woman. Especially not with the kid sister of these tough-as-nails, over-protective brothers.

*It's a little too late for that now, wouldn't you say?*

Randi was a sexy thing. All fire and attitude. A strong woman who would, he suspected, as any self-respecting child of John Randall McCafferty, bulldoze her way through life and do exactly what she wanted to do. She wouldn't like Striker nosing around, prying into her affairs, even if he was trying to insulate her from danger. In fact, she'd probably resent it. Especially now.

"Randi's gonna be ticked." Slade, the youngest McCafferty brother, echoed Striker's thoughts, even though he didn't know the half of it. In jeans and a faded flannel shirt, Slade walked to the window and stared outside at the wintry Montana landscape. Snow covered the fields where a few head of cattle and horses huddled against the cold.

"Of course she'll be ticked. Who wouldn't be?" Matt, brother number two, was seated on the worn leather sofa, the heel of one of his cowboy boots propped onto the coffee table only inches from a check for twelve thousand five hundred dollars. "I'd hate it."

"She doesn't have a choice," Thorne said. CEO of his own corporation, Thorne was used to giving orders and having his employees obey. He'd recently moved to Grand Hope, Montana, from Denver, but he was still in charge. "We agreed, didn't we?" he was saying as he motioned to his younger brothers. "For her protection and the baby's safety, she needs a bodyguard."

Matt nodded curtly. "Yeah, we agreed. That won't make it any easier for Randi to swallow. Even if Kelly's involved."

Kelly was Matt's wife, an ex-cop who was now a private investigator. She'd agreed to work with Striker, especially on this, her sister-in-law's case. Red-haired and quick-witted, Kelly would be an asset. But Striker wasn't convinced Kelly McCafferty would be the oil on troubled waters as far as Randi was concerned. No—having a relative involved would only make a sticky situation stickier.

He glanced to the window, toward the youngest McCafferty brother. The friend who had dragged him into this mess. But Slade didn't meet his eyes, just continued to stare out the frosty panes.

"Look, we've got to do something and we don't have time to waste. Someone's trying to kill her," Thorne pointed out.

Striker's jaw tightened. This was no joke. And deep down he knew that he'd take the job; wouldn't trust anyone else to do it. For as bullheaded and stubborn as Randi McCafferty was, there was something about her, a spark in her brown eyes that seemed to touch him just under the skin, a bit of fire that scorched slightly. It had gotten his attention and hadn't let go.

Last night had been proof enough.

Thorne was agitated, worry evident in the lines of his face, his fingers jangling the keys in his pocket. His stare held Striker's. "Will you take the job, or are we going to have to find someone else?"

The thought of another man getting close to Randi soured Kurt's gut, but before he could respond, Slade finally spoke.

"No one else. We need someone we can trust."

"Amen," Matt agreed, before Slade nodded toward the window where a Jeep was plowing down the lane.

*Trust? Jesus!*

His teeth clenched so hard they ached.

Slade nodded toward the window where an SUV was steadily approaching. "Looks like Nicole's home."

The tension in Thorne's features softened a bit. Within minutes the front door burst open, and a blast of cold Montana air raced into the room. Dr. Nicole McCafferty, still shaking snow from her coat, crossed the entry as the rumble of tiny feet erupted upstairs and Thorne's two stepdaughters, four-year-old-twins, thundered down the stairs. Laughter and shouts added to the din.

"Mommy! Mommy!" Molly cried, while her shier sister, Mindy, beamed and threw herself into Nicole's waiting arms.

"Hey, how're my girls?" Nicole asked in greeting, scooping both twins into her arms and kissing them on the cheeks.

"You're coooooold!" Molly said.

Nicole laughed. "So I am."

Thorne, limping slightly from a recent accident, made his

way into the entry hall and kissed his wife soundly, the girls wriggling between them.

Striker turned away. Felt he was intruding on an intimate scene. It was the same uncomfortable sensation that had been with him from the get-go when Slade had contacted him about helping out the family, and Kurt had first set foot on the Flying M. It had been in October when Randi McCafferty's car had been forced off the road at Glacier Park. She had gone into premature labor and both she and her new baby had nearly died. She'd been in a coma for a while and when she had awoken she'd struggled with amnesia.

Or so she claimed.

Striker thought the loss of memory, though supported by Randi's doctor, was too convenient. He'd also found evidence that another vehicle had run Randi's rig down a steep hillside, where she'd plowed into a tree. She'd survived, though as she'd recovered and regained her memory, she would say nothing about the accident, or guess who might have been trying to kill her. She'd incriminate no one. Either she didn't know or wouldn't tell. The same was true about the father of her kid. She'd told no one who had sired little Joshua. Kurt scowled at the thought. He didn't want to think of anyone being intimate with Randi, though that was just plain stupid. He had no claim to her; wasn't even certain he liked her.

*Then you should have let it go last night...you saw her on the landing, watched her take care of her child, then waited until she'd put him to bed...*

In his mind's eye, Kurt remembered her sitting on the ledge, humming softly, her white nightgown clinging to her body as she cradled her baby and fed him. He'd been upstairs, looking down over the railing and moonlight had spilled over her shoulders, illuminating her like a madonna with child. The sight had been almost spiritual, but also sensual, and he'd slowly eased his way into the shadows and waited. Telling himself he just wanted to walk down the stairs unnoticed, one of the floorboards had creaked and Randi had looked up, seen him there on the upper landing, his hands over the railing.

"Come on, let's see what Juanita's got in the kitchen," Nicole was saying, bringing Kurt crashing back to the here and now. "Smells good."

"Cinn-da-mon!" the shier twin said while her sister rolled her eyes.

"Cinn-a-mon," Molly corrected.

"We'll find out, won't we?" Nicole shuffled the girls down the hallway toward the kitchen while Thorne returned to the living room.

The smile he'd reserved for his wife and family had faded and he was all business again. "So what's it gonna be, Striker? Are you in?"

"It's a helluva lot of money," Matt reminded him.

"Look, Striker, I'm counting on you." Slade gave up his position near the window. Lines of worry pinched the corners of his eyes. "Someone wants Randi dead. I told Thorne and Matt that if anyone could find out who it was, you could. So are you gonna prove me right or what?"

With only a little bit of guilt he slid the check into the battered leather of his wallet. There wasn't really any point in arguing. There hadn't been from the get-go. Striker could no more let Randi McCafferty take off with her kid and face her would-be killer alone than he could quit breathing.

He planned on nailing the son of a bitch.

Big-time.


"Great!" Randi hadn't gotten more than forty miles out of Grand Hope when her new Jeep started acting weird. The steering was off, and when she pulled to the side of the snow-covered road to survey the damage, she realized that her front left tire was low. And it hadn't been when she'd left. She'd passed a gas station less than a mile back, so she turned her vehicle around, only to discover that the station was closed. Permanently. The door was locked and rusted, a window cracked, the pumps dry.

So far her journey back to civilization wasn't going as planned—not that she'd had much of a plan to begin with. That was the problem. She'd intended to return to Seattle, of course, and soon, but last night...with Kurt...oh, hell. She'd gotten up this morning and decided she couldn't wait another minute.

All of her brothers were now married. She was, once again, the odd woman out, and she was the reason that they were all in danger. She had to do something about it.

*But you're kidding yourself, aren't you? The real reason you left so quickly has nothing to do with your brothers or the danger, and everything to do with Kurt Striker.*

She glanced in the rearview mirror, saw the pain in her eyes and let out her breath. She was no good at this, and had never wanted to play the martyr.

"Get on with it," she muttered. She'd just have to change the damn tire herself. Which should be no problem. She'd learned a lot about machinery growing up on the Flying M. A flat tire was a piece of cake. The good news was that she was off the road and relatively dry and protected from the wind under the overhang of the old garage.

With her baby asleep in his car seat, she pulled out the jack and spare, then got to work. Changing the tire wasn't hard, just tedious, and her gloves made working with the lug nuts a challenge. She found the problem with the tire: somewhere she'd picked up a long nail, which had created the slow leak.

It crossed her mind that maybe the flat wasn't an accident,

that perhaps the same creep who had forced her off the road at Glacier Park, then attempted to kill her again in the hospital, and later burned the stable might be back to his old tricks. She straightened, still holding the tire iron.

Bitterly cold, the wind swept down the roadway, blowing the snow and lifting her hair from her face. She felt a frisson of fear slide down her spine as she squinted, her gaze sweeping the harsh, barren landscape.

But she saw no one.

Heard nothing.

Decided she was just becoming paranoid.

Which was a really bad thought.

Huddled against the rain, the intruder slid a key into the lock of the dead bolt, then with surprising ease broke into Randi McCafferty's Lake Washington home.

The area was upscale, and the condo worth a fortune. Of course. Because the princess would have no less.

Inside, the unit was a little cluttered. Not too bad, but certainly not neat as a pin. And it had suffered from neglect in the past few months. Dust had settled on the surface of a small desk pushed into the corner, cobwebs floated from a high ceiling, and dust bunnies had collected in the corners. Three-month-old magazines were strewn over a couple of end tables and the meager contents of the refrigerator had spoiled weeks ago. Framed prints and pictures splashed color onto warm-toned walls, and an eclectic blend of modern and antique furniture was scattered around the blackened stones of a fireplace where the ashes were cold.

Randi McCafferty hadn't been home for a long, long time.

But she was on her way.

Noiselessly, the intruder stalked through the darkened rooms, down a short hallway to a large master suite with its sunken tub, walk-in closet and king-size bed. There was an-other bath, as well, and a nursery, not quite set up but ready for the next little McCafferty. The bastard.

Back in the living room there was a desk and upon it a pic-ture, taken years ago, of the three McCafferty brothers—tall, strapping, cocky, young men with smiles that could melt a woman's heart and tempers that had landed them in too many barroom brawls to count. In the snapshot they were astride horses. In front of the mounted men, in bare feet, cutoff jeans, a sleeveless shirt and ratty braids, was Randi. She was squint-ing hard, her head tilted, one hand over her eyes to shade them, that same arm obviously scraped. Twined in the fin-gers of her other hand she held the reins of all three horses, as if she'd known then that she would lead her brothers around for the rest of their lives.

The bitch.

Disturbed, the intruder looked away from the framed pho-tograph, quickly pushed the play button on the telephone an-swering machine and felt an instant of satisfaction at having the upper hand on the princess. But the feeling was fleeting. As cold as the ashes in the grate.

As the single message played, resounding through the vaulted room, it became evident that there was only one thing that would make things right.

Randi McCafferty had to pay.

And she had to pay with her life.

# Chapter 2

Less than two hours after his conversation with the McCafferty brothers, Striker was aboard a private plane headed due west. A friend who owned this prop job owed him a favor and Striker had called in his marker. He'd also taken the time to phone an associate who was already digging into Randi's past. Eric Brown was ex-military, and had spent some time with the FBI before recently going out on his own. While Striker was watching Randi, Brown would track down the truth like a bloodhound on the trail of a wounded buck. It was just a matter of time.

Staring out the window at the thick clouds, listening to the steady rumble of the engines, Striker thought about Randi McCafferty.

Beautiful. Smart. Sexy as hell.

Who would want her dead?

And why?

Because of the kid? Nah…that didn't wash. The book she'd been writing? Or something else, some other secret she'd kept from her brothers.

She was an intriguing, sharp-tongued woman with fire in her brown eyes and a lightning-quick sense of humor that kept even her three half brothers at bay. True, Thorne, Matt and Slade could have held a grudge. All three of them had ended up sharing half the ranch while she, John McCafferty's only daughter, had inherited the other half. Though some of the townspeople of Grand Hope thought differently, Striker knew that the brothers were clean, their motives pure. Hadn't they hired him for the express purpose of saving their half sister's lovely hide? No, they were out as suspects. They weren't trying to murder her.

Chewing on a toothpick, he frowned into the clouds that were visible through the window. Most murders were committed because of greed, jealousy or revenge. Sometimes a victim was killed because they posed a threat, had something over on the killer. Once in a while someone was murdered to cover up other crimes.

So why would someone want to kill Randi? Because of her inheritance? Because of her son? A love affair gone sour? Had she swindled someone out of something? Did she know too much? Unconnected motives rattled through his brain. He scratched the side of his face.

There were two mysteries surrounding Randi. The first was the paternity of her child, a closely guarded secret. The second was about a book she'd been writing around the time of the accident.

None of her brothers, nor anyone close to her, professed to know who had sired the baby, probably not even the father. Randi had been tight-lipped on the subject. Striker wondered if she was protecting the father or just didn't want him to know.

He thought it wouldn't be too hard to figure out who was little Joshua's daddy. Striker had already found out the kid's blood type from the hospital and he'd managed to get a few hairs from Joshua's head...just in case he needed a DNA match.

There were three men who had been close to Randi, close enough to be lovers, though he, as yet, had not substantiated which—if any—she had been intimate with. At that thought his gut clenched. He felt a jolt of jealousy. Ridiculous. He wouldn't allow himself to get emotionally involved with Randi McCafferty, not even after last night. She was his client, even though she didn't know it yet. And when she found out, he was certain the gates of hell would spring open and all sorts of demons would rise up. No, Randi McCafferty wouldn't take kindly to her brothers' safeguards for her.

He tapped his finger on the cold glass of the plane's window and wondered who had warmed Randi's bed and fathered her son.

Bile rose in his throat as he thought of the prime candidates.

Sam Donahue, the ex-rodeo rider, was at the top of the list. Kurt didn't trust the rugged cowboy who had collected more women than pairs of boots. Sam had always been a rogue, a man none of Randi's brothers could stomach, a jerk who had already left two ex-wives in his dusty wake.

Joe Paterno was a freelance photographer who sometimes worked for the *Seattle Clarion*. Joe was a playboy of the worst order, a love-'em-and-leave-'em type who'd been connected to women all over the planet, especially in the political hot spots he photographed. Joe would never be the kind to settle down with a wife and son.

Brodie Clanton, a shark of a Seattle lawyer who'd been born with a silver spoon firmly wedged between his teeth, was the grandson of Judge Nelson Clanton, one of Seattle's most prestigious lawmakers. Brodie Clanton looked upon life as if it owed him something, and spent most of his time defending rich clients.

Not exactly a sterling group to choose from.

What the hell had Randi been thinking? None of these guys was worth her looking at a second time. And yet she'd been linked to each of them. For a woman who wrote a column for singles, she had a lousy track record with men.

*And what about you? Where do you fit in?*

"Damn." Striker wouldn't think about that now. Wouldn't let last night cloud his judgment. Even if he found out who was the father of the baby, that was just a start. It only proved Randi had slept with the guy. It didn't mean that he was trying to kill her.

Anyone might be out to get Randi. A jealous coworker, someone she'd wronged, a nutcase who had a fixation on her, an old rival, any damn one. The motive for getting her out of the way could include greed or jealousy or fear…at this point no one knew. He shifted his toothpick from one side of his mouth to the other and listened as the engines changed speed and the little plane began its descent to a small airstrip south of Tacoma.

The fun was just about to begin.

Rain spat from the sky. Bounced on the hood of her new Jeep. Washed the hilly streets of Seattle from a leaden sky. Randi McCafferty punched the accelerator, took a corner too quickly and heard her tires protest over the sound of light jazz emanating from the speakers. It had been a hellish drive from Montana, the winter weather worse than she'd expected, her nerves on edge by the time she reached the city she'd made her home. A headache was building behind her eyes, reminding her that it hadn't been too many months since the accident that had nearly taken her life and robbed her of her memory for a while. She caught a glimpse of her reflection in the rear-view mirror—at least her hair was growing back. Her head had been shaved for the surgery and now her red-brown hair was nearly two inches long. For a second she longed to be back in Grand Hope with her half brothers.

She flipped on her blinker and switched lanes by rote, then eased to a stop at the next red light. Much as she wanted to, she couldn't hide out forever. It was time to take action. Reclaim her life. Which was here in Seattle, not at the Flying M Ranch in Montana with her three bossy half brothers.

And yet her heart twisted and she felt a moment's panic. She'd let herself become complacent in the safety of the ranch, with three strong brothers ensuring she and her infant son were secure.

No more.

*You did this, Randi. It's your fault your family is in danger. And now you've compounded the problem with Kurt Striker. What's wrong with you? Last night…remember last night? You caught him watching you on the ledge, knew that he'd been staring, had felt the heat between the two of you for weeks, and what did you do? Did you pull on your robe and duck into your bedroom and lock the door like a sane woman? Oh, no. You put your baby down in his crib and then you followed Striker, caught up with him and—*

A horn blasted from behind her and she realized the light had turned green. Gritting her teeth, she drove like a madwoman. Pushed the wayward, erotic thoughts of Kurt Striker to the back of her mind for the time being. She had more important issues to deal with.

At least her son was safe. If only for the time being. She missed him horridly already and she'd just dropped him off at a spot where no one could find him. It was only until she did what she had to do. Hiding Joshua was best. For her. For him. For a while. A short while, she reminded herself. Already attempts had been made upon her life and upon the lives of those closest to her, she couldn't take a chance with her baby.

As she braked for a red light, she stared through the raindrops zigzagging down the windshield, but in her mind's eye she saw her infant son with his inquisitive blue eyes, shock of reddish-blond hair and rosy cheeks. She imagined his soft little giggles. So innocent. So trusting.

Her heart tore and she blinked back a sudden spate of hot tears that burned her eyelids and threatened to fall. She didn't have time for any sentimentality. Not now.

The light changed. She eased into the traffic heading toward Lake Washington, weaving her way through the red taillights, checking her rearview mirror, assuring herself she wasn't being followed.

*You really are paranoid,* her mind taunted as she found the turnoff to her condominium and the cold January wind buffeted the trees surrounding the short lane. But then she had a right to be. She pulled into her parking spot and cranked off the ignition of her SUV. The vehicle was new, a replacement for her crumpled Jeep that had been forced off the road in Glacier Park a couple of months back. The culprit who'd tried to kill her had gotten away with his crime.

*But not for long,* she told herself as she swung out of the vehicle and grabbed her bag from the backseat. She had work to do; serious work. She glanced over her shoulder one last time. No shadowy figure appeared to be following her, no footsteps echoed behind her as she dashed around the puddles collecting on the asphalt path leading to her front door.

*Get a grip.* She climbed the two steps, juggled her bag and purse on the porch, inserted her key and shoved hard on the door with her shoulder.

Inside, the rooms smelled musty and unused. A dead fern

in the foyer was shedding dry fronds all over the hardwood floor. Dust covered the windowsill.

It sure didn't feel like home. Not anymore. But then nowhere did without her son. She kicked the door behind her and took two steps into the living room, then, seeing a shadow move on the couch, stopped dead in her tracks.

Adrenaline spurted through her bloodstream.

Goose bumps rose on the back of her arms.

*Oh, God,* she thought wildly, her mouth dry as a desert.

The killer was waiting for her.

# Chapter 3

"Well, well, well," he drawled slowly. "Look who's finally come home."

In an instant Randi recognized his voice.

Bastard.

His hand reached to the table lamp. As he snapped on the lights, she found herself staring into the intense, suspicious gaze of Kurt Striker, the private investigator her brothers had seen fit to hire.

She instantly bristled. Fear gave way to outrage. "What the hell are you doing here?"

"Waitin'."

"For?"

"You."

Damn, his drawl was irritating. So was the superior, know-it-all attitude that emanated from him as he lounged on her chenille couch, the fingers of one big hand wrapped possessively around a long-necked bottle of beer. He appeared as out of place in his jeans, cowboy boots and denim jacket as a cougar at a pedigreed-cat show.

"Why?" she demanded as she dropped her bag and purse on a parson's table in the entry. She didn't step into the living room; didn't want to get too close to this man. He bothered her. Big-time. Had from the first time she'd laid eyes on him when she'd still been recuperating from the accident.

Striker was a hardheaded, square-jawed type who looked like Hollywood's version of a rogue cop. His hair, blond streaked, was unruly and fell over his eyes, and he seemed to have avoided getting close to a razor for several days. Deep-set, intelligent eyes, poised over chiseled cheeks, were guarded by thick eyebrows and straight lashes. He wore faded jeans, a tattered Levi's jacket and an attitude that wouldn't quit.

Resting on the small of his back, sprawled on her couch, he raked his gaze up her body one slow inch at a time.

"I asked you a question."

"I'm trying to save your neck."

"You're trespassing."

"So call the cops."

"Enough with the attitude." She walked to the windows, snapped open the blinds. Through the wet glass she caught a glimpse of the lake, choppy, steel-colored water sporting whitecaps and fog too dense to see the opposite shore. Folding her arms over her chest, she turned and faced Striker again.

He smiled then. A dazzling, sexy grin offset by the mockery in his green eyes. It damn near took her breath away and for a splintered second she thought of the hours they'd spent together, the touch of his skin, the feel of his hands...oh, God. If he wasn't such a pain in the butt, he might be considered handsome. Interesting. Sexy. Long legs shoved into cowboy boots, shoulders wide enough to stretch the seams of his jacket, flat belly... Yeah, all the pieces fit into a hunky package. If a woman was looking for a man. Randi wasn't. She'd learned her lesson. Last night was just a slip. It wouldn't happen again.

Couldn't.

"You know," he said, "I was just thinkin' the same thing. Let's both shove the attitudes back where they came from and get to work."

"To work?" she asked, rankled. She needed him out of her condo and fast. He had a way of destroying her equilibrium, of setting her teeth on edge.

"That's right. Cut the bull and get down to business."

"I don't think we have any business."

His eyes held hers for a fraction of a second and she knew in that splintered instant that he was remembering last night as clearly as she. He cleared his throat. "Randi, I think we should discuss what happened—"

"Last night?" she asked. "Not now, okay? Maybe not ever. Let's just forget it."

"Can you?"

"I don't know, but I'm sure as hell going to try."

He silently called her a liar.

"Okay, if this is the way you want to play it."

"I told you we don't have any business."

"Sure we do. You can start by telling me who's the father of your baby."

*Never, buddy. Not a chance.* "I don't think that's relevant."

"Like hell, Randi." He was on his feet in an instant, across the hardwood floor and glaring down his crooked nose at her. "There have been two attempts on your life. One was the accident, and I use the term loosely, up in Glacier Park, when your car was forced off the road. The other when someone tried to do you in at the hospital. You remember those two little incidents, don't you?"

She swallowed hard. Didn't answer.

"And let's not forget the fire in the stable at the ranch. Arson, Randi. Remember? It nearly killed your brothers." Her heart squeezed at the painful memory. To her surprise he grabbed her, strong hands curling around her upper arms and gripping tightly through her jacket. "Do you really want to take any more chances with your life? With your brothers'? With your kid's? Little J.R. nearly died from an infection in the hospital after the accident, didn't he? You went into labor early in the middle of no-goddamn-where, and by the time some Good Samaritan saw you and called for an ambulance, your baby almost didn't make it."

She fought the urge to break down. Wished to heaven that he'd quit touching her. He was too close, his angry breath whispering over her face, the raw, sexual energy of him seeping through her clothes.

"Now, I'm not moving," he vowed, "not one bloody inch, until you and I get a few things straight. I'm in for the long haul and I'll stay here all night if I have to. All week. All year."

Her stupid heart pounded, and though she tried to pull away he wouldn't allow it. The manacles surrounding her arms clamped even more tightly.

"Let's start with one important question, shall we?"

He didn't have to ask. She knew what was coming and braced herself.

"Tell me, Randi, right now. No more ducking the issue. Who the devil is J.R.'s father?"

Oh, God, he was too close. "Let go of me," she said, refusing to give in. "And get the hell out of my house."

"No way."

"I'll call the police."

"Be my guest," he encouraged, hitching his chin toward the phone she hadn't used in months. It sat collecting dust on the small desk she'd crammed into one corner of the living room. "Why don't you tell them everything that's happened to you and I'll explain what I'm doing here."

"You weren't invited."

"Your brothers are concerned."

"They can't control me."

He lifted a skeptical eyebrow. "No? They might disagree."

"Big deal," she said, tossing her head and pretending to be tough. The truth was that she loved all of her older half brothers, all three of them, but she couldn't have them poking around in her life. Nor did she want anything to do with Kurt Striker. He was just too damn male for his own good. Or her own. He'd proved that much last night. "Listen, Striker, this is my life. I can handle it. Now, if you'd be so kind as to take your hands off me," she said, sarcasm dripping from the pleasantry, "I have a lot to do."

He stared at her long and hard, those sharp green eyes seeming to penetrate her own. Then he lifted a shoulder and released her. "I can wait."

"Elsewhere."

His smile was pure devilment. "Is that a hint?" he drawled, and again her heart began to trip-hammer. Damn the man.

"A broad one. Take a hike."

"Only if you show me the city."

"What?"

"I'm new in town. Humor me."

"You mean so you can keep an eye on me."

Curse the sexy smile that crawled across his jaw. "That, too."

"Forget it. I've got a million things to do," she said, flipping up a hand to indicate the telephone where no light blinked on her answering machine. "That's odd," she muttered then glanced back at Striker, whom she was beginning to believe was the embodiment of Lucifer. "Wait a minute. You listened to my messages?" she demanded, fury spiking up her spine.

"No, I actually didn't."

She made her way to the desk and pushed the play button on the recorder. "That's odd," she said as she recognized Sarah Peeples's voice.

"Hey, when are you coming back to work?" Sarah asked. "It's soooo boooring with all these A-type males." She giggled. "Well, maybe not that boring, but I miss ya. Give me a call and kiss Joshua for me." The phone clicked as Sarah hung up.

Randi bit her lower lip. Her mind was spinning as she jabbed a finger at the recorder. "You didn't listen to this?"

"No."

"Then who did?"

"Not you?" he asked and his eyes narrowed.

"No, not me." Her skin crawled. If Striker hadn't listened to her messages, then…who had? Her headache pounded. Maybe she was jumping at shadows. She was worried about her baby, exasperated with the man in her apartment and just plain tired from the long drive and the few hours' sleep she'd had in the past forty-eight hours. That was it, her nerves were just strung tight. Her brothers hiring this sexy, roughshod P.I. only made things worse. She rubbed her temple and tried to think clearly. "Look, Striker, you can't barge in here, help yourself to a beer, then sit back and make yourself at home…"

His expression reminded her that he'd done just that.

"So far," she went on, "I think you've committed half a dozen crimes. Breaking and entering, burglary, trespassing and who knows what else. The police would have a field day."

"So where's your son?" he asked, refusing to be sidetracked. "J.R. Where is he?"

She'd known that was coming. "I call him Joshua."

"Okay, where's Josh?"

"Somewhere safe."

"There is nowhere that's safe."

Her insides crumbled. "You're wrong."

"So you *are* afraid that someone is after you."

"I'm a mother. I'm not taking any chances with him."

"Only with yourself."

"Let's not get into this." She pressed a button and the answering machine rewound.

"Is he with your cousin Nora?"

Her muscles tensed. How had he learned about Nora, on her mother's side? Her brothers had never met Nora.

"Or maybe Aunt Bonita, your mother's stepsister?"

God, he'd done his homework. Her head thundered, her palms suddenly sweaty. "It's none of your business, Striker."

"How about your friend Sharon?" He folded his arms over his chest. "That's where I'm putting my money."

She froze. How could he have guessed that she would leave her precious child with Sharon Okano? She and Sharon hadn't seen each other in nearly nine months, and yet Striker had figured it out.

"You wouldn't take a chance on a relative, or you would have left him in Montana, and your coworkers are out because they might slip up, so it had to be someone you trusted, but not obvious enough that it would be easy to figure it out."

Her heart constricted.

He reached forward and touched her shoulder. She recoiled as if burned.

"If I can guess where you hid him, so can the guy who's after you."

"How did you find Sharon?" she asked. "I'm not buying the 'lucky guess' theory."

Kurt walked to the coffee table and picked up his beer. "It wasn't rocket science, Randi."

"But—"

"Even cell phones have records."

"You went through my mail to find my phone bill? Isn't that a federal offense, or don't you care about that?" she asked, then her eyes swept the desk and she realized that he couldn't have sorted through the junk mail and correspondence that was hers, as she'd had it held at the post office ages ago.

"It doesn't matter how I got the information," he said. "What's important is that you and your son aren't safe. Your brothers hired me to protect you, and like it or not, that's exactly what I'm going to do." He drained his beer in one long swallow. "Fight me all you want, Randi, but I intend to stick to you like glue. You can call your brothers and complain and they won't budge. You can run away, but I'll catch you so quick it'll make your head spin. You can call the cops and we'll get to the bottom of this here and now. That's just the way it is. So, you can make it easy for everyone and tell me what the hell's going on or you can be difficult and we'll go at it real slow." He set his bottle on one end of the coffee table and as he straightened, his eyes held hers with deadly intensity. "Either way."

"Get out."

"If that's the way you want it. But I'll be back."

So angry she was shaking, she repeated, "Get the hell out."

"You've got one hour to think about it," he advised her as he made his way to the door. "One hour. Then I'll be back. And if we have to, we'll do this the hard way. It's your choice, Randi, but the way I see it, you're damn near out of options."

He walked outside and the door shut behind him. Randi threw the bolt, swore under her breath and fought the urge to crumple into a heap. She forced starch into her spine. Nothing was ever accomplished by falling into a million pieces. It was hard to admit it, but Kurt Striker was right about one thing;

she didn't have many choices. Well, that was tough. She wasn't going to be railroaded into making a wrong one.

Too much was at stake.

# Chapter 4

Kurt slid behind the wheel of his rental, a bronze king-cab pickup. The windows were a little fogged, so he cracked one and turned on the defrost to stare through the rivulets of rain sliding down the windshield. He'd give her an hour to sort things out, the same hour he'd give himself to cool off. There was something about the woman that got under his skin and put him on edge.

From the first moment he'd seen her at the Flying M, he'd sensed it—that underlying tension between them, an unacknowledged current that simmered whenever they were in the same room. It was stupid, really. He wasn't one to fall victim to a woman's charms, especially not a spoiled brat of a woman who had grown up as the apple of her father's eye, a rich girl who'd had everything handed to her.

Oh, she was pretty enough. At least she was now that the bruises had disappeared and her hair was growing back. In fact,

she was a knockout. Pure and simple. Despite her recent pregnancy, her body was slim, her breasts large enough to make
a man notice, her hips round and tight. With her red-brown
hair, pointed little chin, pouty lips and wide brown eyes, she
didn't need much makeup. Her mind was quick, her tongue
rapier sharp and she'd made it more than clear that she wanted
him to leave her alone. Which would be best for everyone involved, he knew, but there was just something about her that
kept drawing him in and firing his blood.

*Forget it. She's your client.*

Not technically. She hadn't hired him.

But her brothers had.

*You have to keep this relationship professional.*

*Relationship? What relationship? Hell, she can't stand to be in
the same room with me.*

*Oh, yeah, right. Like you haven't been through this before. And
like last night never happened.*

She'd put Joshua in his room and then after Kurt had
sneaked down the stairway, she'd followed him and found
him in the darkened living room where only embers from a
dying fire gave off any illumination.

He'd already poured himself a drink and was sipping it quietly while staring through the icy window to the blackened
remains of the stable.

"You were watching me," she'd accused, and he'd nodded,
not turning around. "Why?"

"I didn't mean to."

"Bull!"

So she wasn't going to let him off the hook. So be it. He
took a sip of his drink before facing her.

"What the hell were you doing upstairs?"

"I thought I heard someone, so I checked."

"You did. It was me. This house is full of people, you

know." She was so angry, he could feel her heat, noticed that she hadn't bothered buttoning her nightgown, acted as if she was completely unaware that her breasts were visible.

"Do you want me to explain or not?"

"Yeah. Try." She crossed her arms under her breasts, involuntarily lifting them, causing the cleft between them to deepen. Kurt kept his gaze locked with hers.

"As I said, I heard something. Footsteps. I just walked upstairs and down the hall. By the time I started for the stairs you were there."

"And the rest, as they say, is history." She arched an eyebrow and her lips were pursed hard together. "Get a good look?"

"Good enough."

"Like what you saw?"

He couldn't help himself. One side of his mouth lifted. "It was all right."

"What?"

"I've seen better."

"Oh, for the love of St. Jude!" she sputtered, and even in the poor light, he noticed a flush stain her cheeks.

"What did you expect, Randi? You caught me looking, okay? I didn't plan it, but there you were and I was…caught. I guess I could have cleared my throat and walked down the stairs, but I was a little…surprised." His smile fell away and he took another long swallow. "We're both adults, let's forget it."

"Easy for you to say."

"Not that easy."

Her eyes narrowed up at him. "What's that supposed to mean?"

"You're pretty unforgettable."

"Yeah, right." She ran her fingers through her hair and her nightgown shifted, allowing him even more of a view of her breasts and abdomen. As if finally feeling the breeze, she sucked in her breath and looked down to see her breasts. "Oh, wonderful." She fumbled with the buttons. "Here I am ranting and raving and putting on a show and…"

"It's all right," he said. "I lied before. I've never seen better."

She shook her head and laughed. "This is ridiculous."

"Can I buy you a drink?"

"Of my dad's liquor? I don't think so. I…I might do something I'll regret."

"You think?"

She let out a breath, glanced him up and down and nodded. "Yeah, I think."

He should have stopped himself right then while he still had a chance of taking control of the situation, but he didn't and tossed back his drink. "Maybe regrets are too highly overrated," he said, dropping his glass onto a chair and closing the distance between them. He noticed her pulse fluttering on the smooth skin of her throat, knew that she was as scared as he was.

But it had been a long time since he'd kissed a woman and he'd been thinking about how it would feel to kiss Randi McCafferty for weeks. Last night, he'd found out. He'd wrapped his arms around her and as a gasp slipped from between her lips, he'd slanted his mouth over hers and felt his blood heat. Her arms had instinctively climbed to his shoulders and her body had fitted tight against him.

Warning bells had clanged in his mind, but he'd ignored them as his tongue had slipped between her teeth and his erection had pressed hard against his fly. She was warm and tasted of lingering coffee. His fingers splayed across her back and as she moaned against him, he slowly started inching her nightgown upward, bunching the soft flannel in his fingers as her hemline climbed up her calves and thighs. It seemed the most natural thing in the world to use his weight to carry them both to the rug in front of the dying fire…

Now, as he sat in his pickup with the rain beating against his windshield, Striker scowled at the thought of what he'd done. He'd known better than to kiss her, had sensed it wouldn't stop there. He didn't need the complications of a woman.

He hazarded a glance at the third finger of his left hand where he could still see the deep impression a ring had made as it had cut into his skin. The muscles in the back of his neck tightened and a few dark thoughts skated through his mind. Thoughts of another woman…another beautiful woman and a little girl…

Angry with the turn of his thoughts, he forced his gaze to Randi's condominium. This particular grouping of units rested on a hillside overlooking Lake Washington. He'd parked across the street where he had a clear view of her front door, the only way in or out of the condo, unless she decided to sneak out a window. Even then, he'd see her Jeep leaving. Unless she was traveling on foot, he'd be able to follow her.

He glanced at his watch. She had forty-seven minutes to cool off and get herself together. And so did he. Leaning across the seat, he grabbed his battered briefcase and reached inside where he kept an accordion folder on the McCafferty case. With one eye on the condominium, he riffled through the pages of notes, pictures and columns he'd clipped out of the *Seattle Clarion,* columns with a byline of Randi McCafferty and accompanied by a smiling picture of the author.

"Solo," by Randi McCafferty.

Hers was an advice column for singles, from the confirmed bachelors to the newly divorced, the recently widowed or anyone else who wrote in, claimed not to be married and asked for her opinion. Striker reread a few of his favorites. In one, she advised a woman suffering from abuse to leave the relationship

immediately and file charges. In another she told an overly protective single mother to give her teenage daughter "breathing
space" while keeping in touch. In still another, she suggested
a widower join a grief-support group and take up ballroom
dancing, something he and his wife had always wanted to do.
Her columns were often empathetic, but sometimes caustic.
She told one woman who couldn't decide between two men
and was lying to them both to "grow up," while she advised
another young single to "quit whining" about his new girlfriend, who sometimes parked in "his" spot while staying over.
Within each bit of advice, Randi often added a little humor.
It was no wonder the column had been syndicated and picked
up in other markets.

Yet there were rumors of trouble at the *Clarion*. Randi Mc-
Cafferty and her editor, Bill Withers, were supposedly feuding.
Striker hadn't figured out why. Yet. But he would. Randi had
also written some articles for magazines under the name of
R. J. McKay. Then there was her unfinished tell-all book on
the rodeo circuit, one she wouldn't talk much about. A lot
going on with Ms. McCafferty. Yep, he thought, leaning back
and staring at the front door of her place, she was an interesting woman, and one definitely off-limits.

Well, hell, weren't they all? He scowled through the raindrops zigzagging down his windshield and his thoughts started
to wend into that forbidden territory of his past, to a time that
now seemed eons ago, before he'd become jaded. Before he'd
lost his faith in women. In marriage. In life. A time he didn't
want to think about. Not now. Not ever.

"He's okay?" Randi said into her cell phone. Her hands
were sweaty, her mind pounding with fear, and it was all she
could do to try to calm her rising sense of panic. Despite her
bravado and in-your-face attitude with Striker, she was shaky.

Nervous. His warnings putting her on edge, and now, as she held the cell phone to her ear and peered through the blinds to the parking lot where Kurt Striker's pickup was parked, her heart was knocking.

"You dropped him off less than an hour ago," Sharon assured her. "Joshua's just fine. I fed him, changed him and put him down for a nap. Right now he's sleeping like a...well, a baby."

Randi let out her breath, ran a shaking hand over her lip. "Good."

"You've got to relax. I know you're a new mother and all, but believe me, whatever you're caught up in, stressing out isn't going to help anyone. Not you, not the baby. So take a chill pill."

"I wish," Randi said, only slightly relieved.

"Do it... Take your own advice. You're always telling people in your column to take a step back, a deep breath and reevaluate the situation. You still belong to the gym, don't you? Take yoga or tae kwon do or kickboxing."

"You think that would do it?"

"Wouldn't hurt."

"Just as long as I know Joshua's safe."

"And sound. Promise." Sharon sighed. "I know you don't want to hear this, but you might consider going out. You know, with a man."

"I don't think so."

"Just because you had a bad experience with one doesn't mean they're all jerks."

"I had a bad experience with more than one."

"Well...it wouldn't kill you to give romance a chance."

"I'm not so sure. When Cupid pulls back his bow and aims at me, I swear his arrows are poisoned."

"That's not what you tell the people who write you."

"With them, I can be objective." She was staring at Striker's truck, which hadn't moved. The man was behind the wheel. She saw movement, but she couldn't see his facial features, could only feel him staring at her house, sizing it up, just as he'd done with her. "Look, I'll be over tomorrow, but if you need to reach me for anything, call me on my cell."

"Will do. Now, quit worrying."

*Fat chance,* Randi thought as she hung up. Ever since she'd given birth she'd done nothing more than worry. She was worse than her half brothers and that was pretty bad. Thorne was the oldest and definitely type A. But he'd recently married Nicole and settled down with her and her twin girls. Randi smiled at the thought of Mindy and Molly, two dynamic four-year-olds who looked identical but were as different as night and day. Then there was Matt, ex-rodeo rider and serious. Had his own place in Idaho until he'd fallen in love with Kelly, who was now his wife. And then there was Slade. He was a rebel, hadn't grown up worrying about anything. But all of a sudden he'd made it his personal mission to "take care" of his younger, unmarried sister and her child.

A few months ago Randi would have scoffed at her brothers' concerns. But that had been before the accident. She remembered little of it, thank God, but now she had to figure out who was trying to harm her. She could accept Striker's help, she supposed, but was afraid that if she did, if she confided in anyone, she would only be jeopardizing her baby further and that was a chance she wasn't about to take. Regardless of her brothers' concerns.

Frowning, she remembered Matt and Kelly's wedding and the reception afterward. There had been dancing and laughter despite the cold Montana winter, despite the charred remains of the stable, a reminder of the danger she'd brought upon her family. Kelly had been radiant in her sparkling dress, Matt dashing in a black tuxedo, even Slade—who'd been injured in the fire—had forgone his crutches to dance with Jamie Parsons before whisking her away to elope on that snow-covered night. Randi had dressed her son in a tiny tuxedo and held him close, silently vowing to take the danger away from her brothers, to search out the truth herself.

Two days later when a breathless Slade and Jamie had returned as husband and wife, Randi had announced she was leaving.

"Are you out of your ever-lovin' mind?" Matt had demanded. He'd slapped his hat against his thigh and his breath had steamed from his lungs as all four of John Randall McCafferty's children had stood near the burned-out shell of the stable.

"This is beyond insanity." Thorne had glared down at her, as if he could use the same tactics that worked in a boardroom to convince her to stay. "You can't leave."

"Watch me," she'd baited, meeting his harsh gaze with one of her own.

Even Slade, the rebel and her staunchest ally, had turned against her. His crutches buried beyond their rubber tips in a drift of snow at the fence line, he'd said, "Don't do it, Randi. Keep J.R. here with us. Where we can help you."

"This is something I have to do," she'd insisted, and caught a glimpse of Striker, forever lurking in the shadows, always watching her. "I can't stay here. It's unsafe. How many accidents have happened here? Really, it's best if I leave." All of her brothers had argued with her, but Striker had remained silent, not arguing, just taking it all in.

Until last night. And then all hell had broken loose.

So she'd left and he'd followed her to Seattle. Now she realized she'd have one helluva time getting rid of him. It galled her that her brothers had hired him.

"What makes you think you'll be safer in Seattle than Grand Hope?" Thorne had asked as she'd packed her bags in the pine-walled room she'd grown up in. "You're still not healed completely from the accident. If you stayed here, we could all look after you. And little J.R, er, Joshua, would have Molly and Mindy to play with when he got a little bigger."

Randi's heart was torn. She'd eyed her bright-eyed nieces, Molly bold and impudent, Mindy hiding behind Thorne's pant leg, and known that she couldn't stay. She had things to do; a story to write. And she knew that if she stayed any longer, she'd only get more tangled up with Striker.

"I'll be all right," she'd insisted, zipping up her bag and gathering her baby into her arms. "I wouldn't do anything to put Joshua in danger." As she'd clambered down the stairs, she'd heard the twins asking where she was going and had spied their housekeeper, Juanita, making the sign of the cross over her ample bosom and whispering a prayer in Spanish. As if she would haul her own child into the maw of danger. But they didn't understand that in order for everyone to be safe, she had to get back to her old life and figure out why someone was trying to harm her.

*And Joshua. Don't forget your precious son. Whoever it is means business and is desperate.* She noted that Striker was still seated in his truck. Waiting. Damn the man. Quickly she closed the blinds, then took a final glance around the small nursery. Hardwood floors that were dusty, a cradle stuck in a corner, a bookcase that was still in its box as "some assembly" was required and she hadn't had time.

*Because you were in the hospital.*
*Because you nearly died.*
*Because someone is determined to kill you.*
*Maybe, just maybe, your brothers have a point.*
*Maybe you should trust Kurt Striker.*

Again she thought of the night before. Trust him? Trust herself?

What other choice did she have?

Much as she hated to admit it, he was right. If Kurt could figure out where she'd hidden Joshua, then the would-be killer, whoever he was, could, as well. Her insides knotted. Why would anyone want to harm her innocent baby? Why?

*It's not about Joshua, Randi. It's about you. Someone wants you dead. As long as the baby isn't with you, he's safe.*

She clung to that notion and set about getting her life in order again. She made herself a cup of instant coffee and dialed the office. Her editor was out, but she left a message on his voice mail, checked her own email, then quickly un-packed and changed into a clean sweater, slacks and boots. She wound a scarf around her neck and finger combed her short hair, looking into the hall mirror and cringing. She'd lost weight in the past five months, indeed she now weighed less than before she'd gotten pregnant, and she was having trou-ble getting used to the length of her hair. She'd always worn it long, but her head had been shaved before one of her life-saving surgeries to alleviate the swelling in her brain and the resulting grow-out was difficult to adjust to though she'd had it shaped before leaving Montana. Instead, she went into the bathroom, found an old tube of gel and ran some of the goop through her hair. The result was kind of a finger-in-the-light-socket look, but was the best she could do. She was just rinsing her hands when her doorbell buzzed loudly several times, an-nouncing a visitor. She didn't have to be told who was ringing the bell. One quick look at her watch showed her that it had been one hour and five minutes since she'd last faced Striker. Apparently the man was prompt.

And couldn't take a hint.

"Great," she muttered, wiping her hands on a towel and discarding it into an open hamper before hurrying to the front door. What she didn't need was anyone dogging her, bothering her and generally getting in the way. She was a private person by nature and opposed anyone nosing into her business, no matter what his reasons. Reining in her temper, she yanked open the door. Sure as shootin', Kurt Striker, all six feet two inches of pure male determination, was standing on her doorstep. His light brown hair had darkened from the raindrops clinging to it, and his green eyes were hard. Wearing an aging bomber jacket and even older jeans, he was sexy as hell and, from the looks of him, not any happier at being on her stoop than she was to find him there.

"What's with ringing the bell?" she asked, deciding not to mask her irritation. "I thought you had your own key, or a pick, or something. Compliments of my brothers."

"They're only looking out for you."

"They should mind their own business."

"And for your kid."

"I know." She'd already stepped away from the door and into the living room. Striker was on her heels. She heard the door slam behind him, the lock engage and the sound of his boots ringing on her hardwood floors.

"Look, Randi," he said as she stopped at the closet and found her raincoat. "If I can break in, then—"

"Yeah, yeah, I'm way ahead of you." She slid her arms through the sleeves and glanced up at him. "I'll change the locks, put on a dead bolt, okay?"

"Along with putting in an alarm system and buying a guard dog."

"Hey—I've got a baby. Remember?" She walked to the couch, found her purse and grabbed it. Now...the computer. Quickly she tucked her laptop into its case. "I don't think an attack dog would be a good idea."

"Not an attack dog—a guard dog. There's a big difference."

"If you say so. Now, if you'll excuse me, I've got to go to the office." She anticipated what he was about to say. "Look, it wouldn't be a good idea to follow me, you know? I'm already in enough hot water with my boss as it is." She didn't wait for him to answer, just walked back to the door. "So, if you'll excuse me—" She opened the door again in an unspoken invitation.

His lips twisted into a poor imitation of a smile. "You're not going to get rid of me that easily."

"Why? Because of the money?" she asked, surprised that the mention of it bothered her, cut into her soul. "That's what this is all about, isn't it? My brothers have paid you to watch over me, right? You're supposed to be...oh, hell...not my bodyguard. Tell me Thorne and Matt and Slade aren't so archaic, so controlling, so damn stupid as to think I need a personal bodyguard... Oh, God, that's it, isn't it?" She would have laughed if she hadn't been so furious. "This has got to end. I need privacy. I need space. I need—"

His hand snaked out, and fast as lightning, he grabbed her wrist, his fingers a quick, hard manacle. "What you need is to be less selfish," he finished for her. He was so close that she felt his hot, angry breath wafting across her face. "We've been through this before. Quit thinking about your damn independence and consider your kid's safety. Along with your own." He dropped her arm as suddenly as he'd picked it up. "Let's go. I won't get in the way."

The smile he cast over his shoulder was wicked enough to take her breath away. "Promise."

# Chapter 5

"Don't even think about riding with me," she warned, flipping the hood of her jacket over her hair as she dashed toward her Jeep. The rain had softened to a thick drizzle, a kind of mist that made visibility next to nil. It was early evening, the sky dark with heavy clouds.

"It would make things a helluva lot easier."

Obviously, Striker wasn't taking a hint. Collar turned up, he kept with her as she reached the car.

"For whom?" She shot him a look and clicked on her keyless remote. The Jeep beeped and its interior lights flicked on.

"Both of us."

"I don't think so." She climbed into her car and immediately locked her doors. He didn't move. Just stood by the Jeep. As if she would change her mind. She switched on the ignition as she tossed off her hood. Then, leaving Striker standing in the rain, she backed out of her parking spot, threw the Jeep into

Drive and cruised out of the lot. In the rearview mirror, she caught a glimpse of him running toward his truck, but not before she managed to merge into the traffic heading toward the heart of the city. She couldn't help but glance in her mirrors, checking to see if Striker had followed.

Not that she doubted it for a minute. But she didn't see his truck and reminded herself to pay attention to traffic and the red taillights glowing through the rain. She couldn't let her mind wander to the man, not even if she had acted like a fool last night.

She'd let him kiss her, let him slide her nightgown off her body, felt his lips, hot and hard, against the hollow of her throat and the slope of her shoulder. She shouldn't have done it, known it was a mistake, but her body had been a traitor and as his rough fingers had scaled her ribs and his beard-rough face had rubbed her skin, she'd let herself go, kissed him feverishly.

She'd been surprised at how much she'd wanted him, how passionately she'd kissed him, scraped off his clothes, ran her own anxious fingers down his hard, sinewy shoulders to catch in his thick chest hair.

The fire had hissed quietly, red embers glowing, illuminating the room to a warm orange. Her breathing had been furious, her heart rocketing, desire curling deep inside her. She'd wanted him to touch her, shivered when his tongue brushed her nipples, bitten her bottom lip as his hot breath had caressed her abdomen and legs. She'd opened to him easily as his hands had explored and touched. Her mind had spun in utter abandon and she'd wanted him… Oh, God, she'd wanted him as she'd never wanted another man.

Which had been foolish…but as he'd kissed her intimately and slid the length of his body against her, she'd lost all control. All her hard-fought willpower…

She nearly missed her exit as she thought about him and

the magic of the night, the lovemaking that had caused her to steal away early in the morning, before dawn. As if she'd been ashamed.

Now she wended her way off I-5 and down the steep streets leading to the waterfront. Through the tall, rain-drenched buildings was a view of the gray waters of Eliot Bay—restless and dark, mirroring her own uneasy feelings. She pulled the Jeep into the newspaper's parking lot, grabbed her laptop and briefcase and faced a life that she'd left months before.

The offices of the *Seattle Clarion* were housed on the fifth floor of what had originally been a hotel. The hundred-year-old building was faced in red brick and had been updated, renovated and cut into offices.

Inside, Randi punched the elevator button. She was alone, rainwater dripping from her jacket as the ancient car clamored upward. It stopped twice, picking up passengers before landing on the fifth floor, the doors opening to a short hallway and the etched-glass doors of the newspaper offices. Shawn-Tay, the receptionist, looked up and nearly came unglued when she recognized Randi.

"For the love of God, look at you!" she said, shooting to her feet and disconnecting her headset in one swift movement. Model tall, with bronze skin and dark eyes, she whipped around her desk and hugged Randi as if she'd never stop. "What the devil's got into you? Never callin' in. I was worried sick about you. Heard about the accident and…" She held Randi at arm's length. "Where's that baby of yours? How dare you come in here without him?" She cocked her head at an angle. "The hair works, but you've lost too much weight."

"I'll work on that."

"Now, about the baby?" Shawn-Tay's eyebrows elevated as the phone began to ring. "Oh, damn. I gotta get that, but you come back up here and tell me what the hell's been going on with you." She rounded the desk again and slid lithely into her chair. Holding the headset to one ear, she said, *"Seattle Clarion, how may I direct your call?"*

Randi slid past the reception desk and through the cubicles and desks of coworkers. Her niche was tucked into a corner, in the news section, behind a glass wall that separated the reporters from the salespeople. In the time she'd been gone, the walls had been painted, from a dirty off-white to different shades at every corner. Soft purple on one wall, sage on another, gold or orange on the next, all tied together by a bold carpet mingling all the colors. She passed by several reporters working on deadlines, though much of the staff had gone home for the day. A few night reporters were trickling in and the production crew still had hours to log in, but all in all, the office was quiet.

She slid into her space, surprised that it was just as she'd left it, that the small cubicle hadn't been appropriated by someone else, as it had been months since she'd been in Seattle or sat at her desk. She'd set up maternity leave with her boss late last summer and she'd created a cache of columns in anticipation of taking some time off to be with the baby and finishing the book she'd started. Between those new columns and culling some older ones, hardly vintage, but favorites, there had been enough material to keep "Solo" in the Living section twice a week, just like clockwork.

But it was time to tackle some new questions, and she spent the next two hours reading the mail that had stacked up in her in box and skimming the emails she hadn't collected in Montana. As she worked, she was vaguely aware of the soft piped-in music that sifted through the offices of the *Clarion,* and the chirp of cell phones in counterpoint to the ringing of landlines to the office. Conversation, muted and seemingly far away, barely teased her ears.

In the back of her mind she wondered if Kurt Striker had followed her. If, even now, he was making small talk with Shawn-Tay in the reception area. The thought brought a bit of a smile to her lips. Striker wasn't the type for small talk. No way. No how. For the most part tight-lipped, he was a sexy man whose past was murky, never discussed. She had the feeling that at one point in his life, he'd been attached to some kind of police department; she didn't know where or why he was no longer a law officer. But she'd find out. There were advantages to working for a newspaper and one of them was access to reams of information. If he wasn't forthcoming on his own, she'd do some digging. It wouldn't be the first time.

"Hey, Randi!" Sarah Peeples, movie reviewer for the *Clarion,* was hurrying toward Randi's desk. Sarah's column, "What's Reel," was published each Friday and was promoted as "hip and happening." A tall woman with oversize features, a wild mop of blond curls and a penchant for expensive boots and cheap jewelry, Sarah spent hours watching movies in theaters and on DVDs. She lived and breathed movies, celebrities and all things Hollywood. Today she was wearing a choker that looked as if it had been tailored for a rottweiler or a dominatrix, boots with pointed toes and silver studs, a gray scoop-necked sweater and a black skirt that opened in the front, slitted high enough to show off just a flash of thigh. "I was beginning to think I might never see you again."

"Can't keep a good woman down," Randi quipped.

"Amen. Where the hell have you been?"

"Montana with my brothers."

"The hair is new."

"Necessity rather than fashion."

"But it works for you. Short and sassy." Sarah was bobbing her head up and down as if agreeing with herself. "And you look great. How's the baby?"

"Perfect."

"And when will I get to meet him?"

"Soon," Randi hedged. The less she spoke about Joshua, the better. "How're things around here?"

Sarah rolled her eyes as she rested a hip on Randi's desk. "Same old, same old. I've been bustin' my butt...well, if you can call it that, rereviewing all the movies that are Oscar contenders."

"Sounds exhausting," Randi drawled.

"Okay, so it's not digging ditches, I know, but it's work."

"Has anything strange been going on around here?" Randi asked.

"What do you mean? Everyone who works here is slightly off, right?"

"I guess you're right."

Sarah picked up a glass paperweight and fiddled with it. "Now, when are you going to bring the baby into the office and show him off?" Sarah's grin was wide, her interest sincere. She'd been married three years and desperately wanted a baby. Her husband was holding out for the big promotion that would make a child affordable. Randi figured it might never come.

"When things have calmed down." She considered confiding in Sarah, but thought better of it. "He and I need to get settled in."

"Mmm. Then how about pictures?"

"I've got a ton of 'em back at the condo. Still packed. I'll bring them next time, I promise," she said, then leaned back in her chair. "So fill me in. What's going on around here?"

Sarah was only too glad to oblige. She offered up everything from office politics, to management changes, to out-and-out gossip. In return, she wanted to know every detail of Randi's life in Montana, starting with the accident. Finally, she said, "Paterno's back in town."

Randi felt the muscles in her back grow taut. "Is he?" Forty-five, twice divorced with a hound-dog face, thick hair beginning to gray and a razor-sharp sense of humor, the freelance photographer had asked Randi out a few years back and they'd dated for a while. It hadn't worked out for a lot of reasons. The main reason being that, at the time, neither one of them had wanted to commit. Nor had they been in love.

"He's been asking about you." Sarah set the paperweight onto the desk again. "You know, unless you're involved with someone, you might want to give him another chance."

Randi shook her head. "I don't think so."

"You hiding something from him?"

"What?" Randi asked, searching her friend's face. "Hiding something? Of course not... Oh, I get it." She shook her head and sighed. No one knew the identity of her son's father; not even the man himself. Before she could explain, Sarah's cell phone beeped.

"Oops. Duty calls," Sarah said, eyeing the face of the phone as a text message appeared. "New films just arrived. Well, old ones really. I'm doing a classic film noir piece next month and I ordered a bunch of old Peter Lorre, Bette Davis and Alfred Hitchcock tapes to review." She cast a smile over her shoulder as she hurried off. "Guess what I'll be doing this weekend? Drop by if you don't have anything better to do...."

"Yeah, yeah, I know. I won't hold my breath."

Good thing, Randi thought, as she didn't seem to have a moment to breathe. She had way too much to do, she thought as she turned on her computer.

And first item on her agenda was finding a way to deal with Kurt Striker.

"...that's right. All three of 'em are back in Seattle," Eric Brown was saying, his voice crackling from his cell phone's connection to that of Striker's. "What're the chances of that? Clanton lives here but the other two don't. Paterno, he's at least got a place here, but Donahue doesn't."

Striker didn't like it.

"Paterno arrived three days ago and Donahue rolled into town yesterday."

Just hours before Randi had returned. "Coincidence?" Striker muttered, not believing it for a second as he stood on the sidewalk outside the offices of the *Clarion*.

There was a bitter laugh on the other end of the line. "If you believe that, I've got some real estate in the Mojave—"

"—that you want to sell me. Yeah, I know," Striker growled angrily. "Clanton lives here. Paterno does business in town. But Donahue…" His jaw tightened. "Can you follow him?"

"Not if you want me to stick around and watch the condo."

Damn it all. There wasn't enough manpower for this. Striker and Brown couldn't be in three places at once. "Just stay put for now. But let me know if anything looks odd to you, anything the least bit suspicious."

"Got it, but what about the other two guys? Paterno and Clanton?"

"Check 'em out, see what they're up to, but it's Donahue who concerns me most. We'll talk later." Striker hung up, then called Kelly McCafferty and left a message when she didn't answer. Angry at the world, he snapped his phone shut. All three of the men with whom Randi had been involved were here. In the city. Great… Just…great. His shoulders were bunched against the cold, his collar turned up and inside he felt a knot of jealousy tightening in his gut.

Jealousy, and even envy for that matter, were emotions Striker detested, the kind of useless feelings he'd avoided, even while he'd been married. Maybe that had been the problem. Maybe if he'd felt a little more raw passion, a little more jealousy or anger or empathy during those first few years of marriage, shown his wife that he'd cared about her, maybe then things would have turned out differently... Oh, hell, what was he thinking? He couldn't change the past. And *the accident,* that's how they'd referred to it, *the accident* had altered everything, created a deep, soul-wrenching, damning void that could never be filled.

And yet last night, when he'd been with Randi... Touched her. Kissed her. Felt her warmth surround him, he'd felt differently. *Don't make too much of it. So you made love to her. So what?* Maybe it had just been so long since he'd been with a woman that last night seemed more important than it was.

Whatever the reason, he couldn't stop thinking about it. Couldn't forget how right it had felt.

And it had been so wrong.

In an effort to dislodge images of Randi lying naked in front of the fire, staring up at him with those warm eyes, Striker bought coffee from a vendor and resumed his position not far from the door, protected by the awning of an antique bookstore located next door to the *Clarion*'s offices.

A familiar ache, one he rarely acknowledged, tore through him as he sipped his coffee. Leaning a shoulder against the rough bricks surrounding plate-glass windows etched in gold-leaf lettering, he watched the door of the *Clarion*'s building through a thin wisp of steam rising from his paper cup. Pedestrians scurried past in trench coats, parkas or sweatshirts, some wearing hats, a few with umbrellas, most bareheaded, their collars turned to the wind and rain that steadily dripped from the edge of the awning.

His cell phone rang and he swung it from his pocket. "Striker."

"Hi, it's Kelly."

For the first time in hours, he smiled as Matt's wife started rattling off information. The men at the Flying M were still upset about Randi's leaving. Kelly was working to find a maroon Ford, one that was scraped up and dented from pushing Randi's vehicle off the road in Glacier Park. Kelly was also double-checking all of the staff who had been on duty the night that Randi was nearly killed in the hospital. So far she'd come up with nothing.

Striker wasn't surprised.

He hung up knowing nothing more than when he'd taken the call. Whoever was trying to kill Randi was either very smart or damn lucky.

So far.

Cars, vans and trucks, their windows fogged, sped through the old, narrow streets of this part of the city. Striker glared at the doorway of the hotel, drank coffee and scowled as he considered the other men in Randi McCafferty's life, at least one of whom had bedded her and fathered her son.

Paterno. Clanton. Donahue. Bastards, every one of them.

But he was narrowing the field. He'd done some double-checking on the men who had been involved with Randi. It was unlikely that Joe Paterno had fathered the kid. The timing was all wrong. Kurt had looked into Paterno's travel schedule and records. Paterno had been in Afghanistan around the time the baby had been conceived. There had been rumors that he'd been back in town for a weekend, but Kurt had nearly ruled out the possibility by making a few phone calls to Paterno's chatty landlady. Unless Paterno hadn't shown his face at his apartment and holed up for a secret weekend alone with Randi, he hadn't fathered the kid. Since Randi had been out of town most of the month, it seemed Joe was in the clear.

Leaving Brodie Clanton, the snake of a lawyer, and Sam Donahue, a rough-around-the-edges cowboy; a man whose shady reputation was as black as his hat. Again jealousy cut through him. Clanton was so damn slick, a rich lawyer and a ladies' man. It galled Striker to think of Randi sleeping with a guy who could barely start a sentence without mentioning that his grandfather had been a judge.

A-number-one jerk if ever there had been one, Clanton had avoided walking down the aisle so far, the confirmed-bachelor type who was often seen squiring around pseudo-celebrities when they blew into town. He was into the stock market, expensive cars and young women, the kind of things a man could trade in easily. Clanton had been in town around the time Joshua had been conceived, but, with a little digging into credit card receipts, Striker had determined that Randi, at that time, had been in and out of Seattle herself. She'd never traveled as far as Afghanistan or, presumably, into Paterno's arms, but she'd been chasing a story with the rodeo circuit, where Sam Donahue was known for breaking broncs and women's hearts.

If Striker had been a betting man, he would have fingered Donahue as the baby's daddy. Twice married, Donahue had cheated on both his wives, leaving number one for a younger woman who'd grown up in Grand Hope, Montana, Randi's hometown. And now he just coincidentally had shown up here. A day before Randi.

Striker's jaw tightened so hard it hurt.

DNA would be the only true answer, of course, unless he forced the truth from Randi's lips. Gorgeous lips. Even when she was angry. Her mouth would twist into a furious pout that Striker found incredibly sexy. Which was just plain nuts. He couldn't, *wouldn't* let his mind wander down that seductively dark path. No matter how attractive Randi McCafferty was, he was being paid to protect her, not seduce her. He couldn't let it happen again.

He felt a bit of hardening beneath his fly and swore under

his breath. He shouldn't get an erection just thinking of the woman... Hell, this was no time. None whatsoever for ridiculous fantasies. He had a job to do. And he'd better do it quickly before there was another unexplained "accident," before someone else got hurt. Or before the would-be murderer got lucky and this time someone *was* killed.

# Chapter 6

She pushed open the revolving glass doors and found him just where she'd expected him, on a rain-washed Seattle street, looking damnably rough-and-tumble and sexy as ever. Obviously waiting for her. Great. Just what she *didn't* need, an invitation to trouble in disreputable jeans and a beat-up jacket.

Yep. Kurt Striker in all his damn-convention attitude was waiting.

Her stupid pulse quickened at the sight of him, but she quickly tamped down any emotional reaction she felt for the man. Yes, he was way too attractive in his tight jeans, leather jacket and rough-hewn features. His face was red with the cold, his hair windblown and damp as he leaned a hip against the bricks of a small shop, his eyes trained on the main door of the building. He was holding a paper cup of coffee, which he tossed into a nearby trash can when he spotted her.

Why did she have a thing for dangerous, sensual types?

What was wrong with her? Never once in her life had she been attracted to the boy next door, nor to the affable, respectable, dedicated man who worked nine to five, nor the warm, cuddly football-watching couch potato who would love her to the end of time and never once forget an anniversary. The very men she lauded in her column. The men she advised women to give second glances. The salt-of-the-earth, give-you-the-shirt-off-his-back kind of guy who washed his car and the dog on Saturdays, the guy who wore the same flannel shirt that he'd had since college—the regular Joe of the world. One of the good guys.

Maybe, she thought, crossing the street, that was why she could give out advice to the women and men who were forever falling for the wrong kind. Because she was one of them and, she realized, skirting a puddle as she jaywalked to the parking lot where Striker was posed, she knew the pitfalls of hot-wired attraction. She bore the burn marks and scars to prove it.

"Fancy meeting you here," she said, clicking her Jeep's keyless remote. "You just don't seem to get it, do you? I don't want you here."

"We've been through this."

"And I have a feeling we'll go through it a dozen more times before you get the message." She opened the car door, but he was quick, slamming it shut with the flat of his hand.

"Why don't you and I start over," he suggested, forcing a smile, his arm effectively cutting off her ability to climb into the Jeep. "I'll take you to dinner—there's a nice little Irish pub around the corner—and you can fill me in on your life before you got to Montana."

"There's nothing to tell."

"Like hell." His smile slid away. "It's time you leveled with me. I'm sick to the back teeth of the clamped-lip routine. I need to find out who's been trying to hurt you and your brothers. If you weren't so damn arrogant to think this is just about you, that I'm only digging into all this to bother you, then you'd realize that you're the key to all the trouble that's been happening at the Flying M. It's not just your problem, lady. If you remember, Thorne's plane went down—"

"That was because of bad weather. It was an accident."

"And he was flying in that storm to get back to Montana because of you and the baby, wasn't he? And what about the fire in the stable? God, woman, Slade nearly lost his life. The fire was ruled arson and it's a little too convenient for me to believe that it was coincidence, okay?"

"Drop it, Striker," she warned, whirling on him.

"No way."

"Why do you think I left the ranch?" she demanded.

"I think you left because of me."

That stopped her short. Standing in the dripping rain with his gaze centered directly on hers, she nearly lost it. "Because of you?"

"And last night."

"Don't flatter yourself."

"The timing is right."

Dear Lord. Her stomach twisted. "Let's get something straight, shall we? I left Montana so that the 'accidents' at the Flying M would stop and my brothers and their families would be safe. Whoever is behind this is after me."

"So you think you're what? Drawing the fire away from your family?"

"Yes."

"What about you? Your kid?"

"I can take care of myself. And my baby."

"Well, you've done a pretty piss-poor job of it so far," he said, his skin ruddy with the cold, his eyes flashing angrily.

"And you think that confiding in you would help? I don't

even know anything about you other than Slade seems to think you're okay."

"You know a helluva lot more than that," he said, and she swallowed against the urge to slap him.

"If you're talking about last night…"

"Then what? Go on."

"I can't. Not here. And…and besides, that's not the kind of knowing I was talking about. So don't try to bait me, okay?"

His jaw slid to one side and his eyes narrowed. "Fair enough and you're right. You don't know me, but maybe it's time. Let's go. I'll tell you anything you want to know." His grin was about as warm as the Yukon in winter. "I'll buy dinner."

Before she could argue, he grabbed the crook of her arm and propelled her around the corner, down two blocks and toward a staircase that led down a flight to a subterranean bar and restaurant. He helped her to a booth in the back before she finally yanked her arm away. "Where'd you learn your manners? At the Cro-Magnon School of Etiquette?"

"Graduated cum laude." One eyebrow cocked disarmingly.

She chuckled and bit back another hot retort. Goading him was getting her nowhere fast. But at least he had a sense of humor and could laugh at himself. Besides which, she was starved. Her stomach started making all sorts of vile noises at the smells emanating from the kitchen.

Kurt ordered an ale, and she, deciding a drink wouldn't hurt, did the same. "Okay, okay, so you've made your point," she said when he leaned back in the booth and stared at her. "You take your job seriously. You're not going away. What-ever my brothers are paying you is worth putting up with me and my bad attitude, right?"

He let it slide as the waitress, a reed-thin woman with curly red hair tied into a single plait, reappeared with two frosty glasses, twin dinner menus and a bowl of peanuts. She slid all onto the table, then ambled toward a table where a patron was wagging his finger frantically to get her attention.

The place was dim and decorated with leatherlike cushions, mahogany wood aged to near black, a scarred wooden floor and a ceiling of tooled-metal tiles. It smelled of beer and ale, with the hint of cigar smoke barely noticeable over the tang of food grilling behind the counter. Two men were playing darts in a corner and the click of billiard balls emanated from an archway leading to other rooms. Conversation was light, patrons at the long, battered bar tuned in to a muted Sonics basketball game.

"I'm going to check on the baby." She reached into her bag, retrieved her cell phone and punched out Sharon Okano's number.

Sharon picked up on the second ring and was quick to reassure her that Joshua was fine. He'd already eaten, been bathed and was in his footed jammies, currently fascinated by a mobile Sharon had erected over his playpen.

"I'll be by to see him as soon as I can," Randi said.

"He'll be fine."

"I know. I just can't wait to hold him a minute." Randi clicked off and tried to quell the dull ache that seemed forever with her when she was apart from her child. It was weird, really. Before Joshua's birth she had been free and easy, didn't have a clue what a dramatic change was in store for her. But from the moment she'd awoken from her coma and learned she'd borne a son, she could barely stand to be away from him, even for a few hours.

As for being with him and holding him, the next few weeks promised to be torture on that score. Until she was certain he was safe with her. She slid the phone into her purse and turned to Kurt, who was studying her intently over the rim of his mug. Great. Dealing with him wasn't going to be easy, either. Even if she didn't factor in that she'd made love to him like a wanton in the wee hours of this very morning.

They ordered. Two baskets of fish and chips complete with sides of coleslaw and a second beer, even though they weren't quite finished with the first, were dropped in front of them.

"Why are you keeping your kid's paternity a secret?" Kurt finally asked. "What does it matter?"

"I prefer he didn't know."

"Why not? Seems as if he has a right."

"Being a sperm donor isn't the same as being a father." Her stomach was screaming for food but the conversation was about to kill her appetite.

"Maybe he should be the judge of that."

"Maybe you should keep your nose in your own business." She took a long swallow from her drink and the guys at the bar gave up a shout as one of the players hit a three pointer.

"Your brothers made it my business."

"My brothers can't run my life. Much as they'd like to."

"I think you're afraid," he accused, and she felt the tightening of the muscles of her neck, the urge to defend herself.

"Of what?" she asked, but he didn't answer as the waitress appeared and slid their baskets onto the plank table, then offered up bottles of vinegar and ketchup. Only when they were alone again did Randi repeat herself. "You think I'm afraid of what?"

"Why don't *you* tell me. It's just odd, you know, for a woman not to tell the father of her child that he's a daddy. Goes against the grain. Usually the mother wants financial support. Emotional support. That kind of thing."

"I'm not usual," she said, and thought he whispered "Amen" under his breath, though she couldn't be certain as he covered up his comment with a long swallow of ale. She noticed the movement of his throat—dark with a bit of beard shadow as he swallowed—and something deep inside her, something dusky and wholly feminine, reacted. She drew her eyes away and told herself she was being a fool. It had been a long time since she'd been with a man, over a year now, but that didn't give her the right to ogle men like Kurt Striker nor imagine what it would feel like for him to touch her again, to kiss her, to press hot, insistent lips against the curve of her neck and push her sweater off her shoulder...

She caught herself and realized that he was watching her face, looking for her reaction. As if he could read her mind. To her horror she felt herself blush.

"Penny for your thoughts."

She shook her head, pretended interest in her meal by shaking vinegar over her fries. "Wouldn't sell 'em for a penny, or a nickel, or a thousand dollars."

"So tell me about the book," he suggested.

"The book?"

"The one you're writing. Another one of your secrets."

How could one man be so irritating? She ate in silence for a second and glowered across the table at him. "It's not a secret. I just didn't want to tell anyone about it until it was finished."

"You were on your way to the Flying M to finish it when you were forced off the road at Glacier National Park, right?" He dredged a piece of fish in tartar sauce.

She nodded.

"Think that's just a coincidence?"

"No one knew I was going to Montana to write a book. Even the people at work thought I was just taking my maternity leave—which I was. I was planning to combine the two."

"Juanita at the ranch knew about it." He'd polished off one crispy lump of halibut and was working on a second.

"Of course she did. I already explained, it really wasn't a secret."

"If you say so." He ate in silence for a minute, but she didn't feel any respite, knew he was forming his next question, and sure enough, it came, hard and fast. "Tell me, Randi," he said, "who do you think wants to kill you?"

"I've been through this dozens of times with the police."

"Humor me." He was nearly finished with his food and she'd barely started. But her appetite had crumpled into nothing. She picked at her coleslaw. "Who are your worst enemies? You know, anyone who has a cause—just or not—for wanting you dead."

She'd considered the question over and over. It had run through her mind in an endless loop from the moment her memory had started working again when she'd awoken from her coma. "I...I don't know. No one has any reason to hate me enough to kill me."

"Murderers aren't always reasonable people," he pointed out.

"I can't name anyone."

"How about the baby's father? Maybe he found out you were pregnant, is ticked that you didn't tell him and, not wanting to be named as the father, decided to get rid of you both."

"He wouldn't do that."

"No?"

She shook her head. She wasn't certain about many things, but she doubted Joshua's father would care that he'd fathered a child, certainly wouldn't go through the steps to get rid of either of them. She felt a weight on her heart but ignored it as Striker, leaning back in the booth, pushed his near-empty basket aside. "If I'm going to help you, then I need to know everything that's going on. So who is he, Randi? Who's Joshua's daddy?"

She didn't realize she'd been shredding her napkin in her lap, but looked down and noticed all the pieces of red paper. She supposed she couldn't take her secret with her to the grave, but letting the world know the truth made her feel more vulnerable, that she was somehow breaching a special trust she had with her son.

"My money's on Donahue," he said abruptly.

She froze.

He winked though his expression was hard. "I figure you'd go for the sexy-cowboy type."

"You don't know what my type is."

"Don't I?"

"Unfair, Striker, last night was…was…"

"What about it?"

"It was a mistake. We both know it. So, let's just forget it. As I said, you don't have any idea what 'my type' is."

One side of his mouth lifted in an irritating, sexy-as-hell smile. Green eyes held hers fast, and a wave, warm as a desert in August, climbed up her neck. "I'm workin' on it."

Her heart clenched. *Don't do this, Randi. Don't let him get to you. He's no better than…than…* Her throat tightened when she considered what a fool she'd been. For a man who'd seduced her. Used her. Cared less for her than he did for his dog. Silly, silly woman.

"Okay, Striker," she said, forcing the words through her lips, words she'd vowed only hours ago never to utter. "I'll tell you the truth," she said, hating the sense of relief it brought to be able to confide in someone. "But this is between you and me. Got it? I'll tell you and you alone. When the time comes I'll tell Joshua's father and my brothers. But only when I say."

"Fair enough," he drawled, leaning back in his chair and folding his arms over his chest, all interest in his remaining French fries forgotten.

Randi took in a deep breath and prayed she wasn't making one of the biggest mistakes of her life. She stared Striker straight in the eye and admitted to him something she rarely acknowledged herself. "You're right. Okay? Joshua's father, and I use the term so loosely it's no longer coiled, is Sam Donahue." Her tongue nearly tripped over Sam's name. She didn't like saying it out loud, didn't like admitting that she, like too many others before her, had been swept off her feet by the charming, roguish cowboy. It was embarrassing and, had it not been for her precious son, a mistake she would have rued until her dying day. Joshua, of course, changed all that.

Striker didn't say a word. Nor had his lips curled in silent denunciation. And he didn't so much as lift an eyebrow in mockery. No. He played it straight, just observing her, watching her every reaction.

"So now you know," she said, standing. "I hope it helps, but I don't think it means anything. Thanks for dinner." She walked out of the bar and up the steps to the wet streets. The rain had turned to drizzle again, misting around the street lamps, and the air was heavy, laced with the brine from Puget Sound. Randi felt like running. As fast and far as she could. To get away from the claustrophobic feeling, the fear that compressed her chest, the very fear she'd tried to flee when she'd left Montana.

But it was with her wherever she went, she thought, her boots slapping along the rain-slick sidewalk as she hurried to her car. The city was far from deserted, traffic rushed through the narrow old streets and pedestrians bustled along the sidewalks. She carried no umbrella, didn't bother with her hood, let the dampness collect on her cheeks and flatten her hair. Not that she cared. Damn it, why had she told Striker about Sam Donahue? Her relationship with Sam hadn't really been a love affair, more of a fling, though at one time she'd been foolish enough to think she might be falling in love with the bastard. The favor hadn't been returned and she'd realized her mistake. But not before the pregnancy test had turned out positive.

She hadn't bothered to tell Donahue because she knew he wouldn't care. He was a selfish man by nature, a rambler who followed the rodeo circuit and didn't have time for the two ex-wives and children he'd already sired. Randi wasn't about to try to saddle him with the responsibility of another baby. She figured Joshua was better off with one strong parent than two who fought, living with the ghost of a father whom he would grow up not really knowing.

She knew her son would ask questions and she intended to answer them all honestly. When the time came. But not now... not when her baby was pure innocence.

"Randi!" Striker was at her side, his bare head as wet as her own, his expression hard.

"What? More questions?" she asked, unable to hide the sarcasm in her voice. "Well, sorry, but I'm fresh out of shocking little details about my life."

"I didn't come all the way to Seattle to embarrass you," he said as they rounded a final corner to the parking lot.

"That's how it seems."

"No, it doesn't. You know better."

She'd reached her Jeep and with a punch of the button on her remote, unlocked it once more. "Why do I have the feeling that you're not finished? That you won't be satisfied until you've stripped away every little piece of privacy I have."

"I just want to help."

He seemed sincere, but she'd been fooled before. By the master, Sam Donahue. Kurt Striker, damn him, was of the same ilk. Another cowboy. Another rogue. Another sexy man with a shadowy past. Another man she'd started to fall for. The kind to avoid. "Help?"

"That's right." His eyes shifted to her lips and she nervously licked them, tasting rainwater as it drizzled down her face. Her heart thudded. She knew in that second that he was going to kiss her. He was fighting it; she saw the battle in his eyes, but in the end raw emotion won out and his lips crashed down on hers so intensely she drew in a swift breath and it was followed quickly by his tongue. Slick. Sleek. Searching. The tip touched her teeth, forcing them apart as he grabbed her. Leather creaked, the sky parted, rain poured and Randi's foolish, foolish heart opened.

She kissed the rogue back, slamming her mind against thoughts that she was making the worst mistake of her life, that she was crossing a bridge that was burning behind her, that her life, from that moment on, would be changed forever.

But there, in the middle of the bustling city, with raindrops falling on them both, she didn't care.

# Chapter 7

*Stop this! Stop it now! Don't you remember last night?*

Blinking against the rain, fighting the urge to lean against him, Randi pulled away from Kurt. "This is definitely not a good idea," she said. "It wasn't last night and it isn't now."

His mouth twisted. "I'm not sure about that."

"I am." It was a lie. Right now she wasn't certain of anything. She reached behind her and fumbled with the door handle. "Let's just give it a rest, okay?"

He didn't argue, nor did he stop her as she slid into the Jeep and, with shaking fingers, found her keys and managed to start the ignition. Lunacy. That's what it was. Sheer, unadulterated, pain-in-the-backside lunacy! She couldn't start kissing the likes of Kurt Striker again.

Dear God, what had she been thinking?

*You weren't thinking. That's the problem!*

She flipped on the radio, heard the first notes of a sappy love song and immediately punched the button to find talk radio, only to hear a popular program where a radio psychologist was giving out advice to someone who was mixed up with the wrong kind of man, the same kind of advice she handed out through her column in the *Clarion*, the very advice she should listen to herself.

First she'd made the mistake of getting involved with Sam Donahue and now she was falling for Kurt Striker... No! She pounded a fist on the steering wheel as she braked for a turnoff.

Cutting through traffic, she made a call on her cell phone to Sharon, was assured that Joshua was safe, then stopped at a local market for a few groceries.

Fifteen minutes later she pulled into the parking lot of her condo. Now away from the hustle and bustle of the city, the dark of the night seemed more threatening.

The parking lot was dark and the security lamps were glowing, throwing pools of light onto the wet ground and a few parked cars. The parking area was deserted, none of her neighbors were walking dogs or taking out trash. Warm light glowed from only a few windows, the rest of the units were dark.

*So what? This is why you chose this place. It was quiet, only a few units overlooking the lake.*

For the first time since moving here, Randi looked at her darkened apartment and felt a moment's hesitation, a hint of fear. She glanced over her shoulder, through the back windows of the Jeep, wondering if someone was watching her, someone lurking in a bank of fir trees and rhododendron that ringed the parking lot, giving it privacy. She had the uneasy sensation that hidden eyes were watching her through a veil of wet needles and leaves.

"Get a grip," she muttered, hoisting the bag and holding

tight to her key ring. As if it was some kind of protection. What a laugh!

No one was hiding. No one was watching her. And yet she wished she hadn't been so quick to put some distance between herself and Striker. Maybe she did need a bodyguard, someone she could trust.

*Someone you can't keep your hands off of?*

*Someone you've made love to?*

*Someone that even now, even though you know better, you'd love to take to bed?* In her mind's eye she saw the image of Kurt Striker, all taut skin and muscle as he held her in front of the dying fire.

Oh, for the love of St. Peter! Hauling her laptop, the groceries, her briefcase and her rebellious libido with her, she made her way to the porch, managed to unlock the door and snap on the interior lights. She almost wished Kurt was inside waiting for her again. But that was crazy. Nuts! She couldn't trust herself around that man.

"You're an idiot," she muttered, seeing her reflection in the mirror mounted by the coatrack in the front hall. Her hair was damp and curly with the rain, her cheeks flushed, her eyes bright. "This is just what got you into trouble in the first place." She dropped her computer and bag near her desk, shook herself out of her coat and heard a pickup roaring into the lot. Her silly heart leaped, but a quick glance through the kitchen window confirmed that Striker had returned. He was already out of the truck and headed toward the condo.

She met him at the front door.

"You don't seem to take a hint, do you?" she teased.

"Careful, woman, I'm not in the mood to have my chain yanked," he warned. "Traffic was a bitch."

He was inside in a second and bolted the door behind him. "I don't like it when you try to lose me."

"And I don't like being manhandled." She started unpacking groceries, stuffing a carton of milk into the near-empty refrigerator.

"I kissed you."

"On the street, when I obviously didn't want you to."

One of his eyebrows lifted in disbelief. "You didn't want it?" He snorted. "I'd love to see what you were like when you did."

"That was last night," she reminded him, then mentally kicked herself. Lifting a hand, she stopped any argument he might have. "Let's not talk about last night."

He kicked out a bar stool and plopped himself at the counter that separated the kitchen from the living room. "Okay, but there is something we need to discuss."

She braced herself. "Which is?"

"Sam Donahue."

"Another off-limits subject." She pulled a loaf of bread from the wet sack.

"I don't think so. We've wasted enough time as it is and I'm getting sick of you not being straight with me."

"I should never have told you."

He shot her a condemning look. "I'd already guessed, remember?" He took a deep breath and ran stiff fingers through his hair. "You got any wood for that?" he asked, hitching his chin toward the fireplace.

"A little. In a closet on the back deck."

"Get me a beer, I'll make a fire and then, whether you like it or not, we're going to discuss your ex-lover."

"Gee," she mocked, "and who said single women don't have any fun? You know, Striker, you've got a helluva nerve to barge in here and start barking orders. Just because...because of what happened last night, you don't have the right to start bossing me around in my own home."

"You're right," he said without a trace of regret carved into his features. "Would you please get me a beer and I'll get the firewood."

"I might be out of beer. I didn't pick any up at the store."

"There's one left. In the door of the fridge. I checked earlier." The empty bottle on the coffee table stood as testament to that very fact.

"When you practiced breaking and entering," she muttered as he kicked back the stool and made his way to the deck. She opened the refrigerator again and saw the single long-neck in the door. The guy was observant. But still a bully who had barged unwelcome into her life. A sexy bully at that. Her worst nightmare.

She yanked out the last beer, twisted off the top and, as he carried in a couple of chunks of oak to the fire, took a long swallow. The least he could do was share, she decided, watching as he bent on the tiled hearth, his jacket and shirt riding up over his belt and jeans, offering her the view of a slice of his taut, muscular back. Her throat was suddenly dry as dust and she took another pull from the long-neck. What the hell was she going to do with him? She'd already bared her soul and her body, then, after insisting that she wasn't interested in him, kissed him on the street as if she never wanted to stop, and now... She slid a glance toward the cracked door of her bedroom and in her mind she saw them together, wrapped in the sheets, sweaty bodies tangled and heaving as he kissed her breasts. Her heart pounded as he pulled at her nipple, his hands sliding down to sculpt her waist as he mounted her, gently nudging her knees apart, readying himself above her, his erection stiff, his green gaze fiery. Then, eyes locked, he entered her in one long, hard thrust—

He cleared his throat and she was brought back to the living area of her condo where he was still tending to the fire. Turning, she blushed as she realized he'd said something to her. For the life of her she couldn't remember a word. "Wh-what?"

"I asked if you had a match." His gaze was on her face, then traveled down the short corridor to the bedroom. Amusement caused an eyebrow to arch and she wanted to die. No doubt he could read her embarrassing thoughts.

"Oh, yeah…" While she'd been fantasizing, he'd crumpled old newspaper and stacked the firewood, even splintering off some pieces of kindling.

She took another swallow, handed him the bottle and hurried into the kitchen where she rummaged through a drawer. *Don't go there. You're not going to tumble into bed with him. Not again. You're not even going to kiss him again. You're not going to do anything stupid with him. No more.* She found a pack of matches and tossed them over the counter to him, all the while trying to quell the hammering of her heart. Time to go on the offensive.

"Okay, Striker, so now I've told you my darkest secret. What's yours?"

"None of your business."

"Wait a minute. That's not fair."

"You're right, it's not." He struck a match and the smell of sulfur singed the air as he touched the tiny flame to the dry paper and the fire crackled to life. "But then not much is."

"You said I could ask you anything when we were in the pub."

"I changed my mind."

"Just like that?" she asked incredulously as she snapped her fingers.

"Uh-huh." He took a long pull from the bottle.

"No way. I think I deserve to know who the hell you are."

Rocking back on his heels as the fire caught, he looked up at her standing on the other side of the counter. "I'm an ex-cop turned P.I."

"I already figured that much. But what about your personal life?"

"It's private."

"You're single, right? There's no Mrs. Striker."

He hesitated enough to cause her heart to miss a beat. *Oh, God, not again,* she thought as she leaned against the counter for support. He'd kissed her. Touched her. Made love to her.

"Not anymore. I was married but it ended a few years back."

"Why?"

His jaw tightened. "Haven't you read the statistics?"

"I'm talking about the reason behind the statistics, at least in your case."

A shadow passed behind his eyes and he said, "It just didn't work out. I was a cop. Probably paid more attention to the job than my wife."

"And you didn't have any kids?"

Again the hesitation. Again the shadow. His lips tightened at the corners as he stood and dusted his hands. "I don't have any children," he said slowly, "and I never hear from my ex. That about covers it all, doesn't it?" There was just a spark of challenge in his eyes, daring her to argue with him. A dozen questions bubbled up in her throat, but she held them back. For now. There were other ways to get information about him. She was a reporter, for God's sake. She had the means to find out just about anything that had happened to him. Newsworthy articles would be posted on the internet, personal stuff through other sources.

With Sam Donahue she'd been trusting and it had backfired in her face, but this time… Oh, God, why was she even thinking like this? There was no *this time!* There was no Kurt Striker in her life except as an irritating bodyguard her brothers had hired. That was it. He was here because he was hired to be here; she was a job to him. Nothing more.

"Look, I've got to get some work done," she said, motioning to her laptop. "I've been gone for months and if I don't answer some email and put together a new column or two, I'm going to be in big trouble. My boss and I are already not real tight. So, if you don't mind…well, even if you do, I'm going to start plowing through what's been piling up. I understand that you think you've got to be with me 24/7, but it's not necessary. No one's going to take a potshot at me here."

"Why would you think that?" Striker drained the rest of his beer.

"Because there are too many people around, there's a security guard for the condos always on the premises, and most importantly, Joshua is safe with Sharon."

The expression on his face told her he was of another mind. And wasn't she, really? Hadn't she, just minutes ago in the parking lot, sensed that someone had been watching her? She rounded the counter as he straightened and crossed the room.

"Look, I do know that I'm in some kind of danger," she said. "Obviously I know it or I wouldn't have taken the time to hide the baby. I came back here to try to figure this out, to take the heat off my brothers, to get on with my life and let them get on with theirs. And yeah, I'd be lying if I didn't say I was nervous, that I wasn't starting to jump at shadows, but

I need to sort through some things, get a handle on what's happening."

"That's why I'm here. I'm thinking that maybe if we work together, we can make some sense of what's going on." He was close to her, near enough that she could smell the wet leather of his jacket, see the striations of color in his green eyes, feel the heat of his body.

She couldn't even make sense of the moment. "That might be impossible. I've been thinking about what happened from every angle and I come up with the same conclusion. I don't have any real enemies that I know of. At least not anyone who would want to hurt me and my family. It doesn't make any sense." To put some distance between her body and his, she walked to the couch and flung herself onto the cushions. *Who? What? Why?* The questions that had haunted her nights and caused her to lose sleep were still unanswered as they rolled around in her brain.

"So what does make sense?" he demanded. "Someone followed you from Seattle and on your way to Grand Hope, Montana, forced you off the road. Why?"

"I told you, I don't know. Believe me, I've been thinking about it."

"Think harder." He frowned and rammed stiff fingers through hair that was still damp. "If it doesn't have to do with the baby, then what about your job? Did you give someone bad advice and really tick someone off?"

She shook her head. "I thought about that, too. When I was back in Montana, I got online and searched through the columns for the two months prior to the accident and I couldn't find anything that would infuriate a person."

His head snapped up. "So you are worried?"

"Of course I'm worried. Who wouldn't be? But there was

nothing in any of the advice I gave that would cause someone to snap."

"You think. There are always nutcases." He set his empty
bottle on the counter.

That much was true, she thought wearily. "But none who
have emailed me, or called me or contacted me in any way. I
double-checked every communication I received." He nodded and she realized that he'd probably been privy to that information, as well.

"Well, there's got to be a reason. We're just missing it."
He was thinking hard; she could tell by the way he rubbed
his chin. "You write magazine articles under a pseudonym."

"Nothing controversial."

His eyes narrowed. "What about the book you were working on?"

She hesitated. The manuscript she was writing wasn't finished and she'd taken great pains to keep it secret while she
investigated a payola scam on the rodeo circuit. It was while
researching the book that she'd met Sam Donahue, a friend,
he'd claimed, of her brothers'. As it turned out he hadn't been
as much a friend as an acquaintance and somehow she'd ended
up falling for him, knowing him to be a rogue, realizing that
part of his charm was the hint of danger around him, and
yet she'd tumbled into bed with him anyway. And ended up
pregnant.

Which had been a blessing in disguise, of course. Without
her ill-fated affair with Sam, she never would have had Joshua,
and that little guy was the light of her life.

"What's in the book that's so all-fired important?"

Sighing, she walked to the couch and dropped into the soft
cushions. "You know what's in it for the most part."

"A book on cowboys."

"Well, a little more than that." Leaning her head back, she closed her eyes. "It's about all aspects of rodeos, the good, the bad, the ugly. Especially the ugly. Along with all the rah-rah for a great American West tradition, there's also the dark side to it all, the seamy underbelly. As I was getting information, I learned about the drugs, animal abuse, cheating, payola, you name it."

"And let me guess, most of the information came from good old Sam Donahue."

"Some of it," she admitted, opening an eye and catching Kurt scowling, as if the mere mention of Donahue's name made Striker see red. "I was going to name names in my book and, I suppose, I could have made a few people nervous. But the thing of it was, no one really knew what I was doing."

"Donahue?"

She shook her head and glanced to the window. "I told him it was a series of articles about small-town celebrations, that rodeos were only a little bit of the slice of Americana I was going to write about. Sam wasn't all that interested in what I was doing."

"Why not?"

"Oh, I don't know," she said, turning her attention to Kurt. The fire was burning softly, casting golden shadows on the cozy rooms. She snapped on a table lamp, hoping to break the feeling of intimacy the flames created. "Maybe it's because Sam's an egomaniac and pretty much consumed with his own life."

"Sounds charming," he mocked.

"I thought so. At first. But it did wear thin fast."

Striker lifted an eyebrow and she added, "I'd already realized that it wasn't going to work out when I suspected I was pregnant."

"What did he say about it?"

"Nothing. He never knew."

"You didn't tell him."

"That's right. Didn't we go over this before?"

Striker looked as if he wanted to say something but held his tongue. For that she was grateful. She didn't need any judgment calls.

"Besides," she added with more than a trace of bitterness, "I figure we're even now. He forgot to mention that he wasn't really divorced from his last wife when he started dating me." She wrinkled her nose and felt that same old embarrassment that had been with her from the moment she'd realized Sam had lied, that he'd been married all the time he'd chased after her, swearing that he was divorced.

Fool that she'd been, she'd fallen for him and believed every word that had tripped over his lying tongue.

Now a blush stole up her neck and she bit down on her back teeth. She'd always been proud of her innate intelligence, but when it came to men, she'd often been an idiot. She'd chosen poorly, trusted too easily, fallen harder than she should have. From Teddy Sherman, the ranch hand her father had hired when she was seventeen, to a poet and a musician in college, and finally Sam Donahue, the rough-and-tumble cowpoke who'd turned out to be a lying bastard if ever there was one. Well, no more, she told herself even as Kurt Striker, damn him, threatened to break down her defenses.

He walked to the fire, grabbed a poker and jabbed at the burning logs. Sparks drifted upward through the flue and one of the blackened chunks of oak split with a soft thud.

Randi watched him and felt that same sense of yearning, a tingle of desire, she'd experienced every time she was around him. She sensed something different in Kurt, a strength of character that had been lacking in the other men she'd found enchanting. They had been dreamers, or, in the case of Donahue, cheats, but she didn't think either was a part of Striker's personality. His boots seemed securely planted on the ground rather than drifting into the clouds, and he appeared intensely honest. His eyes were clear, his shoulders straight, his smile, when he offered it, not as sly as it was amused. He appealed to her at a whole new level. Man to woman, face-to-face, not looking down at her, nor elevating her onto a pedestal from which she would inevitably fall.

"So what do you think about your kid?" he asked suddenly as he straightened and dusted his hands.

"I'm nuts about him, of course."

"Do you really think he's safe with the Okano woman?"

"I wouldn't have left him there if I didn't."

"I'd feel better if he was with you. With me."

"No one followed me to Sharon's. Not many people know we're friends. She was in my dorm in college and just moved up here last fall. I…I really think he's safer there. I've already driven her nuts calling her. She thinks I'm paranoid and I'm not so sure she's wrong."

"Paranoid isn't all that bad. Not in this case." Striker reached into his jacket pocket, flipped open his cell and dialed. A few seconds later he was engrossed in a conversation, ordering someone to watch Sharon Okano's apartment as well as do some digging on Sam Donahue. "…that's right. I want to know for certain where he was on the dates that Randi was run off the road and someone attempted to kill her in the hospital… Yeah, I know he had an alibi, but double-check and don't forget to dig into some of the thugs he hangs out with. This could have been a paid job… I don't know but start with Marv Bates and Charlie… Damn, what's his name, Charlie—"

"Caldwell," Randi supplied, inwardly shuddering at the thought of the two cowboys Sam had introduced her to. Marv was whip thin with lips that barely moved when he talked and eyes that were forever narrowed. Charlie was a lug, a big, fleshy man who could surprise you with how fast he could move if properly motivated.

"That's right, Charlie Caldwell. Check prison records. See if any of Donahue's buddies have done time.... Okay... You can reach me on the cell, that would be best." He was walking to the desk. "I'll be in the condo, but let's not use the land-line. I checked, it doesn't appear bugged, but I'm not sure."

Randi's blood chilled at the thought that someone could have tampered with her phone lines or crept into her home while she was away. But then Striker hadn't had any problem getting inside. He might not have been the first. Her skin crawled as she looked over her belongings with new eyes. Suede couch, faux leopard-print chair and ottoman, antique rocker, end tables she'd found in a secondhand store and her great-grandmother's old treadle sewing machine that stood near the window. The cacti were thriving, the Boston fern shedding and near death, the mirror over her fireplace, the one she'd inherited from her mother, still chipped in one corner. Nothing out of place. Nothing to give her pause.

And yet...something wasn't right. Something she couldn't put her finger on. Just like the eerie sensation that she was being watched when she parked her Jeep.

"Later." Striker snapped the phone shut and watched as Randi walked to her desk, double-checking that nothing had been disturbed. She'd already done a quick once-over when she'd come home earlier, but now, knowing that her phone could have been tapped, her home violated, her life invaded

by an unknown assailant, she wanted to make certain that everything was as it should be.

Her phone rang and she nearly jumped through the roof.
She snagged the receiver before it could jangle a second time.

"Hello?" she said, half expecting a deep-throated voice on
the other end to issue a warning, or heavy breathing to be her
only response.

"So you did get home!"

Randi nearly melted at the sound of Slade's voice. He was
her youngest half brother, closest to her in age. Slade had been
born with the same McCafferty wild streak that had cursed
all of John Randall's children. Slade had just held on to his
untamed ways longer than his older brothers.

"I thought you'd have the brains to call and tell us you'd
arrived safely," he admonished, and she felt a twinge of guilt.

"I guess I hadn't gotten around to it," she said, smiling at
the thought of her brothers, who had once resented her, now
fretting over her.

"Is everything all right?"

"So far, although I have a bone to pick with you."

"Uh-oh."

"And Matt and Thorne."

"It figures."

"Who the hell do you think you are hiring a bodyguard
for me behind my back?" she demanded and saw, in the mirror's reflection, Kurt Striker standing behind her. Their eyes
met and there was something in his gaze that seemed to bore
straight into hers, to touch her soul.

Slade was trying to explain. "You need someone to help
you—"

"You mean I need a *man* to watch over me," she cut in, irritated all over again. Frustrated, she turned her attention to

the window, where just beyond the glass she could make out the angry waters of Lake Washington roiling in the darkness. "Well, for your information, brother dear, I can take care of myself."

"Yeah, right."

Slade's sarcasm cut deep.

Involuntarily, she squared her shoulders. "I'm serious."

"So are we."

Randi heard conversation in the background, not only the deep rumble of male voices, but others as well, the higher pitches of her sisters-in-law, no doubt, and rising above the rest of the conversation, the sharp staccato burst of Spanish that could only have come from Juanita, the housekeeper.

"You tell her to be careful. *Dios!* What was she thinking running off like that!"

More Spanish erupted and Slade said, "Did you hear that? Juanita thinks—"

"I heard what she said." Randi felt a pang of homesickness, which was just plain ludicrous. This was her home. Where she belonged. She had a life here in Seattle. At the newspaper. Here in this condo. And yet, as she stared out the window to the whitecaps whirling furiously on the black water, she wondered if she had made a mistake in returning to this bustling city that she'd fallen in love with years before. She liked the crowds. The noise. The arts. The history. The beauty of Puget Sound and the briny smell of the sea when she walked or jogged near the waterfront.

But her brothers weren't here.

Nor were Nicole, Kelly or Jamie, her new sisters-in-law. They'd become friends and she missed them as well as Nicole's daughters and the ranch and...

Suddenly stiffening her spine, she pushed back all her maudlin thoughts. She was doing the right thing. Reclaiming her life. Trying to figure out who was hell-bent on harming her and her family. "Tell everyone I'm fine. Okay? A big girl. And I don't appreciate you and Thorne and Matt hiring Striker."

"Well, that's just too damn bad now, isn't it?" he said, re-igniting her anger.

Her headache was throbbing again, she was so tired she wanted to sink into her bed and never wake up and, more than anything, she wished she could reach through the phone lines and shake some sense into her brothers. "You know, Slade, you really can be a miserable son of a bitch."

"I try," he drawled in that damnable country-boy accent that was usually accompanied by a devilish twinkle in his eyes.

She imagined his lazy smile. "Nice, Slade. Do you want to talk to your new employee?" Without waiting for an answer, she slammed the phone into Kurt Striker's hand and stormed to her bedroom. This was insane, but she was tired of arguing about it, was bound and determined to get on with her life. She had a baby to take care of and a job to do.

*But what if they're all right? What if someone really is after you? After Joshua? Didn't you think someone had already broken into this place?*

Her gaze swept the bedroom. Nothing seemed disturbed… or did it? Had she left the curtains to the back deck parted? Had her closet door been slightly ajar…? She lifted her eyes, caught a glimpse of her reflection and saw a shadow of fear pass behind her own eyes. God, she hated this.

She heard footsteps approaching and then, in the glass, saw Kurt walking down the short hallway and stop at the bedroom door.

Her throat was suddenly dry as cotton and inadvertently she licked her lips. His gaze flickered to the movement and the corners of his mouth tightened, and just the hint of desperation, of lust, darkened his eyes.

For a split second their gazes locked. Held. Randi's pulse jumped, as if it were suddenly a living, breathing thing. Her heartbeat thundered in her ears. Inside, she felt a twinge, the hint of a dangerous craving she'd experienced last night.

She knew that it would only take a glance, a movement, a whisper and he would come inside, close the door, take her into his arms and kiss her as if she'd never been kissed before. It would be hard, raw, desperate and they would oh, so easily tumble onto the bed and make love for hours.

His lips compressed.

He took a step inside.

She could barely breathe.

He reached forward, grabbed hold of the doorknob.

Her knees went weak.

Oh, God, she wanted him. Imagined touching him, lying with him, feeling the heat of his body. "Kurt, I..."

"Shh, darlin'," he said, his voice as rough as sandpaper. "It's been a long day. Why don't you get some rest." He offered her a wink that caused her heart to crack. "I'll be in the living room if you need me." He pulled the door shut tight and she listened to the sound of his footsteps retreating down the short hallway.

Slowly she let out the breath she'd been holding and sagged onto the bed. Disappointment mingled with relief. It would be a mistake of epic proportions to make love to him. She knew it. They both did. On unsteady legs she walked into the bathroom and opened the medicine cabinet. She reached for a bottle of ibuprofen and stopped short.

What if someone had been in her home?

What if someone had tampered with her over-the-counter medications? Her food?

"Now you really are getting paranoid," she muttered, as she poured the pills into the toilet and flushed them down.

Paranoid, maybe.

But alive for certain.

Making her way back to the bedroom, she slid under the covers and decided that she could work with Striker or against him.

With him would be a lot more interesting.

And together they might be able to get through the nightmare that had become her life.

# Chapter 8

*He was lying next to her, his body hard and honed, skin stretched taut over muscles that were smooth and fluid as he levered up on one elbow to stare down at her. Green eyes glittered with a dark seductive fire that thrilled her and silently spoke of pleasures to come. With the fingers of one callused hand he traced the contours of her body. She tingled, her breasts tightening under his scrutinizing gaze, her nipples becoming hard as buttons. He leaned forward and scraped a beard-roughened cheek over her flesh. Deep inside, she felt desire stretching as it came awake.*

*This was so wrong. She shouldn't be in bed with Kurt Striker. What had she been thinking? How had this happened? She barely knew the man...and yet, the wanting was so intense, burning through her blood, chasing away her doubts, and as he bent to kiss her, she knew she couldn't resist, that with just the brush of his hard lips on hers she would be lost completely—*

Bam!

Her eyes flew open at the sound. Where was she? It was dark. And cold. She was alone in the bed—her bed—and she felt as if she'd slept for hours, her bladder stretched to the limit, her stomach rumbling for food.

"Let's go, Sleeping Beauty," Kurt said from the vicinity of the doorway. She blinked and found him standing in the doorway, his shoulders nearly touching each side of the frame, his body backlit by the flickering light still cast from the living-room fire. In relief he seemed larger, more rugged. The kind of man to avoid.

So she'd been dreaming about making love to him again. Only dreaming. Thank God. Not that the ache deep within her had subsided. Yes, she was in her own bed, but she was alone and fully dressed, just the way he'd left her minutes—or had it been hours—before?

"Wha—What's the rush?" she mumbled, trying to shake off the remainder of that damnably erotic fantasy even though a part of her wanted to close her eyes and call it back. "So what happened to 'shh, darlin', you should get some rest'?" she asked sarcastically.

He took a step into the room. "You got it. Slept for nearly eighteen hours, now it's time to rock 'n' roll."

"What? Eighteen hours...no..." She glanced at the bedside clock and the digital display indicated it was after three. "I couldn't have..." But the bad taste in her mouth and the pressure on her bladder suggested he was right.

Groaning, she thought about her job and the fact that she was irreparably late. Bill Withers was probably chewing her up one side and down the other. "I'm gonna get fired yet," she muttered, then added, "Give me a sec."

Scrambling from beneath the warmth of her duvet, she stumbled over one of her shoes on her way to the bathroom. Once inside, she shut the door, snapped on the light and

cringed at her reflection. Within minutes she'd relieved herself, splashed water onto her face and brushed her teeth. Her
face was a disaster, her short hair sticking up at all angles. The
best she could do was wet it down and scrub away the smudges
of mascara that darkened her eyes.

Thankfully her headache was gone and she was thinking
more clearly as she opened the door to the bedroom and found
Kurt leaning against the frame, a strange look on his face. She
yawned. "What?" she asked and then she knew. With drop-
dead certainty. Her heart nearly stopped. "It's the baby," she
said, fear suddenly gelling her blood. "Joshua. What's wrong?
Is he okay?"

"He's fine."

"How do you know?"

"I'm having Sharon Okano's place watched."

She was stunned and suddenly frantic and reached for the
shoe she'd nearly tripped over. "You really think something
might happen to him?"

"Let's just say I don't want to take any chances."

She crammed the shoe onto her foot, then bent down, peering under the bed for its mate. Her mind was clearing a bit as
she found the missing shoe and slid it on. Striker was jumping
at shadows, that was it. Joshua was fine. Fine. He had to be.

"Donahue's in town."

She rocked back on her heels.  The news hit her like a ton
of bricks, but she tried to stay calm. "How do you know?"

"He was spotted."

"By whom?"

"Someone working for me."

"Working for you. Did my brothers hire an entire platoon
of security guards or something?"

"Eric Brown and I have known each other for years. He's
been watching Sharon Okano's place."

"What? Wait! You've got someone spying on her?"

His face was rigid. "I'm not ready to take any chances."

"Don't you think someone lurking around will just draw attention to the place? You know, like waving some kind of red flag."

"He's a little more discreet than that."

She shook her head, clearing out the cobwebs, trying to keep her rising sense of panic at bay. "Wait a minute. This doesn't make any sense. Sam doesn't know about Joshua. He has no idea that I was pregnant...and probably wouldn't have cared one way or the other had he found out."

"You think."

"I'm pretty damn sure." She straightened.

"Then why would he be cruising by Sharon Okano's place?"

"Oh, God, I don't know." Her remaining calm quickly evaporated. She had to get to her baby, to see that he was all right. She made a beeline for the closet. "This is making less and less sense," she muttered and was already reaching for a jacket. Glancing at her shoes, she saw a pair of black cowboy boots, one of which had fallen over. Boots she hadn't worn since high school. Boots her father had given her and she'd never had the heart to give away. Ice slid through her veins as she walked closer and saw that the dust that had accumulated over the toes had been disturbed. Her throat went dry. "Dear God."

Kurt had followed her into the walk-in. He was pulling an overnight bag from an upper shelf. "Randi?" he asked, his voice filled with concern. "What?"

"Someone was in here." Fear mixed with fury. "I mean... unless when you got here you came into my closet and decided to try on my cowboy boots."

"Your boots?" His gaze swept the interior of the closet to land upon the dusty black leather.

"I haven't touched them in months and look—"

He was already bending down and seeing for himself. "You're sure that you didn't—"

"No. I'm telling you someone was in here!" She tamped down the panic that threatened her, and fought the urge to kick at something. No one had the right to break into her home. No one.

"Who else has a key?"

"To this place?"

"Yes."

"Just me."

"Not Donahue?"

"No!"

"Sharon? Your brothers?"

She was shaking her head violently. Was the man dense? "I'm telling you I never gave anyone a key, not even to come in and water the plants."

"What about a neighbor, just in case you lost yours?"

"No! Jeez, Striker, don't you get it? It's just me. I even changed the locks when I bought the place so the previous owner doesn't have a set rattling around in some drawer somewhere."

"Where do you keep the spare?"

"One with me. One in the car. Another in my top desk drawer."

He was already headed down the hallway and into the living room with Randi right on his heels.

"Show me."

"Here." Reaching around him, she pulled open the center drawer, felt until her fingers scraped against cold metal, then pulled the key from behind a year-old calendar. "Right where I left it."

"And the one in your car."

"I don't know. It was with me when I had the accident. I assume it was in the wreckage."

"You didn't ask the police?"

"I was in a coma, remember? When I woke up I was a mess, broken bones, internal injuries, and I had amnesia."

"The police inventoried everything in the car when it was impounded, so they must've found the key, right?" he insisted.

"I... Jeez, I'm not sure, but I don't think it was on the report. I saw it. I even have a copy somewhere."

"Back at the Flying M?"

"No—I cleared everything out when I left. It's here somewhere." She located her briefcase and rifled through the pockets until she found a manila envelope. Inside was a copy of the police report about the accident and the inventory receipt for the impounded car. She skimmed the documents quickly.

Road maps, registration, insurance information, three sixty-seven in change, a pair of sunglasses and a bottle of glass cleaner, other miscellaneous items but no key ring. "They didn't find it."

"And you didn't ask."

She whirled on him, crumpling the paper in her fist. "I already told you, I was laid up. I didn't think about it."

"Hell." Kurt's lips compressed into a blade-thin line. His eyes narrowed angrily. "Come on." He pocketed the key, slammed the drawer shut and stormed down the hallway to the bedroom. In three swift strides he was inside the closet again. He unzipped the overnight bag and handed it to her. "Here. Pack a few things. Quickly. And don't touch the damn boots." He disappeared again and she heard him banging in the kitchen before he returned with a plastic bag and started carefully sliding it over the dusty cowboy boots. "I've already got your laptop and your briefcase in the truck."

Suddenly she understood. He wanted her to leave. Now.

His jaw was set, his expression hard as granite. "Now, wait a minute. I'm not leaving town. Not yet." Things were moving too quickly, spinning out of control. "I just got home and I can't up and take off again. I've got responsibilities, a life here."

"We'll only be gone for a night or two. Until things cool off."

"We? As in you and me?"

"And the baby."

"And go where?"

"Someplace safe."

"This is my home."

"And someone's been in here. Someone with the key."

"I can change the locks, Striker. I've got a job and a home and—"

"And someone stalking you."

She opened her mouth to argue, then snapped it closed. She had to protect her baby. No matter what else. Yes, she needed to find out who was hell-bent on terrorizing her, but her first priority was to keep Joshua safe, and the truth of the matter was, Randi was already out of her mind with worry. Striker's concerns only served to fuel her anxiety. She was willing to bet he wasn't the kind of man to panic easily. And he was visibly upset. Great. She began throwing clothes into the overnight bag. "I can't take any chances with Joshua," she said.

"I know." His voice had a hint of kindness tucked into the deep timbre and she had to remind herself that he'd been hired to be concerned. Though she didn't believe that the money he'd been promised was his sole motivation in helping her, it certainly was a factor. If he kept both her and her son's skins intact, Striker's wallet would be considerably thicker. "Let's get a move on."

She was through arguing for the moment. No doubt Striker had been in more than his share of tight situations. If he really felt it was necessary to take her and her son and hide out for a while, so be it. She zipped the bag closed and ripped a suede jacket from its hanger. Was it her imagination or did it smell slightly of cigarette smoke?

Now she was getting paranoid. No one had been wearing her jacket. That was nuts.

Gritting her teeth, she fought the sensation that she'd been violated, that an intruder had pried into her private space. "I assume you've got some kind of plan."

"Yep." He straightened, the boots properly bagged.

"And that you're going to share it with me."

"Not yet."

"You can't tell me?"

"Not right now."

"Why not?"

"It's better if you don't know."

"Oh, right, keep the little woman in the dark. That's always a great idea," she said sarcastically. "This isn't the Dark Ages, Striker."

If possible, his lips compressed even further. His mouth was the thinnest of lines, his jaw set, his expression hard as nails. And then she got it. Why he was being so tight-lipped. "Wait a minute. What do you think? That this place is bugged?"

When he didn't answer, she shook her head. Disbelieving. "No way."

He threw her a look that cut her to the bone. "Let's get a move on."

She didn't argue, just dug through the drawers of her dresser and threw some essentials into her bag, then grabbed her purse.

Within minutes they were inside Kurt's truck and roaring out of the parking lot. Yesterday's rain had stopped, but the sky was still overcast, gray clouds moving slowly inland from the Pacific. Randi stared out the window, but her mind was racing. Could

Sam have found out about Joshua? It was possible, of course, that he'd somehow learned she'd had a baby, but she doubted he would do the math to figure out if he was the kid's father. The truth of the matter was that he just didn't give a damn. Never had. She drummed her fingers against the window.

"I don't know why you think just because Donahue's in town that Joshua's not safe. If he drove by, it was probably just a fluke, a coincidence. Believe me, Sam Donahue wouldn't give two cents that he fathered another kid." She leaned against the passenger door as Kurt inched the pickup through the tangle of thick traffic.

"A truck belonging to Donahue has cruised by Sharon Okano's apartment complex twice this afternoon. Not just once. I wouldn't call that a coincidence. Would you?"

"No." Her throat went dry, her fingers curled into balls of tension.

"Already checked the plates with the DMV. That's what tipped Brown off, the license plates were from out of state. Montana."

Randi's entire world cracked. She fingered the chain at her throat. "But he's rarely there, in Montana," she heard herself saying as if from a long distance away. "And I didn't tell him about Joshua."

"Doesn't matter what you told him. He could have found out easy enough. He has ties to Grand Hope. Parents, an ex-wife or two. Gossip travels fast. It doesn't take a rocket scientist to count back nine months from the date your baby was born." Striker managed to nose the truck onto the freeway where he accelerated for less than a mile, then slammed on the brakes as traffic stopped and far in the distance lights from a police car flashed bright.

"Great," Striker muttered, forcing the truck toward the next exit. He pulled his cell phone from the pocket of his jacket and poked in a number. A few seconds later, he said, "Look, we're caught in traffic. An accident northbound. It's gonna be awhile. Stay where you are and call me if the rig goes by or if there's any sign of Donahue."

Randi listened and tried not to panic. So Sam Donahue was in the area. It wasn't as if he never came to Seattle. Hadn't she hooked up with him here, in a bar on the waterfront? She'd been doing research on her book and had realized through the wonders of the internet that he'd been in a rodeo competition in Oregon and was traveling north on his way to Alberta, Canada. She'd emailed him, met him for a drink and the rest was history.

"Good. Just keep an eye out. We'll be there ASAP." Striker snapped the phone shut and slid a glance in her direction. "Donahue hasn't been back."

"Maybe I should call him."

A muscle in Kurt's jaw leaped as he glared through the windshield. "And why the hell would you want to do that?"

"To find out what he's doing in town."

Striker's eyes narrowed. "You'd call up the guy who's trying to kill you."

"We don't know that he's trying to kill me." She shook her head and leaned the back of her crown against the seat rest. "It doesn't make sense. Even if he knew about Joshua, Sam wouldn't want anything to do with him."

"So why did you two break up—wait a minute, let's start with how you got together."

"I'd always wanted to write a book and my brothers had not only glamorized the whole rodeo circuit but they had also told me about the seedy side. There were illegal wagers, lots of betting. Some contestants would throw a competition, others drugged their horses, or their competitors' mounts. The animals—bulls, calves, horses—were sometimes mistreated. It's a violent sport, one that attracts macho men and competitive women moving from one town to the next. There are groupies and bar fights and prescription and recreational drug abuse. A lot of these cowboys live in pain and there's the constant danger of being thrown and trampled or gored or crushed. High passion. I thought it would make for interesting reading, so, while interviewing people, I came across Sam Donahue." Her tongue nearly tripped on his name. "He grew up in Grand Hope, knew my brothers, was even on the circuit with Matt. I started interviewing him, one thing led to another and... well, the rest, as they say, is history."

"How'd you find him?"

"I read about a local rodeo, down towards Centralia. He was entered, so I got his number, gave him a call and agreed to meet him for a drink. My brothers didn't much like him but I found him interesting and charming. We had a connection in that we both grew up in Montana, and I was coming off a bad relationship, so we hit it off. In retrospect, I'd probably say it was a mistake, except for the fact that I ended up with Joshua. My son is worth every second of heartache I suffered."

"What kind of heartache?" Striker asked, his jaw rock hard.

She glanced through the window, avoiding his eyes. "Oh, you know. The kind where you find out that the last ex-wife wasn't quite an ex. Sam had never quite gotten around to signing the divorce papers." She felt a fool for having believed the lying son of a bitch. She'd known better. She was a journalist, for crying out loud. She should have checked him out, seen the warning signs, because she'd always made a point of dating men who were completely single—not engaged, not separated, not seriously connected with any woman. But she'd failed with Sam Donahue, believing him when he'd lied and said he'd been separated two years, divorced for six months.

Striker was easing the truck past the accident where the

driver of a tow truck was winching a mangled Honda onto its bed and a couple of police officers were talking with two men near the twisted front end of a minivan of some kind. A paramedic truck was parked at an angle and two officers were talking with several boys in baseball hats who appeared unhurt but shaken. As soon as the truck was past the accident, traffic cleared and Striker pushed the speed limit again.

"So you didn't know he was married."

"Right," she replied, but couldn't stop the heat from washing up the back of her neck. She'd been a fool. "I knew that he was divorced from his first wife, Corrine. Patsy was his second wife. Might still be for all I know. Once I found out he was still married I was outta there." With one finger she drew on the condensation on the passenger-door window.

"You loved him." There it was. The statement she'd withdrawn from; the one she couldn't face.

Striker's fingers were coiled in a death grip around the steering wheel, as if somehow her answer mattered to him.

"I thought I loved him, but...even while we were seeing each other, I knew it wasn't right. There was something off." It was hard to explain that tumble of emotions. "The trouble was, by the time I'd figured it out, I was pregnant."

"So you decided to keep the baby and the secret."

"Yes," she admitted, strangely relieved to unburden herself as Striker took an off-ramp and cut through the neighborhood where Sharon Okano's apartment was located. She hesitated about telling him the rest of the story, but decided to trust him with the truth. "Along with the fact that Sam didn't tell me he was married, he also failed to mention that he and some of his friends had actually drugged a competitor's animals just before the competition. One bull reacted violently, injuring himself and his rider. The Brahman had to be put down, but not before throwing the rider and trampling him. The cowboy survived, but barely. Ended up with broken ribs, a shattered wrist, crushed pelvis and punctured spleen."

"So why wasn't Donahue arrested?"

"Not enough proof. No one saw him do it. He and his friends came up with an alibi." She glanced at Striker as he pulled into a parking space at Sharon's apartment building. "He never admitted drugging the bull, and I'm really not sure that it wasn't one of his buddies who actually did the injecting, but I'm sure that he was behind it. Just a gut feeling and the way he talked about the incident." She mentally chastised herself for being such a fool, and stared out the passenger window. "I'd already decided not to see him anymore and then, on top of all that, I discovered he was still married. Nice, huh?"

Striker cut the engine. "Not very."

"I know." The old pain cut deep, but she wasn't about to break down. Not in front of this man; not in front of anyone. Her jaw slid to one side. "Man, can I pick 'em."

Kurt touched her shoulder. "Just for the record, Randi. You deserve better than Donahue." She glanced his way and found him staring at her. His gaze scraped hers and beneath the hard facade, hidden in his eyes, a sliver of understanding, a tiny bit of empathy. "Come on. Let's go get your kid." He offered her the hint of a smile, then his grin faded quickly and the moment, that instant of connection, passed.

Her silly heart wrenched, and tears, so close to the surface, threatened.

She was out of the truck in a flash, taking the stairs to the upper-story unit two at a time. Suddenly frantic to see her baby, she pounded on the door. Sharon, a petite woman, answered. In her arms was Joshua. Blinking as if he'd just woken up from a nap, his fuzz of red-blond hair sticking straight up, he wiggled at the sight of her. Randi's heart split into a million pieces at the sight of her son. The tears she'd been fighting filled her eyes.

"Hey, big guy," she whispered, her voice hoarse.

"He missed you," Sharon said as she transferred the baby into Randi's hungry arms.

"Not half as bad as I missed him." Randi was snuggling her son, wrapped up in the wonder of holding him, smelling the baby shampoo in his hair and listening to the little coo that escaped those tiny lips, when she heard a quiet cough behind her. "Oh…this is Kurt Striker. Sharon Okano. Kurt is a friend of my brother Slade's." With an arch of her eyebrow, she added, "All of my brothers decided to hire him as, if you'll believe this, my personal bodyguard."

"Bodyguard?" Sharon's eyebrows lifted a bit. "How serious is this trouble you're in?"

"Serious enough, I guess. Kurt thinks it would be best if we kept the baby with us."

"Whatever you want." Sharon gently touched Joshua's cheek. "He's adorable, you know. I'm not sure that if you left him here much longer I could ever give him up."

"You need one of your own."

"But first, a man, I think," Sharon said. "They seem to be a necessary part of the equation." She glanced at Kurt, but Randi ignored the innuendo. She didn't need a man to help raise her son. She'd do just fine on her own.

They didn't stay long. While the women were packing Joshua's things, Kurt asked Sharon if she'd had any strange phone calls or visitors. When Sharon reported that nothing out of the ordinary had happened, Kurt called his partner and within fifteen minutes, Randi, Kurt and Joshua, tucked into his car seat, were on the road and heading east out of Seattle. The rain had started, a deep steady mist, and Striker had flipped on the wipers.

"You're still not going to tell me where we're going?" she asked.

"Inland."

"I know that much, but where exactly?" When he didn't immediately respond, she said, "I have a job to do. Remember? I can't be gone indefinitely." She glanced at her watch, scowled as it was after three, then dug in her purse, retrieved her cell phone and punched out the numbers for the *Clarion*. Within a minute she was connected to Bill Withers's voice mail and left a quick message, indicating she had a family emergency and vowing she would email a couple of new columns. As she hung up, she said, "I don't know how much of that Withers will buy, but it should give us a couple of days."

"Maybe that's all we'll need." He sped around a fuel truck, but his voice lacked conviction.

"Listen, Striker, we've got to nail this creep and soon," Randi said as the wipers slapped away the rain. "I need my life back."

The look he sent her sliced into her soul. "So do I."

*The bitch wouldn't get away with it.*

Three cars behind Striker's truck, gloved hands tight over the steering wheel, the would-be killer drove carefully, coming close to the pickup, then backing off, listening to a CD from the eighties as red taillights blurred. Jon Bon Jovi's voice wailed through the speakers and the stalker licked dry lips as the pickup cut across the floating bridge, over the steely waters of Lake Washington. Who knew where they were headed? To the suburbs of upscale Bellevue? Or somewhere around Lake Sammamish? Maybe farther into the forested hills. Even the Cascade Mountains.

Whatever.

It didn't matter.

Sweet vengeance brought a smile to the stalker's lips.

Randi McCafferty's destination was about to become her final resting place.

# Chapter 9

"Get the baby ready," Kurt said as he took an exit off the freeway. Glancing in the rearview mirror to be certain he wasn't followed, he doubled back, heading west, only to get off at the previous stop and drive along a frontage heading toward Seattle again.

"What are we doing?" Randi asked.

"Changing vehicles." Carefully he timed the stoplights, making certain he was the last vehicle through the two intersections before turning down one street and pulling into a gas station.

"What? Why?"

"I'm not taking any chances that we're being followed."

"You saw someone?"

"No."

"But—"

"Just make it fast and jump into that brown SUV." He nodded toward the back of the station to a banged-up vehicle with tinted windows and zero chrome. The SUV was completely nondescript, the fenders and tires splattered with mud. "It belongs to a friend of mine," Striker said. "He's waiting. He'll drive the truck."

"This is nuts," Randi muttered, but she unstrapped the baby seat and pulled it, along with Joshua, from the truck.

"I don't think so."

Quickly, as Randi did as she was told, Striker topped off his tank.

Eric was waiting for them. He'd been talking on his cell phone and smoking a cigarette, but spying Striker, tossed the cigarette into a puddle and gave a quick wave. Ending his call, he helped Randi load up, then traded places with Kurt. The entire exchange had taken less than a minute. Seconds after that, Kurt was in the driver's seat of the Jeep, heading east again.

"I don't think I can stand all of this cloak-and-dagger stuff," Randi complained, and even in the darkness he saw the outline of her jaw, the slope of her cheek, the purse of those incredible lips. Good Lord, she was one helluva woman. Intriguingly beautiful, sexy as hell, smarter than she needed to be and endowed with a tongue sharp enough to cut through a strong man's ego.

"Sure you can."

"Whatever my brothers are paying you, it's not enough."

"That's probably true." He glanced at her once more, then turned his attention to the road. Night had fallen, but the rain had let up a bit. His tires sang on the wet pavement and the rumble of the SUV's engine was smooth and steady. The baby was quiet in the backseat, and for the first time in years Kurt felt a little sensation of being with family. Which was ridiculous. The woman was a client, the child just part of the package. He told himself to remember that. No matter what else. He was her bodyguard. His job was to keep her alive and find out who was trying to kill her.

Nothing more.

*What about the other night at the ranch?* his damning mind taunted. *Remember how much you wanted her, how you went about seducing her? How can you forget the thrill of slipping her robe off her shoulders and unveiling those incredible breasts. What about the look of surprise and wonder in her eyes, or the soft, inviting curve of her lips as you kissed the hollow of her throat. Think about the raw need that drove you to untie the belt at her waist. The robe gave way, the nightgown followed and she was naked aside from a slim gold chain and locket at her throat. You didn't waste any time kicking off your jeans. You wanted her, Striker. More than you've ever wanted a woman in your life. You would have died to have her and you did, didn't you? Over and over again. Feeling her heat surround you, listening to the pounding of your heart and feeling your blood sing through your veins. You were so hot and hard, nothing could have stopped you. What about then, when you gave in to temptation?*

The back of his neck tightened as he remembered and his inner voice continued to taunt him.

*If you can convince yourself that Randi McCafferty is just another client, then you're a bigger fool than you know.*

It was late by the time the Jeep bounced along the rocky, mossy ruts that constituted the driveway to what could only be loosely called a cabin. Set deep in the forest and barricaded by a locked gate to which Kurt had miraculously had the key, the place was obviously deserted and had been for a long time. Randi shuddered inwardly as the Jeep's headlights illuminated the sorry little bungalow. Tattered shades were drawn over the windows, rust was evident in the few downspouts that were still connected to the gutters, and the moss–covered roof sagged pitifully.

"You sure you don't want to look for a Motel 6?" she asked. "Even a Motel 2 would be an improvement over this."

"Not yet." Kurt had already pulled on the emergency brake and cut the engine. "Think of it as rustic."

"Right. Rustic. And quaint." She shook her head.

"This used to be the gatekeeper's house when this area was actively being logged," he explained.

"And now?" She stepped out of the Jeep and her boots sank in the soggy loam of the forest floor.

"It's been a while since the cabin's been inhabited."

"A long while, I'd guess. Come on, baby, it's time to check out our new digs." She hauled Joshua in his carrier up creaky porch steps as Kurt, with the aid of a flashlight and another key, opened a door that creaked as it swung inward.

Kurt tried a light switch. Nothing. Just a loud click. "Juice isn't turned on, I guess."

"Fabulous."

He found a lantern and struck a match. Immediately the room was flooded with a soft golden glow that couldn't hide the dust, cobwebs and general malaise of the place. The floor was scarred fir, the ceiling pine was stained where rainwater had seeped inside and it smelled of must and years of neglect.

"Home sweet home," she cracked.

"For the time being." But Kurt was already stalking through the small rooms, running his flashlight along the floor and ceiling. "We won't have electricity, but we'll manage."

"So no hot water, light or heat."

"But a woodstove and lanterns. We'll be okay."

"What about a bathroom?"

He shook his head. "There's an old pump on the porch and, if you'll give me a minute—" he looked in a few cupboards and closets before coming up with a bucket "—voila! An old fashioned Porta Potti."

"Give me a break," she muttered.

"Come on, you're a McCafferty. Rustic living should be a piece of cake."

"Let me give you a clue, Striker. This is *waaaay* beyond rustic."

"I heard you were a tomboy growing up."

"Slade talks too much."

"Probably. But you used to camp all the time."

"In the summers. I was twelve or thirteen."

"It's like riding a bike. You never forget how."

"We'll see." But she didn't complain as they hauled in equipment that had been loaded into the Jeep. Sleeping bags, canned goods, a cooler for fresh food, cooking equipment, paper plates, propane stove, towels and toilet paper. "You thought this through."

"I just told Eric to pack the essentials."

"What about a phone?"

"Our cells should work."

Scrounging in her purse, she found her phone, yanked it out and turned it on. The backlit message wasn't encouraging. "Looking for service," she read aloud, and watched as the cell failed to find a signal. "Hopefully yours is stronger."

He flashed her a grin that seemed to sizzle in the dim light. "I already checked. It works."

"So what about a phone jack to link up my laptop?"

He lifted a shoulder. "Looks like you're out of luck unless you've got one of those wireless hookups."

"Not a prayer."

"Then you'll have to be out of touch for a while."

"Great," she muttered. "I don't suppose it matters that I could lose my job over this."

"Better than your life."

She was about to reply, when the baby began to cry. Quickly, Randi mixed formula with some of the bottled water she'd brought, then pulled off dust cloths from furniture that looked as if it was in style around the end of World War II. Joshua was really cranking it up by the time Randi plopped herself into a rocking chair and braced herself for the sound of scurrying feet as mice skittered out from the old cushions. Fortunately, as she settled into the chair, no protesting squeaks erupted, nor did any little scurrying rodent make a mad dash to the darker corners. With the baby's blanket wrapped around him, she fed her son and felt a few seconds' relaxation as his wails subsided and he ate hungrily from the bottle. There was a peace to holding her baby, a calm that kept her fears and worries at bay. He looked up at her as he ate, and in those precious, bonding moments, she never once doubted that her affair with Sam Donahue was worth every second of her later regrets.

Kurt was busy checking the flue, starting a fire in an antique-looking woodstove. Once the fire was crackling, he rocked back on his heels and dusted his hands. She tried not to notice how his jacket stretched at the shoulders or the way his jeans fit snug around his hips and buttocks. Nor did she want to observe that his hair fell in an unruly lock over his forehead, or that his cheekbones were strong enough to hint at some long-forgotten Native American heritage.

He was too damn sexy for his own good.

As if sensing her watching him, he straightened slowly and she was given a bird's-eye view of his long back as he stretched, then walked to a black beat-up leather case and unzipped it. Out came a laptop computer complete with wireless connection device.

He glanced over his shoulder, his green eyes glinting in amusement.

"You could have said something," she charged.

"And miss seeing you get ticked off? No way. But this isn't the be-all and end-all. I have one extra battery. No more. Since there's no electricity here, the juice won't last forever."

"Wonderful," she said, lifting her baby to her shoulder and gently rubbing his back.

"It's better than nothing."

"Can I use it?"

"For a small fee," he said as the corners of his mouth twitched.

"You are *so* full of it."

"Wouldn't want to disappoint."

"You never do, Striker."

"Good. Let's keep it that way."

Joshua gave a loud burp. "There we go, big guy," she whispered as she spread his blanket on a pad and changed his diaper. The baby kicked and gurgled, his eyes bright in the firelight. "Oh, you're full of the devil, aren't you?" She played with him a few more minutes until he yawned and sighed. Randi held him and swayed a little as he nodded off. She couldn't imagine what life would have been like without this precious little boy. She kissed his soft crown, and as his breathing became regular and his head heavy, she placed him upon the makeshift crib of blankets and pillows, then glanced around the stark, near-empty cabin. "We really are in the middle of no-darned-where."

"That was the general idea."

She ran a finger through the dust on an old scarred table. "No electricity, no indoor plumbing, no television, radio or even any good books lying around."

"I guess we'll just have to make do and find some way to amuse ourselves." His expression was positively wicked, his eyes glittering with amusement. That he could find even the tiniest bit of humor in this vile situation was something, she thought, though she didn't like the way her throat caught when he stared at her, nor the way blood went rushing through her veins as he cocked an arrogant eyebrow.

"I think we'll do just fine," she said, hoping to sound frosty when, in fact, her voice was more than a tad breathless. Damn it all, she didn't like the idea of being trapped here with him in the middle of God-only-knew-where, didn't like feeling vulnerable not only to whoever was stalking her, but also to the warring emotions she felt whenever she was around Striker. *Don't even go there,* she told herself. *All you have to do is get through the next few days. By then, if he does his job the way he's supposed to, he'll catch the bad guy and you can reclaim your life. Then, you'll be safe. You and your baby can start over.*

*Unless something goes wrong. Terribly, terribly wrong.*

She glanced again at Striker.

Whether she liked it or not, she was stuck with him.

Things could be worse.

Less than two hours later, Striker's phone jangled.

He jumped and snapped it open. "Striker."

"It's Kelly. I've got information."

*Finally!* He leaned a hip against an old windowsill and watched as Randi, glasses perched on the end of her nose, looked up from his laptop. "News?"

He nodded. "Go on," he said into the phone and listened as Matt McCafferty's wife began to explain.

"I think I've located the vehicle that forced Randi off the road in Glacier Park. A maroon Ford truck, a few years old, had some dents banged out of it in a chop shop in Idaho. All under-the-table stuff. Got the lead from a disgruntled employee who swears the chop shop owner owes him back wages."

Striker's jaw hardened. "Let me guess. The truck was registered to Sam Donahue."

"Close. Actually was once owned by Marv Bates, or, precisely, a girlfriend of his."

"Have you located Bates?"

Randi visibly stiffened. She set aside the laptop and crossed the few feet separating them. "We're working on it. I've got the police involved. My old boss, Espinoza, is doing what he can." Roberto Espinoza was a senior detective who was working on Randi's case. Kelly Dillinger had once worked for him, but turned in her badge about the time she married Matt McCafferty. "But so far, we haven't been able to locate Mr. Bates."

"He had an alibi."

"Yeah," Kelly said. "Airtight. Good ol' boys Sam Donahue and Charlie Caldwell swore they were all over at Marv's house when Randi was forced off the road. Charlie's girlfriend at the time, Trina Spencer, verified the story, but now Charlie and Trina have split, so we're looking for her. Maybe she'll change her tune now that Charlie's no longer the love of her life and the truck she owned has been linked to the crime. We're talking to the employees of the chop shop. I figure it's just a matter of time before one of 'em cracks."

"Good. It's a start."

"Finally," Kelly agreed. "I'll keep working on it."

"Want to talk to Randi?"

"Absolutely." Striker handed the phone to Randi and listened to her end of the conversation as she asked about what Kelly had discovered, then turned the conversation to her family. A few minutes later, she hung up.

"This is the break you've been waiting for," she said, and he heard the hope in her voice.

God, he hated to burst her bubble. "It's a start, Randi. Time will tell if it pans out, but yeah, it's something."

He only hoped it was enough.

"Why don't you turn in." He unrolled a sleeping bag, placing it between the baby's makeshift crib and the fire.

"Where will you be?"

"Here." He shoved a chair close to the door.

She eyed the old wingback. "Aren't you going to sleep?"

"Maybe doze."

"You're still afraid," she charged.

"Not afraid. Just vigilant."

She shook her head, unaware that the fire's glow brought out the red streaks in her hair. Sighing, she started working off one boot with the toe of another. "I really can't believe this is my life." The first boot came off, followed quickly by the second. Plopping down on the sleeping bag, she sat cross-legged and stared at the fire. "I just wanted to write a book, you know. Show my dad, my boss, even my brothers that I was capable of doing something really newsworthy. My family thought I was nuts when I went into journalism in college—my dad in particular. He couldn't see any use in it. Not for his daughter, anyway. And then I landed the job with the paper in Seattle and it became a joke. Advice to single people. My brothers thought it was just a lot of fluff, even when the column took off and was syndicated." She glanced at Striker. "You know my brothers. They're pretty much straight-shooter, feet-on-the-ground types. I don't think Matt or Slade or Thorne would ever be ones to write in for advice on their love lives."

Kurt laughed.

"Nor you, I suppose?"

He arched an eyebrow in her direction. "Not likely."

"And the articles I did for magazines under R. J. McKay, it was all woman stuff, too. So the book—" she looked up at the ceiling as if she could find an answer in the cobwebby beams and rafters "—it was an attempt to legitimatize my career. Unfortunately Dad died before it was finished and then all the trouble started." She rubbed her knees and cocked her head. Her locket slipped over the collar of her shirt and he noticed it winking in the firelight. His mouth turned dry at the sight of her slim throat and the curve of her neck where it met her shoulder. A tightening in his groin forced him to look away.

"Maybe the trouble's about to end."

"That would be heaven," she said. "You know, I always liked living on the edge, being a part of the action, whatever it was, never set my roots down too deep."

"A true McCafferty."

She chuckled. "I suppose. But now, with the baby and after everything that happened, I just want some peace of mind. I want my life in the city back."

"And the book?"

Her smile grew slowly. "Oh, I'm still going to write it," she vowed, and he noticed a determined edge to her voice, a steely resolve hidden in her grin. "Bedtime?"

The question sounded innocent, but it still created an image of their lovemaking. "Whenever you want."

"And you're just going to play security guard by the door."

"Yep." He nodded. "Get some sleep."

"Not until you tell me what it is that makes you tick," she said. "Come on, I told you all about my dreams of being a journalist and how my family practically laughed in my face. You know all about the men I've dated in recent history and I've also told you about my book and how I got involved with a man who was still married and might be trying to kill me. Whatever you're hiding can't be that bad."

"Why do you think I'm hiding something?"

"We all have secrets, Striker. What's yours?"

*That I'm falling for you,* he thought, then clamped his mind shut. No way. No how. His involvement with Randi McCafferty had to remain professional. No matter what. "I was married," he said, and felt that old raw pain cutting through him.

"What happened?"

He hesitated. This was a subject he rarely bridged, never brought up on his own. "She divorced me."

"Because of your work?"

"No." He glanced at her baby sleeping so soundly in his blankets, remembered the rush of seeing his own child for the first time, remembered the smell of her, the wonder of caring too much for one little beguiling person.

"Another woman?" she asked, and he saw the wariness in the set of her jaw.

"No. That would have been easier," he admitted. "Cleaner."

"Then, what happened? Don't give me any of that 'we grew away from each other' or 'we drifted apart.' I have readers who write me by the dozens and they all say the same thing."

"What happened between me and my ex-wife can't be cured by advice in your column," he said more bitterly than he'd planned.

"I didn't mean to imply that it could." She was a little angry. He could feel it.

"Good."

"So what happened, Striker?"

His jaw worked.

"Can't talk about it?" She rolled her eyes. "After I explained about Sam Donahue? That I was sleeping with him and he was still married. How do you think I feel, not seeing the signs, not reading the clues. Jeez, whatever it is can't be that humiliating!"

"We had a daughter," he said, his voice seeming to come from outside his body. "Her name was Heather." His throat tightened with the memories. "I used to take her with me on the boat and she loved it. My wife didn't like it, was afraid of

the water. But I insisted it would be safe. And it was. Until..."
His chest felt as if the weight of the sea was upon it. Randi
didn't say a word but she'd blanched, her skin suddenly pale,
as if she knew what was to come. Striker closed his eyes, but
still he could see that day, the storm coming in on the hori-
zon, remember the way the engine had stalled. "Until the last
time. Heather and I went boating. The engine had cut out and
I was busy fiddling with it when she fell overboard. Somehow
her life jacket slipped off. It was a fluke, but still... I dived in
after her but she'd struck her head. Took in too much water."
He blinked hard. "It was too late. I couldn't save her." Pain
racked through his soul.

Randi didn't move. Just stared at him.

"My wife blamed me," he said, leaning against the door.
"The divorce was just a formality."

# Chapter 10

Dear God, how she'd misjudged him! "I'm so sorry," she whispered, wondering how anyone survived losing a child.

"It's not your fault."

"And it wasn't yours. It was an accident," she said then saw recrimination darken his gaze.

"So I told myself. But if I hadn't insisted upon taking her..." He scowled. "Look, it happened. Over five years ago. No reason to bring it up now."

Randi's heart split. For all of his denials, the pain was fresh in him. "Do you have a picture?"

"What?"

"Of your daughter?"

When he hesitated, she crawled out of the sleeping bag. "I'd like to see."

"This isn't a good idea."

"Not the first," she said as she crossed the room. Reluctantly he reached into his back pocket, pulled out his wallet and flipped it open. Randi's throat closed as she took the battered leather and gazed at the plastic-encased photograph of a darling little girl. Blond pigtails framed a cherubic face that seemed primed for the camera's eye. Under apple cheeks, her tiny grin showed off perfect little baby teeth. "She's beautiful."

"Yes." He nodded, his lips thin and tight. "She was."

"I apologize if I said anything insensitive before. I didn't know."

"I don't talk about it much."

"Maybe you should."

"Don't think so." He took the wallet from her fingers and snapped it shut.

"If I'd known…"

"What? What would you have done differently?" he asked, a trace of bitterness to his words. "There's nothing you can say, nothing you can do, nothing that will change what happened."

She reached forward to stroke his cheek and he grabbed her wrist. "Don't," he warned. "I don't want your pity or your sympathy."

"Empathy," she said.

"No one who hasn't lost a child can empathize," he said, his fingers tightening, his eyes fierce. "It's just not possible."

"Maybe not, but that doesn't mean I can't feel some of your pain."

"Well, don't. It's mine. You can do nothing." A muscle worked in his jaw. "I shouldn't have told you."

"No…it's better."

"How?" he demanded, his nostrils flaring. "Tell me how you knowing about Heather helps anything."

"I understand you better."

"Jesus, Randi. That's woman patter. You don't need to figure out what makes me tick or even know about what I've been through. You weren't there, okay? So I'd rather you not try to 'feel my pain' or any of that self-aggrandizing pseudo-psychological, television talk-show crap. You just need to do what I tell you to do so that we can make certain that you and your son are safe. End of story."

"Not quite," she whispered, and without thinking, placed a kiss on the corner of his mouth. The need to soothe him was overpowering, nearly as intense as her own need to be comforted. To be held. "If we're going to be sequestered from the rest of the world, I do need to understand you." She kissed him again.

"Don't do that." His voice was hoarse and she noticed that he shifted, as if his jeans were suddenly too tight.

"Why?" she asked, not budging an inch, so close she smelled the rain drying on his jacket. She felt reckless and wild and wanted to touch him and hold him close, this man who had seen so much of life, felt so much pain.

"You know why."

"Kurt, I just want to help."

"You can't." He turned to look her square in the eye, his nose only inches from hers. "Don't you know what you're dealing with here?"

"I'm not afraid." She kissed his cheek and he groaned.

"Don't do this, Randi," he ordered, but it sounded like a plea.

"You can trust me."

"This isn't about trust."

"No? Then why are we here? Alone together? If I didn't trust you, you can bet I wouldn't be locked away from the world like this. Believe me, Striker, this is all about trust. That's why you told me about Heather."

"Let's leave her out of this!" he growled.

"You have a right to be angry about what happened to your daughter."

"Good. 'Cuz I am and you're not helping!"

"No?" she said, her temper snapping. "Then I don't suppose I helped the other night, either?"

"Hell," he muttered, glancing away. His fingers were still surrounding her wrist, her pulse beating wildly beneath the warm pads.

"You remember that night, don't you?" she reminded him. "The one where you were watching me from the second story? *That* night, you didn't have any of these reservations."

"That night is the reason I'm having these reservations. It was a mistake."

"You didn't think so at the time."

"You're right, I didn't think period. But I'm trying to now."

"So it's okay for you to seduce me, but not the other way around."

He closed his eyes as if to gain strength. "I didn't bring you up here to sleep with you."

"No?" She kissed him again, behind his ear, and this time his reaction was immediate.

He turned swiftly, pinning her onto the floor and leaning over her. "Look, woman, you're pushing it with me. A man can only take so much."

"Same with a woman," she said. "You can't just—"

The rest of her sentence was cut off as his lips clamped over hers. Fierce. Hot. Hard. Desperate. He kissed her long and wildly and she responded, opening her mouth, feeling his tongue slide into her, arching as it probed. Her breath was trapped, her blood on fire, her bones melting as he slid his hands up and down her body. No longer did he deny what they both wanted. No longer did he say a word, just kissed and touched and tugged at her clothes.

She had no regrets. This was what she wanted. To touch him, physically and emotionally. Her own fingers struggled with the zipper of his coat and the shirt buttons below. She felt strong sinewy muscles covered by taut skin and chest hair that was stiff. Her fingertips grazed nipples that tightened at her touch.

"Oh, God," he rasped as he yanked off his shirt, then worked at the hem of her sweater. Strong, callused hands rubbed her skin as he scaled her ribs. She cried out as he touched beneath her bra, skimming the underside of her breasts. Her nipples tightened. Her breasts filled and she wanted him. With every breath in her body, she needed to feel him inside her, to have him rubbing and moving and balming the ache growing deep within. He peeled away her bra and scooped her into his strong arms, climbed to his feet and carried her to the sleeping bag, where they fell into a tangle of arms and legs. His mouth was ravenous as he kissed her face and breasts. Hard fingers splayed against the small of her back, pulling her tight against him, pressing her mound into the hardness of his fly, rubbing her sensually.

She moaned softly as he kissed her nipples, teasing them with his tongue and lips, biting softly before he nuzzled and sucked. Her mind spun in dizzying fragments of light and shadow. She saw his face buried into her breasts, felt his fingertips probing beneath the waistband of her pants, burned with a want so hot she was sweating in the cold room, aching for him, her fingers reaching for his fly. "Randi," he whispered across her wet breasts. "Oh, God, darlin'..." His hand slid down the slope of her rump, fingers stretching to find that sweet spot within her. She cried out and moved her hips as he yanked off her pants with his free hand and continued to explore with his other. Parting her. Delving deep. Causing her to gasp and throw her head back as she arched and he suckled at her breast. He scratched the surface of her need. Liquid warmth seared her.

"More," she whispered, lost.

He stripped her panties from her.

She fumbled with the buttons of his fly, but they came undone and, with amazing agility, he kicked out of his jeans to be naked with her. Skin on skin. Flesh on flesh. Blood heating, he pulled her atop him, and in one quick movement removed his hand and replaced it with his thick, hard erection.

"Oh!" she cried as he pushed her hips down and raised his buttocks in one swift motion. The world melted away as they began to move. Slowly at first. Friction and fire. Heat and want. All emotion and need. Randi closed her eyes and heard a slow, long moan. From her throat or his? She didn't know, didn't care. Nothing mattered but the man beneath her, the man she wanted, the man she feared she loved. This small moment in time could very well be their last, but she didn't care, just wanted to feel him within her.

Deep inside something snapped. She wanted more of him. More. So much more. Opening her eyes, she saw him staring at her, his own gaze bright with the same desire as her own. "That's it, baby," he whispered as she increased the tempo. He caught up quickly and took command, his hands tight on her as he began pumping furiously beneath her. Beads of sweat dotted his forehead, his skin tight, his hair damp with perspiration. Yet he didn't stop.

Hotter. Faster. The world spinning. "Oh, God, oh, God, oh...oh..." she cried as the world seemed to catch fire and explode around her. She convulsed, but still he held her upright, still he thrust into her, and though she'd felt complete surrender a minute before, she met each of his jabs with her own downward motion. Again. And again... Over and over until the heat rose in her in such a rush that she bucked. This time he came with her, his breath screaming out of his lungs, his body straining upward as he let go and finally emptied himself into her.

"Randi!" he cried hoarsely, his voice breaking, "Oh, love..."

She fell against him and felt his strong arms surround her and hold her close. One hand cradled her head, the other was wrapped around her waist. Tears sprang unbidden to her eyes as his words echoed through her head. Though they were spoken in the throes of passion, though she knew she would never hear them again, she clung to them. *Randi... Oh, love.*

They would be meaningless in the morning, but for now, for all of this night, they sustained her. She cuddled up against him, and knew a few moments' peace. For tonight, she would indulge herself. For tonight, she would sleep with this man she could so easily love. For tonight she'd forget that he was her bodyguard, paid to protect her, a man who no woman in her right mind would allow herself to fall for.

Lovers.

She and Kurt had become lovers.

The thought hit her hard, battering at her before she opened her eyes and knew that he wasn't in the sleeping bag with her. They'd made love over and over the night before and now... She opened one eye to the cabin as morning light streamed through the dusty windows. If anything, the dilapidated old cottage looked worse in the gloom of the day. The baby was rustling. It had probably been his soft cries that had cut through her thick slumber and roused her. So here she was, naked, cold, no sign of Kurt, in the middle of nowhere.

"Coming," she called to the baby as she found her clothes and slid into them. As she felt a slight soreness between her legs, a reminder of what had happened, what she'd instigated last night. What had she been thinking? Embarrassed at her actions, she crawled over to her baby and smiled down at his beatific face. "Hungry?" she asked, though she was already changing him. How quickly she'd become adept at holding him in place, talking to him, removing the old diaper, cleaning him and whipping a new diaper around him.

She found premixed formula in a bottle and, singing softly, fed her child. She heard the door open and looked over her shoulder to spy Kurt, carrying an armload of split kindling into the cabin. She felt heat wash up the back of her neck, but he didn't seem embarrassed. "Mornin'," he drawled, and the look he sent her reminded her of their lovemaking all over again. She'd been the aggressor. She'd practically begged him to make love to her. She'd definitely seduced him and now she felt the fool.

"I think I should say something about last night," she offered.

"What's to say?"

"That I'm not usually like that…"

"Too bad." One side of his mouth lifted. "I thought it was pretty damn nice."

"Really? But you…I mean you acted like it was a mistake. You *said* it was one."

"But it happened, right? I think we shouldn't second-guess ourselves."

"So it was no big deal?" she asked, and felt slightly deflated.

"It was a big deal, but let's not start the morning with recriminations, okay? I don't think that would solve anything. As I said, I'm not into overanalyzing emotions." He stacked the kindling in an old crate that was probably home to several nests of spiders. "I was hoping to make coffee before you woke up."

"Mmm. Sounds like heaven," she admitted.

"It'll be just a second." He dusted his hands and found a packet of coffee.

"I don't suppose you have a nonfat, vanilla latte with extra foam and chocolate sprinkles?" she asked, and he snorted a laugh.

"You lived in Seattle too long."

"Tell that to my boss," she muttered. "Actually, when I'm finished here…" She inclined her head toward her son. "I want to call him. If I'm allowed," she added.

"Just as long as you don't divulge our whereabouts."

"That would be tough considering that I don't know where we are." Randi finished feeding the baby and played with him as she changed his clothes. While Kurt heated water for the instant coffee, she balanced her son to her shoulder and put in another call to Bill Withers, only to leave another voice message when the editor didn't pick up his phone. "Withers must be ducking me," she muttered as she redialed and connected with Sarah.

"Where've you been?" Sarah demanded once she realized she was talking to Randi. "Bill gave me the third degree, and whenever your name is mentioned, he looks as if he's having a seizure."

"I can't really say, but I'll be back—" she glanced at Kurt who was shaking his head "—soon. I don't really know when. In the meantime I'm going to email my stories. It shouldn't be that big of a deal, most of the questions I get come in over the internet."

"It's a control issue with Bill, but then it is with most men."

"Especially if the man happens to be your boss," Randi said. "Look, if he talks to you, tell him I'm trying to get hold of him. I've called twice and I'm going to email in a couple of hours."

"Well, hurry back, okay?"

"I'll be back as soon as I can," Randi assured her.

"Should I tell Joe?"

"What?"

"Paterno's back in town and he's been asking about you."

Randi and Joe had never been lovers, their relationship hadn't blossomed in a romantic way. She was surprised that he'd be looking for her. "Well, tell him I'll get back to him when I'm in town," she said, and saw Striker stiffen slightly. He couldn't help but overhear her conversation and she didn't like the fact that she had so little privacy. "Look, Sarah, I've got to run." She hung up, hoping to save as much battery as possible before Sarah could argue. Exchanging the phone for a cup of coffee, she said, "So I didn't lie, did I? This will end soon."

"I think so, but I did some checking this morning before you woke and so far no one's been able to locate Sam Donahue."

"You think he's hiding?"

"Maybe."

"Or...?" She didn't like the feeling she was getting. "Or you think he's followed us?"

"I don't know. Did he come looking for you at the office? I heard you tell your friend that you'd get back with him."

"That wasn't Sam." She hesitated, then decided to come clean. "It was Joe Paterno. We were...are...friends. That's all. That's all there ever was between us."

He looked as if he didn't believe her.

"Really." She lifted a shoulder. "Sorry to disappoint you. I get the feeling that you think I had this incredible love life, that I slept with every man I dated, but that just wasn't the case. I let everyone wonder about my baby's paternity to protect him. The fewer people who knew that Sam was the baby's father, the better it was for me and Joshua. At least that's what I thought, so I let people draw their own conclusions about my love life." She arched an eyebrow at him. "I might not have the best taste in men, but I am somewhat picky."

"I guess I should feel flattered."

"Damn straight," she said, sending a look guaranteed to kill, then took a long swallow of coffee before turning her attention to her baby. After all, he was the reason that everything was happening and Randi wouldn't have changed a thing. Not if it meant she never would have had her son. Joshua made it all worthwhile.

Even the accident, she thought as the baby giggled and cooed.

Late last fall she'd left Seattle intending to return to the ranch she'd inherited from her father. She'd just wanted some peace of mind and time alone in Montana where she intended to write her book and do some serious soul-searching. Once on the ranch, she'd made some stupid mistakes including firing Larry Todd, the foreman, and even letting Juanita Ramirez, the housekeeper, go. Those decisions had been stupid, as Larry had known the livestock backward and forward and Juanita had not only helped raise Randi and her half brothers but had put up with their father until the grumpy old man had died. But Randi had been on a mission and had believed that before she could take care of a baby, she had to prove to herself that she could be completely self-reliant.

She'd thought that living on the Flying M, returning to her roots and running the ranch while writing her book might be the right kind of therapy she needed. After the baby came, she'd figured she could look after her child and raise him where she'd grown up, away from the hustle and bustle of the city. Plus, she still had her job at the *Clarion,* using email and a fax machine, until she could return to Seattle every other week or so if need be.

The prospect of becoming a mother—a single mother— had been daunting. How would she deal with her son's inevitable questions about his father? When she finished the book and the scam was exposed, many people in the rodeo world, including Sam Donahue, would be investigated and possibly indicted. How would she feel knowing that she'd sent her son's father to prison?

Nevertheless, because she'd been born a McCafferty, the kind of person who never shied away from the truth or tough decisions, she'd come to the conclusion that she had to let the truth be known and let the chips fall where they may.

But she hadn't gotten the chance. On her way back to Grand Hope, she'd had the accident that had nearly taken her life and sent her into premature labor. She'd been laid up in a coma, woken up to find out that she couldn't remember anything and that she had this wonderful infant son. As she'd recovered and her memory had returned in bits and snatches, she was horrified to realize that she'd been played for a fool, that Sam Donahue was Joshua's father and that he was a heartless criminal.

And now... *And now what?* She leaned closer to the baby and her locket swung free of her shirt. Joshua giggled and smiled, kicking and reaching for the glittering gold heart. "Silly boy," she said, leaning over to buss him in the tummy. He chortled and she did it again, making a game of it, closing out her doubts and worries as she played with her child.

Striker's cell phone rang, disturbing the quiet.

He flipped it open and answered, "Kurt Striker... Yeah, she's right here... I don't know if that's such a great idea.... Fine. Just a sec."

Randi turned her head and saw Striker glowering through the window, his cell phone pressed against his ear. He glanced her way and her heart nearly stopped. Something had happened. Something bad. "What?"

"Okay, put him on, but I don't have much battery left, so he'd better keep it short." He held the phone toward Randi. "That was Brown. He found Sam Donahue."

The floor seemed to wobble. "And?"

"It's for you, darlin'." Kurt's smile was cold as ice. "Seems as if good ol' Sam wants to talk to you."

# Chapter 11

"What the hell's going on, Randi?" Sam Donahue shouted through the phone wires.

Randi braced herself for the onslaught. And it came.

"I've got some crazy son of a bitch telling me that I'm gonna be arrested because I tried to kill you or some damn thing and that's all a pile of crap. You *know* it's crap. Why would I want to hurt you? Because of the kid? Oh, give me a break! That story you're writing? Who would believe it? I've got an iron-clad alibi, so call off your dogs!"

"My dogs?" she repeated as static crackled in her ear. The signal was fading and fast. Thankfully.

"Yeah, this guy. Brown."

"I can't hear you, Sam."

"...nuts! Crazy! He's talkin' about the police... Oh, God, they're here... Look, Randi, I don't know what this is all about, maybe some personal vendetta or something... This is all wrong," he said, swearing a blue streak that broke up as the battery in the phone began to give out. "...damn it...sue you and anyone...false arrest...no way... Leave me the hell alone! Wait...Randi..." His voice faded completely and the connection stopped just as the cell phone beeped a final warning about its battery running low.

Numbly, she handed the phone back to Striker.

"What did he want?"

"To protest his innocence," she said. "He told me to call off my dogs."

"They aren't yours."

"I didn't have time to explain. He didn't give me much of a chance and the connection was miserable." She shoved her hands into the pockets of her jeans. "Not that I wanted to straighten him out." She glanced at her baby, sleeping again, so angelic, so unaware.

"You okay?" Kurt asked, rubbing the back of her neck in that comforting spot between her shoulder blades.

"Yeah. It wasn't all that emotional for me. I was surprised." She managed a sad smile. "You know, I thought I'd feel something. Anger, maybe, or even wistfulness, *any* kind of emotion because he *is* the father of my child, but I just felt...empty. And maybe a little sad. Not for me, but for Joshua." She shrugged. "Hard to explain." She glanced around the cabin, her gaze landing on her baby, who despite the tense conversation had fallen asleep. "But the odd thing about the phone call was that I believed him."

"Donahue?" Striker snorted as he walked to the fire and warmed his hands.

"Yes. I mean, he was so vehement, so outraged that he was being arrested. It didn't seem like an act."

Striker barked out a laugh. "You thought he'd go quietly?"

"No, of course not, but—"

"You're still protecting him," Kurt said with a frown. "You know, just because he's the father of your child doesn't mean you owe him any allegiance or anything."

That stung. "Are you kidding? The last thing I feel for Sam Donahue is allegiance. He was married when he and I met. *Married.* Not just going with someone, or even engaged. When I asked him about it, he'd said he was divorced, that they'd been separated for some time and the divorce had been final for months. He flat-out lied. Silly me. I believed him," she admitted, but that old pain, the embarrassment of falling for Donahue's line and lies wasn't as deep. She'd fantasized about meeting or talking with him again, of either telling him to go to hell or advising him that he had a son who was the most precious thing on earth. And she'd hoped to feel some satisfaction in the conversation, but instead, all she'd felt was relief that she wasn't involved with him, that she was here, with Kurt Striker, that in fact, she'd moved on.

*To what? A man who has been up front about his need to be independent; a sexy, single man who had no intention of settling down; a man who was so hurt after losing his child that he's formed a wall around his heart that no sane woman would try to scale. He's your bodyguard, Randi. Bought and paid for by your brothers. Don't be stupid enough to throw love into the mix. You'll only get hurt if you do.*

Kurt added a chunk of wood to the fire. The mossy fir sizzled and popped. "And still you believe him. Defend him."

"That's not what I was doing. I was just...I mean, if he's guilty, okay. But...I still believe in innocent until proven guilty. That's the law, isn't it?"

"Right. That's the law. I'll just have to prove that he's the culprit."

"If you can."

A muscle jumped in Striker's jaw as he glanced over his

shoulder. "Watch me." He swung the door of the woodstove shut so hard it banged, and Joshua, startled, let up a little cry.

Randi shot across the room and scooped up her baby. "It's all right," she whispered, holding him close and kissing a downy-soft cheek. But Joshua was already revving up—his cries, originally whimpers, grew louder, and his nose was beginning to run.

Striker looked at the baby and an expression of regret darkened his gaze. "I'll go see if I can recharge the cell's battery in the truck. I've got a second phone, but it doesn't hold a charge worth crap." With that he was out the door, letting in a gust of damp, cool air before the door slammed shut behind him.

"Battery, my eye," Randi confided to her tousle-haired son. "He just wants to put a little space between us." Which was fine. She needed time to think about the complications that had become her life and to hold her child. What was it about Striker that got to her? It seemed that they were always making either love or war. With Kurt, her passions ran white-hot and ice cold. There was nothing in between. And her emotions were always raw, her nerves strung taut whenever she was around him.

*Because you're falling in love with him, you idiot. Don't you see? Even now you're sneaking peeks out the window, hoping to catch a glimpse of him. You've got it bad, Randi. Real bad. If you don't watch out, Kurt Striker is going to break your heart.*

From a van near Eric Brown's apartment, the would-be killer hung up the phone and didn't bother smothering a smile. High tech was just so damn great. All one needed to know was how to tap into a cellular call, and that was pretty basic stuff these days. Easy as pie.

A fine mist had collected on the windshield and traffic, wheels humming against the wet pavement, spun by the parking lot of the convenience store where the van was parked. No one looked twice at the dark vehicle with its tinted windows. No one cared. Which made things so much easier.

Taking out a map, the stalker studied the roads and terrain of central Washington. So the bitch and her lover were in the mountains. With the kid. Hiding out like scared puppies. Which was fine and dandy. It wouldn't take long to flush her out and watch her run. The only question was, which way would Randi McCafferty flee?

To her condo on the lake?

Or back to Daddy's ranch and that herd of tough-as-nails brothers?

West?

Or east?

It didn't matter. What was the old saying? Patience was a virtue. Yeah, well, probably overrated, but there was another adage... Revenge is best served up cold.

Hmmph. Cold or hot, it didn't matter. Just as long as vengeance was served.

And it would be. No doubt about it.


The baby was fussy as if he, too, could feel the charged atmosphere between Randi and Kurt.

Randi changed Joshua's diaper and gave up on the column she'd been composing on Striker's computer. The article would have to wait. Until her son was calmer. Quieter.

Joshua had been out of sorts for two days now and Randi didn't blame him. Being here, trapped with Kurt Striker, was driving her crazy. It was little wonder her baby had picked up on the emotional pressure. But Randi was afraid there was more to the baby's cries than his just being out of sorts.

Joshua was usually a happy infant but now he cried almost constantly. Nothing would calm him until he fell asleep. His face seemed rosier than usual and his nose ran a bit. Randi checked his temperature and it was up a degree, so she was watching her child with an eagle eye and trying like crazy not to panic. She could deal with this. She was his mother. Okay, so she was a *new* mother, but some things are instinctive, right? She should know what to do. Women raised babies all the time, married women, single women, rich women, poor women. Surely there wasn't a secret that had somehow, through the ages, been cosmically and genetically denied to her and her alone. No way. She could deal with a little runny nose, a slight fever, the hint of a cough. She was Joshua's mother, for God's sake.

While trying to convince herself of her maternal infallibility, she wrapped Joshua in blankets, held him whenever she could, prayed that he'd snap out of it and generally worried that she was doing everything wrong.

"If he doesn't get better, I want to take him to a pediatrician," she told Kurt on the third day.

"You think something's wrong?" Striker had just finished stoking the fire and was obviously frustrated that he'd not heard back from the police or Eric Brown.

"I just want to make certain that he's okay."

"I don't think we can leave just yet." Striker walked over to the baby. With amazing gentleness, he plucked Joshua out of Randi's arms and, squatting, cradled Randi's son as if he'd done it all his life. "How're ya doin', sport?" he asked, and the baby blinked, then blew bubbles with his tiny lips. With a smile so tender it touched Randi's heart, Striker glanced up at her. "Seems fine to me."

"But he's been fussy."

"Must take after his mother."

"His temperature is running a little hot."

He crooked an eyebrow and his gaze raked her from her

feet to her chest, where he stopped, pointedly, then finally looked into her eyes.

"Say it and die," she warned.

"Wouldn't dare, lady. You've got me runnin' scared." He handed Joshua back to her.

"Very funny." She pretended to be angry, though she couldn't help but smile. "Okay, okay, so maybe I'm overreacting."

"Give the kid a chance. He might have a little cold, but we'll keep an eye on it."

"Easy for you to say. You're not a parent..." She let her voice fade as she saw Striker flinch. "Oh, God, I'm sorry," she whispered, wishing she could take back the thoughtless comment. But it was too late. The damage had been done. No doubt Kurt was reminded of the day he'd lost his own precious daughter.

"Just watch him," Striker advised, then walked outside.

Randi mentally kicked herself from one side of the cabin to the other. She thought about running after him, but decided against it. No...they all needed a little space. She thought of her condo in Seattle. If she were there...then what would she do? She'd be alone and have to leave Joshua with a babysitter.

*Yeah, a professional. Someone who probably understands crying, fussy babies with runny noses a helluva lot better than you.*

But the thought wasn't calming

And there still was the issue of someone having been inside her place. Someone having a key. The more she considered it, the more convinced she was that someone had broken in—or just walked in—and made himself at home. A shiver ran across the nape of Randi's neck. The thought of someone being so bold, so arrogant, so damn intrusive bothered her. Of course, she could change the locks, but she couldn't change the fact that she and the baby were alone in a city of strangers. Yes, she had a few friends, but who could she really depend upon?

She glanced at the window and saw Kurt striding to his truck. Tall. Rangy. Tough as nails, but with a kinder, more human side, as well. Sunlight caught against his bare head, glinting the lighter brown strands gold and the dusting of beard shadowing his chin. He was a handsome, complicated man but one she felt she could trust, one she could easily love. She thought of their nights together, sometimes tempestuously hot, other times incredibly tender. Biting on her lower lip, she told herself he wasn't the man for her. Theirs was destined to be one of those star-crossed affairs that could never develop into a lasting relationship.

She twisted the locket in her fingers as she watched Kurt climb into the truck. She tried not to notice the way his jeans fit tight around his long, muscular legs, or the angle of his jaw—rock-hard and incredibly masculine. She refused to dwell on the fact that his jacket stretched over the shoulders she'd traced with her fingers as she'd made love to him. Oh, Lord, what was she doing?

It didn't feel right.

Something about the way the case was coming down felt disjointed, out of sync.

Two days had passed since Eric Brown had called and the police had taken Donahue into custody, and yet Striker had the niggling sensation that wouldn't let go of him that something was off. That he was missing something vital.

He stood on the porch of the cabin and stared into old-growth timber that reached to the sky. The air was fresh from a shower earlier. Residual raindrops slid earthward from the fronds of thick ferns and long needles. Earlier, as he'd sat in the broken-down porch swing, he'd spotted a doe and her fawns, two jackrabbits and a raccoon scuttling into the thickets of fir and spruce. The sun had been out earlier, but now was sinking fast and the gloom of night was closing in. Striker was restless, felt that same itch that warned him trouble was brewing. Big trouble.

He hankered for a cigarette though he'd given up the habit ten years earlier. Only in times of stress or after two beers did he ever experience the yen for a swift hit of nicotine. Since he hadn't had a drop of liquor in days, it had to be the stress of the situation. Maybe it was because both he and Randi were experiencing a bad case of cabin fever.

Even the baby was cranky. No doubt the little guy had picked up on the vibes within the cabin. During the days the tension between him and Randi had been so thick a machete would have had trouble hacking through it. And the nights had been worse. Excruciating. Sheer damn torture as he'd tried, and failed, to keep his hands off her. Though neither one of them admitted the wanting, it was there, between them, enticing and erotic, and each night they'd given in to the temptation, making love as intensely as if they both thought it would be the last time.

Which it should be, all things considered.

But the fire he felt for her, the blinding, searing passion, wasn't an emotion easily dismissed; especially not in the cold mountain nights when she was so close to him, as willing, as eager as he to touch and reconnect.

Just thinking of the passion between them caused a stiffening between his legs, a swelling that was so uncomfortable, he had to adjust himself.

Hell.

Just like a horny teenager.

He ran frustrated fingers through his hair.

Soon this would be over.

*Yeah, and then what?*

*Are you just going to walk away?*

He clenched his jaw so hard it ached, and kicked a fir cone with enough force to send it shooting deep into the woods. Not that anything was going to end soon. Unbelievable as it might seem, it looked as if Randi might be right about her ex-lover. Donahue's alibi for the day she'd been run off the road was airtight. Unbreakable. Donahue's two best friends swore that all three of them had been together in a Spokane tavern at the time. Though the border town was close enough to the Idaho panhandle and not that far from Montana, the time it would have taken Donahue to make the round-trip made it near-impossible for the cowboy or either of his cohorts to have actually done the deed.

Coupled with his friends' dubious testimony, a bartender at the tavern remembered the nefarious trio. Two other guys playing pool that day also acknowledged that the boisterous bunch had been downing beers like water that afternoon and into the evening.

Striker leaned against the weathered porch railing. There wasn't much chance that Sam Donahue had forced Randi off the road that day.

Unless he'd paid someone to try to kill her.

Kurt couldn't let it go.

*Because you want it to be Donahue. Admit it. The fact that he's a mean son of a bitch and the father of Randi's baby bugs the hell out of you. You don't like to think of Randi making love to Donahue or anyone else for that matter. Just the thought of it makes you want to punch Donahue's lights out. Jeez, Striker, you'd better get out now. While you still can. The longer you're around her, the harder it's going to be to give her up.*

Angry at the turn of his thoughts, he spat into the forest and rammed his hands deep into the back pockets of his jeans.

*You have no right getting involved with her. She's your client and you don't want a woman fouling up your life. Especially not a woman with a kid.* He thought of his own daughter and realized the pain he usually felt when he remembered her was fading. Oh, there were still plenty of memories, but they were no longer clouded in guilt. That seemed wrong. He could never forget the guilt he carried. And it stung like the bite of a whip when he realized that some of his pain had been eased by being near Randi's child. As if letting little Joshua into his heart allowed him to release the pain over Heather's loss.

"Kurt?"

The door creaked open and Randi appeared. Stupidly, his heart leaped at the sight of her.

Tousled red-brown locks, big eyes and a dusting of freckles assaulted him and he felt his gut tighten. She'd spent the morning on his computer working on a couple of new columns that she planned to email when they reached a cyber-café, and now, smiling enough to show off impossibly white teeth, she looked incredible. As sexy and earthy as the surrounding forest.

"How's the baby?" he asked, his voice a tad hoarser than usual.

"Sleeping. Finally." Arms huddled around her as if to ward off the cold, she walked outside and he noticed how her jeans fit so snugly over her rounded hips. The weight she'd gained while pregnant had disappeared quickly because she'd been in the hospital, on IVs while in a coma; hence her inability to breast-feed, though she'd tried diligently once she'd awoken. So now she was slim and, if the little lines puckering her eyebrows could be believed, worried.

He felt the urge to wrap an arm over her shoulders, but didn't give in to the intimacy.

"Can we get out of here?" she asked.

"What? And leave all this luxury?" He forced a smile he

didn't feel and noticed that her lips twitched despite the creases in her forehead.

"It'll be hard, I know. A sacrifice. But I think it's time."

"And go where?"

"Home."

"I'm not sure your condo is safe."

"I'm not talking about Seattle," she admitted, her brown eyes dark with thought. "I think I need to go home. Back to Montana. Until this is all sorted out. I'll call my editor and explain what's going on. He'll have to let me work from the ranch. Well, he won't have to, but I think he will."

"Wait a minute. I thought you were hell-bent to start over. To prove yourself. Take command of your life again."

"Oh, I am. Believe me." She nodded as if to convince herself. "But I'm going to do it closer to my family." Staring at him, she inched her chin up in a gesture he'd come to recognize as pure unabashed McCafferty, a simple display of unbridled spirit, the kind of fortitude that made it impossible for her to walk away from a challenge. "Come on, Striker, let's get a move on."

He glanced around the cabin and decided she was right. It was time to return to Montana. This case had started there... and now it was time to end it. Whoever had first attacked Randi had done it when she'd attempted to go back to her roots at the Flying M. Somehow that had to be the key. Someone had felt threatened that she was returning. Someone didn't want her back at the ranch... Someone hated her enough to try to kill her and her unborn child....

His mind clicked.

New images appeared.

The baby. Once again, Striker thought Joshua was the center of this maelstrom. Didn't children bring out the deepest of emotions? Hadn't he felt them himself?

It was possible that whoever had started the attacks on Randi had done so with a single, deadly purpose in mind that Kurt hadn't quite understood. Perhaps Striker, Randi, the McCaffertys and even Sam Donahue had been manipulated. If so… there was only one person who would take Randi's fame and pregnancy as a personal slap in the face. And Kurt felt certain he knew who the culprit was.

"What do you know about Patsy Donahue?" he asked suddenly.

Randi started. "Sam's wife, or ex-wife, or whatever she is?"

"Yeah."

"Not a lot." Lifting a shoulder, Randi said, "Patsy was a year ahead of me in high school, the family didn't have much money and she got married right after she graduated, to her first boyfriend, Ned Lefever."

"You weren't friends with Patsy?"

"Hardly." Randi shook her head. "She never liked me much. Her dad had worked for mine, then her folks split up and I think she even had a crush on Slade, before Ned…well, it's complicated."

"Explain. We've got time."

"I won some riding competition once and edged her out and…oh, this is really so high school, but Ned asked me to the prom. He and Patsy were broken up at the time."

"Did you go?"

"To the prom, yes. But not with Ned. I already had a date. And I wasn't interested in Ned Lefever. I thought he was a blowhard and a braggart." Randi rested a hand against the battle-scarred railing as she rolled back the years. "It was weird, though. All night long, during the dance, I was on the receiving end of looks that could kill. From Patsy. As if I was to blame for Ned's—" She froze. "Oh, God, you think Patsy's behind the attacks, don't you?"

Kurt's eyes held hers. "I'd bet my life on it."

# Chapter 12

"How could she let herself get tangled up with the likes of Donahue?" Matt grumbled to his brother as he uncinched Diablo Rojo's saddle. For his efforts, the Appaloosa swung his head around in hopes of taking a nip out of Matt's leg. Deftly Matt sidestepped the nip. "You never learn, do you?" he muttered to the fiery colt.

Rojo snorted, stamping a foot in the barn and tossing his devilish head. Matt, Slade and Larry Todd, the recently rehired foreman, had been riding nearly all day, searching for strays, calves who might have been separated from the herd in the cold Montana winter. Spring was still a few months off and the weather had been fierce since Christmas, snow drifting to the eaves of some of the outbuildings.

Larry had already taken off, but Slade and Matt were cooling down their horses now that three bawling, near-frozen calves had been reunited with their mothers. The barn was warm and smelled of dust, dry straw and horseflesh. The same smells Matt had grown up with. Harold, their father's crippled old spaniel, was lying near the tack-room door, his tail thumping whenever Matt glanced in his direction.

Slade unhooked The General's bridle and the big gelding pushed against Slade's chest with his great head. He rubbed the horse's crooked white blaze and said, "I don't think Randi planned on getting involved with Donahue." The brothers had been discussing their sister's situation most of the day, hoping to find some answers to all of their questions.

"Hell, the man was married. I bet Patsy put up one helluva ruckus when she found out."

Slade nodded.

"She always was a hothead. She never liked Randi, either, not since Randi beat her out of some competition when they were in high school."

"What competition?" Slade scooped oats from a barrel with an old coffee can. The General, always eager for food, nickered softly. As Slade poured the grain into the manger, the old chestnut was already chomping.

"I can't remember. I wasn't around, but Dad mentioned it once. Something about horse racing, yeah, barrel racing, when they were kids. Randi beat Patsy, and Patsy did something to her at school the next week."

Slade began rubbing The General down. "Wasn't that Patsy Ellis? Jesus, I think she had a thing for me once."

"You always think women are interested in you."

"Don't tell Jamie."

"Right." Matt was feeding Rojo. Thankfully the colt was finally more interested in food than in taking a nip out of Matt's hide. "That was her maiden name. Right after high school she married Ned Lefever. A few years later they were divorced and a while after that she took up with Donahue, married him. It must really have teed her off that he ended up cheating on her with an old rival."

"A woman scorned," Slade muttered as the barn door opened and Kelly, her eyes bright, her cheeks nearly as red as the strands of hair escaping from her stocking cap, burst inside. Harold gave off a gruff bark.

"Shh," Kelly reprimanded, though she bent over to pat the old dog's head. Snow had collected on her eyelashes and was melting on her skin. To Matt, as always, she looked sweet and sexy and was the most incredible woman to walk this earth. "I just got a call from Striker," she announced breathlessly as she straightened. "He and Randi are on their way back here, and guess what? They think Patsy Donahue is behind all this."

Matt and Slade exchanged glances.

"I've already checked with Espinoza, and the police are looking for her, just to ask her some questions. I put a call in to Charlie Caldwell's ex-girlfriend and guess who handed her over the keys to the maroon Ford van that edged Randi's Jeep off the road? Good old Patsy."

Slade's grin moved from one side of his face to the other. "Your husband and I had just come up with the same idea," he said.

"No way."

"Honest to God." Matt held up a gloved hand as if he was being sworn in at a trial.

"Great. Now you can both be honorary detectives and form your own posse or something."

Matt tossed aside the brush and walked out of Diablo Rojo's stall. "Don't I at least get a kiss for being so smart?" he teased.

"If you were so smart why didn't you come up with this idea months ago and save us all a lot of grief. Forget the kiss, McCafferty." She winked at him and his heart galumphed. He'd never figured out why she got to him so, how when she

walked into the room, everything else melted into the background. "Besides," she said coyly, "I expected smart when I
married you."

"And good-looking and sexy?" he asked, and heard his
brother guffaw from The General's stall.

"Minimum requirements," she teased. Matt dropped a kiss
on her forehead and molded his glove over the slight curva-
ture of her belly where his unborn child was growing. "Come
on, you good-looking, sexy son of a gun," she began, pulling
on the tabs of his jeans.

"On my way," Slade intercepted.

"I think she was talking to me." Matt shot his brother a
look that could cut through steel.

"Both of you!" Kelly insisted, backing toward the door.
"Let's go have a little heart-to-heart with Patsy Donahue."

"I think you'd better leave that to the police," Matt said.

"I was the police, remember?"

"Yeah, but now you're my wife, the mother of my not-yet-
born child and Patsy could be dangerous."

"I'm not afraid."

"Spoken like a true McCafferty," Slade said as he slipped
from The General's stall and tested the latch to make certain
it was secure. "But maybe you should leave this to the Brothers McCafferty."

"We're like the Three Musketeers," Matt said.

"I won't say the obvious about a certain trio of stooges,"
she baited, and for her insolence, Matt whipped her off her
feet and hugged her.

"Sometimes, woman, you try my patience."

She laughed and winked up at him with sassy insolence as
he set her on her feet.

"Leave this to the men," Matt insisted as he held the barn
door open and a blast of icy Montana wind swept inside.

"In your dreams, boys." Kelly adjusted the scarf around her neck as she trudged through the snow toward the ranch house. Not far from the barn stood the remains of the stables, blackened and charred, in stark contrast to the pristine mantle of white and a glaring reminder of the trouble that had beset the family ever since Randi's fateful drive east. "Look," Kelly said, sending her husband a determined glare. "I've been involved with this case since the beginning. Patsy Donahue is mine."

"Guess what?" Kurt asked as he clicked off the cell phone. They were driving east through Idaho, closing in on the western Montana border. Night was coming and fast, no moon or stars visible through the thick clouds blanketing the mountains. "That was Kelly. She and Espinoza and your brothers went over to Patsy Donahue's place."

"Let me guess." Randi adjusted the zipper of her jacket. "Patsy is missing."

"Hasn't been at her house for days, if the stacked-up mail is to be believed."

"Great." Randi was disheartened. Would this nightmare never end? It was unbelievable to think that one woman could wreak such havoc, be so dangerous or so desperate. Could Patsy hate her that much as to try to kill her? Kill her baby? Harm her brothers?

"I just don't get it," Randi said as she turned toward the backseat to check on Joshua. The baby, lulled by the hum of the truck's engine and the gentle motion of the spinning wheels, was sleeping soundly, nestled in his car seat. "Why take it out on the ranch...I mean, if she had a thing against me, why harm my brothers?"

"The way I figure it, Thorne's plane crash was an accident. Patsy wasn't involved in that. But the attacks on you were personal and the fire in the stable was to keep you frightened, maintain a level of terror."

"Well, it worked. Slade nearly lost his life and the livestock… Dear God, why put the animals in jeopardy?" She bit her lip and stared at the few flakes of snow slowly falling from a darkening sky. Sagebrush and scrub pine poked through the white, snow-covered landscape, but the road was clear, the headlights of Striker's truck illuminating the ribbon of frigid pavement stretching before them.

"She's angry. Not just at you but at your family. Probably because she doesn't have much of one. Besides, you own the lion's share of the ranch. She must've figured that hurting the ranch and hurting your brothers was hurting you." He flicked a look through the rearview mirror. "I just feel like a fool for not seeing it sooner."

"No one did," she admitted, though that thought was dismal. Maybe when they arrived at the ranch, Patsy would be in custody. Silently Randi crossed her fingers. "So what's going to happen to Sam?"

"He's being questioned. Just because he wasn't responsible for harming you doesn't mean he's not a criminal. If you testify about his animal abuse, illegal betting and his throwing of the rodeo competitions, we'll have a good start in bringing him to justice. There's no telling what the authorities will dig up now that they've been pointed in the right direction."

"Of course I'll testify."

"It won't be easy. He'll be sitting at the defense table, staring at you, hearing every word."

"I know how it works," she retorted, then softened her tone as they passed through a small timber town where only a few lights were winking from the houses scattered near the road and a sawmill stood idle, elevators and sheds ghostlike and hulking around a gravel parking lot and a pile of sawdust several stories high. "But the truth is the truth," Randi continued, "no matter who's listening. Believe me, I'm over Sam Donahue. I would have taken all of the evidence I'd gathered against him to the rodeo commission and the authorities if I hadn't been sidetracked and sent to the hospital." She leaned back against the seat as the miles sped beneath the truck's tires. "I had worried about it. Wondered how I would face Joshua's father. But that's over. Now I'm sure I can face him. The way I look at it, Sam Donahue was the sperm donor that created my son. It takes a lot more to be a real father."

The baby started coughing and Randi turned to him. Kurt glanced back, as well. Joshua's little face was bright red, his eyes glassy. "How much longer until we get to Grand Hope?"

"Probably eight or nine hours."

"I'm worried about the baby."

"I am, too," Kurt admitted as he glared at the road ahead.

Joshua, as if he knew they were talking about him, gave off a soft little whimper.

"Give me the cell phone," Randi said. She couldn't stand it another minute. Joshua wasn't getting any better; in fact, he was worsening, and her worries were going into overdrive. Kurt handed her the phone, and she, trying to calm her case of nerves, dialed the ranch house as she plugged in the adapter to the cigarette lighter.

"Hello. Flying M Ranch," Juanita said, her accent barely detectible.

Randi nearly melted with relief at the sound of the housekeeper's voice. "Juanita, this is Randi."

"Oh, Miss Randi! *¡Dios!,* where are you? And the *niño.* How is he?"

"That's why I'm calling. We're on our way back to the ranch, but Joshua's feverish and I'm worried. Is Nicole there?"

"Oh, no. She is with your brother and they are at their new house, talking with the builder."

"Do you have her pager number?"

"¡Sí!" Quickly, Juanita rattled off not only the telephone number for Nicole's pager, but Thorne's cell phone, as well. "Call them now, and you keep that baby warm." Juanita muttered something in Spanish that Randi interpreted as a prayer before hanging up. Immediately Randi dialed Thorne's cell and once he answered, she insisted on talking to his wife. Nicole had admitted Randi into the hospital after the accident, and with the aid of Dr. Arnold, a pediatrician on the staff of St. James, had taken care of Joshua during the first tenuous hours of his young life.

Now, she said, "Keep fluids in him, watch his temperature, keep him warm, and I'll put a call into Gus Arnold. He's still your pediatrician, right?"

"Yes."

"Then you're in good hands. Gus is the best. I'll make sure that either he or one of his partners meets us at the hospital. When do you think you'll get here?"

"Kurt's saying about eight or nine hours. I'll call when we're closer."

"I'll be there," Nicole assured her, and Randi was thankful for her sister-in-law's reassurances. "Now, how are you doing?"

"Fine," Randi said, though that was a bit of a stretch. "Eager to get home, though."

"I'll bet—oh! What...?" Her voice faded a bit as if she'd turned her head, and Randi heard only part of a conversation before Nicole said, "Look, your brother is dying to talk to you. Humor him, would you?"

"Sure."

"Randi?" Thorne's voice boomed over the phone and Randi felt the unlikely urge to break down and cry. "What the hell's going on?" Thorne demanded. "Kelly seems to think that Patsy Donahue is the one behind all this trouble."

"It looks that way."

"And now Patsy's gone missing? Why the hell hasn't Striker found her?"

"Because he's been babysitting me," Randi said, suddenly defensive. No one could fault Kurt; not even her brothers. From the corner of her eye Randi noticed Kurt wince, his hands gripping the steering wheel even harder. "He's got someone on it."

"Hell's bells, so does Bob Espinoza, but no one seems to be able to find her. It's time to call in the FBI and the CIA and the state police and the damn federal marshals!"

"She'll be found," Randi assured him, though she, herself, doubted her words. "It's just a matter of time."

"It can't happen soon enough to suit me." He paused, then, "Tell me about J.R. How is he?"

"*Joshua's* running a temperature and has a cold. I'm meeting Nicole at St. James Hospital."

"I'll be there, too."

"You? A big corporate executive? Don't you have better things to do?" she teased, and he laughed.

"Yeah, right now I'm discussing the kind of toilet to go into the new house. Believe me, it's a major decision. Nicole's leaning toward the low-flow, water-conservation model, but I think we should go standard."

"I think I've heard enough," Randi said, giggling. Some of her tension ebbed a bit.

"You and me both. We haven't even started with colors yet. I'm leaning toward white."

"Big surprise, oh, conservative one."

He chuckled. "Well, it's too damn dark and cold to make many more decisions tonight. That's what happens when you're married to a doctor who works sixty or seventy hours a week and then gets detained at the hospital."

"Poor baby," Randi mocked.

"Uh-oh, they need me," he said, but his voice was fading, the connection breaking up. "I think…going to check into… sinks and…see you in a few hours…"

"Thorne? Are you there?"

Only crackle.

"I'm losing you!"

"Randi?" Thorne's voice was suddenly strong.

"Yeah?"

"I'm glad you're coming home."

"Me, too," she said, and her throat caught as she envisioned her oldest half brother with his black hair and intense gray eyes. She imagined the concern etched on his strong features. "Give my love to…" but the connection was lost, as they were deep in the mountains. Reluctantly, she clicked the cell phone off.

"He wants to know why I haven't tracked Patsy down yet," Striker surmised, his lips blade-thin.

"He wants to know why *no one's* tracked Patsy down. Your name came up, yes, but so did Detective Espinoza's, along with every government agency known to man. You have to understand one thing about Thorne. He gives an order and he expects immediate, and I mean im-me-di-ate, results. Which, of course, is impossible."

"I'm with him, though," Kurt said. "The sooner we nail Patsy Donahue, the better."

Randi wanted to agree with him, but there was a part of her that balked, for she knew that the minute Patsy was located and locked away, Kurt would be gone. Out of her life forever. Her heart twisted and she wondered how she'd ever let him go. It was silly really. She'd only known him for a month or so and only intensely for a week.

And yet she would miss him.

More than she'd ever thought possible.

This entire midnight run to Montana seemed doomed. Joshua's fever was worsening, there was talk of a blizzard ahead, and somewhere in the night, Patsy Donahue was planning another attack. Randi could feel it in her bones. She shivered.

"Cold?" Kurt adjusted the heater.

"I'm fine." But it was a lie. They both knew it. Every time a vehicle approached, Randi tensed, half expecting the driver to crank on the wheel and sideswipe Striker's truck. Silently she prayed that they'd reach Grand Hope without any incident, that her baby would recover quickly and that Kurt Striker would be a part of her life forever. It was a hard fact to face, one she'd denied for a long time, but no protests to herself or anyone else could overcome the God's honest truth: Randi McCafferty had fallen in love with Kurt Striker.

Patsy drummed gloved fingers on the wheel of her stolen rig, an older-model SUV that had been parked for hours at a bar on the interstate in Idaho. No one would be able to connect her to the theft. She'd ditched her van on an abandoned road near Dalles, Oregon, gotten on a bus and traveled east until the truck stop, where she'd located the rig and switched license plates with some she'd lifted while in Seattle. By the time anyone pieced together what she'd done, it would be too late. She was behind Striker's pickup, probably by an hour or so, but she figured she could make up the distance. It would take time, but eventually she'd be able to catch the bitch.

And then there would be hell to pay.

Her speedometer hovered near seventy, but she pushed on the accelerator and pumped up the volume on the radio. An old Rolling Stones tune reverberated through the speakers. Mick Jagger was screaming about getting no satisfaction. Usually Patsy identified with the song. But not tonight. Tonight she intended to get all the satisfaction she'd been lacking in recent years.

The SUV flew down the freeway. Patsy didn't let up for a second. She'd driven in dry snow all her life and felt no fear.

By daybreak her mission would be accomplished.

Randi McCafferty and anyone stupid enough to be with the bitch would be dead.

# Chapter 13

The baby wouldn't stop crying.

Nothing Randi did stopped the wails coming from the backseat and Striker felt helpless. He drove as fast as he dared while Randi twisted in her seat, trying to feed Joshua or comfort him, but the baby was having none of it.

Striker gritted his teeth and hoped that the baby's fever hadn't climbed higher. He thought of the pain of losing a child and knew he had to do something, *anything* to prevent the little guy's life from slipping away.

He gunned the pickup ever faster, but the terrain had become rough, with sharp turns and steep grades as they drove deep into the foothills of the Montana mountains.

"He's still very warm," Randi said, touching her son's cheek.

"We'll be there in less than an hour," Striker assured her. "Hang in there."

"If he will," Randi whispered hoarsely, and it tore his heart to hear her desperation.

"I think it's better that he's crying rather than listless," Striker offered, knowing it was little consolation.

"I guess. Maybe we should get off and try to find a clinic."

"In the rinky-dink towns around here? At three in the morning? St. James is the nearest hospital. Just call Nicole and tell her we'll be there in forty-five minutes."

"All right." She reached for the phone just as Striker glanced in the rearview mirror. Headlights were bearing down on them and fast, even though he was doing near sixty on the straight parts of this curving, treacherous section of interstate. At the corners he'd had to slow to near thirty and he'd spotted the vehicle behind him gaining, taking the corners wide. "Hang on," he said.

"What?"

"I've got someone on my tail and closing fast. It would be best if I let them go around me." He saw a wide spot in the road, slowed down, and the other vehicle shot past, a blur of dark paint and shiny wheels.

"We'll probably catch up to him rolled over in the ditch ahead."

"Great," she whispered.

He took a turn a little fast and the wheels slid, so he slowed a bit. As he passed by an old logging road, he thought he saw a dark vehicle. Idling. No headlights or taillights visible, but exhaust fogging the cold night air. The same fool who'd passed them? The hairs on the back of his neck lifted.

It was too dark to be certain and he told himself that he was just being paranoid. No one in his right mind would be sitting in their rig in the dark. His gut clenched. Of course no one in his *right mind* would be there. But what about a woman no longer in control of her faculties, a woman hell-bent for revenge, a woman like Patsy Donahue?

*No way, Striker. You're tired and jumping at shadows. That's all. Pull yourself together.*

He peered into the rearview mirror and saw nothing in the darkness. No headlights beyond the snow flurries...or did he? Was there a vehicle barreling after him, one with no head-lights, one using his taillights to guide it? His mouth was sud-denly desert dry. The image took shape then faded. His mind playing tricks on him. Nothing more. God, he hoped so.

"What?" Randi asked, sensing his apprehension. The baby was still crying, but more softly now. The road was steep and winding and he cut his speed in order to keep the truck on the asphalt.

"Look behind us. See anything?"

Again Randi twisted in her seat and peered through the window over the back of the king cab. She squinted hard. "No. Why?"

He scowled, saw his own reflection in the mirror. "I thought I saw something. A shadow."

"A shadow?"

"Of a car. I thought someone might be following us with his lights out."

"In this terrain? In the dark?" she asked, and then sucked in her breath and stared hard through the window. "I don't see anything."

"Good." He felt a second's relief. This would be the worst place to encounter danger. The road was barely two lanes with steep mountains on one side and a slim guardrail on the other. Beyond the barrier was a sheer cliff where only the tops of trees were visible in the glare of his headlights as he swept around the corners.

Randi didn't stop looking through the window, searching the darkness, and he could tell by the way she held on to the back of the seat, her white-knuckled grasp a death grip, that, she, too, was concerned. His hands began to sweat on the wheel, but he told himself they were all right, they would make it, they only had a few more miles. He thought of how, in the past few weeks, he'd fallen for Randi McCafferty hook, line and proverbial sinker. With a glance in her direction, his heart filled. He couldn't imagine life without her or without little Joshua. As much as he'd sworn after Heather's death never to get close to a woman or a child again, he'd broken his own pact with himself. And it was too late to change his mind. His stubborn heart just wouldn't let him. Maybe it was time to tell her. To be honest. Let her know how he felt.

*Why?*

*Come on, Striker, are you so full of yourself to imagine she loves you? And what about the kid? Didn't you swear off fatherhood for good? What are you doing considering becoming a father again? Why would you set yourself up for that kind of heartache all over again? Remember Heather? Do you really think you have it in you to be a parent?*

The arguments tore through his mind. Nonetheless, he had to tell her. "Randi?"

"What?" She was still staring out the back window.

"About the last few nights—"

"Please," she said, refusing to look his way. "You don't have to explain. Neither of us planned what happened."

"But you should know how I feel."

He noticed her tense. She swallowed hard. "Maybe I don't want to," she whispered before she gasped. "Oh, God, no!"

"What?"

"I think…I think there *is* someone back there. Every once in a while I see an image and then it fades into the background. You don't think…"

Kurt stared into the rearview mirror. "Hell." He saw it too. The outline of a dark vehicle without its lights on, driving blind, bearing down, swerving carelessly from one side of the road to the other and then melding with the night. He pressed hard on the accelerator. "Keep your eye on it and call the police."

She reached for the phone. Dialed 911.

Nothing.

"Damn."

She tried again and was rewarded by a beeping of the cell. "No signal," she said, staring through the window as the baby cried.

"Keep trying." Kurt took a corner too fast, the wheels spun and they swung wide, into the oncoming lane. "Damn it."

"It's getting closer!"

Kurt saw the vehicle now, looming behind them, dangerously close as they screeched around corners. "Hell."

"Do you think it's Patsy?"

"Unless there's some other nutcase running loose."

"Oh, God…" Randi sounded frantic. "What's she going to do?"

"I don't know." But he had only to think of the accident where Randi was forced off the road to come up with a horrific scenario.

Randi punched out the number of the police again. "The call's going through! Where are we? I'll have to give our location…oh, no…lost the signal again."

"Hit redial!" Kurt ordered. A sign at the edge of the road warned of a steep downgrade.

"Maybe you should just slow down," Randi said. "Force her to slow."

"What if she's got a gun. A rifle?"

"A gun?"

The vehicle switched on its lights suddenly and seemed to leap forward.

Kurt swung to the inside, toward the mountain.

The SUV bore down on them.

A sharp corner loomed. A sign said that maximum speed for the corner was thirty-five. The needle of his speedometer was pushing sixty. He shifted down. Pumped the brakes. Squealed around the corner, fishtailing.

The SUV didn't give up. "She's getting closer," Randi cried as she kept redialing. "Oh, God!"

*Bam!*

The nose of the trailing vehicle struck hard as Kurt hit a pothole. The truck shuddered, snaking to the guardrail, wheels bouncing over a washboard of asphalt and gravel. Kurt rode out the slide, easing into it, only changing direction at the last minute. His heart was pounding, his body sweating. He couldn't lose Randi and the baby!

"Hello! Hello! This is an emergency!" Randi cried, as if she'd gotten through to police dispatch. "Someone's trying to kill us. We're on the interstate in northern Montana." She yelled their approximate location and the highway number, then swore as the connection failed.

*Thud!*

Again they were battered from behind.

The front wheel hit a patch of ice and the truck began to spin, circling in what seemed like slow motion. Kurt struggled with the steering wheel, saw the guardrail and the black void beyond. Gritting his teeth, trying to keep the truck on the road, he felt the fender slam into the railing and heard the horrid groan of metal ripping. Over it all the baby cried and Randi screamed. "Come on, come on," Kurt said between clenched teeth, willing the pickup to stay on the road, his shoulders aching. He couldn't lose the woman he loved, nor her child. Not now. Not this way. Not again.

"Oh, my God, look out!" Randi cried, but it was too late.

The SUV hit the truck midspin, plowing into the passenger side with a sickening crash and the rending of steel. Kurt's fingers clenched over the wheel, but the truck didn't respond. The SUV's bumper locked to the truck and together the two vehicles spun down the road, faster and faster. Trees and darkness flashed by in a blur.

Randi screamed.

The baby wailed.

Kurt swore. "Hold on!" The two melded vehicles slammed into the side of the mountain and ricocheted across the road with enough force to send the entangled trucks through the guardrail and into the black void beyond.

Somewhere there was a bell ringing…steady…never getting any louder…just a simple bleating. It was so irritating. *Answer the phone, for God's sake…answer it!* Randi's head ached, her body felt as if she'd been beaten from head to toe, there was an awful taste in her mouth and… She opened an eye and blinked. Everything was so white and blinding.

"Can you hear me? Randi?" Someone shined a light into her eyes and she recoiled. The voice was a woman's. A voice she should recognize. Randi closed her eyes. Wanted to sleep again. She was in a bed with rails…a hospital bed…how did she get here? Vaguely she remembered the smell of burning rubber and fresh pine…there had been red and blue lights and her family…all standing around…and Kurt leaning over her, whispering he loved her, his face battered and bruised and bleeding… Or had it been a dream? Kurt…where the hell was Kurt? And the baby? Joshua. Oh, God!  Her eyes flew open and she tried to speak.

"Jo...Joshua?"

"The baby's okay."

Everything was blurry for a minute before she focused and saw Nicole standing in the room. Another doctor was examining her, but her eyes locked with those of her sister-in-law. Memories of the horrible night and the car wreck assailed her.

"Joshua is at home. With Juanita. As soon as you're released you can be with him."

She let out her breath, relieved that her child had survived.

"You're lucky," the doctor said, and Nicole was nodding behind him. *Lucky? Lucky?* There didn't seem anything the least bit lucky about what happened.

"Kurt?" she managed to get out though her throat was raw, her words only a whisper.

"He's all right."

Thank God. Slowly turning her head, Randi looked around. The hospital room was stark. An IV dripped fluid into her wrist, a monitor showed her heartbeat and kept up the beeping she'd heard as she'd awoken. Flowers stood in vases on a windowsill.

"I...I want to see...my baby...and...and Striker."

"You've been in the hospital two days, Randi," Nicole said. "With a concussion and a broken wrist. J.R., er, Joshua, had a bad cold but didn't suffer anything from the accident. Luckily there was an ambulance only fifteen minutes away from the site of the accident. Police dispatch had gotten your message, so they were able to get to you fairly quickly."

"Where's Kurt?"

Nicole cleared his throat. "Gone."

Randi's heart sank. He'd already left. The ache within her grew.

"He had some eye damage and a dislocated shoulder."

"And he just left."

Little lines gathered between Nicole's eyebrows. "Yes. I know that he went to Seattle to see a specialist. An optic neurologist."

Randi forced the words over her tongue. "How bad is his vision?"

"I don't know."

"Is he blind?"

"I really don't know, Randi."

She felt as if her sister-in-law was holding back. "Kurt's not coming back, is he?"

Nicole took her hand and twined strong fingers between Randi's. "I'm not certain, but since you're going to ask, if I were a betting woman, I'd have to say 'No, I don't think so.' He and Thorne had words. Now, please, take your doctor's advice and rest. You have a baby waiting for you at the Flying M and three half brothers who are anxious for you to come home." Nicole squeezed Randi's fingers and Randi closed her eyes. So they'd survived.

"What about Patsy?" she asked.

"In custody. As luck would have it, she got away unscathed."

The doctor attending her cleared his throat. "You really do need to rest," he said.

"Like hell." She scrabbled for the button to raise her head. "I want to get out of here and see my baby and—" Excruciating pain splintered through her brain. She sank back on her pillow. "Maybe you're right," she admitted. She had to get well. For Joshua.

*And what about Kurt?* Her heart ached at the thought that she might never see him again. Damn it, she couldn't just let him walk away.

Or could she?

★ ★ ★

Three days later she was released from the hospital and reunited with her family. Joshua was healthy again, and it felt good to hold him in her arms, to smell his baby-clean scent. Juanita was in her element, fussing and clucking over Randi and the baby, generally bossing her brothers around and running the house.

Larry Todd seemed to have forgiven Randi for letting him go, though he insisted on a signed contract for his work, and even Bill Withers, after hearing of the accident, had agreed to allow Randi to write her column from Montana. "Just don't let it get out," he said over the phone. "People around here might get the idea that I'm a softie."

"I wouldn't lose any sleep over it if I were you," Randi said before hanging up and deciding to tackle her oldest brother. She checked on the baby and found him sleeping in his crib, then, with her arm in a sling, made her way downstairs. The smells of chocolate and maple wafted from the kitchen where Juanita was baking.

Though Slade and Matt were nowhere to be found, she located Thorne at his desk in the den. He sat at his computer, a neglected cup of coffee at his side. No doubt he was working on some corporate buyout, a lawsuit, the ever-changing plans for his house, or concocting some new way to make his next million. Randi didn't care what he was doing. He could damn well be interrupted.

"I heard you gave Striker a bad time." She was on pain medication but was steady enough on her feet to loom above the desk in her bathrobe and slippers.

Thorne looked up at her and smiled. "You heard right."

"Blamed him for what happened to me and Joshua."

"I might have come down on him a little hard," her brother admitted with uncharacteristic equanimity.

"You had no right, you know. He did his best."

"And it wasn't good enough. You were nearly killed. So was Joshua."

"We survived. Because of Kurt."

A smile twitched at the corners of his mouth. "I figured that out."

"You did?"

"Yep." He reached into his drawer and held out two pieces of a torn check. "Striker wouldn't accept any payment. He felt bad about what happened."

"And you made it worse."

"Nah." He leaned back in the desk chair until it squeaked and tented his hands as he looked up at her. "Well, okay, I did, but I changed my mind."

"What good does that do?"

"A lot," he said.

She narrowed her eyes. "You're up to something."

"Making amends."

"That sounds ominous."

"I don't think so." He glanced to the window and Randi heard it then, the rumble of an engine. "Looks like our brothers are back."

"They've been away?"

"Mmm. Come on." He climbed out of his desk chair and walked with her to the front door. She looked out the window and saw Matt and Slade climb out of a Jeep. But there was another man with them and in a pulse beat she recognized Kurt. Her heart nearly jumped from her chest and she threw open the door, nearly tripping on Harold as she raced across the porch.

"Wait!" Thorne cried, but she was already running along

the path beaten in the snow, her slippers little protection, her robe billowing in the cold winter air.

"Kurt!" she yelled, and only then noticed the eyepatch. He turned and a smile split his square jaw. Without thinking, she flung herself into his arms. "God, I missed you," she whispered and felt tears stream from her eyes. His face was bruised, his good eye slightly swollen. "Why did you leave?"

"I thought it was best." His voice was husky. Raw. The arm around her strong and steady.

"Then you thought wrong." She kissed him hard and felt his mouth mold to hers, his body flex against her.

When he finally lifted his head, he was smiling. "That's what your brothers said." He glanced up at Thorne who had followed Randi outside. He stiffened slightly.

"I'm glad you're back," Thorne said. "I made a mistake."

"What? You're actually apologizing?" Randi, still in Kurt's arms, looked over her shoulder. "This," she said to Kurt, "is a red-letter day. Thorne McCafferty never, and I mean, never, admits he's wrong."

"Amen," Matt said.

"Right on," Slade agreed.

Thorne's jaw clenched. "Will you stay?" he asked Striker.

"I'll see. Give me a second, will you." He looked at all the brothers, who suddenly found reasons to retreat to the house. "It's freezing out here and you're hurt…" He touched her wrist. "So I'll keep this simple. Randi McCafferty, will you marry me?"

"Wh-what?"

"I mean it. Ever since I met you…and that kid of yours, life hasn't been the same."

"I can't believe this," she said breathlessly.

"Do. Believe, Randi."

Her heart squeezed. Fresh tears streamed from her eyes.

"Marry me."

"Yes. Yes! Yes!" She threw her good arm around his neck and silently swore she'd never let go.

# Epilogue

"I do," Randi said as she stood beneath an arbor of roses. Kurt was with her, the preacher was saying the final words and Kelly was holding Joshua as Randi's brothers stood next to Kurt and her sisters-in-law surrounded her. The backyard of the ranch was filled with guests and the summer sun cast golden rays across the acres of land.

It had been over a year since John Randall had passed on. The new stable was finished, if not painted, and Thorne and his family had moved into their house. Both Nicole and Kelly were nearly at term in the pregnancies.

"I give to you Mr. and Mrs. Kurt Striker…" The preacher's final words echoed across the acres and somewhere from Big Meadow a horse let out a loud nicker.

Randi gazed up at her bridegroom and her heart swelled. He had healed from the accident, only a small scar near one

eye reminding her that his peripheral vision had been com-
promised.

Both Patsy and Sam Donahue had been tried and convicted
and were serving time. Sam had agreed to give up all paren-
tal rights and Kurt was working with an attorney to legally
adopt Joshua.

They lived here at the ranch house and Randi was able to
keep working, though Kurt thought she should give up her
column entitled "Solo" and start writing for young marrieds.

"Toast!" Matt cried as she and Kurt walked toward the
table where a sweating ice sculpture of two running horses
was melting and pink champagne bubbled from a fountain.

"To the newlyweds," Thorne said.

Randi smiled and fingered the locket at her throat. Once
it had held a picture of her father and son. Now John Randall
had been replaced by a small snapshot of her husband.

"To my wife," Kurt said, and touched the rim of his glass
to hers.

"And my husband."

She swallowed a glass of champagne and greeted their guests.
Never had she felt such joy. Never had she felt so complete.
She held her son and danced on a makeshift floor as the band
began to play and shadows began to crawl across the vast acres
of the Flying M.

"I love you," Kurt whispered to her and she laughed.

"You'd better! Forever!"

"That's an awful long time."

"I know. Isn't it wonderful?" she teased.

"The best." He kissed her and held her for a long minute,
then they walked through the guests and she saw her brothers with their wives… Finally all of the McCafferty children
were married. As John Randall McCafferty had wanted. More
grandchildren were on the way.

She could almost hear her father saying to her, "Good goin', Randi girl. About time you tied the knot."

As she danced with her new husband, she could feel her father's presence and she didn't doubt for a second that had he been here, the old man would've been proud.

Another generation of McCaffertys was on its way.

★ ★ ★ ★ ★

# The past can catch up to you....

# MARTA PERRY

Rachel Weaver Mason is finally going home to Deer Run, the Amish community she left behind so many years ago. Recently widowed, she wants desperately to create a haven for herself and her young daughter.

But the community, including Rachel's family, is anything but welcoming. The only person happy to see her is her teenage brother, Benjamin, and he's protecting a dark secret that endangers them all.

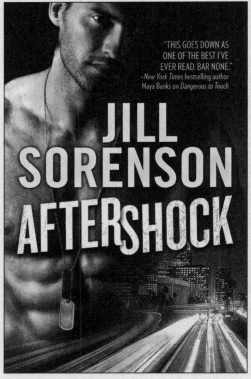

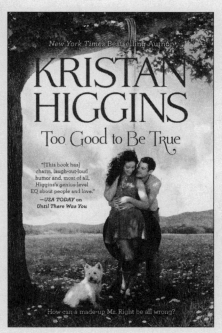